THE MAGICIANS OF VENICE, BOOK 1

THE IMMORTAL CITY

AMY KUIVALAINEN

bhc
press

Livonia, Michigan

Editor: Hayley Stone
Proofreader: Amanda Lewis

Quotation from *Bibliotheca* by Pseduo-Apollodorus.
Public domain.

Quotation from *The Illiad* by Homer. Public domain.

Quotation from "The Heroic Enthusiasts (Gli Eroici Furori) Part
the First / An Ethical Poem" by Giordano Bruno. Public domain.

THE IMMORTAL CITY
Copyright © 2020 Amy Kuivalainen

Published by BHC Press

Library of Congress Control Number: 2018948478

ISBN: 978-1-947727-77-9 (Hardcover)
ISBN: 978-1-64397-263-3 (Large Print Hardcover)
ISBN: 978-1-947727-79-3 (Trade Softcover)
ISBN: 978-1-64397-262-6 (Mass Market Paperback)
ISBN: 978-1-947727-78-6 (Ebook)

Also available in Audio

For information, write:
BHC Press
885 Penniman #5505
Plymouth, MI 48170

Visit the publisher:
www.bhcpress.com

ACKNOWLEDGMENTS

I wanted to extend a very special thank you to Jenn Trevaskis for the loan of multiple text books on Venice and Renaissance life in Italy, glasses of scotch and the Saint Mark's bell. Without them I doubt I would've gotten as far as I did with this series. Buckets of gratitude is also extended to Hayley Stone for all of the pragmatic advice and helping me push this story to where it needed to be.

PART ONE

THE
BULL

"And in sacrificing to Poseidon he prayed
that a bull might appear from the depths,
promising to sacrifice it when it appeared.
Poseidon did send him up a fine bull."
~ Pseudo-Apollodorus ~

PROLOGUE

I N THE FLOODED catacombs of San Zaccaria, the Acolyte bent his head and prayed to the darkness.

"*Maestro oscuro, ascolta la mia preghiera…*"

He picked up a knife and cut a shallow line across his thigh. With a handful of blood, he slowly began sketching ancient and twisting glyphs across his bare chest. A ripple of power, ancient and terrible, rose up from the ground, curling around his legs and chest.

"Dark Master, hear my prayer," he repeated, "I am your tool. Take me to do your will. My body is your body, flesh of my flesh."

Images flickered through his mind, thick and fast.

"A sacrifice? Yes, of course."

The Demon God replied in gentle whispers, encouragement from master to beloved servant.

"Yes, Master, I understand," the Acolyte answered dutifully. "Take my body. Guide me to your chosen sacrifice."

The grounds outside of the Chiesa di San Giacomo dell'Orio had emptied for the night. The Acolyte waited patiently, strength and desire burning in his veins.

There, the voice said from deep inside of him as a woman appeared from around the corner of the church. Her slow stride and black eyes spoke of exhaustion, but she still wore a pleased smile, as if the quiet walk through the streets of Santa Croce was some guilty pleasure. Under her knit sweater her breasts were heavy, and there was a telling swell to her stomach and hips.

Can you not smell her fertility? That aroma of milk and blood and sex.

The Acolyte smiled as he approached her with an unlit cigarette in his hand. "*Mi scusi, hai da accendere?*"

She returned his smile with an apologetic, "*Io non.*"

He gave a disappointed shrug, waiting until she reached the shadows of the church before following her.

It was dawn when the Demon left the Acolyte naked and shivering on the floor of his apartment, his hands and clothes covered in blood and clay, his soul on fire inside of him.

ONE

THE WIND WAS howling off the canal as Inspector Marco Dandolo wrapped his coat tightly around himself and lit a cigarette. He'd been trying to quit—his third time that year using Isabella's hypnotist—and it had been going well until he'd received a call about two distraught Americans. The unfortunate students had been taking photos of the canal entrances when they had seen a body hanging inside.

"What do you think, *Inspecttori*?" Beppe asked nervously. As one of the Polizia di Quartiere for Santa Croce, Beppe had been the first officer the Americans had alerted. They had been loud and hysterical, and by the time Marco had arrived, Beppe was pale with sweat and breathing heavily.

"Your first body?" Marco asked.

"*Si*," Beppe admitted. Marco passed him his packet of cigarettes and Beppe lit one gratefully. "I never thought people could be so horrible to each other."

Marco grunted. "I've seen some terrible murders, but this…this is something else."

"A good thing they have *Le Doge Cane* on the case," Beppe said brightly. Marco smiled weakly at him.

Le Doge Cane was a nickname he had acquired as much for his famous ancestor, Doge Francesco Dandolo, known as *the dog* after he chained himself while

petitioning the pope to remove Venice's excommuni-
cation, as for Marco's ability to focus on a case like a
bloodhound. He hated it but did his best not to let
the banter between officers get to him. As reputations
went, it wasn't a bad one.

They finished their cigarettes in silence before
ducking back under the police tape, walking along the
narrow strip of stone and into the canal entrance of the
palazzo.

"Have we found out who owns the palazzo yet?"
Marco asked a nearby female police officer. She was
young and pretty, and he always managed to forget her
name.

"The Tintoretto's, a celebrity couple," she replied.

"Are they here yet?"

"No, but their alibi is solid. They're in Milano
where she's doing a photo shoot for *Vogue*."

"Does anybody else have access to the house?"

"Only their sixty-year-old housekeeper who didn't
see or hear anything."

"*Grazie*," Marco replied, waving her on.

Steeling himself with a deep breath, he finally
looked up at the body hanging in front of him.

The woman was naked, a bull's head pulled over her
own. Her arms had been stretched out and tied above
her head. In one hand she held a goblet, in the other an
elaborate Greek urn painted with sea creatures.

An umbilical cord fell from her vagina, terminat-
ing at an embryonic sac and calf fetus resting in a copper pan at water level. The victim's heart had been

removed, but the wound had also been cleaned. On the stone wall behind the body were three massive symbols encircled by a script unlike any Marco had ever seen.

"It looks a little like Sanskrit, but it's wrong," a masked forensics officer commented. He and the rest of the forensics team were working quickly to beat the next high tide, due in two hours. "I studied some of it for my degree, but this looks too jagged, almost like a mutated cuneiform."

Marco pulled out his phone and took multiple photos of the wall. "I might know someone who can help."

IT WAS midnight when Doctor Alessa Christiano's phone rang in her office at Sapienza in Rome.

"*Pronto*?" she answered, barely looking up from her computer screen where she was composing a lecture on the Roman conquest of Egypt.

"Alessa, I'm glad you are awake," a painfully familiar voice said. "I should've known you would still be working."

"Says the man also still working. What do you want, Marco?" Her ex-lover's voice didn't sound drunk, but she detected a note of trouble in it.

"I need your expertise, *Dottore*. I've emailed you some photos I need you to look at."

"Marco, I really don't have time—"

"It's a case, Alessa," he insisted. "This is the Polizia de Strato asking, not Marco Dandolo the *coglione*. *Per favore bella*, a woman is dead."

"Fine, fine, I'll take a look," Alessa sighed and clicked through the pages on her screen to bring up her emails.

"I need to warn you, the pictures—" Marco began, but she had already opened the first one.

"*Mio Dio*," Alessa cried, crossing herself twice. "Who would do such a thing?"

"A sick bastard. Click on the other attachments. There is some script I'm hoping you can decipher; it might give me an idea who did this."

Alessa downloaded and scrolled through the other photos, zooming in on the graffitied wall.

"It's a hoax."

"What do you mean?" Marco asked.

"I mean apart from the three main symbols, which are alchemical, the rest of the script is completely made up."

"What do the three main symbols mean?"

"I don't know alchemy, Marco. Look them up. I've seen them before, but the rest is bullshit."

"How do you know?"

"A few years ago a fragment of a stone tablet was found near Crete. It had a similar sort of disjointed cuneiform style of writing. Your wall looks like a fanatic has created a full alphabet from it and finger painted it on his murder site." Alessa looked at the next picture. "It's all gibberish, Marco."

There was a long pause and then the sound of a metal lighter flicking open from the other line. They'd broken up years ago but, whenever Alessa smelled MS tobacco, she still thought of him. "I see your sister's hypnotist has failed again. You need to stop paying her."

"She's Isabella's wife's sister. If I don't let her hypnotize me, they will try and set me up on a date with her."

"If she were any good, she could just hypnotize you into sleeping with her."

"You said fanatic," Marco commented thoughtfully. "Why that word?"

"Only someone obsessed with the legends would go to that much effort to create a full alphabet over an artifact that doesn't prove a thing." She rubbed the lenses of her glasses before putting them back on. "Worse than a fanatic, I think you have a true believer."

"In what? What legend?"

Alessa couldn't hold in a snort. "The Lost City. Atlantis."

"And you say they found evidence of it?" asked Marco, sounding not at all phased by her revelation.

"No, I said they found a fragment of a stone tablet. The person who found it claimed it was evidence that Atlantis existed. She wanted funding to do an underwater dig at the site."

"What happened?"

"Nothing. No professional scholar would take Atlantis seriously. She is a pariah in her field." Alessa shook her head. "It's a shame. Both her parents are brilliant scholars. Anyway, there were some who believed her. They were more the New Age crowd, and a few mythologists hunting the dream."

"And you think one of them could be our killer?"

"I don't know, Marco. The only place I've ever seen anything like this was an attachment to the paper about the Tablet."

"Where can I get a copy of it?"

"I can email it to you." Alessa took one last look at the mutilated woman and shook her head. "Her contact details should be at the bottom of the paper if you want to talk to her yourself. I'm sorry I can't be more helpful, *mio amico*."

"You have been an incredible help to me tonight. I knew you were the right person to call. Next time you are in Venezia, I will buy you the best meal of your life," he promised.

Despite their separation, they still ate together whenever she was in Venice, or he was in Rome. Inevitably, it always ended with them in bed together that night, and by morning, agreeing how it was better they had broken up.

"It's a deal. I hope you catch them soon, Marco," Alessa said solemnly.

"*Grazie Dottore.*" He hung up, and she sent him the paper as promised before heading out to midnight mass.

Alessa wasn't God's most pious servant, but after seeing the bull-headed woman, she couldn't shake the taint of evil from her mind.

TWO

BREATHE SLOWLY, TAKE *in the sound of nothing,* Penelope told herself as the weights on her belt drew her down into the dark blue water. She adjusted her mouthpiece and goggles more comfortably before checking her watch. Beginning now, she would have two hours of blessed silence with nothing but tropical fish for company.

Penelope had just started her first holiday in two years when a friend working at James Cook University in Cairns had called to tell her that some coins had been brought in to his office by a pair of free divers.

"They look Phoenician, Pen," he'd revealed. "I know you have your theories about Egyptians and Phoenicians coming this far so I thought I'd let you know. See if you're interested."

Get your ass back on the horse, Pen, her best friend and flatmate Carolyn had said. *You just need a win.*

She had watched Penelope's downward spiral after losing out on investors and grants for the past two years. Carolyn was an academic. She knew the score when it came to research funding, but when Penelope had mentioned the coins and a trip to the warm sunshine of Queensland, Carolyn had all but packed her bag for her. Hunting Phoenician coins on the Great Barrier Reef seemed exactly like the right kind of holiday.

Still chasing ridiculous dreams, Penelope. When are you ever going to grow up? Her father's voice echoed in her head.

Penelope ground her teeth around the rubber of her regulator. It had been six months since their argument, but the words still stung. Professor Stuart Bryne was known for his prowess as a lecturer, but what people didn't know was that he had practiced those skills by lecturing Penelope.

"He's only worried about you," her mother, Kiri, had consoled her that afternoon when Penelope had called in tears. Kiri was back in her native New Zealand working on her newest book about gender roles in Māori culture.

"He's worried I'm going to tarnish his reputation. He's an anthropologist, for God's sake. We aren't even in the same field!" Penelope snapped. "He needs to calm his shit and let me live my own life."

"Hey! Don't you use that kind of language about your father," Kiri defended. "He loves you and doesn't want you throwing your career away."

"They thought Schliemann was crazy, too, until he found Troy. I know it exists, Mom. I can feel it. It's like an extra heartbeat inside my chest. It's *mine*. I know it is."

"Maybe it's not the right time for you to find it yet," sighed Kiri. "Take a job teaching for a while until you can figure out your next steps."

Like usual, Penelope only decided to take her mother's advice once she'd run out of other options and lost any hope of getting funding.

At least under the water, the only thing she needed to worry about was drowning.

Penelope breathed slowly through her regulator, counting down from ten to soothe her anxiety. *There's nothing around or over you. Straight dive. Nothing to get caught on.*

Three years ago, she'd nearly drowned while diving through an old ship, and it had taken her months to get the courage to put a pair of goggles on again. Penelope hated being afraid of anything, so she'd quickly forced herself back into the ocean, starting small with lifeguard courses before moving on to snorkeling, and then finally back to deep diving. As long as she had open water, and wasn't moving through wrecks or caves, her fear of drowning remained in check.

It had been on her first real dive since the incident that Penelope had discovered the corner of a stone tablet. It was on a research trip to Crete, and she thought her luck couldn't have been better. She was wrong.

And didn't that just send my anxiety off in a whole new direction. She thought the Atlantis Tablet would be the key to her Troy, but all it'd done was set her up for more disappointment and frustration.

One of the free divers, Sam, swam past her, making her start. *Phoenician coins, Pen, no mysterious tablets with mixed origins.* It didn't matter that finding Phoenician coins in Australia would launch a whole new line of inquiry for her to be ridiculed over. *These mysteries keep finding you, not the other way around.*

Sam waved at her and pointed to an outcrop of coral and rock before he shot up to the surface for another breath of air. Penelope shut out her thoughts, letting the eerie silence of the ocean fill her as she searched the rocks, brushing the seabed with her gloved hands.

Three hours underwater produced four startled stingrays and two tarnished coins and Penelope couldn't have been happier.

By the time she got back to her hotel, she felt calmer than she had in months. Her chestnut hair was a riot of salty curls, and her body was physically exhausted. She showered and made sure her heavy silver ring was secure on her finger. It was a replica of the Phaistos Disc, and she had bought it on the same trip to Crete that she had found the Tablet. The Disc had been discovered in a Minoan temple in 1908 and researchers still had no idea what it meant. It was a reminder that some mysteries fought against being solved.

After pouring herself a glass of wine, Penelope opened her laptop. Despite being on a semester break until March, Penelope's university inbox had a way of becoming flooded with emails if she didn't clear it out daily.

Her Atlantis Tablet had gained her notoriety with all the wrong people. The mystery of Atlantis called to ufologists, New Agers, and Lemurian theorists alike.

They all wanted to know about the magic, about the secret hidden knowledge the Atlanteans had allegedly possessed. It felt like Penelope spent half of every day emailing the enthusiasts back politely to say that she had no new information for them.

In her defense, Penelope had done everything she could not to get caught up in what she couldn't prove. She had stuck to facts, scraping away at the added mystery of the few primary sources she had, such as the one from Plato, trying to get to the heart of the mythic civilization.

Forever the realist, her father did his best to disregard the esoteric. The fact that Penelope's dream had been to find Atlantis since she was ten years old had caused him countless headaches. He couldn't look at her bookshelves, crammed with as many mythology collections and fantasy novels as academic textbooks and journals, without rolling his eyes.

"You're just like your grandmother," he often muttered in his Irish brogue. "She was mad by the time she died, leaving milk out for brownies and God knows what else." At times like that, Penelope regretted never having the chance to meet her grandmother. Both her parents were painfully atheist, believing only what could be proven by scientific theory.

Scrolling through her inbox, Penelope deleted the university newsletter and staff room spam until an unknown name caught her attention.

Who on earth is Marco Dandolo?

She opened the email, silently hoping he wasn't another crazy person.

Dear Doctor Bryne,

My associate, Doctor Alessa Christiano, gave me your paper on the Atlantis Tablet. She believes you might be able to assist in identifying markings I encountered this evening at a crime scene. Please forgive me for contacting you so directly, but our experts are at a loss and time is particularly short regarding this case. Please find the attached photo of a sample of the writing. I would appreciate any help you might be able to provide.

Regards,
Inspector Marco Dandolo

A crime scene? Penelope read the email twice. The footer had his official titles, the police station, and its crest. It wasn't spam. Penelope prayed it wasn't a virus before opening the attachment. The glass of wine fell from her hand, splattering red all over the tiles.

"Impossible. This can't…" Penelope zoomed in, trying to get a closer look, but the resolution of the photo only blurred. Five minutes later Penelope picked up her phone and called Carolyn.

"I knew you couldn't go three days without ringing!" Carolyn said triumphantly, "What's up, Bryne? Have another panic attack caused by your shit brain father?"

"Carolyn, don't freak out"—Penelope took a steady breath—"but I'm going to Venice."

THREE

HE LECTURE ROOM at the State Library was filled with students, scholars, and the curious. Penelope squeezed her notes together and tried to remind herself that this was not the first time she'd been forced to stand in front of people.

"You're going to be fine," Carolyn had assured her. She had a doctorate in Esoteric Religions and knew a tough crowd when she saw one. "This is a great turnout, Pen. The more people who know how brilliant you are, the more money they will give you to continue your research."

"Thanks, Caro," Penelope replied, her mouth dry. She tightened her ponytail and smoothed the lapels of her blazer again.

It was the first time she was going to present her paper on the Atlantis Tablet, and she was a bundle of tightly wound nerves. There were people in the audience who could help fund her dig off the islands of Crete. She had to be brave and confident. The Tablet demanded it of her.

Carolyn gave her a helpful shove after she was announced, and Penelope mumbled her thanks to the university and the State Library for allowing her to use the space for the lecture.

She began by providing a brief overview of the days leading up to the discovery. She had been diving off the islands of Crete after a statue of Poseidon had been found in a fisherman's net. Underwater shots were projected behind her as she moved through each slide of her PowerPoint.

"When I first discovered the stone fragment it was almost invisible due to the coral surrounding it," Penelope said, a trickle of sweat sliding down her back. "But this symbol here in the corner caught my eye."

She clicked to the next slide. A magnified version of the glyph appeared.

"As some of you may be aware, it looks like Sumerian cuneiform with its straight lines and triangle accents, but this curve at the end of the glyph doesn't fit. In fact, it looks almost like Sanskrit. You might be thinking, 'this is an absolute hoax,' which was my first thought too, until I read the results of the carbon dating tests we did at a lab in Athens."

Penelope clicked to the slide of the detailed report, and a rolling murmur went through the room as one by one the academics realized what they were looking at.

"As you can see, the stone dates from anywhere between 9000–10,000 BC. The oldest form of written text found so far has been protowriting, pictographs or symbol systems, like the Jiahu symbols found at Neolithic sites in China. The Bronze Age is where we see different alphabets emerging, one of the oldest being these hieroglyphs on the seal impression of the tomb of Seth-Peribson, dated at 2690 BC. Like the Phaistos

Disc found at Knossos, the Atlantis Tablet is an anomaly, completely unusual and undocumented. As the Tablet is fragmented, we may never be able to decipher a full alphabet without further research into the site where it was found."

Penelope continued her hypothesis of how the tides could have been responsible for the location of the Tablet from a different site lost under the waves.

"Forgive the interruption, Doctor, but are you talking about Atlantis right now?" Doctor Phillip Brown's voice was filled with mock amazement. Of course, he would have to be in attendance. He had been one of Penelope's teachers long ago, and she had never forgotten the arguments they had about Mycenaean cultures. They had quarreled about Atlantis even then.

"As a matter of fact, Doctor Brown, I am," Penelope replied. "I want you all to forget the stories and fairy tales. I want you to think about the possibility of a highly civilized culture on a group of islands located in the Mediterranean between Crete and Egypt. We have enough evidence from the island of Thera that proves a large-scale volcanic eruption occurred that could have been enough to destroy a culture already weakened by civil war. It is highly likely that the islands themselves would have had their own volcanos as they would have been on the same fault lines as Crete and Thera."

The room grew deathly silent as she continued, and Penelope wished someone would interrupt her again, even if it were the insipid Phillip Brown.

"What about magic?" an accented voice said from the back of the room.

Penelope lifted a hand against the spotlight but was unable to find him against the glare.

"Pardon me, did you say magic?" Penelope could barely keep the disbelief from her voice.

"You are claiming that the Atlanteans not only existed but that they were highly advanced. Surely you have read studies about them being a people of magic and science," the man persisted from the shadows.

Penelope tried to stay professional. "I'm talking about a *real* civilization, sir. I don't believe in magic, though their science could've been perceived as magic by outsiders who were less advanced. I don't believe in a city powered by magical crystals or theories of black magicians, such as Madame Blavatsky peddled to her followers."

"But you would have us believe you have uncovered a lost Atlantean language? I don't think considering the possibility of magic is much of a stretch," he argued, prompting chortles of laughter from the room.

"I see you're going to be persistent until you get my personal opinion." Penelope smiled at the shadow. "To answer you honestly, if the Atlanteans existed and they had magic and science, I believe they would've been intelligent enough to know the difference between an aqueduct and astral travel. They would've been completely different branches of study. My Tablet proves there was another people, a lost people, living in the Aegean before 10,000 BC and the only lost cul-

ture from that area that we have ever heard of, albeit
through academically unreliable sources, is Atlantis.
My hypothesis isn't unbelievable…"

"I don't believe the possibility of magic is either.
The Atlanteans are meant to be the precursors to the
Greeks, a highly magical and religious society," the man
argued, and Penelope ground her teeth. "This Tablet
looks religious to me."

"I didn't realize I had another Atlantis expert in the
audience," Penelope said, covering the bite in her tone
with a nervous laugh. "I would be happy to discuss any
theories once the lecture is over, sir. I'll even listen to a
magical theory if there is wine involved."

The audience chattered politely, but the white smile
at the back of the room only grew wider.

PENELOPE JERKED awake as the wheels of the
plane hit the tarmac with a hard bump. She ran a hand
through her loose curls, trying to shake the dream and
memories from her head. She wouldn't forget that
night as long as she lived. If she'd known ahead of time
how poorly it would go, she would never have agreed
to do that stupid lecture.

Penelope had done her best to dismiss all the unex-
plainable aspects of Atlantean culture, including the
odd events surrounding the discovery, such as the way
the dive crew had been forced to a different site due to
unusually high tides and choppy weather, or that the
water had been so cloudy she could barely see meters

in front of her, how it felt like an invisible line had tugged her toward an outcrop, how when her hand had touched the stone she felt a pulse pass through her.

Penelope shouldn't have been able to free the heavy block from the tight coral it was stuck in, but she'd only had to wriggle it once before it came loose. She had been fiercely protective of it, but the curators on Crete refused to let her leave the country with it. The government let her claim the find and permitted her to study it for as long as she wished, but her finances soon forced her back to Melbourne and into a contract role writing and tutoring students on Mediterranean history and archaeology. Her Tablet was to remain in Greece, and she had felt the ache of being apart from it. *It's just a bit of rock*, her father had said, *one that doesn't prove your theory on where the city is located.*

Penelope had only agreed to the lecture to try and raise financial support to get herself back to Greece. It was just her luck that there had to be an argumentative nut in the crowd. *That fucking guy*. She had seen him across the foyer after the event, but the glare on her face must have scared him away because he never did try and discuss his magical theory with her.

In the weeks after the lecture and her publication in the *Journal of Oceanic Cultural Research* she had a few potential investors interested, but one by one they had disappeared, along with the possibility of any grant money. She was rejected more than once on the basis that it wasn't an Australian discovery and she was acting like a treasure hunter, not an academic.

The black moleskin notebook Penelope had bought at the airport on her connecting flight in Sydney had fallen to the floor, and she placed it securely in her handbag. She had been filling the thick, lined pages with notes and initial observations about the wall in Venice. Penelope took out her phone and looked at the photo again. Should she dare to get excited? *It was that over-ambition that you hung yourself with last time, Penelope.*

It took an hour to get through customs at the Marco Polo Airport and find a bathroom. Penelope put on some eyeliner, mascara, and lip gloss to get the look of travel off her face. She was about to charge into a police station. It couldn't hurt to look good.

It took twenty minutes of her taxi's rally driving through tight motorway traffic to reach the Questura di Venezia in Santa Croce. It was only when she was clinging for dear life to the door of the Alpha Romeo that Penelope realized just what she had done. The terra-cotta roofs and blue canals of Venice loomed in front of her, and her heart began to race, sweat moistening the back of her neck as panic gripped her. This was, even by Penelope's standards, one of the most impulsive things she had ever done.

They parked in front of the police station and Penelope all but leapt from the car in her eagerness to be on solid ground. She took a deep, steadying breath, picked up her small suitcase, and opened the door of the ochre brick building. The officer behind the desk eyed Penelope as she approached. He looked her over distrustfully, and Penelope tried not to flinch.

"*Mi scusi, parla inglese?*" Penelope asked nervously.

"How can I assist?" the officer said.

"I'm looking for Inspector Marco Dandolo. Is he here at the moment?" Penelope opened the email Marco had sent her and showed it to the officer. "This is the right police station isn't it?"

"Take a seat." The officer gestured to some uncomfortable waiting room chairs and picked up the phone. Penelope didn't sit. She'd been sitting for hours. Instead, she filled a plastic cup with water from a cooler and slowly paced. The officer's eyes watched her as he spoke rapid Italian, too fast and low for Penelope to catch the gist of the conversation.

Finally, he hung up and glared at her. "He's coming."

Ten minutes later a man appeared, cursing at the duty officer who pointed toward Penelope with a smirk. This time she caught part of the conversation. The duty officer thought she was a disgruntled lover and Marco was trying to deny that he knew her.

Unlike the officer wearing the blue and gray uniform of the Polizia de Strato, Marco Dandolo dressed in a black suit with a white button-down shirt. With only a few gray hairs in his curling black hair and some minor stress lines around his mouth, he looked about forty. He had olive skin, black stubble, and probably would have been handsome if he smiled, but at the moment he wore a deep, intimidating scowl.

"You are Penelope Bryne, the archaeologist?" he asked as he joined her in the waiting room.

Penelope held out her hand. "I got your email, Inspector Dandolo."

He took her hand and reluctantly shook it. "You received my email and came to Venice to see me?" His frown deepened, and Penelope laughed nervously.

"Of course! You can't send a photo like that to an expert and not get a response."

"I expected a response, just not a visit." He took a deep breath and gestured toward the door. "Come on. I need a smoke."

Marco led her to a smoking area that looked out over the police boats and offered her his packet of cigarettes.

"No, thank you." Penelope smiled politely. "So, the photo you sent me, are there any more?"

"Why? Can you read it?"

"Not the bad resolution you sent me," Penelope replied as she opened the photo on her phone and held it out to him. "See that large fork-like glyph? That's an alchemical symbol for Neptune or Poseidon. This one here is the water of life. The third is for a vessel or a woman. What was the crime? Was there a bull involved?"

Marco choked on his cigarette smoke. "Why would you ask that?"

"The symbols together allude to a sacrifice. People loved to sacrifice bulls during the Neptunalia to ensure fertility and a good harvest, but that is in July, not February. They liked to sacrifice horses, too, because Poseidon was the God of Atlantis, and it is said they were the first people to tame horses. It might be relevant."

"What about the rest of the script?" he asked. His tone was bored, but Penelope saw the flash of interest in his eyes.

"You were right. It's the same language I found on the Atlantis Tablet, but there's far more of it. If I could have a look at the site, I might be able to help with a translation."

"You flew all this way to offer your services as a consultant?"

"No. I flew all this way because that language hasn't been seen in ten thousand years and I want to find out who the hell wrote it," Penelope replied bluntly. "But I will also agree to be your consultant if it means we can find them."

Marco Dandolo studied her slowly and won extra points by not letting his gaze drift down from her face. "Let me go and talk to the Questore and see what he thinks. He can decide if you'll be worth it."

"If I'm not, you can tell him good luck on finding anyone else who can help him understand a dead language from a lost civilization." Penelope folded her arms stubbornly, but because she had bills to pay, she added, "You can tell him my consultation fees start at €300 a day. The longer he makes me wait, the higher it will go up."

Marco let out a surprised bark of laughter. "Ha! I think I'm going to like you, *Dottore*."

QUESTORE ADALFIERI of Venice was a rotund man with oiled white hair and a thick mustache. He eyed Penelope shrewdly as Marco introduced her in Italian twenty minutes later.

"*Buon pomeriggio,*" she said with a friendly smile. He gave her the slightest nod before talking to Marco in a deep bass voice, Penelope forgotten.

You have insinuated yourself into a police investigation in a foreign country. You didn't think it was going to be easy did you, Pen? She wasn't bothered by their dismissive attitude toward her. She had spent her entire life around patriarchal academics who looked down their noses at her breasts and outspoken ways. She wanted to see the graffitied wall. Her mind burned with the images she had been shown, and if that meant playing nice, she was going to do it.

Marco protested loudly as the word DIGOS was mentioned, but the Questore merely shrugged and pointed to the door. Marco threw up his hands in exasperation.

"What's going on?" Penelope asked, still smiling nervously.

"He's agreed to pay you, provided you produce something useful toward the case. I'm going to take you to your hotel," he said as he directed her back toward the busy offices.

"Does that mean you are finally going to tell me what type of crime scene it is?" she asked.

"I'll tell you on the way."

Outside, Marco led her down to the docks where a blue-and-white patrol boat was being refueled.

"We go by water from here," he said, placing her suitcase on the deck before offering her a hand as she stepped in. "Adalfieri's sister owns a hotel in Dorsoduro and has a room for you. Carnevale is a terrible time for space so it's lucky she had some visitors leave for a family emergency, otherwise you probably would have been stuck on my couch."

"I've slept in worse places," Penelope said. "I was on a dig in Israel once, and I had to sleep under the Jeep."

"Don't tell Adalfieri that, or he'll stop paying for the hotel." Marco laughed, and her anxiety eased. With well-practiced precision, he maneuvered the boat onto the canals.

Penelope tried not to appear overly impressed as the buildings and boats of Venice flashed by. She hadn't been to Venice in ten years and couldn't believe she was here now. A part of her had wanted to return for years; she had missed the warm terra-cotta roofs, inverted cone chimneys, colorful boats, and the dilapidated grandeur of its buildings.

Venice had survived like a small pocket of the decadent past, its mythology only enhanced by the world that loved and protected her, even if they were not Venetian. It was a city that still welcomed all and stole their hearts as easily as it relieved the money from their giving pockets. Penelope fought hard to contain her excitement, reminding herself of the unusual circumstances that had inspired her to come.

"It was a murder," Marco said, steering with one hand and passing her his phone with the other. "I hope you have a strong stomach, *Dottore*."

"Jesus," Penelope whispered as she scrolled through the photos. A woman was strung up and wearing a bull's head. "Can you email me these?"

"Now that Adalfieri has cleared you, I'll send you the entire report. I have been working this job for over twenty years, and I haven't seen anything like it."

"And you have no idea who did it?"

"There was no DNA evidence found at the scene. Whoever the killer is, they knew what they were doing. The woman is the daughter of a prominent judge. We are trying to keep it out of the media as much as we can because he has such a high profile, and it's a sensitive time here in Venice."

"Why is that?"

"He was in charge of the corruption cases against the MOSE project," Marco explained over the roar of the engine. "It officially comes online in a fortnight. It is why they might make us work with DIGOS."

"I'm sorry, DIGOS?"

"The Divisione Investigazioni Generali e Operazioni Speciali is the anti-terrorism branch here in Italy, and they are *arrogante*."

"It was one murder. That doesn't sound like terrorist activity to me," Penelope replied.

"They are more nervous than usual because of the MOSE launch, and they are worried about someone trying to sabotage it."

Penelope had heard of the billion-dollar MOSE project designed to keep Venice and the lagoon from flooding during the Adriatic Sea's high tides. Multiple gates had been installed at the Lido, Malamocco, and Chioggia inlets that would be able to temporarily isolate Venice and protect it from being damaged.

"I managed to convince the Questore to dissuade them as much as he can. DIGOS will only get in the way," added Marco. "You better be as useful as I hope so we can solve this quickly."

"You and me both," Penelope muttered. She looked at the photos again and swallowed the lump in her throat. *What the hell have you put your foot into now?*

Within seconds of stepping off the boat, Penelope was grateful for Marco's lead through the perplexing maze of streets. The hotel was a neat bed-and-breakfast on the Fondamenta Eremite. It smelled of coffee and the rosemary and lavender bunches that hung above the doors to mask the tang of the briny canal outside.

Marco flirted outrageously with Louisa, the Questore's younger sister, who smiled widely when Marco kissed both of her round cheeks in greeting. She had twenty years at least on his age, but it didn't stop her blushing and sweet talking him.

"I'll give you tonight to sleep and get over your jet lag," Marco said as Louisa went to retrieve the room key. "Tomorrow I'll take you to the site."

"I don't need to sleep," Penelope protested. "I did on the plane. This writing isn't going to be easy to translate and as soon as I can get started—"

Marco held up a hand. "Tomorrow. I need to check with forensics about some things before I let you into the crime scene. I'll send you a full report on what they learned about the body in case something is relevant. I need to sleep, too." He must've sensed Penelope's hesitation because he let out an exhausted huff, adding, "The wall will still be there in the morning, *Dottore*. Sleep. I need you at your best." He kissed Louisa Adalfieri once more before leaving Penelope in her matronly hands.

Penelope's room was clean and simple with a large wardrobe, narrow desk, and a double bed, its headboard painted in a homely cream-and-gold. Louisa handed her a key with a wide red tag and left her with an open invitation for dinner.

It was five o'clock in Venice, and well past midnight in Australia, but Penelope was too wired to sleep. She opened her bag and unpacked her laptop.

Surely Marco could've taken her to see the wall! It was ridiculous that she had traveled all this way only to get dumped in a hotel. *You should be grateful they didn't kick you out of the police station.*

She set up her toiletries in the bathroom in a neat row before peeling off her traveling clothes and taking a hot shower to ease the cramped muscles in her shoulder and the anxiety in her stomach. Penelope always had problems with nerves before starting a big project, and a murder only added to that. She hoped the faith Marco and Adalfieri were placing in her abilities wouldn't be in vain.

Penelope dried her hair and dressed in a pair of leggings and a baggy T-shirt. She shut the glass window that looked out over the Rio de le Romite and set her suitcase out of the way. Gradually, she folded herself down into a downward facing dog pose, her back clicking twice before her hands reached the floor.

Like most academics, Penelope's posture wasn't the best, and Carolyn had convinced her to start yoga to prevent getting a hunchback. At the end of a long day, yoga was the only exercise Penelope could do that successfully cleared the white noise from her mind. Thirty minutes of yoga followed by fifteen minutes of meditation was her sweet spot. If she was going to get any sleep at all that night, she needed to relax her mind.

Penelope moved through the series of poses slowly, controlling her breathing. She struggled to quiet her mind. Carolyn believed she had undiagnosed ADHD, but Penelope had never bothered to get it checked, owing her restlessness to boredom. She had to be thinking or moving or creating in some way. Meditation and sleep were the only times she was still.

After twenty minutes of yoga to unkink her traveler's back, Penelope sat down on the soft bed.

In the early days of meditation practice, she used to focus on the Greek word *akinitos* (meaning still) in order to command her body to relax. Now she only had to focus on her breath for a few moments before the calm settled over her.

Meditation had saved her over the past two years as she watched her research ridiculed throughout the academic world. After the lecture, her reputation had fallen apart, and she had borne it with as much stubborn grace that she could muster. It was only through contacts of her father's that she had gotten a job teaching online university courses. It wasn't glamorous, but she was lucky to still be allowed to teach at all.

Penelope listened to the sound of the boats out on the water, voices in the street, and the faint strains of a Paganini concerto Louisa was playing while she cooked. She filtered each sound out, one at a time, until a deep calm pulled her under a blanket of silence.

A few moments later, her mind's eye snapped open unexpectedly.

She was standing in a circular room at the top of a tower. White marble arches opened out to the sky, with views of the Venice lagoon on one side and the city on the other.

Penelope had experienced different visions of places while in meditations for as long as she had been practicing. The only difference this time was the man sitting cross-legged in the center of the room. She had never seen anyone but herself in her meditations. Not ever. Carolyn had mentioned guides, but Penelope was skeptical about the idea of metaphysical beings interested in helping her out.

The man in front of her didn't look like a mystical guide. He looked like a Turkish corsair, dressed in *entari* robes from the late Ottoman era. He wore loose white trousers of finely woven linen, and his long bare feet were tucked under his crossed legs.

Fascinated by his unexpected appearance, Penelope walked over to study him. His dark brown chest was bare, tattooed with designs and symbols she had never seen before in blue ink. As she studied the symbols, they disappeared into his skin, and others appeared in their place.

Penelope circled him as quietly as she could. His robe was magnificent. The silk was peacock blue with a variety of embroidered symbols trailing down the back. From her studies, she recognized them as a blending of magical symbolism; a star and crescent from Islamic and Byzantine cultures, an Egyptian Wadjet eye and Shen Ring, a complex Indian hamsa hand, and an Icelandic Veldismagn Rune, as well as many others she didn't recognize.

He had a narrow face with high cheekbones, a closely trimmed beard, and a thick riot of black hair that curled around his face and neck. His long back was perfectly straight, and his eyes were closed, lost in a meditation of his own.

If I touch him, will my hand go straight through? As Penelope reached out to poke his shoulder, his eyes snapped open with sharp awareness. They were such a startling blue that Penelope jumped backward. The smile, when it came, was slow and devious.

"Who are you?" Penelope asked, too shocked to move.

"How did you get in here?" he said, his Turkish accent a dangerous purr.

He reached out to her, but Penelope's body jolted awake back in her hotel room. Heart racing, she jumped to her feet, unsure of what to do with the sudden adrenaline pouring through her.

Who the hell was that?

FOUR

WHEN MARCO DANDOLO arrived at the hotel at 9:00 a.m., he found Penelope awake and drinking strong coffee with Louisa. She looked exhausted, which didn't bode well for the day. He had been skeptical when she first arrived at the station, but after seeing how she handled Adalfieri, he was learning a quick mind and a temper to match lingered under her distractingly pleasant frame.

"What's happened? Did you not sleep at all?" he asked after accepting a coffee from Louisa.

"A new city and nerves prevented it," Penelope said. "Don't let it bother you. I'm an academic. We are used to being sleep deprived." She smiled.

"You sound like my ex-girlfriend; Alessa was the same. Her breakthroughs always seemed to occur at three in the morning." Marco shook his head in sympathy. Those crazy working hours were probably the only thing he didn't miss about her.

"I am keen to see the wall," Penelope stated before draining her coffee. "I want to know if the language is real or made up. If it's fake, I want to know how they got access to the Atlantis Tablet long enough to get the glyphs right. It's locked up in an archive in Crete, and the samples we published weren't complete."

Marco could see the frustration in her hazel green eyes. Dressed in black boots, tight black jeans, a T-shirt and blazer, she looked almost too fashionable for an academic. He had expected a pinch-faced old lady or a pale young spinster. Doctor Bryne was fit, with a pretty smattering of freckles over her light brown skin. If he wasn't working with her, he would have asked her out for a drink. He liked smart women. Unfortunately, they were always smart enough to leave him and his hectic life.

Penelope wrapped a dark red scarf around her throat to keep the canal wind at bay and followed him to the patrol boat he had waiting. Tourists were already pouring into Santa Croce, but Marco and Penelope avoided most of the crowd thanks to the Tintoretto's giving the Polizia de Strato permission to use their private dock.

Beppe met them at the palazzo, having already spoken with the housekeeper to let her know that there would be more *polizia* arriving. The formidable, gray-haired woman seemed to enjoy having so many young officers around to flirt with and had brought them biscotti and espresso on more than one occasion.

Beppe greeted Penelope with a blushing, "*Buongiorno Dottore.*"

"Hello," Penelope replied, aiming a smile at the young man. "Marco tells me you were the first person on the scene when the body was found."

"*Si.* I'm glad they have taken it away, *signorina*," Beppe said. "I'll show you the way." She followed him through the palazzo without batting an eye at the frescoed roofs or priceless antiques. Behind them Marco smiled; she had a one-track mind. It was going to be good working with another hound.

Out in the courtyard, Beppe stepped down onto the damp pavement of the canal entrance.

"Watch your step, *signorina*. It is still slippery from the high tide," he warned, but Penelope was already walking toward the wall with wide eyes. Marco watched her take in the iron rings where the body had been raised up against the stonework. She took an Olympus camera out of her bag and started photographing the wall from top to bottom.

"Have you analyzed what they used to write the script?" she asked, her voice heavy with emotion.

"Forensics said it was a mix of the bull and the victim's blood. She was almost drained entirely, but that's hardly surprising with her feet severed," Marco replied.

"Was her throat cut?" Penelope asked, barely looking up from the small screen on her camera.

"No. Her cause of death was asphyxiation from the bull's head. It had been hollowed out, like a mask, but it was still…meaty." Beppe paled beside him. He hadn't been privy to the autopsy, and Marco was starting to wonder if Beppe had the right sort of stomach for police work.

"You didn't send me the forensics report last night," Penelope stated disapprovingly. "I would like you to do that now, *per favore*."

"Why would you want to know all the gory details? Isn't this horrible wall enough?" Beppe asked.

"No," replied Penelope sharply. "We already know it was ritualistic but to go to this much effort...every piece is important and symbolic. The writing will give meaning to the body and vice versa. There is such a collision of symbols and chthonic religion here, I need every piece to figure out what it is. These alchemical symbols are the only thing that remotely makes sense."

"How so?" asked Marco.

"As I told you yesterday, this symbol here"— Penelope pointed to the large trident intersected with a cross—"this is Neptune, or more likely Poseidon, as the other elements are more Greek than Roman. This V here top and center..."

"It is for a woman like in *The Da Vinci Code*," Beppe chimed in. The look that Penelope gave him was so pitiful that Marco struggled to keep a straight face.

"Sometimes, yes, this V is used for women and a chalice," she said indulgently, "but in this context, I think it's more relevant as the alchemical symbol for water. The same with this other V with the circles on the points, except it is *aqua de vida*, the water of life. One could assume this was a sacrifice to Poseidon, but it's unlike anything I've read about before. The script could change the meaning of it, translate as something completely different."

"But your first guess is a sacrifice to Poseidon? I didn't think anyone still worshipped the old gods." Marco rubbed his chin thoughtfully.

"Some do. The person who did this isn't just a believer. They are obsessed. I'm not even sure it's to

Poseidon; it seems too dark." Her brows pulled tightly together as she studied the symbols, leaning in so the wall was only inches from her face. "It is the same writing as the Atlantis Tablet, but it's so intricate, so complete. How could anyone know this language still?"

"Maybe it's a smaller dialect you didn't know about?" suggested Marco.

"It's not possible, trust me. This has been my work for the past two years. I have cross-checked with every dialect and alphabet from the Aegean to Egypt and the Middle East, and every sea-trading people on earth." She pushed a hand through her thick curls in frustration. "My reputation depended on it, and I did the research, Inspector." She had the fire of obsession in her eyes. It was a look Marco was familiar with, so he dropped it and let her work.

After a trip to the Questura to print photos and get a hard copy of the forensics file, Marco took Penelope back to her hotel so she could study the records and cross-reference them with her research. He had wanted to use her as an excuse to get out of paperwork, but the good doctor had rejected his offer of lunch, preferring to keep researching on her own. Marco didn't mind the rejection. She was onto something, and he knew that it was wise not to get in the way of a smart woman when she was working.

WITH YEARS of academic study under her belt, Penelope spread out the photos she had taken and began methodically tacking them in order onto the wall of the hotel. When it was completed, she had a small recreation of what she was calling "The Bull Wall." She had tried to keep on a professional face while Marco had patiently waited for her to study the scene, but inside she had been screaming with excitement and terror. The writing emanated menace.

Beside it, she stuck up photos of the original hanging of the body and the analysis reports of the remains as well as the other items found at the scene. Finally, she dragged the narrow desk to the center of the room facing the wall of information and set up her laptop.

"Okay, let's start with what we know, Bryne," she said aloud to herself as she typed bullet points onto a blank document. "A woman, recently given birth, was taken from outside of the Chiesa di San Giacomo dell'Orio. Her feet were removed and replaced with feet of clay. The umbilical cord had been forced inside of her vagina, and the bull fetus was placed where the tide would fill the bowl and pull it back out to sea. Calves were sacrificed throughout the world, especially by placing them in the sea. Her heart was removed and is still missing. A trophy? The goblet she held in one hand contained blood, wine, and seawater, which they are still analyzing. The amphora held bull's blood…"

Penelope was reaching for another memory of Aegean cults when her mobile rang.

"Hello, this is Doctor—"

"Penelope," a hard voice interrupted her. Stuart Bryne's Irish brogue was thick and angry, causing

Penelope to cringe. "Where are you? Your mother has been calling your phone for two days."

"I've been traveling," Penelope replied, trying to sound calm as her mind went from academic to scolded daughter. "I was going to give her a call tonight, but the time differences are off in Italy and—"

"Italy! What the hell are you doing there? You were supposed to meet your mother in Wellington next week."

"I'm in Venice working with the police," Penelope said with a burst of frustration. "Shopping in Wellington can wait."

"Working with the police?" Stuart Bryne's voice didn't lose any of its edge. "What's happened, Pen? How could you possibly help them?"

"A woman has been murdered, and it's connected to my Tablet. You'll never believe it but—"

"That bloody Tablet has ruined your career, and still you're pursuing it! Let it go, Pen. Separate yourself from this fairy tale once and for all, for your own sake."

"It's my career to burn, Stuart, not yours. A woman is dead, and if I can help I will," she said coldly, knowing that using his first name would annoy him. "Tell Mom I'll speak to her soon."

Penelope hung up before she lost her temper and said something she couldn't take back. She had inherited her anger from him, and she hated it about herself. She hated even more that he could still provoke that reaction from her. *I'm thirty-five for fuck's sake. Why can't he treat me like it?*

Penelope tried to focus on the case for another ten minutes before giving up and putting on her jacket. Her concentration had been shot to hell, and she needed to walk it off. With any luck, it would exhaust her enough that she might get some sleep. She wasn't about to try meditation again after yesterday. She couldn't get the mystery man out of her head and had spent the previous evening staring at the ceiling. Walking was the next best thing.

Penelope strolled casually up the Fondamenta Eremite, taking in the architecture around her and letting the bunched muscles in her shoulders relax. Despite the phone call from her father and the case, she was in Venice, and there were few cities in the world as beautiful as La Serenissima. She admired the facade of the Chiesa delle Eremite before crossing the small bridge over the Rio de le Romite.

As Penelope walked, she thought of the murder and the script on the wall. She wasn't a linguist, but ancient alphabets were familiar to her. Her father used to challenge her continually as a child, leaving messages written in Greek, Hebrew, and cuneiform. He had a brilliant child who unfortunately had a brilliant imagination to go with it. At an early age, Penelope had turned to the myth that fascinated her most—Atlantis—and she had been obsessed ever since.

Penelope was walking past a bar on the Fondamenta Toletta when a tall man stepped out in front of her with an espresso in his hand. She collided hard with his chest and he only just managed to prevent spilling his coffee all over her.

"*Mi scusi signore*," she apologized quickly, blushing furiously.

"It's okay, it's okay, not a drop was spilled." He looked down at her and smiled. He was striking in only the way an Italian man could be in bone-white trousers and a blue dress shirt. He had curling black hair and a charming white smile.

"*Posso offrirti una bevanda calda per sciogliere il ghiaccio?*" he asked flirtatiously. Penelope picked up the offer of a drink and ice melting, but the rest of the pickup line was lost on her.

"No thank you, maybe some other time," she said politely as she moved around him. "Sorry again." She continued her walk, an unexpected smile on her face.

Penelope reached the end of the lane before her mind caught up and she stopped dead in her tracks.

He had been wearing different clothes, and his eyes had been brown instead of blue, but the man from her meditation had just run straight into her. Penelope hurried back to the café but he was gone, only an empty espresso cup to show he'd been there at all.

FIVE

"HAS IT FINALLY happened, Bryne? Have you finally gone crazy?" Carolyn asked from the other side of the world.

"I haven't left the hotel in two days, does that count?" Penelope replied from her position on the floor. She stared up at the photos of the Bull accusingly.

"I still can't get over the fact that you are in Italy. I mean, it takes a lot for you to do anything impulsive, Pen. When you do, it's an epic runaway to Venice to solve crimes with a hot cop."

"What makes you think he is hot?" Penelope laughed.

"I have Google, Pen. Marco Dandolo was hailed a hero two years ago when he rescued a child from a kidnapper. There are pictures. If he hasn't gained thirty kilos and lost all of his hair since this picture was taken, then he is a hottie."

"Venice is filled with good-looking men. I bumped into one the other day, and he asked me out. The Italians do love to flirt." A small part of Penelope wished her brain had been fast enough to realize he was the man from her meditation.

"You are so clueless. Why are you hiding out in a city of beautiful men?"

"I'm busy working. It's driving me crazy. A year ago I would have died for a breakthrough like this. It's my script! It's all there so why can't I decipher it?"

"Maybe you are too close to it? I don't know, Pen, you don't exactly have a Rosetta Stone to help you out. This is a dead language we are talking about."

"But it's not dead! It's right here in front of me. Someone knows it and is using it. I don't want to mess this up. We need to find the sicko who did this."

Carolyn let out a tired sigh. "Look, I know how much being awesome at everything means to you but cracking a language takes time. You don't want to disappoint Inspector Hottie, so maybe you need to focus on the things you *do* know. Leave the stupid wall. Tell him what you are sure about while you figure out the rest."

Penelope sat up and pulled her notebook out from under the bed where it had fallen.

"God, I hate it when you're right," she groaned.

"You rang me for advice. You can't complain about the quality of said advice," Carolyn said. "By the way, you sound totally wired. Have you been keeping up with your meditations?"

"Ha! After last time I'm too nervous to meditate," replied Penelope.

"What happened last time? Did you see something cool?"

"Not really, just some Turkish corsair in a tower." Penelope bit her lip. "I didn't think he could see me, but then he talked to me. I freaked out."

"Woah! It sounds like you might have astral projected for the first time. Intense, isn't it? I don't think it's anything to be afraid of though," Carolyn replied enthusiastically. "I've spoken to plenty of people in meditations. The images can't hurt you. And hey, you never know, maybe he has a message for you."

"Unless he has a message that includes this stupid wall, I don't want to hear it."

"Maybe you should ask him," said Carolyn thoughtfully.

"Sure thing. I just need to jump back into mediation land and say, 'Hey, Hot Turkish corsair guy, come help a sister out by checking out my wall, and buy me a coffee while you are at it.'"

"Pen, what's wrong?"

"Can I tell you something weird without you judging me?"

"Depends on how weird it is. You just told me you met a dark, mysterious stranger in your head."

"I think I saw him in the street," admitted Penelope. "The guy I bumped into, his eyes were different, but I *swear* it was him."

"And he didn't recognize you?"

"I don't think so. He didn't say anything. It sounds crazy." Penelope let out an exasperated sigh.

"Maybe it wasn't an astral projection. Maybe it was like a premonition," Carolyn said seriously. "Maybe you were meant to meet him."

"Why would I need to meet some stranger? It doesn't make sense." Penelope tapped her pen on her notebook. "And if it *was* so I could meet him, I blew it and kept walking."

"If he's important, you'll see him again."

Penelope knew better than to argue with Carolyn about premonitions and déjà vu. "Look, Caro, I need to go. You're right. I should put a report together for Marco."

"Take care of yourself, Bryne. I've got to admit I don't have the greatest feeling about you being caught up in a case with a murdering nut bag."

Penelope promised to watch her back and hung up. After two days of staring at the photos, she needed to touch base with reality. She texted Marco, asking if he felt like dinner and a debriefing. She needed to get out of the hotel and away from the symbols for a bit, away from the dead eyes of the Bull which seemed to follow her around the room.

The feeling that she had met the man from the meditation on the streets refused to go away, however. Dinner was three hours away; she had time for more meditation. *Better that you make the first move than leave it to him.*

Penelope showered and dressed in her favorite black jeans and red sweater while debating whether or not to follow Carolyn's suggestion and ask the man flat out who he was or if he had a message for her. Her hands trembled as she applied her makeup, a sure sign that her anxiety was ramping up.

Giving in, Penelope sat down on her bed and shut her eyes. Instead of focusing on a word, she focused on the man, pulling up details of his face and voice. She was about to give up when she felt a small tug inside of her chest like an invisible line had straightened, and she was suddenly sitting in a café under a large cream umbrella, the man sitting opposite her.

He pushed a small cup of espresso across the table toward her. "I was waiting to see if you would turn up again." He wore a cream suit and a shirt the same gray-blue as the sea in front of them. His dark curls were tied back in a stylishly lazy bun.

Penelope could smell the sharp sea air, the hot, fragrant coffee, and her companion's aftershave; a curious, alluring combination that reminded her of firecrackers, cinnamon, and sandalwood.

"Is this real?" she asked, her mouth dry. Being pulled out of her hotel room had left her dizzy.

"As in are we physically at a café right now? No. This is a space created so we can talk," he replied.

"Created by who?" Penelope glanced around at the tourists taking photos and the waiters serving food. It seemed so real.

"By me, of course. I thought this would be more suitable than my tower." He sipped his coffee, watching her curiously with his violently blue eyes. "I thought it would be obvious considering it's my meditation you keep interrupting."

"Your meditation! You are interrupting mine," she protested. She touched the side of her espresso, the heat seeping through the porcelain and into her skin. *Impos-*

sible. "I don't know who you are or what you want. My friend said to ask if you had a message for me. She is more used to this kind of thing happening."

Something in his mocking expression softened. "Be careful what you dig into. You will only find death on the other side of it."

Penelope looked down at the slender, brown hand that had come to rest over hers. "If we aren't really here, how come I can feel you?"

"This is my space. I want you to feel it when I touch you."

"Are you a real person? Here in Venice?"

"Does it matter?" His fingers drifted up her forearm, gently stroking. "How do you have the ability to break into a magician's mind, Penelope?"

"Magician?" Penelope jumped as his hand tightened unexpectedly, pinning it to the table. "What are you talking about? And how do you know my name?"

"You really have no idea what's going on, do you? Regardless, I will find out where you got your abilities," he promised seriously. "I will find out what you really are."

"No, you won't." She yanked her hand out of his grasp, and before he could stop her, she forced herself awake.

Her eyes opened, and the room spun around her. She looked down at her arm. There was no mark from where he had held her, only the faint smell of spice and firecrackers lingering on her skin.

"I WAS happy to get your message," Marco said an hour later as they walked through the narrow streets. "I was starting to think I was going to have to drag you away from that wall myself."

"I'm not going to lie to you, I haven't cracked the language, but I thought you deserved an update so you know I'm not wasting your time," Penelope said, pushing her hands deeper into the pockets of her coat. The sun hadn't quite set, and all of Venice was filled with a misty orange light. Despite the cold sea breeze and her bad mood, it was devastatingly beautiful.

"You don't strike me as a time waster, Doctor Bryne," answered Marco. "I don't expect you to solve this case on your own, only give insight into what you can. We both have our areas of expertise. I'm trying to keep you out of the routine police work, so you have space to focus on the rest."

"You are remarkably understanding, Inspector Dandolo," she said.

He laughed loudly. "Can I get that in writing so I can email it to all of my ex-girlfriends?"

They found a small restaurant and sat at a table away from other customers so details of the case wouldn't be overheard.

"I've written you a report that I'll email to you," Penelope explained as Marco poured her red wine.

"Tell me about our killer, in your own words, not a report. I hate reports. I want to understand your thoughts and process in your own words."

"Okay, the killer is obsessed to an extreme level," she began, toying with the stem of her glass. "Not a Christian in any religious sense. He is a practitioner of a religion as dead as the language he was writing in."

"What religion?" Marco asked.

Penelope swallowed a mouthful of wine, hoping it would give her courage. "Do you believe in demons, Inspector?" She expected him to laugh in her face, but instead, his expression darkened.

"Yes. I'm a Catholic and if angels and saints can influence people, why not devils and demons? I've certainly seen enough in my time to convince me that both are real."

"Have you ever heard of the name Thevetat?"

"No, should I have?"

"I should point out there's no real academic evidence for what I'm about to say but try and keep an open mind. A lot of what people know of Atlantis is pure myth. There are stories about information being channeled through spiritual mediums like Helena Blavatsky, who wrote how Atlanteans lived before the cataclysm and what happened to them afterward. One of the theories is that worshippers of a powerful demon called Thevetat arose within their society. Magicians, or good priests, whichever you prefer, stood against them but ultimately the power struggle led to the destruction of Atlantis. There are stories of survivors coming to the other continents, and I suppose that would mean the good with the bad."

"And you think our killer believes some of this?" Marco asked.

"From what I can tell he's worshipping Thevetat or trying to. I can't figure out if he's part of a cult, or if he was simply taken in by the theories and decided to do it on his own. It might not be academically sound, but it's true to him."

A waiter arrived before Marco had a chance to reply and Penelope tried not to fall on her *risotto al nero di seppie*. She had been living off coffee, toast, and biscotti for the last two days and her stomach knew it. The wine was warming her and helping her to relax. Marco still hadn't called her crazy, so she took it as a good sign.

"Do you think our killer has friends?" he asked.

"From the way the body was positioned, he either had to have a helper, or he's freakishly strong. The victim had given birth less than a week beforehand. She wasn't exactly petite."

"What about the murder itself? Do you think it was a ritual to this Thevetat?"

"Most definitely, though the connection it had with the water makes me think it was more than a common practice ritual. It's something…special. It has intent, but…" Penelope hesitated, unable to say the words.

"It's a spell," Marco finished. "They are doing *la magia*."

"I'm sure the killer believes he is. What he thinks the magic can do I won't know until I crack the language. There are so many symbols to Poseidon, which almost makes it seem like a petition from demon god to sea god." Penelope shook her head. "I know it sounds completely cracked."

"It does but as you say, it makes sense to the killer," Marco replied. "Now, for the harder question: do you think he's likely to kill again?"

"I have a hunch that he will, but I'm no police officer for that to be reliable. The murder was shamelessly bold, a spectacle. Nothing about it was random. It was carefully planned in every detail."

"I'll keep looking into the woman and see if I can find any connection that might be suitable for a motive. Her father is a very well-connected man so it might lead to more speculation. Who knows what these rich people are into."

They talked for another hour and were waiting for their coffee to arrive when Marco's phone rang.

"I have to go back to work," he complained. "The Questore wants a progress report in person. He's too lazy to read them."

"Sounds like you," Penelope teased. "Do you want me to come with you?"

"No, no. Stay and enjoy your night. We shouldn't both have to suffer from more after-hours work."

"I'm more than happy to stay here and eat your *zaeti*." Penelope grinned. She loved the raisin and polenta cookies.

"*Va bene*. You have good taste, like a Venetian." He smiled back at her approvingly. "I'll give you a call tomorrow and check in. Don't hide for days at a time, *Dottore*, it's not healthy. Do you know your way back to the hotel?"

"I'll be fine, don't leave the Questore waiting. I don't want him to have any reason to think I'm not keeping up my end of our deal."

"I believe he's a little intimidated by you," Marco replied. He went to kiss her cheek, hesitated, and held out his hand instead.

Penelope shook it. "We'll talk tomorrow, Inspector. Thank you for dinner."

"*Prego*. Be careful walking back."

"Don't worry. I'm a big tough girl who can handle herself."

Penelope watched him leave and for a moment felt remarkably lonely. While he was around, she wasn't thinking of the man from her meditation or contemplating if she was losing her mind. A waiter brought her coffee and *zaeti* that she broke into pieces to dunk.

Penelope had tried hard not to get caught up in superstitions and new age philosophies, but a secret part of her wanted to believe in the stories of a magical Atlantis. It just wasn't the way to get anywhere in academia. After her astral projection and meeting the stranger, she was seriously reassessing what she believed. Carolyn was always insisting that the world was far weirder and more magical than what it appeared. Maybe it was time she started to listen.

Penelope remembered the strange tug inside of her that had taken her to the café that didn't exist. It had been like an invisible line that had pulled on her the same way the Atlantis Tablet had done the day she had found it.

What was it? She closed her eyes and tried to focus, imagining it in front of her, and tugged back experimentally. When nothing happened, she shrugged and went back to her espresso.

The stranger had said he was a magician, and she'd just spent an hour describing a killer trying to do magic. Her squid ink risotto shuddered in her stomach. Was he the one they were hunting? She rubbed her arm where he had touched it, trying to forget the phantom sensation of his hand. He hadn't felt like a creepy murderer, but then what did evil feel like?

Draining her coffee, Penelope got up and went to pay the bill, only to discover Marco had covered it on the way out. *Keep this up, and we may even become friends, Marco.* She smiled to herself and pocketed one of the restaurant's business cards as a keepsake.

Penelope strolled along the canal way until she reached a bridge over the Rio de la Toletta, and then stood admiring the lights of the houses reflecting on the night-blue water.

A sudden sharp sting in her side caused her to gasp, and Penelope turned to see the glint of a small blade in the hand of a stranger. She gripped her ribs in shock, pain shooting through her as hot blood gushed between her fingers.

"You are no seeker," the man said, and as he made to stab her again, Penelope threw herself at him, trying to unbalance him.

"Help!" she tried to yell, her voice a hoarse gasp. Her legs started to buckle, and she grabbed vainly at the stone rail for support.

"Pathetic," the man said. His smile was cold in the lamplight as he shoved her hard.

Penelope toppled over the side of the bridge into the water, the freezing salty blackness of the canal dragging her under.

SIX

PENELOPE FELT WARM light before something heavy crashed into her and dragged her up
and out of the darkness. Wet, hot lips pressed insis-
tently against hers moments before water rushed out
of her lungs. She flickered in and out of consciousness as someone carried her through the gate of a canal
entrance.

A deep voice shouted commands as she was placed
on something dry and soft. With blurry vision, she saw
the face of an older woman hovering over her. Behind
her, a soaked man was speaking swiftly in a language
she didn't understand.

"Be quiet, she's trying to say something," the
woman commanded him.

Penelope looked up at his familiar blue eyes and
whispered, "Firecrackers," before her world went dark
once more.

The next time Penelope woke, the pain in her side
had faded to a dull throb. A man sat in a chair beside
her. She blinked rapidly, trying to focus on him. He
had long, curling blond hair and amber eyes as keen
as a wolf's.

"Well, well, look who is awake. The mystery woman
that has everyone so excited," he said with a smile.

Penelope tried to move, but her limbs refused to budge under the thick blanket that had been placed over her. *Where am I?*

"I don't recommend moving just yet, your body is trying to heal a fatal knife wound and won't be rushed." The stranger reached out a hand and ran it two inches above her body. "Your flesh is mending, but your chakras are shot. Your root chakra doesn't seem to be working at all. Once you are feeling up to it, I could help you get it going again."

Penelope had no idea what he was talking about, but the way he said it made it sound suggestive. "Where is my phone?"

The golden-haired man pointed to a small table next to the couch. "You are lucky Galenos is so good with electronics. Otherwise it would have been completely wrecked." Penelope snatched her phone and held it protectively to her chest. She was about to ask him who he was when a door opened, and the man from her meditation came into the room. Her eyes went wide with angry recognition.

"Oh, my mistake. There it goes, your chakra flaring red hot," the golden-haired man said suddenly. He looked over his shoulder, following Penelope's gaze, and his beautiful face pulled back in a snarl. "Why am I not surprised?"

"Who *are* you? And where am I?" Penelope demanded, not looking away from the Turkish man. "Is this real or am I...?"

"You aren't dead," the man from her meditations said, his rolling accent more pronounced than she remembered. "I'm Alexis, and this's Phaidros. You seem to have survived an attempted murder."

The golden-haired man got up with a disgusted snort. "I still think you should've let her die. This drowned rat hardly seems worth the magic we spent on healing her."

"Get out, Phaidros, before you make matters worse," Alexis said. His tone was soft, but the threat in it made the hair on Penelope's arms stand on end.

"Where am I?" Penelope repeated, her hands bunching into fists. Alexis sat down in Phaidros's chair, his expression guarded.

"My palazzo in Dorsoduro. I brought you here so that my friend Nereus could save you. You were stabbed and tossed into the canal like garbage. Any idea why?"

Penelope remembered the sensation of the cold blade sliding between her ribs. Her hand reached under the blanket and touched the fresh, tender scar on her left side. *I should be dead.*

"How did you find me?" she asked, even as she tried pushing her way further up her pillows so that she could face him. He leaned over to help her, and she caught the sandalwood scent that seemed to emanate from him.

"Phaidros and I were out walking when I felt you pull on our…connection. I felt your pain," he admitted slowly, straightening the cuffs of his white shirt. "I sent Phaidros after the man who did this to you, but someone had gotten to him first. He had his throat cut in the middle of the street, so we can assume he was a hired blade."

"I don't understand why anyone would attack me. I am no one; I don't know anyone in Venice. I wasn't even wearing jewelry to rob."

"But you are working on a murder investigation and hunting dark priests of Thevetat. That's more than enough reason to want you dead."

"How do you know that?" Penelope asked suspiciously. *Who is this guy?*

His smile was mysterious as he said, "Magic."

"Did you kill that woman?" Penelope asked, trying to calculate how far she could get from the couch to the door on the other side of the room. She glanced at a glass vase not far from her; if she had to defend herself, it would be the closest weapon she had.

"If I was the murderer you are hunting, do you think I would have bothered to dive into a freezing canal to save you?"

"Then why did you?" she demanded. "And why do you keep turning up in my meditations?"

Alexis crossed his long legs in front of him. "I don't know. It has never happened before."

"You should kill her," a sharp female voice interrupted them.

A black woman appeared in the room, but no doors had opened. She looked like she had been cut from a swathe of shadow with intricate white tattoos decorating her muscled arms. She had long silver hair and gray eyes. Blades glimmered in her hands as she approached them at a silent stalk.

Adrenaline dumped down Penelope's spine, and she struggled to sit up, grinding her teeth against the pain in her side.

"Stay back, Lyca," Alexis warned, his whole body stiffening.

"It would be best for all of us, Alexis, you know this. Leave, and I'll make it quick and painless."

Alexis was suddenly on his feet and standing between them, a strange blue light shimmering under the skin of his arms. "I won't warn you again."

"You dare threaten me…" Lyca growled.

An older woman materialized between them. "That's enough." She hadn't raised her voice, but the pair of them obeyed instantly. "Lyca, you're forbidden to touch Penelope, do you understand?"

"My lady," Lyca hissed as she bowed low, her blades disappearing into her robes. The light coming from Alexis vanished, and he stepped back to let the older woman pass. Her gray hair was long and loose, and she had a brown, lined face of unknowable age. She wore a green-and-blue dress and had the bearing of a queen.

"Doctor Bryne, I apologize for their behavior. They aren't used to guests," the woman told her. When she got close enough, Penelope realized she could see the faint outline of Lyca's figure through her. *She's astral projecting!*

"You aren't really here, are you?" Penelope asked.

"She's quick, Alexis," the woman said approvingly, "and she isn't screaming, a sign of good sense. I'm Nereus. How are you feeling?"

"A little sore and I've got a headache," she answered. "I'm mostly confused about waking up in a house full of strangers. Thank you for helping me, though."

"Thank Alexis. He's the one who believed you were worth saving," Nereus replied.

"My lady, we need to wipe her memory and dump her outside," Lyca interrupted. "This woman exposes all of us."

"I understand your concern, but you forget something vital. The palazzo let Penelope in. Not only in physical form, but also metaphysically. You know the safeguards are still in place. You have checked them yourself." Nereus gave Penelope a once-over. "She's important somehow."

"If she is important, we let fate decide," Alexis said, folding his arms stubbornly. "I'll wipe her memory and put her back in her hotel as Lyca says. If she finds her way back to us again, then we accept her. We haven't let a human live among us for a long time, and as Nereus says, she's important."

"*She* is sitting right here—" Penelope began.

"Agreed," Lyca replied, ignoring her. "But you aren't allowed to appear to her in any way to spark her search."

"I never did in the first place," Alexis replied coolly.

A snort of disbelief announced Phaidros's reappearance. Penelope wondered how many more of them there were.

"Look, I'm not a threat to anyone," she interrupted. "I don't care who any of you are, and you have no right to tell me what to do. I'm not interested in coming back here, and I'm certainly not going to let you wipe—"

Alexis touched her head, and her world spun once more.

Penelope felt someone scoop her up out of the chair. With bleary eyes, she could make out the sharp line of Alexis's jaw and stern eyes as he carried her through a door and out into the street. Penelope looked behind her as the blue-and-gold door shut, bright Roman numerals XXXIX shining before the door disappeared.

"Pretty door," she mumbled. The street lantern above her flickered, and suddenly they were in her hotel room.

"I do wish you would take those evil photos down," Alexis muttered under his breath. "Black magic is bad for you, Doctor Bryne." He placed her on the bed and pulled off her boots. "Rest now."

Penelope reached out and grabbed his hand tightly. "Don't want to forget…you…bastard," she mumbled before the magic overwhelmed her.

SEVEN

PENELOPE WOKE TO the sound of frantic knocking on her hotel room door. "*Signorina* Penelope!" Louisa yelled. "*Inspecttori* Dandolo is here! Are you in there?"

"I'm here. I'll be down in a moment!" she called back as she tried to get her bearings.

Penelope climbed out of bed, swaying unsteadily, and headed for the bathroom. She had slept in her clothes that smelled like salt and something burnt, and her hair was riotously frizzy even though she knew she had straightened it before going out to dinner the previous night. She found her phone crammed into her back pocket, the battery flat.

What happened last night? She searched her hazy memory as she stripped and climbed into the hot shower. She soaped herself down, touching her left side, and then again as if she expected it to feel differently.

Ten minutes later she pulled on fresh clothes and ran downstairs. Marco was waiting at the kitchen table, looking out of sorts.

"How much did you drink last night?" he asked which told her that she looked far worse than he did.

"Only what I had at dinner," Penelope replied, taking her coffee from Louisa and downing it.

"I suppose you have your phone off too?" he asked irritably.

"It's dead...Why? What happened?"

"There was another murder last night. I've been trying to reach you since 5:00 a.m."

"Five! Shit. I'm sorry. I must have fallen asleep last night and forgot to charge it," Penelope fumbled. But wait—how had she gotten back to the hotel? She remembered having her dessert and leaving the café, but the rest was a blank.

Marco's anger faded when he realized she wasn't faking it. "It's okay. There isn't much you could've done with all the *polizia* in the way. You look like you are going to be sick...Maybe a tourist drugged you."

"I can't remember drinking anything that tasted weird. Is there such a thing as delayed jet lag?"

"It doesn't matter. This body won't wait." Marco drained his coffee and got to his feet.

The cold air outside did nothing to clear the sleep or confusion from Penelope's mind.

"Where are we going?" she asked as she stepped unsteadily into the boat.

"Cannaregio," Marco replied grimly. "The body was found by an elderly nun visiting the Isola di San Michele. They've had to treat her for shock, and the whole island has been closed."

Penelope didn't ask him any more questions; she was too focused on breathing, so she didn't throw up over the side of the boat.

She saw a flicker of lapis blue in the corner of her eye but when she turned it was only a woman's sweater and not...what? There was something...something important about that blue. She had never been particularly attracted to the color, and now she was like a bowerbird.

Maybe you ate bad squid risotto last night. Food poisoning would explain her nausea. She focused on the horizon and tried to clear her head. She didn't want to embarrass herself at the crime scene by not being able to give any insight or by being unable to stand straight.

The red walls of the Isola di San Michele rose up in front of them, police boats floating offshore to dissuade any civilian sailors from getting too close. Marco pulled the boat closer to dock at a small jetty. The iconic white domes were painfully bright in the early morning glare, and Penelope tried not to look up at them.

San Michele was an island of the dead, the famous cemetery including the likes of Stravinsky and Ezra Pound. It had been one of the highlights of her previous trip, and ten years later, she was back to look at a body.

How life had changed from a month ago when she was receiving emails telling her that she was either a flunky historian or a prophetess for the Lemurians.

A crowd of police officers opened a path for Marco and Penelope as they walked through the garden entrance and down to a small stretch of beach.

The retaining wall had been graffitied with the now familiar, but no less maddening Atlantean script.

Pegged into the tiny stretch of sand was a horse constructed of burnt bones and driftwood. Bent over and fed through an enormous rib cage, hands tied upward to make a neck, was the body of a man crowned with a black stallion's head. Its hooves had been hacked off… and…and…

The sand swayed under Penelope's feet, and she bent over and vomited in the waves.

"GOD, I'M embarrassed," Penelope complained from the shade of the trees. Instead of being openly ridiculed by the group of police, a young officer had loaned her a spare Italia National Football T-shirt from his gym bag. It hung to her knees, and she tried not to ruin it with vomit as well.

Marco handed Penelope a bottle of water. "You aren't the first person to be sick at a murder scene, *Dottore*, and you won't be the last. I thought you were only hungover this morning. I didn't realize you were so ill."

"I blame seafood dinners in dodgy Venetian cafés," Penelope said, her head between her knees. "I should be okay soon."

Marco rested his large hand on her forehead. "You are burning with fever. I'm going to get someone to take you back to Dorsoduro. I can come by the hotel tonight and bring you photos. Go back to bed. You are no use to me or the case like this."

Marco walked Penelope down to the dock and instructed an officer in a patrol boat to return her to Dorsoduro.

"Make sure you take photos of the wall in order this time," Penelope said as she climbed into the boat. "There are more alchemical symbols that would—"

"Yes, yes. I'll see you tonight and bring you some soup," Marco said.

"*Le Doge Cane* likes you," the young officer, Francesco, noted with a sly smile as the boat pulled from the dock.

"How can he resist when I'm at my most charming?" Penelope quipped.

Francesco looked at the football shirt she was wearing, staring at her chest a fraction too long. "That's his favorite team."

Penelope wanted to reply with something clever, but all that came out was a scathing, "Fuck off and drive."

Francesco laughed loudly over the roar of the engines, and Penelope wished the gray-blue water of the lagoon would rise up and swallow her whole.

MARCO KNEW there was going to be trouble the moment he saw the tall blonde step onto the beach. She was dressed in a neat blue suit with a pressed white shirt. She was in plain clothes, but there was no mistaking what she was. It was in her walk, the way she held herself above everyone else. Marco groaned inwardly. DIGOS.

Marco went to approach her, but she detoured around the crowd and headed straight for the body. He arrived just as she looked at the face of the dead man.

"*Vaffanculo*," she hissed.

"*Scusi Signora—*"

"Agent Bianchi," she cut him off, still studying the body, brown eyes taking in every detail.

"May I ask what you are doing at my crime scene, apart from contaminating it?" he demanded. It must've been the tone that made her finally stop and look at him. Her eyes made an equally scathing assessment of him.

"I was led to believe that the scene had already been contaminated by your consultant," she countered smoothly. "Did you ever stop to think that a civilian would need a debriefing after being exposed to the first body, let alone this one?"

"She was cleared to assist by Adalfieri."

"So was I. I'll be with you on this case until it is over."

"Why are you stepping in now? How does it even involve DIGOS?"

Agent Bianchi handed him her phone where a photo glowed. It was of a young man, handsome and having fun with a group of friends. "Look familiar?"

Marco looked up at the body. "Who is he?"

"His name is Juliano. He was in Venice working as an engineering assistant with his father."

"Let me guess, the MOSE project?"

"*Bravo.*" Agent Bianchi pocketed her phone. "We believe a group is targeting MOSE to stop its launch. Tony Duilio is in Venice and is stirring up protestors too, making publicity difficult. This killer means to spread terror, and we need to stop him before anyone else dies."

Marco had heard of Duilio. He was an upstart entrepreneur with a genius mind for engineering. His company was creating floating resorts in the Bahamas and had pitched an alternative project to the City of Venezia. Duilio had wanted to raise the city, suspending the buildings on cables that could be lengthened as the ocean rose. He had been the loudest and most public protestor on the MOSE, claiming it was a waste of funds for a Band-Aid job. When the oceans rose due to global warming, the MOSE gates would be useless.

"Penelope—Doctor Bryne—believes they are cult killings," said Marco.

"Or they just want to make them as scandalous and sacrilegious as possible to incite more fear into people." Agent Bianchi walked around the body, her face stony. "She was allowed onto this case as a consultant with no background checks or the proper clearance. She hasn't had any success deciphering the language because it's *fake*. I read her report, and I'm surprised a seasoned inspector like yourself bought into ridiculous theories about Atlantean scripts and cults to dead gods."

"Her theories aren't ridiculous. She's qualified in areas we aren't, and that includes giving us valuable insight into the murderer's motivations. Whether they're killing to stir up MOSE supporters doesn't matter. There's enough evidence to prove they believe in this demon god."

"I don't care about their beliefs," she said, her ponytail flicking over her shoulder as she stood. "I only want them caught. Help me, Inspector, or stay out of my way."

PENELOPE WAS caught in a world of heat and confused consciousness. In her hotel room, she thrashed in her sheets, sweating and shaking in the grips of a fever.

With the fever came the dreams. In them Penelope twisted in a pale blue ribbon of light, drowning in salty blackness. Flashes of golden hair caught her eyes, along with curious symbols on a robe. She woke sporadically, the smell of spicy gunpowder mixed with something sweet in her nose.

And those were just the dreams that didn't involve her reliving the fate of the murder victims, slowly suffocating as a bloody mask was pulled down over her head, combined with the knowledge that she was dying and leaving her baby without her mother. Her fear was real and raw as she was forced into a rib cage, the burning eyes of a god watching from above as it constructed a prison of bone and driftwood around her.

She screamed then; a name she could never remember. Waking, she expected to see someone in the room with her, but she was always alone.

"Where are you?" Penelope whispered, expecting a reply. She touched a place in the middle of her chest, searching for something she felt should be attached there. "Who are you?"

"Penelope?" Marco's voice came through the door before it opened. No, it wasn't him she was looking for. Her heart slowed as she lay back down.

"Hey," she managed, pushing her hair back from her damp forehead.

"You look like death," he said as he placed a brown takeaway bag on the bedside table. "I brought you some soup, as promised."

"Thanks." She smiled weakly. "I'm sorry about today."

"Don't be. It was going to be a bad day with or without you there," he replied as he moved a chair beside her bed and sat down.

"I hope you brought me a case file and not just food," she said.

He made a face and took a folder out of his satchel, placing it on her desk. "I shouldn't give you these in your current state, but I'm a man of my word. Please don't look at them until you feel better. We have more than enough people working this case for the time being."

"What else has happened? You look...angry." Penelope didn't know if it was the fever still, but he seemed to have a frustrated crimson and gray light buzzing around him.

"DIGOS happened. There's an agent that they're going to force me to work with, and she doesn't think much of us so far."

"You mean she doesn't think much of me," Penelope stated.

"She doesn't know you. She thinks this killer is a part of a group that wants to terrorize people involved with MOSE. Some plot to try and stop it from coming online," Marco explained. He folded his arms. "She's ignorant and believes it's so clear-cut. You and I know otherwise."

"You still believe me? Even after the demon worship conversation?"

"Of course. Faith is an extremely powerful thing, and I don't think we'll be able to figure this out without you." He fidgeted slightly. "But Adalfieri has agreed with Agent Bianchi that you aren't allowed onto the crime scenes anymore, at least until the body has been removed. I've brought you photos, and they have said you can keep consulting, but you aren't allowed to be involved so directly."

"And you agree with them?"

"Not so much, but I do know that if this killer is connected enough to know who has been directly involved with MOSE and their families, then I don't want you being caught in any crossfire. You're an academic, not police."

"If he's that well-connected, then he already knows I'm involved." Penelope rubbed a hand along her left ribs, something itchy under her skin.

"Perhaps." Marco frowned. "But you need to get well. That should be your only priority for the next few days. Have a look at the photos when you are more clearheaded and tell me what you think."

"Will you put them on the wall for me?" she asked, pointing at the blank space on the other side of a bay of windows.

Marco sighed. "The Stallion of San Michele is as horrible as the Bull. Do you really want to be surrounded by so much death when you are running a fever?"

"Perhaps I'll gain insight in my hallucinatory state," she joked and hoped it wasn't too horrific. *Black magic is bad for you,* a voice whispered in the back of her mind. She shook her head.

"Fine! But if you end up going crazy, you can't sue me."

"I promise." She laughed weakly.

They talked easily, Marco telling her all about the arrogant DIGOS agent while he pinned the photos to the wall in order. Penelope's brain fired as she watched the retaining wall from San Michele take shape. Something was needling her, something new she had learned about magic.

"It's another spell," she said, sitting up slowly. "And I'm certain that it's about Thevetat. San Michele wasn't a random place to select."

"What do you mean?"

"Thevetat was a death cult. San Michele is an island of bones and ghosts." Penelope licked her lips and forced herself to say, "I think they believe they are doing magic and this's another part of a spell."

"And because it's a death cult, being at a cemetery the spell would be more powerful?" Marco guessed. She smiled, loving how quick he was.

"Exactly, and the fact that he used a horse instead of a bull this time confirms the petition to Poseidon," Penelope replied. "He's upping his game, or maybe a second layer to the same spell? Argh, I wish my head wasn't so fuzzy. I feel like the answer is at the tip of a tongue I don't have."

Marco chuckled softly as he picked up his coat. "It'll come to you. Eat and rest. I'll keep you posted if we learn anything else."

"Marco? One other thing. I've been thinking about the meat."

"The meat? What do you mean?"

"First, parts of a bull and now a horse carcass? Those aren't cuts you can buy just anywhere."

"We've been looking into meat suppliers and butcher shops in Venice—"

"No, you need to look further afield." Penelope sat up, holding her pounding head as she tried to focus. "For these kinds of sacrifices, you wouldn't go to any old butcher. Animals used in sacrifice were special. Top grade, like prize bulls, the finest stallions. You wouldn't offer up any old nag if you were trying to get favors out of the gods."

"So maybe check with the farmers on the mainland?" Marco thought aloud. "There are quite a few within an hour of here."

"It would be a good place to start. He would've had to have killed it somewhere else and transported it to the city. Too many people would notice a live bull on a boat around Santa Croce."

"I'll make some calls and see what I can dig up. You really need to get some sleep and feel better. Let the *polizia* worry about things for a few days."

"Thank you for the soup and for defending me to Agent Bianchi," Penelope said.

"I've learned to trust my instincts over the years, and something tells me we won't be able to solve this without you." He flashed her a smile. "I'll make sure Louisa checks in on you."

"It's just the stomach flu, I'll get over it," Penelope said as he shut the door. She got out of bed and stumbled to the bathroom to pee and wash her face. Her clothes from the night before sat on the floor in a pile where she had left them that morning.

What had happened to her?

She searched the pocket of her jeans and found a crumpled business card of the restaurant where they'd eaten and a soggy packet of gum. She had gotten wet, that much was obvious. But how, and why?

Penelope picked up her red sweater and checked it. There was a hole in the fabric, and it was stained with…

"Holy shit—is that *blood*?" She held it out at arm's reach but didn't let it go. Avoiding the stain, she sniffed the soft fabric. It smelled salty like canal water and underneath that iron, something sweet like spice and…

"Firecrackers?" she murmured. It was Carnevale. Maybe she had stumbled into a street party when they were releasing fireworks? It seemed unlikely. She lifted up her shirt, checking for cuts or scratches that would explain the hole and the blood, but found none. She tossed the sweater and jeans into a laundry bag, hiding them from sight before she bent over to clutch her knees. A wave of nausea flooded her, and she curled up on the tiles and tried to breathe.

"You're okay, Penelope. The blood wasn't yours. Everything's fine. You're okay," she said before she reached for the toilet bowl to throw up.

TWO DAYS passed before Penelope's fever broke. She woke with a clearer head in a bed covered with photos and scribbled notes. She had been writing ideas down as they came to her during her brief periods of wakefulness, and as she went through them, less than half made sense.

"That was some epic stomach flu," Penelope mumbled as she tried to sort them. Something square flashed in the corner of her eye, and she lifted a torn page from her notebook. It was a sketch of a door, the numerals for thirty-nine scribbled in black ink. Where had she seen that before? There was something about the night she'd gotten sick and the days before it that didn't feel right.

It wasn't just her fevered scribblings. She had received a message from Carolyn asking her if she'd seen the man from her meditation again, but she couldn't remember doing a meditation since she had arrived in Venice, let alone telling Carolyn about it. Penelope took a hot shower and dressed warmly.

After making sure that Louisa wasn't around, Penelope ducked into the hotel kitchen and looked through the cutlery drawers. Someone had drugged her, that was the only solid explanation that made sense, and she'd be damned if she let it happen again. Penelope took out a sharp oyster knife and tucked it into her coat pocket, its shape reassuring against her thigh.

Exiting the kitchen, Penelope collided with Louisa coming in from the markets.

"Ah, *Dottore*! You are looking much better," Louisa said, patting Penelope's cheek. "What were you doing in the kitchens?"

"Looking for you, of course!" Penelope lied. "I wanted to thank you for all of the soup you made me while I was unwell."

"*Prego bella*. But where are you going in this dreadful weather?"

"Just need some fresh air," Penelope assured her. She had started to believe Louisa was reporting back to Marco on her condition.

"Be back by dark," Louisa replied as she shuffled off to the warm kitchen.

Outside the sky was gray and the streets of Dorsoduro were damp with mist. Penelope breathed in the salty air and tightened the scarf around her neck. It took her twenty minutes of wandering the streets before she came to the café where she had eaten with Marco.

"Okay, Penelope, let's retrace your steps and figure this out," she said to herself, anger clearing her mind. "Someone messed with you and you are going to find out who. You had your coffee, went to pay the bill... Marco had already paid it, and you went for a walk. Which way?"

Penelope headed toward a small bridge. She loved the boats that lined the canals at night. She stood at the top of it, reaching for a memory. There was a rusty smear on the stone at her feet that looked like...blood? Her hand shot to the side of her ribs as something silver flashed in her mind's eye.

Her body jerked, remembering the feeling of shock as the blade had entered her. She slid her hand inside her coat and felt her ribs as she had done obsessively over the last few days. Not caring who was watching, Penelope lifted her shirt to see the purple line stretch along her heart.

"What's happening to me?" she whispered, her pulse racing. She followed the Fondamenta Eremite before turning left onto the Calle dei Cerchieri.

Penelope took the crumpled drawing of the door
out of her coat pocket, déjà vu snapping at her brain
like an electric shock. She had been there; she *knew* it.
She walked from one end of Calle dei Cerchieri to the
other searching for a blue door that wasn't there. She
retraced her steps and ended up at the Rio de la Toletta,
upstream from the bridge she had been stabbed on.

Someone had pulled her from the water. They had
taken her…where? She knew the door from her drawing was connected. She remembered the blue paint, the
golden Roman numerals and the lamp that hung on
the side of the building. She turned and looked back
down the alley. Not far from her was a blank, brick wall
with a lamp hanging from it. No door. Penelope hurried over to it, her memory stretching and tearing.

"I know it was here," she muttered, resting her hand
on the damp bricks. Something trembled beneath her
fingers. "Pretty door." She had been carried through it,
and then…it had simply vanished like magic.

How can you break into a magician's mind? a male
voice asked through her memories. She couldn't recall
his face, but his voice made something inside of her
burn. *I must still be sick to believe any of this*, Penelope
thought as she rested her head on the bricks. But she
knew, deep in her gut, that she hadn't imagined it. The
man, the magician…her fever dreams came back to her
carrying with them a name.

"Alexis," she whispered, the name tumbling from
her freezing lips against the stonework. "Are you there?"

There was no reply.

Frustration and anger rolled through her. Something had happened to her and whoever was the cause of it was going to pay.

Penelope beat her fist against the wall. "God damn it, Alexis! What did you do to me? I swear, if you don't let me in I'll get a sledgehammer and knock this fucking wall down! Let me in, you bastard!"

Bricks crumbled beneath her fists as a blue door pushed its way through them. The Roman numerals gleamed in the gray light. A golden handle appeared and without knocking she opened it.

A tall man with brown skin and black hair stood on the other side, his lapis blue eyes matching the shirt he wore. Emanating from him was the spicy firecracker smell that had haunted her dreams.

"Doctor Bryne, what a pleasure to see you again," he said in his deep Turkish accent.

Penelope stood frozen as memories flooded back to her. The man in the tower; drinking espresso in a café that didn't exist; Nereus, Phaidros, and Lyca all arguing whether she should die; and *him*. She remembered him pulling her from the canal, the feel of his wet lips as he breathed life back into her, a string of light joining them together and pulsing with energy.

Breathing heavily and fighting tears, Penelope lifted her trembling hand and slapped him hard across the face.

PART TWO

TWILIGHT
OF THE
IMMORTALS

"There flash'd, like autumn's star, that brightest shines, when newly risen from his ocean bath."

~ Homer ~

EIGHT

THE DOCTOR AND the magician eyed each other, neither moving. Alexis's cheek stung, but he was more shocked than in pain. He couldn't remember the last time someone had slapped him. Or the last time he'd let them.

"What did you do to me? Who the hell are you?" Penelope asked through gritted teeth.

"You are understandably angry, Penelope, and I owe you an explanation." He gestured in the direction of the kitchen. "Come with me, and I'll make us something warm to drink while we talk." They held each other's gaze a moment longer, Alexis waiting to see if she would yield or run.

He didn't want her to leave. This human woman with her dark hair tousled by the salt wind was the realest thing that had stepped through the door in over a century.

But she had to choose to stay of her own accord, and he wasn't allowed to influence her decision as part of his agreement with Nereus.

"I could use a coffee," Penelope relented, taking a nervous step forward. The door shut silently behind her.

"Me too," he admitted, giving her a small smile.

Alexis didn't turn to see if she was following as he led the way to the kitchen; he could feel the heat of her angry aura pulsating six feet from her body. If she stayed, he would have to make sure Phaidros didn't start rubbing up against her like a cat in heat.

Alexis opened a cupboard and took down his favorite copper *cezve* pot.

"Would you like sugar?" he asked as if he'd had her around for casual drinks a thousand times before. He wanted her to be at ease, and it surprised him. He should be terrifying her, so she never bothered them again.

"Sugar would be good. Answers would be better," replied Penelope sharply. She hesitated before sitting down on a stool on the opposite side of the blond timber bar, closest to the door. Alexis tried not to smile at how cautious she was. She was brave enough to walk through the front door and yet drinking coffee worried her. *What an interesting creature you are shaping up to be.*

"This is a nice kitchen," she said, likely trying to fill the awkward silence.

Alexis looked around at the mosaic of bluestone tiles, white cupboards, and timber accents. Nereus always liked fresh flowers in the house, and bright blooms sat in crystal vases around them.

"Zotikos redecorates it nearly every time he visits Venice. He thinks himself a chef and insists on a fresh creative space." Alexis scooped the finely ground coffee and sugar into the pot and mixed it with filtered water before setting it on the stove.

"Zotikos is another…magician?" Penelope asked hesitantly as if she had to force herself to say the word.

He could see the questions wanting to explode out of her. *So the memory spell has shredded enough for her to remember that we are magicians. Interesting.*

"Yes, he is. He's younger than the rest of us and prefers focusing his art on poetry."

"Is he any good?"

Alexis took a copper spoon from a drawer as he considered the question. "His poetry is better than his cooking."

Penelope smiled unexpectedly before she tried to hide it. He poured her coffee into a blue-and-gold ceramic cup and placed it on a saucer in front of her.

"I can't remember the last time I had coffee made like this," she said, lifting it to her nose to smell its rich, strong scent. Alexis waited until she had taken her first small sip, taking pleasure in the way her cheeks warmed in response to the heat. "This is really good coffee," she said begrudgingly. "My mother would love this cup; can I ask where you bought it?"

Alexis touched the ceramic saucer, shutting his eyes a moment as he read its history. "Kotiaion in the 14th century, just before the Ottomans made the city a part of the empire."

The cup and saucer rattled in her hands as she placed it back on the counter.

"Is something the matter?"

"Fourteenth century Ottoman ceramics should be in a museum, not in a kitchen cupboard," squeaked Penelope.

"If they were in a museum, what would we drink out of?" Alexis replied. "Drink, Penelope. It has been handled by rougher hands than yours."

"Extraordinary," she said, picking up the cup again, her historian eyes taking in the fine golden pattern.

"I assure you, Doctor Bryne, the coffee cups are the least extraordinary thing in this house."

This time her smile was open as she said, "I'm starting to figure that out for myself. How—*why* did you take my memories away?"

"I removed your memories, or tried to, to protect those like me."

"From me? What possible threat am I to you? I'd never hurt anyone. I'm an academic, I'm as harmless as they come."

"If that were true, he wouldn't have been trying to trash your career for years," Phaidros said as he came into the kitchen, dressed in a gold-silk robe and nothing else.

I am going to kill you. Alexis glared at Phaidros as he took the remaining coffee from the pot. Alexis turned just in time to dodge the cup that Penelope just claimed was priceless. She was shaking with fury.

"*What the actual fuck*," Penelope ground out through clenched teeth.

"Whoa! Look at that aura flare!" Phaidros laughed as he stepped over the broken china. "He didn't tell you? Alexis, you should be more honest. We've known about you for some time, Doctor Bryne. Alexis even traveled to Australia to see you a few years ago, and you've had him all tied up in anxious knots since."

Penelope picked up the saucer, and her eyes went wide in sudden recognition. "*You.* You were that crazy guy at my lecture arguing about magic and trying to make me look like an ass."

"You pulled the corner of a sacred Tablet from the sea," Alexis replied, folding his arms. "Of course I asked you about bloody magic."

Anger and curiosity warred on Penelope's face. "How do you know it was a sacred Tablet? No one knows what it is. People still want to believe it's a fake."

"It's not a fake at all," Phaidros said, leaning toward her. "Has anyone ever told you that you're radiant when you are angry?"

"Has anyone ever told you wearing all gold makes you look like a rejected Christmas tree decoration?" Penelope snapped. Alexis choked on his coffee as unexpected laughter bubbled up through him.

Phaidros grinned like a shark. "We might just keep you yet, Penelope Bryne."

"Go away, Phaidros. You've done enough," Alexis said.

"*He's* done enough? What about you?" Penelope rounded on him, the saucer in her hand trembled as if she was still fighting the urge to throw it.

"I do hate arguments, even if I could just *lick* all of your lovely energy up," Phaidros purred. "*Ciao bella.*" He sauntered out of the room, and Penelope's hazel eyes narrowed.

"You might want to be careful. If you keep talking like that to him, he'll fall in love with you," Alexis teased. "And there is nothing worse than Phaidros in love."

"Oh, I don't know, sabotaging someone's career for no good reason seems a hell of a lot worse to me."

Alexis leaned against the bench opposite her, trying to make his body language nonthreatening. She was angry, but there was a bruised look in her eyes and her tone, and he knew her career wasn't the only thing he'd damaged. *What did you think would happen? That she would just pick herself up and find another dream?*

"You were getting too close," he admitted softly. "Give me the afternoon to explain. I'll show you my reasons, and then you may begin to understand."

"I'm going crazy, aren't I? This is another fever dream, and I'm back in my hotel, and I'm dying of some viral—"

Alexis took her hand. He did it before even considering the consequences fully. She looked down at his ink-stained fingers covering hers, and Alexis felt the tug of the twisting line of light that connected them. His third eye opened and he saw it reconnecting, pulsing brighter than before. It was that line that had led her to his tower during her meditation, like a beautiful Theseus heading into the den of the Minotaur. Her hand curled under his, and the way she was looking at him, Alexis knew she felt it too.

"You're safe here, Penelope. Let me show you who we are, and why I have been working so hard to protect us," he said and slowly moved his hand away. "Or I can show you the way out, and you'll never see us again."

Penelope studied him silently before finally putting the saucer down. "Okay. You have one afternoon, but I swear you better have the best explanation in the history of explanations."

"Curiosity wins the day," Alexis replied as he stepped over the broken china.

"I'm...sorry I broke your cup."

"But not that you threw it?"

"Obviously," Penelope said as they made for the kitchen door.

Alexis snapped his fingers behind him, and the broken cup mended itself and moved back to the saucer.

"I wouldn't worry about it too much." It was a silly piece of showmanship, but the look on her face was too priceless for him to resist.

Alexis walked slowly through the house allowing Penelope to stop and look at the Caravaggio, Titian, and Tintoretto paintings, along with some Athenian vases, marble sculptures, and a set of bronze Minoan bull statues.

"*All* of this stuff should be in museums," Penelope said as she studied a perfectly persevered Spartan helmet from the Persian wars.

"These are trinkets compared to some of the other things in the house," Alexis teased. He was slightly surprised to find how much he enjoyed her curiosity and how much he wanted to show her.

You are getting too old to be this delighted by a stranger. "We had better get a move on. Otherwise, you will be here a lot longer than an afternoon."

"Fair enough," Penelope said with a sigh, her head turned awkwardly as she studied the inside of the helmet.

When they arrived at a set of brilliant blue-and-gold doors, Alexis found himself unexpectedly nervous.

"Before you go in I want you to know that you are an incredible scholar," he said seriously. "Many have studied Atlantis, or tried to, but you are the one that was the closest to the truth."

Penelope folded her arms. "There are a lot of people out there who would disagree with you."

Alexis smiled smugly and opened the blue doors. "Trust me, I am the leading authority."

Penelope's arms fell to her sides as she took in the contents of the room, her aura flaring in surprise and pleasure.

She gripped the door frame to steady herself and whispered, "Holy Atlantis."

NINE

THE LONG SET of chambers before Penelope was filled with books, scrolls, tablets, sculptures, paintings, films, and music. All of it was on Atlantis. There were vases and sculptures covered in barnacles, pieces of broken mosaic tiles, and fragile papyrus pressed under planes of glass. But that wasn't what captured Penelope's attention.

Resting on a coffee table was the *Journal for Oceanic Cultural Research Volume 27*. Penelope had the same copy on display in her flat in Melbourne. They had accepted a full paper on her research of the Atlantis Tablet. She was a part of his collection like a creepy trophy.

"This is quite the obsession," she said slowly. In fact, it was the same level of obsessive passion of the killer she had profiled for Marco. Penelope's hand went to the handle of the oyster knife in her pocket, and she moved away from him, putting a lounge and the coffee table between them.

"Stop, Penelope, your mind is making leaps that are false," Alexis said.

"You don't know what my mind is leaping to," she snapped.

Alexis made a frustrated sound at the back of his throat. "I'm no acolyte of Thevetat, and I'm certainly not the murderer you and Inspector Dandolo are looking for."

"How do you know about the murders?" she demanded, holding the knife in front of her. "There has been no media, no police reports that you could've—"

"I had to know why you were in Venice, so I broke into your hotel room and saw the Bull on your wall and the police reports on your desk," Alexis admitted.

"You are a next-level stalker, you know that?" Penelope shook her head. "How did you know where my hotel was?"

"You kept seeking me out in meditations. I followed the path you left when you astral projected into my tower. I thought you were here in Venice because of us. I didn't realize you were helping the *polizia*."

"Why would I be here for *you*? I don't even know you." Penelope sat down on one of the plush chairs on the other side of the room. "Who are you people? And don't give me that vague magician bullshit again. Tell me facts."

"If you can't believe that, Penelope, even after what you have seen with your own eyes, then I don't know if you're ready to hear the truth."

"Jesus, you guys are another cult, aren't you?" groaned Penelope. "I knew it."

"If I sit down, do you promise not to stab me?" he asked. "I'm letting you keep that knife because it makes you feel safe. I don't know how else to convince you that you have nothing to be afraid of."

Penelope wanted to believe him. Everything about him scared and attracted her all at once. She didn't know why she felt connected to him, but she wasn't about to trust him. When she'd seen him standing on the other side of the door, it had taken every ounce of bravery she possessed not to run the other way.

Seeing Alexis in meditations and hazy memories was nothing like being subjected to the full force of his real presence. He was mesmerizing, making everything around him seem a little duller. *It had to be some kind of magic, right?* she thought. Even though she was furious with him, she was also struggling to look anywhere else.

Very slowly, Penelope placed the knife on the coffee table. "Truce. For the next ten minutes only."

"Ten minutes is all I need." Alexis sat down on the chair beside her, and she tried not to move away. "It's okay, Penelope. We aren't a cult. We are magicians."

"And that's better? This room feels pretty culty to me. You said you would give me answers so start giving them. Start with why you thought it was okay to crash my career." *This better be so good.*

"I can show you if you like. Do you trust me?" Alexis said and held out his hand.

"Not even a little bit."

"Well, then you might find this uncomfortable."

Before she could stop him, he took her hand, and she was falling.

Penelope found herself standing in the misting rain of a cold Melbourne night. They stood on the corner of Lonsdale and Swanston Street looking up at the tall gray pillars of the Victorian State Library. It glowed like a defiant beacon of academia amidst the rowdy night-time shoppers and club goers.

"What is this?" she asked, gripping his hand hard.

"This is a memory. One of mine, in fact. You will know and feel this night as I did." He looked about him and pointed out a shadowy reflection of himself dressed in a dark blue suit. "I hope you are ready for this, Penelope Bryne."

"And this is supposed to make me less afraid of you?" she asked, letting his hand go.

"Whatever gave you that idea?" He flashed her an amused look as he crossed the tram line to the State Library. As they caught up to the shadowy version of himself, Alexis nudged her forward.

"Hey, what gives—?" she began but was cut short as she suddenly merged with the second Alexis, becoming him.

A WEEK beforehand an antiques dealer in Florence had told him of a mysterious stone tablet that had been pulled from the sea at Crete. His heart had stopped when he'd heard the name of the lucky diver; Doctor Penelope Bryne. He had been keeping a file on her career as a person of interest, and he was fuming that her discovery hadn't been flagged earlier. The *Journal of Oceanic Cultural Research* had already published a paper, one Penelope was going to present to a crowded lecture hall of academics and students that evening.

He was worried and frustrated, burdened with the knowledge that if she were getting too close to the truth, he would have to kill her to protect his secrets.

Alexis entered the State Library, passing students taking advantage of the free Wi-Fi and warm study space, and followed the small signs that led him to the lecture hall. He took a seat at the back in case he needed to make a quick exit. People filed in around him, his height and dark looks garnering curious glances from a crowd already familiar with each other, either socially or academically. He assumed the air of a wealthy, potential investor as he avoided eye contact and leafed through the glossy brochure that had been left on every chair.

There were photos of the seabed where the dubbed Atlantis Tablet had been found, obscured by sand and rock. *How had she even seen it amongst all of that?* Photographs and artistic renderings of what they could make out of script were in one corner, and on the back was a picture of Penelope with the people she had been diving with. Her face was ecstatic amidst the crowd, her braid over one shoulder and green eyes shining.

You are going to have to crush that hopeful dream from her eyes, Alexis reminded himself. He shuffled in his seat, the thought making him surprisingly uncomfortable.

Alexis sat patiently as the hall filled up and the dean from a local university announced Penelope and her achievements. She was younger than he expected; too young to have achieved so much. He knew from her file that she was brilliant.

Dressed in a knit dress, knee-high boots, and a black blazer she looked too warm and charming to be an academic. Alexis had expected someone withdrawn, soft-spoken, and aloof. She was a strong speaker; casual with the subject, passion giving her lecture a pulse of excitement.

There was something else that was undeniable; Penelope Bryne was nothing short of obsessed with Atlantis and had a relentless hunger to find it. She silenced naysayers in the crowd with an easy grace, unperturbed by the questions. It would have been better to remain anonymous, but Alexis's desire betrayed him.

"What about magic?" he interrupted, his deep voice carrying easily through the room.

"Magic?" Her voice was disbelieving but indulgent. She was polite, but it was obvious from her tone that she thought the question was absurd. She shut him down with a challenging glare. *Wouldn't you be fun to argue with?* Alexis smiled as she moved on, dismissing him.

After the lecture, he had watched her work the crowd. He didn't dare approach her, but their eyes locked once, and the look she gave him was so defiant he could only smile in acknowledgment before heading out of the library.

Outside, the cold, wet air cleared the buzz from his mind. Penelope was getting too close. Obsession was a cruel mistress. Alexis had lived long enough to know how dangerous it could be. He couldn't allow her to find them. With reluctance in his soul, Alexis resigned himself to killing Penelope Bryne.

IT WAS after midnight when the keys rattled in the door, and Penelope entered her dark flat. Alexis had been there for an hour, a blade resting across his knees. He admonished himself for snooping, but he hadn't been able to help it. She lived with another woman who wasn't there that night. The presence of a lover was nowhere to be found, and unlike most academics, Penelope was scrupulously neat. Books were stacked in piles on the floor and inside groaning shelves. A framed copy of the article on the Atlantis Tablet hung above the gas fireplace.

An inspection of her bookshelves proved quite revealing. There were tattered copies of Plato and the Odyssey, textbooks on the Greeks, Phoenicians, and Mycenaeans tabbed with pieces of colored paper. An unopened book on anxiety was tucked in a dusty corner. When Alexis's curious fingers began to touch things, he scolded himself and sat down to wait.

Penelope came into the flat and shut the door behind her without turning on the lights. Her feet were sure of their destination as she placed her black leather satchel bag and keys on the kitchen counter and headed for the bathroom. *Do it now. Stop dragging out the inevitable*, a voice of reason urged him.

But Alexis wasn't listening to reason; he was tapping his blade softly against his knee, waiting for another option to present itself.

Warm light spilled through the bathroom door as Penelope reappeared wearing Wonder Woman pajamas, her hair piled on top of her head, the scent of jasmine, musk, and sea salt lingering in the air. She turned off the light and went to bed.

Alexis waited another thirty minutes before getting up and going into the room after her. She slept in the middle of the bed, stretched out like a long cat, already fast asleep. The knife in his hand twitched once before Alexis sheathed it. He would destroy any chance she would have to continue her search. It would be a way to save her life even if it would destroy her career.

Alexis touched her forehead, sketching a symbol that would be sure to alert him before she got so close again.

PENELOPE WAS pulled out of the memory, gasping for air and thrashing her arms.

"Easy, Penelope, you're okay," Alexis said from the chair beside her. She let go of his hand, pushing him away so she could stick her head between her knees.

"Oh God, oh God," she breathed, a panic attack imminent as her chest tightened, the extra adrenaline making her stomach heave. "You were in my house. You were going to kill me…"

"But I didn't. You could feel my reluctance. You are brilliant, Penelope, and brilliant people are too few in the world to just kill off when they become inconvenient."

"What have you done to her, Alexis?" a woman's voice said sharply, and Penelope looked up to see an old woman striding into the room, face like a thunderstorm. *Nereus, the healer*, she remembered.

"I tried to show her I didn't want to kill her," Alexis said stubbornly.

"By showing me the night you were planning on killing me! Are you insane?" Penelope shouted.

Nereus gave Alexis a look that had him cringing. "You are thoughtless sometimes. Look at the damage you've just done." Nereus crouched down beside Penelope and touched the base of her skull in a gentle twisting motion. Instantly, the adrenaline vanished, the panic and nausea leaving with it.

"Thank you," breathed Penelope.

"I'm sorry, I didn't think—" Alexis said softly, but Nereus hissed at him.

"I thought you liked this girl. What use is scaring the life out of her? You should know better," she chastised before turning to Penelope with a gentle smile. "I'm so sorry my dear, I shouldn't have trusted Alexis to greet you properly. Would you like to come with me and see something that won't send you screaming out of the palazzo? He's doing a terrible job of reassuring you that we aren't involved with Thevetat's band of miscreants."

Penelope got to her feet and slid the knife back into her pocket without looking at Alexis. "Sure, Nereus, I'd like that."

"Sometimes it takes a woman's touch," Nereus muttered as she led Penelope out of the Atlantis Room.

Penelope risked a glance back at Alexis, but he remained glaring at the wall of paraphernalia. Once Penelope had entered the long hallway with her new guide, she felt the connection to him tug again.

Perhaps Nereus could fix that like she did my panic attack, Penelope thought.

She didn't know what to make of Alexis. The trip into his memories was too weird. The lecture night had haunted her for months and seeing it through someone else's eyes left her disorientated.

"Alexis can be brooding and secretive, but his heart is honorable," Nereus said beside her.

"You can read minds?" asked Penelope. *Please don't be able to read minds.*

"I don't have to. Your conflicted emotions are on your face."

"You would be concerned, too, if a strange man claiming to be a magician kept turning your life upside down."

Nereus chuckled under her breath. "According to Alexis, you are the one terrorizing him."

"This is all a big misunderstanding."

"I don't think it is. Sometimes fate and the gods intervene to make our lives more interesting. If you weren't meant to be here, you wouldn't have found the palazzo, and it certainly wouldn't have let you into his tower, even as an astral projection."

"I didn't do it on purpose," argued Penelope.

"Alexis knows that and finds it worse than if you were trained." Nereus smiled mischievously, and it made her appear young and wicked. "He takes himself far too seriously. It'll humble him to know there are things left in this world that he doesn't know. I must say, it's been a delight to see him so rattled recently. It's probably why he thought it would be a good idea to show you the most inappropriate memory he could. The man isn't exactly thinking straight and has forgotten how to make friends."

Despite her words, her tone was thoroughly amused, and Penelope found herself relaxing ever so slightly.

"So you're saying I should trust him?" Penelope asked. "After everything he's done and all the other… weirdness?"

"God no. Never trust a magician just because he asks, Doctor Bryne. I'm merely suggesting that you give him a chance to earn it. He would never do anything intentionally to hurt you. I've known him long enough to know when he's fond of someone."

Nereus pressed a silver button on the wall, and the elevator doors slid silently open. Penelope stepped inside the elaborate cage of iron and glass in a stunning art nouveau design wondering just how big the palazzo was.

The doors were closing when a brown hand caught them. Alexis stepped inside without saying anything.

Nereus looked sideways at Penelope and gave her a secret wink.

The hair on Penelope's arms rose when Alexis leaned on the glass beside her, the proximity and intense hum of his energy making her edgy. *This is real this is real this is real*, she reminded herself. She didn't like that a part of her was fighting the urge to touch him again just to be sure.

"You should turn around," Alexis suggested.

"Why?"

He gave a shrug that could mean anything. "You will enjoy it."

Penelope turned so she was facing the glass through which only the interior of the wall could be seen. The elevator began to drop, and she was surrounded by the blue-gray of the canal water before they descended into the seabed. She looked at him questioningly, but he only smiled. The earth and rock vanished as they descended through the roof of an immense cavern. Elaborate chandeliers and floating orbs of light illuminated shelves upon shelves of books.

"This is a library?" Penelope's voice was small with wonder. She rested her hands on the glass to steady herself as her knees went weak.

"We call it the Archives."

"What's that?" Penelope pointed.

Alexis stood behind her to see, and the hair on the back of her neck rose. In the distance, gold flickered on top of a marble pillar.

"That's the Atlantean symbol for knowledge," he replied, reaching around her to point at another pillar, "and that one over there is for protection. The pillars are carved with stories, but you won't be able to make anything out from this distance."

Penelope looked over her shoulder at him. His blue eyes were calm, and before she could think about it she asked, "Will you show me?"

"If you like."

"You see, Alexis? You just needed to show her some books, and she's friends with you already." Nereus chuckled.

He was so tall she had to tilt her head back, but Penelope stared him dead in the eye. "I'm so not your friend."

"Yet," he replied, the corner of his mouth twitching toward a smile. Penelope's mouth twitched back. *God damn it, I wanted to hate you.*

"You can show her whatever you like *after* we have been to the lab," Nereus interrupted as the elevator doors opened.

Nereus led them into a laboratory that was built out of the cavern rock. It was filled with glass and metal contraptions of varying shapes and colors. Penelope could only speculate what they did.

They found a slender black man standing near a stone slab examining a dead body. "Hello, Penelope," he greeted with a brilliant smile. "I am Galenos."

Penelope tried to smile, but she was doing her best not to balk at the sight of the body. She had seen dead bodies before, especially recently, but this one made her blood run cold. It was the man who had stabbed her on the bridge. His throat was cut, and she turned questioningly to Alexis.

"We didn't kill him," he said innocently. "By the time Phaidros caught up to him, the thug was already dead."

"Why did you bring him back here? Why not call the police?"

"We needed to question him," Nereus said as she tied on a leather butcher's apron.

"But he's dead."

"Good observation," she replied. "I can see why Alexis is so taken with you."

Penelope bit her tongue, chastised.

"Nereus, please. Give her a chance to—" Alexis began, but Nereus silenced him with a sharp glance.

"Sink or swim, Penelope. Sink or swim." Nereus took a knife and sliced the dead man's shirt, pulling it back to examine his skin. "Tell me what you see, Miss Observation. He was sent to kill you, after all."

Penelope stepped forward, determined not to embarrass herself further. The man's skin was pale brown, with a spray of dark hair and a few tattoos, but otherwise unmarked. "He's not part of the Thevetat cult," she said, lifting parts of his shirt away to check as much skin as she could. "At least not directly."

"What makes you sure?" Nereus asked. "Demon worship isn't something people would advertise."

"From my research, and what I know about chthonic cults, there would be a brand," Penelope explained. "I don't know what the brand or mark would look like, but there would be some initiation rite scarring. The ritual murders are steeped in pain and blood because they believe they can draw power from it. If he were a part of it, there would be evidence of self-mutilation."

"Interesting. What other evidence is there?"

"He was a hired thug. I recognize that tattoo of the snake around the lion head. It's the gang sign for the *Sangue di Serpente*. I remember reading an article a few years ago when there was a corruption case against a Sicilian politician. He had hired the *Serpente* to protect some of his properties." Seeing Nereus's disbelieving look, Penelope added, "Too many years looking at ancient texts has given me a curious memory for symbols. My father used to write my household chores out in hieroglyphics. He's a jerk that way."

Alexis looked at Penelope, and though he wasn't smiling, there was something in his stance that seemed smug. "Are you satisfied, Nereus?"

"Let's see if she's right." Nereus rubbed her hands together, static sparks jumping between her fingers. Galenos handed her a small black stone. Nereus dropped it into the dead man's mouth and shut his jaw. The hair on Penelope's arms lifted as energy crackled around the lab. The man on the table started to cough, and she leaped backward, colliding with Alexis.

"It's okay, Penelope, he can't hurt you," Alexis reassured her.

The dead man coughed again and then, in gargling, Sicilian started to curse.

"What's he saying?" Penelope asked, still hanging onto Alexis's arm.

"Something about the son of a pig whore," Nereus said before gripping the man's face and asking a question of him in a stern voice.

"She asked him who hired him to kill you," Alexis translated. "He's not sure of the man's real name because he's known as the Acolyte in gang circles. He's worked for him before."

"Does he know where he lives?" Penelope asked. "If he does, Marco can focus the investigation there."

Nereus asked and whatever the man replied earned him a slap in the face. Apparently, dead men did feel pain as he cursed her even as he gave up the information.

"He met him in San Marco, at the palazzo where there were lots of people. He didn't trust the Acolyte. He was on his way back to meet him there when he was jumped," Alexis said.

"Any other questions, Doctor Bryne?" Nereus asked, and Penelope shook her head. Alexis didn't translate what Nereus asked next, but Penelope heard the word Thevetat, and the man's face twisted in fear.

"He knows nothing, release him," Alexis said.

Nereus eyed the dead man coldly before placing her hand over the man's mouth. Lines of electricity crackled from her palm and the black stone flew into it. The man collapsed back on the slab, dead and broken.

"You were right, Penelope," Nereus said quietly. "He wasn't initiated into the cult, but he did know what Thevetat was and that's cause for some concern. Alexis, show her around. Galenos and I will clean this up." Nereus dismissed them with a wave and started directing Galenos in a strange and lilting language.

"Come on, let me show you something less dreadful than this sad display," Alexis said, his hand on the small of Penelope's back, guiding her from the laboratory.

Penelope took a deep breath and stared up at the floating lights above her. "How is it not cold and damp in here?"

"A simple answer? Magic. We use it to regulate the heat and humidity so none of the books rot," he replied. "You are still not screaming or panicking."

"You expected me to?"

"You seemed to have calmed down quickly." He frowned.

"Maybe I just needed some books," Penelope said, looking at him with a small smile. "Books always make me feel better."

"I'll keep that in mind for future reference. Are you sure you don't have magician blood?"

"Believe me. There's nothing magical about my family. My father thinks I'm a nut case for studying Atlantis," Penelope scoffed, "but I'm pragmatic. If this is a dream, it is a fascinating one. If this is real, then I'm being given the opportunity to brush against true mystery, and hopefully, find the answers that have plagued me since childhood."

Alexis considered this as they walked between the shelves. Penelope had to stop her hands from reaching out to touch the spines of the books. Many were bound in colored leathers, their titles stitched onto the spine in scripts she didn't recognize. She wanted to know what was in them, why there were so many, and what else the Archives held. Shelves were built into the rock from the floor to the roof hundreds of meters above her. *How did you get them down? Who would be game enough to climb a ladder that high?*

"If you were given the option of knowing answers, but never being able to publish or prove them to anyone else, would you still want to know the truth?" asked Alexis, as she paused to study a statue.

"Of course I'd want to know. I only published my work on the Tablet because I wanted to generate interest and funding to search for the rest of it. I'm not interested in fame. I only want to find things," admitted Penelope.

"You still wouldn't have found it," Alexis said with a curious head tilt.

"That's what you think." Penelope folded her arms. "Would you have sabotaged my dig if I *had* received the funding?"

"I wouldn't have had to," he replied confidently. "The rest of the Tablet is here."

"What? *Where?*"

"Behind you," he pointed. "Look."

Penelope turned sharply on her heel. Sure enough, displayed on a wall behind her was a massive stone tablet. It was four meters long and would have been two meters wide except a corner piece was missing.

"Oh my God."

Penelope ran over and immediately began scanning the curves and loops of the script. Unlike the writing at the crime scene, this felt wonderful to look at. She touched it tentatively, running her fingertips over the border carved with intricate, geometric patterns. She felt the same buzzing under her hand as she had the day she found the missing piece. *I found you.*

"You can imagine my surprise when I saw your article claiming you had found the missing piece of my Tablet," Alexis said from behind her. "I thought it was lost forever in a stream of lava."

"It's beautiful…wait, what do you mean *your* Tablet?" She looked at him.

"It's mine. I carved every inch of it. True, it was for the Temple of Poseidon at the time, but it's mine more than anyone else's. Once Zotikos returns from Crete with the other piece, it will be together for the first time in ten thousand years. What?"

"You…" Penelope looked from the Tablet to the man beside her. "But how is that possible? You can't be—"

"Haven't you figured it out yet, Penelope Bryne?" he asked, his voice softening. "You said you wanted answers, even if you couldn't speak of them to anyone. Maybe not even to yourself, because how could you, with your glorious academic mind so filled with science, believe in magic and immortals." He drew close to her, and her fingers tightened on the stone engravings. "You have seen magic, Penelope, and you didn't flinch. Are immortals such a stretch?"

"Immortal magicians from Atlantis. *Atlantis*. That is…" Her breath hitched as her lungs tightened. "Impossible."

"Is it? Would you like proof? I could show you more."

"You mean you can throw me into another memory?"

"It wouldn't be as intense. You wouldn't be me like last time but if you want to see…" Alexis held out his hand and waited.

See Atlantis? Was it possible? Penelope bit her lip and put her shaking hand in his. Slowly, he lowered their hands to the Tablet, and the Archives disappeared.

PENELOPE STOOD in a temple of crystal and marble. Color flooded her eyes as she took in everything, from the murals on the ceilings to the carved pillars and finely woven curtains that blew softly in the mild sea breeze. Oil braziers burned on tall iron stands, filling the rooms with golden light. Alexis stood beside her, holding her hand gently.

"Where are we?" she whispered.

"Atlantis," he said sadly. "This is one of my memories of the Temple of Poseidon." They walked together out onto a large balcony. Beneath them stretched a dark garden and the shimmering ocean.

Voices made her turn, and she saw Alexis and Phaidros, clad in *chitons* of red fabric that fell to their knees with golden belts about their hips. Their skin glowed where gold had been painted in a thick band across their eyes.

Alexis appeared about twenty years old, the soft look of boyhood still about his face even though his long body was filled with the muscles of a man. Phaidros's golden hair shone brightly and hung in looping coiled waves down his shoulders. Teasing banter passed between them in the same lilting language Penelope had heard Nereus speak.

"What are you saying?" Penelope asked, following them.

"I'm teasing him about a girl. He was so in love with one of the priest's daughters he thought he was going to die from desire," Alexis answered.

"Boys." Penelope rolled her eyes. "What were you doing at the Temple?"

"Everyone had training at the Temple before they became a man. We were still seen as boys and had yet to go through our Rites. My father was one of the most famous artisans in all of Atlantis, and I'd made the Tablet as an offering to Poseidon, shaping it with dedication and love in the hopes he would bless my coming of age with a commission."

"And did he?"

"Yes," Alexis said with a broad smile, "but not in stonework. It was my destiny to become a magician."

"Not a priest?"

"I lacked certain disciplines." Alexis's smile was so filthy Penelope blushed. "Nereus was at the selection night. She saw the magic in me and insisted on taking me for the Magicians. The High Priest challenged her, but she was a powerful woman in the capital, and Nereus always has her way."

"I've noticed," laughed Penelope. "I can only imagine the argument."

"I'll show it to you sometime if you like," Alexis said, and then they were back in the Archives in Venice, their hands linked. Penelope stumbled in surprise. "Do you believe me yet?"

"I'm starting to," she said, removing her hand from his. "Not going to lie, I want to believe, but it might take me a few days to wrap my head around all of this."

"That's understandable. It can be overwhelming to have everything you ever thought about magic and Atlantis be entirely incorrect."

"It's not just that, I mean *look* at this place." Penelope waved her hands, gesturing to the books and manuscripts around her. "No libraries are like this anymore, how do you keep track of it all? How is it cataloged?"

"Come, I'll show you," Alexis said, and she followed him eagerly. "Galenos has always kept registers, but as technology advanced, he found different ways of doing things."

They reached another group of rooms and Penelope's mouth fell open. They were filled with servers, computer terminals, and workbenches covered in half-finished electronic gadgets. Galenos sat in front of a group of screens, eyes flicking over code. Apparently, it didn't take long to get rid of a body.

"I never thought a magician from Atlantis would be such a computer geek," Penelope said, trying to reconcile the technology with the trove of manuscripts outside the door.

"One of us needed to be a little more advanced than parchment and ink." Galenos smiled brightly. "I always was fascinated by technology, and when you are immortal, anything new is a novelty."

"What does all of this do? Are you digitizing the Archives?" Penelope asked eagerly, her fingers aching to open a search engine.

"Absolutely not," Alexis huffed. "More copies, the stronger the spells get. Copies of an entire book of spells would be a disaster."

"Well, not exactly," Galenos corrected, earning a warning glare from Alexis. "Alexis is half right. In some cases, making digital copies would duplicate the magic. In others, it would be only the copy of a completed ritual that would make it grow more powerful. What I'm doing, in most cases, is cataloging what's actually in the Archives. Each artifact, manuscript, and book are special."

He pulled up what looked like a blank database entry form with familiar fields such as NAME, AUTHOR, and ORIGIN. Then there were others that were unique such as MAGICAL PROPERTIES, RADIATION LEVEL, DANGER TO HUMANS.

"What does it mean by radiation level?" Penelope asked.

"Some books have a magical aura, and if they are cataloged or stored incorrectly, the magic of the books around them can be affected. It could grow more powerful by draining the other magical auras. By measuring the radiation levels, we can ensure that a balance is kept," Galenos explained, pulling up tables and data and ever-shifting numbers. Penelope took it in with giddy delight.

"If you have recorded radiation, I'm sure you've done enough categories and keywords that I could use a computer to track down certain topics?"

"Of course." Galenos snorted like it was the least exciting thing she could have asked. "I'll get you permissions if Nereus allows it. Perhaps you can show Alexis who still wants to search one bookshelf at a time."

"Well, we will stop disturbing you, Galenos," Alexis cut in. "We'll talk about giving Penelope database access next time *if* she decides to visit again."

"Look at her face." Galenos's smile was knowing. "Of course she is coming back."

ALEXIS LED her back to the Archives, Penelope's head swimming with data and search engines and magical radiation. She was excited, distracted, and a little nauseous like she used to feel on the first day of school.

"It's late, I'll take you back to your hotel so you can…process," Alexis said. "I wanted to ease you in so you weren't frightened, and I'm sorry if I failed at that. Nereus is worried about these murders and thought it best to throw you in."

"Sink or swim. Luckily, I'm an excellent swimmer." Penelope grinned. *When you aren't freaking the hell out of me.*

"I can tell. Still, I will wait a few days before I interrogate you on how you broke into my meditation. You say you don't know what happened, but I'll figure it out."

"Good luck. Finding some Turkish corsair in my meditation was as much of a surprise to me as it was to you."

Alexis roared with laughter. "Turkish corsair! I've never been accused of such a thing in my life."

"I'm glad you're not offended by that," Penelope said.

"How could I be offended? I *was* one for a while. Although nobody knew enough to accuse me of it."

"Really? What did you steal?" she asked as they walked back through the shelves to the elevator.

"Lysippos's statue of Hercules and the most valuable books and scrolls from the Library of Constantinople," Alexis replied without hesitation.

"Lysippos's Hercules was destroyed during the Sack of Constantinople in 1204. Crusaders melted it down."

"Did they now? How interesting. I'm quite sure it's on the other side of the palazzo."

"You stole it from the crusaders?"

"I commandeered it for preservation purposes," Alexis corrected, "and to be fair, they stole it first. I was making sure it wasn't melted down, though they went with that story rather than losing it to pirates."

"No wonder this place is so big," Penelope said as they stepped back into the elevator. "You have been thieving for centuries."

"Preserving, Penelope. Humans can't be trusted with some knowledge, and every time people decide to fight with each other, they seem to want to destroy books and art first."

"It's a shame you couldn't get to Alexandria before they..." Penelope began and then stopped. "You didn't...?"

"Didn't I?" he said, blue eyes filled with innocence.

"Well, fuck me," Penelope whispered, and Alexis laughed at her shocked expression.

"Maybe some other time. I think you've had as many surprises as you can handle tonight."

"Smart-ass," replied Penelope. She leaned against the elevator as it rose, a sea of knowledge and magic beneath and around her. "So you've spent eternity collecting knowledge."

"Collecting and protecting it as I have the other survivors." Alexis looked out at the Archives. "There are seven of us, and I've done my best to ensure that our true natures remain undetected."

"Why? Why not let people know about all of this?"

"Humans destroy what they don't understand. I won't have my brothers and sisters becoming science experiments, or have our treasures burnt, our magic stolen. You know that even the noblest and moral humans can be seduced by the smallest of things. Could you imagine if they had access to this knowledge? To immortality?"

Penelope *could* imagine, and she swallowed the lump in her throat. If anybody knew about the Archives under Dorsoduro, they would plunder and destroy it as well as its guardians. *And he would kill to protect it.* But he hadn't killed her, and now he was trusting her even though she didn't trust him. The enormity of Alexis's decision to share all of this with her knocked the sense from her long enough for her to turn and hug him.

"Thank you for showing me," she said against his chest, before quickly letting him go. "Sorry."

"You're welcome, Doctor Bryne," he replied awkwardly. The elevator doors opened, and she quickly stepped back from him. "I'm just glad you've stopped trying to stab me with your oyster knife."

"For now."

"May I escort you back to your hotel? It's late, and I don't like the idea of having to bring you back from the dead again."

She rubbed her sternum. "I'm not keen on that either."

"There's something I'm curious about that night," he added, taking a coat from a closet as the blue-and-gold door appeared.

"What's that?" Penelope asked, winding her scarf around her neck.

"You came to, spewing canal water and bleeding profusely—"

"I'm charming that way," Penelope added as they stepped into the cold, misty night.

"You were almost dead, and yet the word that came out of your mouth was 'firecrackers.' Why that word?"

Penelope suddenly wished she had rejected his offer for an escort. "If I tell you, you must promise not to hold it against me," she said as they walked under the lamps of the Calle dei Cerchieri.

"You have my word," he said solemnly, a hand over his heart. He went first down a tight alley between the buildings, and Penelope took advantage of the fact that he couldn't see her face.

"It's your aftershave."

"*Scusi?*"

"You smell like firecrackers and some spice, like cinnamon or sandalwood. It's one of the first things I noticed when I came out of the water. I knew it was you because you smelled the same in the meditation."

"How strange," he said.

"After today, I'm reassessing what I find strange."

"It's not that," Alexis said as they crossed a small bridge. "I don't wear aftershave."

"Then what is it? Because people don't naturally smell that way. Especially after a dunk in a canal," argued Penelope.

"What you are smelling is my magic." Alexis shook his head. "Amazing. I haven't known a human who could smell magic in four thousand years."

"Here I thought Dolce and Gabbana had upped their fragrance game," teased Penelope. She would freak out over this later. She looked at him, dark hair tousled around his high cheekbones, and wrapped in double-breasted navy cashmere.

That's magic all right, she heard Carolyn's voice quip in her head.

"Can I ask how you are feeling? Now that you know some of what is happening?" asked Alexis when they reached the hotel.

"Much better. My urge to throw things at you has lessened, and my stomach flu seems to be gone."

"It wasn't the flu. Your body was fighting the memory spell I placed on you." Alexis frowned pensively. "It was fighting even after you forgot what you were fighting. The fever dreams were forcing you to remember."

"Believe it or not, some people don't like their memories messed with."

"I had to do it or Lyca would have killed you."

"What's her deal anyway?"

"Killing is her magic. She has protected Nereus all her life and only answers to her. Taking your memories was a kind of compromise. But you remembered. You came back."

"It was a test, and I passed? Or is it something I should still worry about?"

"You definitely passed."

"What does that mean now?"

"It means tomorrow we are going to start hunting down Thevetat's followers before they hurt anyone else. We'll find out what spells the murderer is using."

Penelope let out a small groan. "Damn it! I was meant to ring Marco. There is some DIGOS agent that's managed to sway the Questore into not letting me back to any of the crime scenes."

Alexis waved dismissively. "I'll fix it. I've some friends who owe me a favor."

"If you think they can help, it would be great. I'm going to get some sleep, and hopefully, when I wake up this won't have been a dream."

"It's not a dream." He turned to leave but hesitated, adding, "I've wanted to talk to you for a long time, Doctor Bryne. I'm happy you found your way back to the palazzo."

"Me too."

"*Buona notte, Dottore.*"

"*A domani,* Alexis," Penelope replied and hurried inside the hotel. She shut the door behind her and leaned against it, dazed.

"Hell of a day, Bryne," she whispered.

Louisa was nowhere to be seen, and when Penelope looked at her phone, she realized why. It was nearly 1:00 a.m. She had somehow lost nine hours inside of the palazzo.

There were four messages and a missed call from Marco, two from Carolyn, and one from her mother. Penelope replied to Marco first as she walked up the steps to her room, apologizing profusely for the time and extending an offer for breakfast.

Penelope opened her door and switched on the light. Her room had been trashed, with clothes pulled out of drawers and papers scattered across the floor.

"What the…?"

She was struck hard from behind, and her world went dark.

TEN

PENELOPE'S HEAD THROBBED, her hair wet with blood. She had been tied to an old wooden chair with duct tape, and her hands ached from the lack of blood flow. She looked at her surroundings, trying to get her bearings.

She was in a damp shed filled with gondolas in need of repair. A small ramp of rotting wooden slats led down into oil-slicked canal water.

"She's awake," a voice said from the shadows. A balding man with thick arms came into sight and pulled down her sticky gag.

"What do you want?" asked Penelope, earning herself a sharp slap.

"I ask the questions, whore," the man said in heavily accented English. "Where is Lorenzo?"

"I don't know anyone called Lorenzo," Penelope answered through bloodied lips. *Lorenzo? Who are these people?*

"He was sent to kill you. Did you kill him first? Did the Acolyte?"

"Do I look like I'm capable of killing anyone?" Penelope said, even as fear filled her stomach. In the hazy light, she saw the lion and serpent tattoo on his forearm. Suddenly, she knew who Lorenzo was. *The dead man in the Archives.* "I think you have me confused with someone else." Her voice shook. "Nobody has tried to kill me. I'm no one—"

"You are Penelope Bryne, an Australian traveling in Venezia and putting her nose into other people's business. Lorenzo was offered a big contract to see you dead." The man loomed over her. "And now he's gone. Who are you working with?"

"No one! I'm here on holiday—"

He seized her little finger and broke it.

"Don't lie to me, *Dottore*."

"I'm not, I swear," she cried, pain riding up her arm. "I'm just a tourist."

"I'll give you ten minutes to think about your answer before I return and break something else. You have a lot of bones, and I have a lot of patience." He calmly took out his phone and began speaking angrily in Italian before disappearing through the doors.

Biting back tears, Penelope strained against the tape, willing her hand to slip free. She only managed to make the pain in her broken finger worse as the tape folded over and cut into her sharply.

Her kidnapper laughed when he came back and saw her struggling.

"Even if you were to escape, I have men surrounding the building." He eyed her in a way that made her skin crawl. "The Acolyte and I have brokered a deal for your life. He said I'm not to injure you any further because he wants to be the one to break you." He grabbed the back of her chair and dragged her down the small ramp to where the tide was coming in. "Fortunately, there are many ways to break someone without ever leaving a mark."

He pushed her backward into the dirty canal water.

Penelope thrashed, trying to flip the chair back upright. Her fear of drowning surged back in a terrifying rush. *I'm going to be taken by the sea after all.*

She fought and struggled, but all of her free diving training was for nothing in a situation like this. Only when she thought she couldn't hold out any longer was she brought back up. Her ribs screamed in agony as she coughed out water and gulped air. Oil from the water slicked her clothes and ran down her arms. *The oil!* Penelope pulled her arms back and forward, the slime on her skin loosening the tape ever so slightly.

"Make this easy on yourself and tell me what happened to Lorenzo," the man said. "He was my best killer; how did you get the better of him? Who are you working for? And why does the Acolyte want you dead so badly? If you tell me the truth, maybe I will kill you quickly before he arrives. I've seen what he does to women in his special sacrifices, *bella.* Believe me, you would be begging me for a blade if you knew the fate that awaited you."

"I—I don't know what you are talking about," Penelope said, shaking. "I'm here on holiday."

"Why would someone like the Acolyte want a *tourista* dead? I'm not that stupid."

Penelope was still shouting her innocence as he kicked her chair, toppling her back into the water. She tried her best to hold her breath as she rolled her oily wrists, loosening the tape further. Inside her mind, she reached for the strange connection that Alexis claimed he had followed to her. *Magic is real. Maybe he'll feel it.* The darkness started to fill her mind, head squeezing from the pressure of holding her breath and she tugged at the string of light. *Alexis, help me…*

Penelope was pulled out of the water again and slapped awake. She coughed up brine and swore at him between breaths. There was another man in the shed with them now, watching her with cold eyes.

"I don't think she knows anything, Giacomo," he said in English. "She would've cracked by now."

"I saw the look in her eye, I know she is holding something back. Why would the Acolyte pay so much for her? What is special about her? Who are you working for, *Dottore*? Who are you protecting? We can do this all night."

"F-fuck you," she mumbled through frozen lips. The man smiled darkly, and she readied herself for a blow that never came. There were voices from outside the shed followed by gunshots.

"What's happening out there?" Giacomo shouted. "Go and see what they are doing."

With their attention elsewhere, Penelope pulled at the tape with all her might, and her bruised hands squeezed out from underneath the damaged plastic. She grabbed the wooden chair and swung it hard, crashing it heavily into Giacomo's back.

"You bitch!" he swore as he stumbled. Penelope hurried to the broken gondolas behind her and found a broken oar.

"You're brave, but that will not save you." The other man held out his knife toward her.

A shadow danced across the lights making both men pause. A thick plume of glittering black sand filled the shed, and Alexis stepped out of it, bringing the blade of his *yataghan* down on Giacomo's skull. The other man threw his knife at him, but Alexis moved like smoke, cutting the man down. Penelope gripped the oar tighter as he turned to her, pale blue light flickering under his skin and making his eyes glow.

"Are you okay, Penelope?" he asked cautiously, the light in his skin disappearing.

"There are other men outside," she said, unable to lower her oar. He rotated the bloody sword once, and it disappeared.

"Not ones that are still breathing," he growled.

"Y-you heard me?"

"I did, though you seem to be doing okay without my help." He held out his hand to her. "Put the oar down, Penelope. It's over now."

Penelope started to tremble all over, the oar clattering to the ground as she collapsed wet and freezing into his arms.

"You're all right, I have you," Alexis said softly. "I called Marco Dandolo. He should be here shortly."

She held onto him, shivering and bleeding until the sirens wailed in the distance. Wrapped in the warm, spicy scent of him, she started to cry.

"You heard me. I can't believe you heard me," Penelope whispered. She tried to remember all of her breathing techniques to lower her adrenaline, but her mind was blank, and her lungs felt like they would never have enough air again.

"We can talk about it later," he said, his grip tightening as her legs gave way. "It's okay. I have you."

Alexis carried her out of the wooden shed as police arrived in boats. He placed her in the care of a paramedic, and someone wrapped a blanket around her. Marco pushed his way through the crowd to get to them.

"Penelope, are you hurt?" he asked urgently, his face filled with worry.

"I'll live," she wheezed as the paramedics inspected her.

"What happened?" Marco asked her before recognizing Alexis standing behind her. "*Signore* Donato! What are you doing here?"

"Alexis helped save me. You know each other?" asked Penelope.

"Only by reputation," replied Marco coolly. "There are seven dead bodies, and you two are the only ones left alive. Tell me everything."

"Doctor Bryne and I are old friends," Alexis lied smoothly. "We had dinner together, and I walked her back to her hotel just after midnight. Some suspicious men passed me as I was leaving, and I heard them mention Penelope's name, so I backtracked. When I arrived at her hotel, I saw them carrying her out, and I followed."

He said it so confidently that even Penelope almost believed him. Marco nodded intently.

Alexis went on. "I called the *polizia* when I found where they were holding her and was waiting for you to arrive when there was shouting and gunfire. When it stopped, I checked the building and found Penelope fighting off two other men with a broken oar, and then you all arrived," he finished, his blue eyes filling with admiration as he turned to look at her. "She was fearsome to behold."

"Is this true?" Marco looked at her questioningly.

"As far as I know. I was grabbed from the hotel. The big one inside said he had sold me to someone called the Acolyte, who had contracted them to kill me." She rubbed the side of her ribs with her good hand. "I think he's the murderer and he knows we are onto them."

Marco ran his hands through his hair. "I'm so sorry this happened to you, Penelope. I'll send men to watch the hotel and—"

"No," Alexis interrupted him. "I want Penelope to stay with me at my palazzo. I have enough private security to protect her from these thugs the Acolyte is sending after her."

"I don't think involving more citizens is the right approach—"

"I don't care what you think. Penelope can make up her mind as to where she would like to stay."

"The both of you can stop talking about me like I'm not here," Penelope interrupted. The two men eyed each other coldly.

"Excuse me, *Signore* Donato, I need to speak with Penelope alone. Due to the confidentiality of the other case," Marco said stiffly. "You understand."

"Of course, I'll be waiting right over there. There are calls I really should make," Alexis said smoothly, and Marco's nostrils flared.

"How in the world do you know Alexis Donato?" he asked once they were alone.

"Academic rivalry in the politest way." It was only half a lie. "He came to a lecture of mine a few years ago. I caught up with him last night, as he said." Penelope thought about going back to the hotel and tightened the blanket around her. The palazzo had a door no one could open unless it allowed it. Staying in an invisible palazzo would be useful. *But would you be safer in a house full of magicians?* Alexis had come to help her when she needed it. He killed her attackers without hesitation to protect her.

"And you trust him?" Marco frowned, as if sensing Penelope's hesitation.

Penelope looked across the crowded jetty to where Alexis was standing, head and shoulders above the officers. He was watching her and the crowd around her, scanning for danger. She thought of the day they'd had and the memories they'd shared. The way he constantly tried to reassure her. He was trusting her with a secret he had done everything in his long life to protect. *Sink or swim, Penelope.*

"Yes, I trust him," she whispered, and by admitting it aloud reaffirmed it to herself.

"I can't force you into police protection, although I don't know if letting you leave with him is a good idea," muttered Marco. "Being involved with a man like Donato is a whole other danger in itself."

There are no men like Alexis Donato, Penelope thought, looking across the crowd and finding his eyes on hers. She turned back to Marco and asked, "Why do you say that? What do you know about him?"

"He's quite notorious here in the north. Extremely well-connected, so much so that there are rumors he is mafia. Everyone knows *of* him—judges, police, politicians—but no one knows him personally, or what he does."

"Being mysterious and having influential friends doesn't make him mafia," Penelope said.

"Is there any way I can convince you not to go with him?"

"No." Penelope cringed at the thought of going back to the hotel. She would never sleep well there again. The fear of having someone waiting behind every door was enough to send her packing right now. "Alexis saved me, Marco. I feel safe with him, and I don't want to be alone. I want to be with friends." *Friends who know magic and can protect me from psycho demon worshippers.*

Marco smiled weakly. "I'm your friend, and I was joking about you sleeping on my couch. I have a spare room if you don't want to stay in another hotel—"

"Let her go home, *Inspecttori*," a blonde woman said brusquely. "I just got off the phone, and the Questore has approved her leaving with Donato."

"Doctor Bryne, meet Agent Bianchi. She's the DIGOS agent that is now assisting with the case," Marco said through gritted teeth.

"Nice to meet you," Penelope said. The woman's brown eyes narrowed when she looked at the bodies being zipped into bags.

"This is why you should never involve civilians, Dandolo," Agent Bianchi growled. "Make sure you get her statement before she leaves." She headed for the shed, leaving them staring after her.

"Wow, I can see why you were so excited to work with her," said Penelope before she started coughing. She would be tasting oily brine at the back of her throat for weeks.

"You are still a consultant on this case," Marco replied firmly. "I don't care what she says."

The paramedic finished numbing and binding Penelope's bruised hands and broken finger before finally clearing her to leave.

The sun was starting to rise over the terra-cotta roofs as Penelope climbed off the gurney. She swayed dangerously as the drugs kicked in, but as she tipped forward, Alexis's arm was there to steady her.

"Will you come with me?" he asked Penelope.

"If you don't think Nereus will mind having me," she replied.

Alexis's smile was remarkably sweet. "Of course she won't mind. She loves guests."

"Would you like to come with me and some other officers and get your luggage from the hotel?" Marco interrupted.

"I'll have someone collect Penelope's things from the hotel so she can rest," Alexis told him. "Her phone was damaged by those thugs, so you can contact her at this number."

Marco accepted the white card Alexis handed him. "I'll call you soon. We will need an official statement once you are feeling better." He let them leave without further argument, but Penelope could see the questions in his dark eyes.

Once they were out of police sight, Penelope steered Alexis over to a canal and wretched up oily water. Her lungs were burning, and her head pounded.

"Oh God, this is so embarrassing," she whimpered when Alexis passed her a crisp blue handkerchief. He looked up and down the alley before scooping her up into his arms.

"Hey! I can walk. Put me down."

"Please, just hold on for one moment," he instructed. Penelope grabbed the lapels of his jacket as he opened a doorway of shadows and they stepped through it, leaving only streaks of sunlight behind them.

ELEVEN

BACK AT THE palazzo in Dorsoduro, Alexis helped Penelope upstairs to a guest room in a wing that overlooked the Grand Canal. The palazzo tended to know exactly where to put people, and this time it had created a room near the entrance of his tower. It would give her space, but she was still close enough if there was an emergency.

She isn't yours to protect all the time, a voice reminded him.

"Apart from breaking your finger, did they stab you with any needles? Or hurt you in any other way?" he asked.

Penelope leaned against the bathroom basin as he turned her shower on and closed the glass doors. She looked pale and unsteady. He had an irrational and inappropriate urge to hold her. *You should have known they would come for her.*

"They only tried to drown me. Apparently, the Acolyte didn't want them marking me up." Penelope pushed damp curls away from her face. "I don't know why. They talked about him making sacrifices. Maybe the *Serpente* gangs work for him as lackeys."

"There are rules about sacrifices being whole from the beginning. It's to do with the ritual." Alexis hated the look in her eyes; she knew full well what would have happened to her. "Have a shower and get warm, Penelope. I'll be outside the door if you need anything." He left her looking like she was going to throw up again.

Outside the bathroom, Alexis slumped against the wall, sliding down to sit on the floor. How had he let this happen? He should've known that if it were so easy for him to find her hotel, others hunting her would too. The *Serpente* gang had more of a presence in Venice than he would have guessed, and it would be something else for him to investigate once the Acolyte was dead. If Penelope was right, and the Acolyte was using them as his group of flunkies, he might be able to get one of them to tell him how to get in contact with their boss. *You can't do that now that they are all dead.*

Alexis had done his best not to show Penelope how angry he was at himself. He had killed people in front of her; what the hell had he been thinking?

But of course, the answer was: he hadn't been.

Alexis had been in his tower, reminiscing about the day and how Penelope had been so openly delighted by everything she had seen. He knew he would enjoy her company, but it had been a surprise to learn how much. Even Nereus had told him to bring her back to the Archives whenever she liked.

Penelope's pain and fear had hit him like a kick to the stomach, and he hadn't paused for a moment to consider what he might be portaling into. Panicked, he had used magic to get to her without thinking about who might see it. He hadn't felt fury that strongly for a long time. Without a second thought, he had killed everyone who had believed her life worth less than theirs. He would never forget the look on her face, either, her bruised and broken hands gripping the oar, ready to attack anyone who went near her. *Brave as well as brilliant—how can I not like her?*

Inside the bathroom, the shower water shut off and the hair dryer switched on. Alexis should've left her alone, but the deeply protective side of his nature wouldn't allow it until he was satisfied that she felt calm and safe.

Alexis tensed as the bathroom door opened and she stepped out in a robe. She spotted him sitting on the floor, and the worried crease on her brow softened.

"Are you going to be guarding my door all night?" she asked, folding her arms.

"Probably," he answered.

"Then you might as well sit in a chair like a person and talk to me for a while. I'm too wired to sleep."

Alexis politely looked away as Penelope took off her robe and slipped under the bright orange bed covers.

"How well-connected do you think the Acolyte is?" she asked as he sat on the chair beside her bed.

"If he has the money to pay off *Serpente* errand boys then we can assume he isn't an amateur at this. He's been planning this display of violence for a long time, and he's not about to let anyone get in his way."

"You can tell from the details in the ritual how careful he is. Every glyph, every element of it is precise.

There is an artistry to the arrangements, despite the horror."

Alexis saw frightened streaks of color in her aura, and felt it pulse through their connection.

"I want you to know there are more than magicians protecting this palazzo. Nothing will harm you while you are under this roof."

"Thank you for coming tonight. I didn't think it would work. I thought…" Tears filled her hazel eyes and Alexis wrapped his hand around hers.

"You don't have to say it, Penelope. I'm only sorry I didn't get there sooner."

"You got there in time, and that is all that matters." Penelope's hand had the slightest of tremors as she asked, "How many people have you killed, Alexis? The way you moved…I've never seen anything like that before."

"I've had a lot of practice. If you want an exact number, I can't give you one." He hoped that his honesty would make her less afraid but, these kind of truths had a way of blowing up in his face. "I have lived a long time, Penelope. I have fought many wars in countries that no longer exist, for kings whose names are dust. I have protected the seven survivors of Atlantis for ten thousand years, and I'm good at it. You found us and are counted as one of our friends, so I'll always come when you need me."

"Is it wrong that I don't feel guilty that I lived while those men died? You killed them, and I'm still more afraid of them than you. That makes me a pretty horrible person, right?"

Penelope didn't meet his eye, so he lifted her chin with his finger so she would see how serious he was.

"It isn't wrong. You feel no guilt because you are innocent. They were not good men, Penelope. Good men don't *sell* people, and they don't profit from murder and death." Her skin warmed beneath his touch, so he let her go. "Sleep, Penelope. I'll be here if you need anything."

ALEXIS WATCHED the rise and fall of Penelope's chest. He could hear the rattle of water in her lungs with each inhale. He couldn't heal her other wounds—there had been too many witnesses to them—but inside was another matter.

Alexis rubbed his palms together and gently placed them on either side of her rib cage. Focusing his energy, he shut his eyes and started to evaporate the water inside of her to prevent infection. It took only a moment, but he left his hands there, feeling the warmth of her body and the steady beat of her heart to remind himself that she was alive.

"She's okay, Alexis," Phaidros whispered beside him. Alexis removed his hands and stepped away from the bed. Phaidros inclined his head, and they left her room, Alexis shutting the door quietly behind them. "Leave her to sleep. The palazzo will look after her."

"She could've died protecting our secrets, Phaidros," Alexis said. His body was starting to ache now that the adrenaline had gone, the price for using so much magic.

"At least now we know we can trust her. She's brave for a human," replied Phaidros.

"Someone called the Acolyte tried to buy her from the *Serpente* to use as a sacrifice like she was some beast at the markets."

"You saved her, Alexis. You killed all of those men tonight to make sure of it." Phaidros watched him carefully. "I haven't seen this side of you for a while, Defender. You've taken the sabotage approach for so long now, I'm surprised you went straight for the sword."

"She's under our protection, whether you like it or not. I acted the same way with her as I would have for any of you," said Alexis. "You saw the Bull. The *Serpente sold* her to that fate. To that death. I won't apologize for taking their lives."

"We've seen a lot of death, Alexis. She has not. She might not look at you in that same wide-eyed, utterly charmed way, and you should be prepared for that."

"She saw, she knew exactly what she was coming home with," Alexis argued, "and she doesn't look at me like that. She's just tolerating me at the moment because she wants to get her hands on the Archives."

"*Everyone* looks at you like that. You're just too stupid to realize. Come on, you need to sleep. I can get her things from the hotel." Phaidros steered him away from her door.

"I don't think…"

"I will watch over her." Lyca stepped from a shadow.

Alexis narrowed his eyes. "Can I trust you to keep your blades to yourself?"

"Of course. Nereus told me I must watch over her because she's your friend. My blade will never touch her skin."

Lyca might not think being friends with curious humans was wise, but she would never disobey Nereus. Alexis nodded his consent and allowed Phaidros to gently push him toward the stairs of his tower.

PENELOPE WOKE in a sea of vermillion sheets made of Egyptian cotton. Outside her window, stormy gray clouds had gathered over the sea. Her clothing, books, and laptop had been placed on a Louis XIV writing desk that hadn't been there at dawn when Alexis had helped her to bed. Only magicians could have moved furniture so quietly.

Magicians.

A week ago, she struggled to believe in astral projection, let alone magic, but after seeing Alexis and what he could do in the last two days, she was now a true believer. He had killed those men with as much detached emotion as Penelope had when grocery shopping. They had fallen to his blade without so much as

laying a single scratch on him. Only centuries of practice and killing could make someone so dispassionate
in a fight. It should have frightened her, but being near
Alexis seemed like the safest place in the world if the
Acolyte and the *Serpente* were after her.

You should come home, her father's voice said, *you
would be safe here, teaching history at a university on the
other side of the world.*

Living in a house of magicians hunting a crazy
murderer was not safe, but Penelope had no intention
of leaving.

The bathroom adjoining her main chambers had
marble floors, large antique mirrors, and a cast-iron tub
that made her sigh with delight. Fresh white roses that
hadn't been there that morning sat in a vase on the long
vanity with an array of shampoos, soaps, and lotions.

Despite the shower at dawn, Penelope could still
smell blood and oily saltwater on her skin and hair. It
made her question the sanity of Lord Byron swimming
the canals after visiting his mistress. She didn't want to
think how much worse the water quality would have
been in 1817.

After selecting a creamy soap that smelled of roses
and honey, she climbed into the shower and let the hot
water from the oversized head pulverize her bunched
muscles. Her lungs ached less than she had expected
them to, and her hands no longer throbbed in pain.
She felt along her new scar, inspecting the purple and
red line over her heart. Alexis had saved her then too.

Another mystery.

If Alexis hadn't wanted her getting any closer to the truth, he could've watched her die. *Maybe he wanted you to find them.*

Penelope thought of the Archives downstairs and trembled at the idea of visiting it again. There were so many secrets and so much history in the palazzo. She itched to know more about everything, including her rescuer.

The magical Turkish corsair who fought crusaders to save books.

Despite the terrifying night she had endured, Penelope couldn't stop the smile that spread across her face. The part of her that tried so hard to deny the magical aspect of Atlantis history had been annihilated. As an undergraduate, she had shut away the wild, irrational belief and yearning for the strange and magical. That wasn't the Atlantis she could prove to others. Stones, relics, temples, only *physical proof* became her obsession instead. Except now the proof she had found was in the form of magic. *Maybe it's time to forget everything you think you know and go and find out the truth.*

Wrapped in a thick robe, Penelope went to search her bag for a pair of clean black leggings and a knit sweater. Sitting on top of her bed was a card with elegant, masculine writing:

Doctor Bryne,

At your convenience, please join me in the courtyard for a late breakfast. The palazzo will show you the way.

Alexis

"Just as long as you have coffee, I'll be there," Penelope said, pulling on her clothes. It might have been vain, considering her busted lip and bruised cheek, but she still applied a little powder and eyeliner before leaving the room. Just because she felt like shit didn't mean she was going to look like it.

Penelope walked down a winding set of stairs and through empty hallways. She tried not to stop every two feet to look at art, sculptures, or bookcases. The breeze that blew through the house was too mild and summery for that time of year, and the speckled floors beneath her bare feet were warm.

Penelope had been staring at the intricate patterns of a Persian rug when she felt the walls shift. At the end of the hallway was now an archway with sunlight and greenery beyond it.

The palazzo will show you the way, the note had said. Penelope thought it was a joke. A house that moved around was going to make life even more confusing. She tried to keep an open mind as she stepped outside into a courtyard filled with leafy green trees and bright flowers. The walls of the house rose around her in an eclectic mix of Byzantine and Western architecture.

The sun was warm overhead even though there had been wet clouds outside of her bedroom minutes ago.

Penelope followed a path of terra-cotta tiles and found Alexis sitting at a glass and wrought iron table, a large white umbrella shielding their breakfast from the sun. He was reading a copy of *La Nazione*, coffee steaming in front of him. He glanced up, and his blue eyes looked at her in a way that exploded her stomach with butterflies.

"I hope you haven't been out here too long," she said, trying to sound relaxed.

"Good afternoon," he replied with a smile. "Did you sleep okay after your night of…adventures?"

"Better than I thought I would." She took a seat beside him. "This is the same table as the café you created in the meditation."

"It is. I'm surprised you remember it." Alexis poured her coffee, black as sin. "I must apologize for my behavior that day. I laid hands on you, and it was uncalled for."

Penelope rubbed her arm, remembering the feeling of his hand on her skin. "You didn't grab me hard. It frightened me more than anything."

"I apologize for it all the same. I was…unsettled by your presence."

"At least you knew I was a real person. I thought you were some imaginary guy I'd dug out of my subconscious."

"Does your subconscious frequently conjure strange men?" he asked, a small smile curling the corners of his mouth.

"You are definitely the strangest."

Penelope sipped her coffee and almost groaned with happiness as the complex flavor hit her taste buds. She didn't know where he got his beans from, but she vowed not to leave Venice without some.

"Do you always pull that face when you drink coffee?" he chuckled.

"Only when I drink your coffee. I swear you must put smack in it."

"A little cinnamon only."

Penelope helped herself to some fruit and tried to be as relaxed as he looked, dressed casually in tan pants and a white shirt rolled to his elbows, his long fingers heavy with silver rings. Alexis's black hair was a tumble of long black curls around his bearded face, and she would've resented his easy Mediterranean style if she didn't enjoy looking at him so much.

"How come it's raining in one part of the house, and perfectly sunny here?" she asked. "And please don't mysteriously smile and say magic."

Alexis smiled mysteriously anyway and replied, "But what if it is magic? Do you want to see how it is done?"

"If it's magic, of course, I want to see!"

"Come on, and I'll show you something you won't find in your universities." Alexis got to his feet and stepped out from the shade of the umbrella, gesturing for her to join him. She put her coffee down and hurried over to his side.

"Stand right here and look up," Alexis said, moving her in front of him. Penelope watched the sky as he lifted his arms upward and the sun above them faded to reveal the cloudy Venetian sky, the rain falling on an invisible barrier. "I chose a particularly beautiful day I remembered from last spring. I thought you would prefer the sun after your ordeal." The clouds were once again replaced by sunshine and Penelope stared at him, blinking in wonder.

"Thank you," she said softly. "That's very thoughtful of you."

Alexis touched her cheek gently, and her skin hummed. "If Marco Dandolo wouldn't become suspicious, I would heal all of your bruising too."

"I would've been a lot worse if you hadn't have turned up. I would have only gotten so far with that oar," Penelope said, her pulse jumping as he lightly touched her bruises. The sandalwood spice smell of him grew stronger. "And despite Marco's suspicions, you're doing healing magic anyway?"

"Only to take the pain away, not the look of it," he admitted. "I don't know how I feel about you knowing when I'm using magic."

"It's your fault for smelling so good."

The words were out before she could stop them. Before either of them replied, Phaidros appeared near the table, his golden skin and hair in the sunshine making him glow like Apollo.

"She only thinks that because she hasn't smelled me yet," he said, helping himself to a croissant.

Penelope took a step back from Alexis. "Hey! That's my breakfast."

"Come and eat it and stop fucking about with my weather." Phaidros sat down in a chair. "Has Alexis given you a phone yet?"

"A phone?"

"I was going to give it to you after you ate." Alexis reached into his pocket and handed her a new iPhone. "Phaidros doesn't believe in patience."

"I don't believe in you hogging the doctor, especially when Inspector Dandolo has been messaging her nonstop," Phaidros replied.

"And how would you know that?" Penelope asked, taking the phone.

"Call it a hunch. If I had your number, I'd be messaging you too." Phaidros smiled flirtatiously and Alexis smacked him lightly on the back of the head.

"Cut it out."

"You want to ruin all of my fun," Phaidros complained as he poured himself coffee.

Penelope turned on the phone, and sure enough, there were ten messages, including two missed calls from Marco checking on her. They had finished at the site where Penelope had been held, and they had recovered phones that they could use to trace numbers.

"I should give him a call back," she groaned before putting the phone down on the table. "Alexis is right.

It can wait until after breakfast. They kicked me off the case after all."

"They still want you consulting, but we are doing an investigation of our own," Alexis said. "Believe me. We will get further and go faster without having to work with the *polizia*. The walls at the crime scene were covered in dark magic. Marco Dandolo is in over his head."

"I've just come from the Archives. Nereus has your photos and has reconstructed the crime scenes," added Phaidros. "I haven't seen her so pissed off in years. It almost makes me want to go back to Florence."

"Florence? Is that where you usually live?" Penelope asked.

"At the moment it is. Alexis summoned me when he figured out you were in Venice." Phaidros gave her a sly smile. "He was quite upset."

"Why?" Penelope turned to Alexis who looked like he was going to stab Phaidros with a fork.

"Because I thought you were going to try and expose us," Alexis said.

"When we broke into your hotel room and saw the sacrifices on your walls, it really got him going," laughed Phaidros. "It's good you have come, Penelope. I haven't been this amused in years."

"You are kind of a dick, aren't you?" said Penelope. "Is he always like this, Alexis?"

"Yes. Always." Alexis smiled over the rim of his coffee cup.

"I'm not a dick. I'm just happy to see Alexis stirred up for once. It's good to know he isn't perfect all the time," Phaidros said as he stole a bunch of grapes from Alexis's plate. "I feel all energized by his frustration and agitation."

"You are one weird guy." Penelope shook her head.

"No, I'm not. Alexis has probably neglected to tell you *anything* about us worth knowing, but we all have different magical abilities," explained Phaidros. "Mine is the manipulation of energy."

"What do you mean? Like a vampire?" Penelope asked, intrigued to know more. Alexis burst out laughing at the look on Phaidros's face.

"No, my darling, not like a vampire," the golden magician said. "Magic is energy. A magician finds different ways to manipulate that energy to achieve the desired outcome. Everything around us, including you, has an aura of energy running through it. I can manipulate that in all sorts of interesting ways."

"Like what?"

"Like I could change it to affect your emotions, making you happy or sad." Phaidros's eyes darkened. "Or I could heat every molecule up in your body, so you boil alive from the inside."

"That seems rather excessive," Penelope murmured, her heart beating faster.

"It can be useful." Phaidros laughed easily. "Don't worry, I would find far nicer ways to manipulate your energy."

Alexis smiled at him threateningly. "Not if you want to keep breathing, you won't."

"He's no fun at all, Penelope," huffed Phaidros. "As amusing as this is, Nereus won't wait patiently for us much longer. Are you coming?"

AFTER BREAKFAST, they went back downstairs to the Archives. Even though Penelope knew what to expect, the sight of the cavern of books spread out beneath her still punched her in the chest. She could spend every day for the rest of her life reading and not get a quarter of the way through the collection. *What secrets and lost mysteries do you hold?*

"If only I could find a woman who looked at me the same way you look at books, Penelope," Phaidros lamented beside her.

"It's so overwhelming, it makes me want to cry," she replied.

"Mortals," Phaidros chuckled as they stepped out of the glass elevator.

"Maybe you are just old and jaded, Phaidros," Alexis said from behind her.

"Old and jaded I may be, but I'm still prettier than you."

Penelope thought it best if she kept her mouth shut, but she still shot a grin at Alexis from behind Phaidros's back.

Phaidros opened a door, and Penelope recoiled at the sight before her. The room was made entirely of shiny black hematite stone. She had never seen so much of it in one place. Inside, Nereus had recreated both crime scenes with perfect 3-D, life-size models.

"Hello again, my dear, do they look about accurate?" Nereus asked Penelope in her no-nonsense way.

"Yes," she managed. "God, it's creepy seeing them like this." Penelope reached out to touch the driftwood of the horse, and her hand slid straight through. "It's a projection?"

"Think of it as magical imaging," Phaidros offered.

"Is that the reason for the hematite room?"

"No, the hematite contains the dark energy generated from the spells," Alexis explained.

"But it isn't the real thing." Penelope frowned.

"It doesn't matter," Nereus interrupted. "Spells don't care, and the more images or recreations, the more power is generated to the spell's purpose."

"So when I had them on my wall…"

"It was like water on a prayer wheel," finished Alexis before adding, "you couldn't have known."

"I hate that. I hate not knowing," Penelope said as she circled the grotesque horse.

"So I've noticed."

Penelope tried not to cringe when she studied the fear etched on the dead man's face. That had almost been her fate, too. She swallowed hard and stepped away, turning her attention to the writing on the sea wall.

"Can you read this?" she asked Nereus. "I've been trying to figure it out, but it's been hopeless."

"I can read some of it, but not all," Nereus admitted. "It's a form of Atlantean. When Thevetat's worship was growing in Atlantis, the temple priests took the Living Language and perverted it. This is the result. I never wanted to learn such a foul thing."

"Living Language?"

"All language is alive," Alexis explained. "Written script, whether scripture or a shopping list, holds emotion, a story, a form of consciousness. In Atlantis, this language was sacred, vibrant, and held power. There was an everyday alphabet, but the Living Language was only written for magic or ritual. They took something used for pure purposes and turned it into something twisted and dark."

"Do you know what they are trying to achieve with it?" Penelope asked.

"What do you think it is? How does it feel to you?" Nereus asked. "I'm curious to see how intuitive you are. You found the Tablet, or the Tablet found you, so there must be some ability locked inside of you."

Penelope tried to sound confident as she replied, "The Acolyte is petitioning Poseidon on Thevetat's behalf. Demon to God. It's using the old sacrifices structure of favor, but like the language, it's distorted. What they are trying to get the God of the Sea to do I'm not sure, but it's a request as well as a threat."

"And isn't that just the crux of it." Nereus frowned. "But why petition a god with a threat? I'm impressed that you figured out it was a spell with no magical training and no knowledge of the language, Penelope. You have good instincts; I like that in a woman. I'm going to need some time to sort through this butchering of Atlantean, and I want you to help. First, I need you and Alexis to make peace with the *polizia*. We don't need to give them any more cause for suspicion."

"They said I'm not allowed near the case—" Penelope began.

"But the case wants to be near you," argued Nereus. "Don't you understand? The Acolyte, whoever he is, wants you. You are useful to the police because of it."

Penelope chewed her lip thoughtfully. If the Acolyte wanted her that bad, would he risk exposing himself to get to her?

"I could get them to use me as bait to lure him out." Penelope hated the idea, but she couldn't deny that it could work.

"You aren't going to act as bait for a follower of Thevetat," said Alexis.

"I don't need your permission," Penelope retorted. "If it stops other people from dying, it's worth the risk."

"Penelope's right," Nereus said as she studied the Bull-headed woman. "I'm sure you'll keep her safe, Alexis, but trust me, the idea would have already occurred to the *polizia* by now, and their new agent is ruthless enough to plan and execute it."

"Marco might be able to hold the police off for a few days so I can recover, but they will want to do some proper questioning. I'll tell them to use me to draw the Acolyte out."

"This's madness," Alexis muttered. "You've already been stabbed and kidnapped in the past fortnight!"

"I'm not a sadist. I don't want to be bait, but I do want to catch this bastard. Even if it's to find out where he learned this language."

"Penelope, you should call Marco Dandolo and let him know you are doing better," Nereus instructed, ignoring Alexis's noises of protest. "I'll keep you down here with me today while we try and figure out this petition."

"That sounds like a good idea," Penelope said and pulled out her phone.

"And me?" Alexis asked.

"You and Phaidros can go back upstairs and summon the others. I've got a bad feeling in my guts about all of this. I want everyone together."

"Zotikos should still be in Crete," Phaidros said. "That is, if he hasn't gotten distracted by beautiful women."

"Any idea where Aelia is?" Alexis asked him. Phaidros's face darkened.

"Vienna, but she won't come. She's better off staying there. She'll only cause trouble."

"Excellent! You know where they are. Get to it," Nereus said. "Talk to Aelia, Alexis. She's always listened to you."

Phaidros turned on his heel and stormed away, cursing vehemently in Greek. Alexis gave Penelope a tight smile before following him out.

"Don't worry about them, Penelope," said Nereus. "Alexis gets moody when he's worried, and Aelia and Phaidros have been at each other's throats for the last ten thousand years. It's been the only constant I've known."

"Should I ask what happened?"

"That's their story to tell, but if you ask me, they should've had sex years ago and got it out of their system." Penelope burst out in surprised laughter. Nereus waved it away. "I'm too old to care about propriety. Right now, you need to call the inspector so we can get to work."

PENELOPE STEPPED out of the lab and found Marco's number in the new phone's contact list. He answered the call within the first ring. "Penelope! *Grazie Dio*. I thought that bastard Donato had given me a false number."

"I'm fine. I've been asleep."

"Of course, of course. I'm sorry. I've been worried since I let you leave with him. To make matters worse, when I got back to the office I was told to let him consult with you. I can't believe he pulled Adalfieri's strings so easily!"

"It's not a bad idea, Marco. He's obsessed with Atlantis and the Aegean almost as much as I am. He's followed my work, and he'll be an asset," Penelope replied. She wasn't surprised that Alexis had maneuvered himself onto the case. He seemed to work four steps ahead of everyone else.

"The only thing that's made me feel any better about it was Agent Bianchi almost turning purple when she was told the good news."

"I can imagine! Don't worry, Alexis and I are already working on decoding the script, and as soon as I have something, I'll let you know."

"Sounds good. Keep in contact, *Dottore*. I still don't like Donato. There's more to him than meets the eye."

You have no idea, Penelope thought as she hung up and hurried back to Nereus's lab.

UPSTAIRS PHAIDROS had gone straight to his rooms to call Zotikos, leaving Alexis sighing in age-old frustration. He couldn't argue with Nereus's decision to keep Penelope downstairs. Together they would pull the spell apart in no time. Despite her terrible idea about being used as bait, he couldn't help but smile with an unexpected, secret warmth.

Back in his tower, Alexis focused on Aelia. She was the type of person who would leave her phone in the bottom of a bathtub if it rang too much. He couldn't risk her ignoring them. If dark priests of Thevetat were on the move, they would try and pick off those outside the pack, and Alexis wasn't about to let that happen.

It took him but a moment to fix on Aelia's mansion. It was in a grand old building, first built when the land was still known as Vindobona, and its Romanesque architecture had taken on other, more baroque styles as she expanded it. Thinking about her music room, he opened a portal and stepped through.

The room was a collection of old and new instruments with a piano once owned by Beethoven (that she won from him in a game of cards), soundboards for mixing digital music, and piles of sheet music written by Vivaldi held down by a used martini glass.

"Defender," said a deep voice behind him, "what a surprise."

Aelia stood in the doorway dressed in a long burgundy robe with heavy golden stitching. She had golden-brown skin, her arms heavy with bronze cuffs, and her burnt-bronze hair was piled elegantly on the top of her head. Her violet eyes were striking in a bed of black eyeliner. Aelia looked him over carefully, holding a martini in one hand and a *gladius* in the other.

"Princess." Alexis bowed. "Is that blade's edge for me?"

"Oh, this?" She looked down at it as if she were surprised to see it. "I felt magic being used and I thought I best be ready to expect the worst."

"You have felt it then? The growing darkness?" he asked, sitting down on one of the plush chaise lounges scattered about the room.

"I'm a princess and High Priestess of Atlantis," she said proudly, placing the *gladius* down on the top of the piano. "Of course I have felt the bloody darkness growing. They are back, aren't they?"

"Thevetat's found some new followers in Venice. There have been…sacrifices. We are trying to stop them."

"After all this time," she said, her voice hollow. "Do you think it has something to do with the tide of magic growing stronger?"

"It wouldn't surprise me. They would want to be as powerful as possible before they make their move on us."

"Fucking Thevetat," Aelia muttered. Her eyes flicked to her sword as if she needed the comfort of its hilt in her hand. Alexis knew Aelia's past with Thevetat's priests, and he wasn't about to judge her uneasiness.

"And what of this pretty human I keep seeing in my dreams?" she asked, changing the subject.

"A scholar I've kept an eye on for a few years. She came to Venice to help with the murder investigation and has gotten tangled up with magic. We made a truce."

"So quickly?" Aelia's coppery brow shot up.

"I found out she was in Venice when she astral projected straight into my tower. Then she found the palazzo, and it let her in."

"I bet you hated that." Aelia laughed.

"That's not all. She also figured out the priests were setting spells and charging them with their sacrifices. All of this with absolutely zero magical ability."

"Impressive little mortal. What do you want from me, Alexis?"

"Come home, Aelia, at least until this matter is sorted out. Nereus wants us together, and I agree that we are safer that way."

Aelia made a face. "If we are together there will be more bloodshed."

"You and Phaidros are the only ones who don't get along."

"That's because he does everything he can to irritate me."

"Why do little boys pull little girls' hair?" teased Alexis.

"Because little boys are assholes raised in a patriarchal society who think it's okay to treat women however they please," Aelia said, finishing her martini. "How many weeks?"

"Two, maybe three. It's Carnevale, your favorite. Besides, Penelope and Nereus are getting to the bottom of this mystery as we speak."

"Nereus is letting her work in the Archives *with* her? Wow, she hasn't liked a human that much since…" Aelia trailed off.

"Da Vinci?" Alexis couldn't quite recall, either, it had been so long.

"Only when he got older," added Aelia. "At least she didn't argue with him the way she did with that Englishman."

"Which one? She's argued with the English more than any others she's known."

Aelia clicked her fingers in frustration before exclaiming, "John Dee! Athena save us from mathematicians and occultists."

"I had hoped she would get along with Penelope, but it seems she has a genuine liking for her."

"It seems Nereus isn't the only one." Aelia's eyes danced. "The stoic Defender has a crush."

"Hardly. The woman is incredibly frustrating, and if she had any sense at all, she would have walked away before she got herself into this mess. Now someone called the Acolyte wants to sacrifice her, and what does she want to do? Offer herself up as bait."

"Gods, Alexis, it sounds like you need one of these more than I do." Aelia sang a few harmonic notes and another martini glass and full shaker appeared on the small table beside her. She poured a drink and passed it to him. "You have got yourself all riled up over some human woman. How very unlike you, Defender."

"I was going to kill her and decided against it. I annihilated her career, and still, she kept coming," Alexis complained. "Relentless, obsessive, frustrating woman."

"Hmm. Doesn't sound like anyone I know at all," Aelia said, sipping her drink.

"At least I can protect myself, and I don't needlessly put myself in harm's way. Bait for Thevetat! The woman is insane. Maybe you can talk some sense into her."

"If you can't, I don't like my chances," said Aelia. "The Alexis I know would never give her the option not to listen. The priests of Thevetat haven't been seen in ten thousand years, and there is no way she could comprehend what it means. You need to explain it to her without losing your temper. Make her understand."

"I would, but she doesn't exactly trust me yet." Alexis drained his glass. "She makes me want to protect her." *And throttle her and kiss her all at once.*

"Well, that is your very nature. Otherwise, you wouldn't be the Defender, would you?" Aelia's purple eyes studied him carefully. "If you didn't like her, she wouldn't drive you so crazy."

"I know that too." Alexis got to his feet and clapped his hands. "Enough about Penelope. Pack up your things, Princess. Dark priests aren't going to hunt themselves."

"Hunting dark priests…it's starting to feel like the old days," Aelia said. "Give me a day or two to get a few things in order, and I'll come. I need to meet this human."

TWELVE

FOR THE NEXT few days, Penelope healed, sent regular updates to Marco, and hung out in the Archives. The black moleskin notebook she had bought at the airport gift store slowly filled with notes.

Knowing only her eyes would see it, she wrote about being amongst the magicians, the Archives, and how time seemed to move slower in the palazzo. A part of her was afraid of forgetting again, or that it was still somehow not happening and the palazzo and Alexis would vanish in the night. The academic side of her had a minor heart attack every time she entered the Archives, and while Nereus had given her permission to touch and read whatever she wished, she was usually so overwhelmed she didn't know where to start.

Penelope wrote about the script at the crime scenes, and how if she looked at it for too long it felt like little burrs were hooking themselves into her mind. In a stream of consciousness, she hypothesized what the spells were for, how they could be connected to MOSE, and why anyone would want to follow a demon god. She sat in Nereus's lab, the magician using her as a sounding board as she tried to unravel the spell work at the sites.

"I don't know who would have been able to teach him all this," Nereus muttered as she and Penelope drank tea. "The Demon could have, I suppose. It explains why it's haphazard even for a dark priest."

"What about other survivors?" Penelope asked. "Atlantis is pretty big for no one else to have managed to escape apart from you seven."

"In the beginning, I thought it was possible," Nereus admitted, "but we searched the world for them. There weren't as many magicians as you might think, and within fifty years or so, any survivors would have died."

"A human follower of Thevetat could've taught others." Penelope tapped her pen thoughtfully on her notebook. "They might have even masqueraded as something else."

"Come again?" Nereus put her tea down.

"If you were a priest or a follower in a new land and you followed a religion that others might not under-stand or be afraid of, wouldn't you keep it quiet?"

"You would if you knew magicians survived who would have hunted you into the ground," said Nereus, getting to her feet. "I want you to follow this line of inquiry with Alexis. He searched for survivors, and he was my best hunter when it came to Thevetat's fol-lowers."

At Nereus's instructions, Alexis began joining Penelope in the Archives, and she finally began to relax in his presence. They claimed a huge study table, and sitting opposite each other, pulled out manuscripts on dark magic and cults that could have been Thevetat worship under a different name.

"What about the Anemospilia site near Herak-lion?" Penelope asked as she used her laptop to search the Archives databases.

"What about it?" Alexis asked, not looking up from his book.

"An excavation took place there in 1979, and the temple they found was completely different from any of the other ancient Minoan sites. The construction itself was odd, less labyrinthine and more symmetrical," Penelope explained. "From the looks of it, the temple was destroyed by an earthquake. They found a statue that had feet made of clay, like our Bull woman."

Alexis's head snapped up from the book. "Sacred Earth. What else did they find?"

"It was full of vases that held traces of blood as well as food and wine." Penelope opened the Internet and pulled up papers and articles written on the dig. "There was a room for sacrificing bulls, but the thing that got everyone in a real tizzy was the body of a young man they found on an altar. His hands and feet were bound, and there was a sacrificial blade on the skeleton. I always thought it strange that they would sacrifice a human when it was obvious everything was designed for bulls."

"If they were concerned about the earthquakes then they might have been pushed to offer a human life to the gods to make them stop." Alexis moved so he could see over her shoulder and study the photos on the screen. "The Greeks weren't shy when it came to sacrificing humans when the need arose, and the Mino-

ans were no different. It's the building structure and its
location that concerns me."

"In what way?"

"*Anemospilia* means 'caves of the wind,' and it's on
the hills of Mount Juktas." Alexis leaned around her
to use the keyboard to bring up maps. Penelope tried
not to breathe in the distracting smell of spice that
emanated from him, but the heat coming off his body
made the hair on her neck stand up.

"It's supposedly where Zeus is buried. It would
make sense to have a temple there to him," argued
Penelope.

"We should look into it further," Alexis said, moving back into his chair and to his book. "Thevetat's
priests liked caves. They could have easily made it look
like a cult to a dead God."

"I'll see what I can find and send an update to
Marco."

"Tell him to look into black market antiques. If
those vases in Santa Croce were authentic, there will be
a trail and a lot of money changing hands."

"I'm on it," Penelope replied. "My brain has been
so focused on the script that I overlooked the antiques."

"Let Nereus worry about the script. She and Galenos will have it cracked soon enough."

WHENEVER PENELOPE needed to reset her
brain, she asked Alexis questions. Lots of questions.

When she had arrived at 39 Calle dei Cerchieri, Alexis had promised her answers, and to her delight and considerable surprise, he gave them up to her. Penelope loved the way his Byzantine accent made whatever he was saying sound mysterious and fantastic. Penelope couldn't help but note everything from the pattern of the embroidery on his never-ending supply of *entari* robes, to the crease in his brow when he was concentrating, as if he was trying to intimidate the manuscript he was studying to yield its secrets.

Penelope always thought her father's hands were typical scholar's hands, their soft, Irish paleness a reminder of his refusal to do any physical labor. Alexis's hands were strong and calloused from sword practice, decorated with rings, smatterings of ink and scars from his adventures. A few times, Penelope's treacherous mind had wandered off to imagine how many other scars decorated his tall, lean body. She wanted to know all the stories behind them.

Like a male Scheherazade, Alexis was *full* of stories, and they appeared sporadically within conversations as if the storytelling was an intrinsic part of whatever he was explaining.

Once she had asked him about horses in Atlantis, and his explanation about how they used to breed and raise them had turned into a recollection of how when he was a child, he and his brother had gone to steal their cousin's mare for a ride. What they hadn't known was that the mare was pregnant and had already begun to give birth. They had feared the horse was dying and went for their uncle, all mischief forgotten. The foal was having trouble getting out of its poor mother, so Alexis, being the youngest and with the skinniest arms, had to reach inside of the mare to pull the long-legged foal free. Both mother and baby lived, and as the foal grew it obsessed over Alexis, following him around like a dog, as if it remembered the great favor he had done for it.

A lot of the stories were simple, but they were always punctuated with something unbelievable or historically fascinating. There was the time Aelia had mentored a child with a prodigious talent for piano who turned out to be Mozart, or how Phaidros had once decided to have a month-long orgy in Greece, and when the local king Pentheus tried to put a stop to it, Phaidros had raised the town, turning the women against the king who was subsequently torn apart.

"Aren't you talking about the Dionysus myth?" Penelope interrupted.

"It survived in that form, but the truth of it was Phaidros had a drunken tantrum." Alexis folded his arms. "I would know, Penelope. I was the one that had to clean up the bloody mess after. Phaidros went through some incredibly dark periods in those days. We had seen and lost so much already. No one grieves like a magician, and a depressed one is volatile. It is lucky for us that humans can't handle what they don't understand, so a drunk magician sparking a riot becomes Dionysus seeking revenge."

When the three of them had dinner that evening, Penelope tried to find that rage-fueled Dionysus behind Phaidros's flirting golden eyes. His stunning gold hair and dark brown skin, paired with the ability to do magic, would have been enough to convince her of his godhood but the rage was not there. Or it was simply buried and dormant.

Penelope knew she was never going to stop being amazed as long as she stayed at the palazzo in Dorsoduro, and as long as Alexis kept telling her what she wanted to know, the less inclination she had to leave.

THE QUESTURA was packed and rowdy when Penelope and Alexis arrived for their formal interviews three days after her kidnapping. Marco took Penelope aside as a smiling female officer escorted Alexis to a separate office.

"How are you feeling, Penelope?" Marco asked.

"Much better. I've been treated like a princess the last few days, so you have nothing to worry about," she assured him. "Are these interviews really necessary?"

"We need to keep everything official in case it all goes to hell. I'll make it quick, I promise." He showed her into one of the sterile interview rooms.

"Tell me again what happened when Alexis Donato arrived." Marco tapped his pen against the table.

Penelope recounted him everything that had happened that day, keeping her story consistent with the one she knew Alexis was telling next door.

"Why are we going through this again? You don't think Alexis or I could've killed them?"

"No, not at all. Men like Donato pay other people to get their hands dirty for them." Marco rolled his eyes at her when she frowned at him. "I'm joking, Penelope."

"No, you aren't. He's not mafia, Marco. If he were, Adalfieri wouldn't allow him to work on this case."

"Maybe he's not mafia, but I know he is hiding something."

"So is everyone," Penelope said. "I've known Alexis long enough to know he's just a rich eccentric. There's nothing mysterious or interesting about him."

Except absolutely everything is interesting and mysterious about Alexis.

"If you say so," he replied. There was a sharp knock on the door, and Agent Bianchi came in, looking about as happy as the last time Penelope saw her.

"Have you asked her yet?" she demanded, sitting opposite Penelope. Her blonde hair was tied in a ponytail so tight and smooth it made Penelope's eyes water in pity.

"Ask me what?"

"Agent Bianchi had an idea—"

"We want your help to get this Acolyte to come to us."

Penelope made a mental note to ask Nereus if she was clairvoyant. Nothing would surprise her. "I was also going to suggest you find a way to use me as bait to lure him out."

"No, not like bait exactly—" began Marco, but Penelope cut him off.

"It's fine, Marco. I expected you to ask, and it's a good idea. I have one condition."

"What?" demanded Agent Bianchi.

"I want Alexis to help with whatever you're planning."

"Why?"

"Because Questore Adalfieri will want him involved," Penelope said sweetly. "He has private security that could also ensure I don't end up at the bottom of a canal."

Again.

"I'll agree to Donato—he has a high-enough profile to get into places others can't—but no to the private security. I don't want any more civilians involved," Agent Bianchi bargained. "I want this to be a proper operation with every angle covered."

"What did you have in mind?" Penelope asked.

AN HOUR later, Penelope left the interview room feeling like she had been raked over the coals. She didn't doubt that Agent Bianchi was an excellent agent, but her people skills lacked Marco's panache. Penelope had to keep reminding herself that she was only trying to do her job, and that deep down she probably wasn't the raging bitch she presented to the world.

They found Alexis sitting with a group of female officers chatting and laughing. By the rosy glow of their cheeks and shy smiles, he wasn't holding back any of his charms.

"I was starting to think they had arrested you for your own kidnapping," he joked when he saw them. Marco waved the women on, and they scattered under his glare.

"They were telling me their plan to use me to attract the Acolyte," Penelope said.

Alexis's eyebrow cocked. "Really? And you believe risking your life again is wise?"

Penelope glared at him. "It's my life to risk."

"She will be perfectly safe," Marco assured him. "There will be lots of *polizia* to protect her, and the venue will have its security."

"What venue?" Alexis asked, a definite tone creeping into his voice. Penelope pulled on their connection, and he looked at her irritably.

"The Arsenale for the masquerade ball," Agent Bianchi said bluntly. "I'm sure you have more than one mask to wear, *Signore* Donato."

"I DON'T like that woman," Alexis stated as they walked through the streets of Santa Croce.

"She's certainly blunt," Penelope replied diplomatically. "You probably don't like her because she's immune to your flirting, unlike every other female in that office."

"This is Italy—flirting is a local custom. Besides, it makes them think I'm something I'm not."

"A playboy instead of a centuries-old magician from Atlantis?" Penelope said as straight-faced as she could.

"Yes, something like that," he replied. "I thought by now you would have reconsidered risking your life to flush out the Acolyte."

"I made it pretty clear how I felt about it. Are you worried about your abilities to protect me?"

"It's not my abilities I'm concerned with. We don't know if this Acolyte has paid off the police. I'll have to watch them as well as watch you."

"I doubt the Acolyte will be stupid enough to try and grab me in the middle of a masquerade ball."

"You don't know how stupid or smart he is and that's the problem," Alexis argued. "There's so much we don't know. I don't like people very often, Penelope. Despite our uneasy beginning, I do like you, and I won't apologize for not wanting you to take unnecessary risks."

Penelope wanted to argue, but his sincerity, and the fact she felt the same about him, doused her fire. "I like you, too, and believe me, I won't do anything stupid to get myself hurt. Nereus has been pretty adamant that I'm meant to follow your lead if a situation arises."

"Did she? And you listened to her?" he teased.

"She told me she'd kick me out of the Archives if I didn't."

Alexis's laugh was loud and easy. "I'll have to remember to use that in future arguments."

"And you think there will be many of those?" Penelope grinned.

"Have you met you?"

The Campo Santa Margarita was packed with tourists, and when Alexis placed her hand over his arm to prevent losing her, Penelope didn't argue. Nor did she let go even once they'd made it past the crush of people. There were worse ways to spend her time than arm in arm with a handsome man in La Serenissima.

"Why Venice?" she asked as they strolled casually. "Of all the places in the world you could all live, why here?"

"We have always been here," Alexis explained. "For many years it was only us and the *incolae lacunae*, the lagoon dwellers. As wars pushed people from their homelands, we began to be inundated with refugees. If you know anything about Venice, you know that its strategic position is a safe and powerful one. To find ways to house everyone, Nereus, Galenos, and I helped develop the idea of building houses and bridges to the islands, the way peasants used to in Atlantis. It made travel and trade between everyone safer and easier."

"So the real reason Venice has never been severely looted or bombed is that you have been protecting it?" asked Penelope.

"Yes and no. Venice itself inspires a fierce loyalty even if the grand old lady is now seen as a decaying relic only fit for tourists." Alexis looked fondly at the buildings around him, their facades tired and weatherworn. "She is still beautiful and safe. We learned our lesson after Alexandria. Humans can't be trusted not to destroy, so we rebuilt here."

"Are you telling me the Library of Alexandria was the original Archives?"

"What they destroyed upstairs was valuable, but it was nothing compared to what lay underneath it. It was enough for Nereus to decide to relocate. Egypt was no longer a place she recognized or liked. The Romans were like rampaging children, and Nereus wanted a place we could protect and defend."

"I'm starting to see why you took on the crusaders for the Library of Constantinople," said Penelope.

"Knowledge is sacred, whether it's magical or not. It's always worth protecting because its value is infinite."

"I can understand not wanting magical knowledge to escape out into the world but what about historical knowledge of Atlantis? That would be fascinating and invaluable."

"There is no way to separate one from the other. It's one of the reasons I've fought so hard to protect it." Alexis frowned, his blue eyes darkening as she watched him. "You will never be satisfied with that answer, will you?"

"Not even a little bit," Penelope stated, giving his arm a playful squeeze. "But that's what you like about me, my academic ability to poke my nose in is one of my charms."

"One of many, and not my favorite," Alexis replied with a smile that seemed to start at his eyes and fill his entire body.

It was but a moment, but it was enough that a long-forgotten part of Penelope woke up with interest.

Shut it down, Pen, she instantly warned herself, but the feeling refused to go away. She couldn't help but be attracted to him, even though no good could come of it.

Christ, if she couldn't keep a normal man interested, what chance did she have with someone like him? Gorgeous, dangerous, magical creature that he was. She blamed La Serenissima and the afternoon light that made everything glow warmer, turning their platonic stroll into something else. Eventually, she looked away from him, common sense winning out.

ALEXIS SAW Penelope brighten with flirtation before something closed behind her eyes. What had happened? She asked him about how Venice began to grow and how it was similar to the peasant housing of Atlantis. Alexis answered her, but his mind turned back to a conversation he had with Nereus.

Penelope had only been in the house for a few days and the growing desire to corner her with questions, to be in her company, was becoming embarrassing. What was worse was he could feel her through the blasted metaphysical connection they shared. It was like a phantom limb he couldn't scratch or cut off.

As always when he was restless and melancholy, Alexis had ended up in the Archives, pulling down books in Atlantean, Greek, Egyptian, and Arabic to try and discover an answer to his problem. Nereus had come and sat with him like she had so many other times.

"How is our guest settling in?" she asked.

"The woman is insatiable for information," Alexis complained, "and it's always the mundane things: what kind of food was grown in Atlantis? How was it harvested? What animals did we have? What were our clothes like? What stories were popular?"

"And you answer these questions?"

"Of course I do!"

"Why?" Nereus pressed.

"Because…" Alexis struggled for the words. "Because I like the look of wonder on her face. I haven't thought about any of this for thousands of years."

"But you are happy to talk about them now, with her?"

"Yes," he said softly. "I have always avoided talking or thinking about those kinds of memories because they hurt too much. Telling Penelope doesn't hurt. Maybe it's her open enthusiasm for it all, her happiness in simply knowing is contagious. *She* is contagious."

"Phaidros is certainly taken with her," Nereus said, studying her nails. "He's in the kitchen with her making Festival Cakes—"

The fountain pen in Alexis's hand snapped in half, sending a flood of ink over his hand and the journal he had been writing in.

"Penelope has had enough shocks over the past few weeks without that idiot making her uncomfortable," he said irritably.

"She didn't look uncomfortable." Nereus handed him a handkerchief. "She's a wise enough woman to make her own decisions when it comes to men. I'm more concerned with what's bothering you. You've been hiding here for hours."

"Show me what I'm not seeing, Nereus. Why her? What the hell is this?" He waved a hand over his chest, and the glowing, complicated weave that tied him to Penelope appeared.

"Oh dear, I haven't seen one of those since the old days," Nereus said, leaning forward. She went to poke it, but he stopped her.

"Don't. Penelope will feel it. There is only one way this could've happened. When I was in Australia listening to her lecture, I may have placed a psychic tracker on her," he admitted. Nereus raised a white eyebrow. "It was only to alert me if she stumbled across anything real. Do you think the spell changed somehow, making it reverse in some way which allowed her to follow it back to me?"

"If that was the case, why didn't it happen sooner? I'm sure Penelope meditated in the past two years. Why did she not find you then?" Nereus asked, making him feel like her student again. Would that feeling ever go away?

"Proximity," he hypothesized. "She wasn't strong enough to do it from the other side of the world but being in Venice gave it the push needed to connect."

"What happened when she almost died?" Nereus sat back in her chair.

Alexis felt that sickening jolt again and rubbed his chest. "It frayed, and then I wiped her memories. When we touched after she found the house it...it reconnected. Even without the connection, her mind fought the spell, locking parts of her memory away so they couldn't be destroyed. That's why she became so ill."

"It takes a special, singular mind to do that." Nereus's smile was slow and sly. "How upset will you be when I tell you that you're wrong?"

"What do you mean wrong? That's the only connection I could've made with her and..." Alexis stopped as her smile widened. He huffed irritably. "Tell me then."

Nereus clicked her fingers, and the connection appeared again. "*Moíra desmós*, it's a destiny knot. Your fates are woven so closely, so intimately and powerfully, that it's manifested as an actual tie. It happened when she found your corner of the Tablet I'd say. It could be why it called to her in the first place. You've seen where it washed up. No one could have spotted it as easily as she did."

"But why has it been found after all this time? Why now?"

Nereus brought out a silver device that looked like a modified astrolabe. She opened it and dials slid, gliding back and forth. "The tide of magic is rising again. You can't have failed to feel it growing."

"Magical tides ebb and flow, Nereus. It's nothing unusual."

"But it is this time. Look." She handed him the glowing silver dials. "It hasn't been this high since Atlantis.

Thevetat might have waited this long to be at his strongest again. Fate always plays its part in these battles. Perhaps Penelope found the Tablet because you are going to need her, or the gods want her by your side."

"But she's only a human. A human's fate can't be tied to an immortal's."

"Looks like it can be." Nereus got up and kissed his cheek, her eyes full of understanding. "Good luck trying to break it, my dear Defender."

As Phaidros would say, he was completely fucked.

"ALEXIS?" PENELOPE'S hand tightened around his arm, jolting him back to the present. "Are you okay?"

"Yes, *mi scusi*, I got a little distracted—what was your question?"

"You said that magic was too tied to the history of Atlantis, can you tell me how? Or is that a secret too?"

"It's a secret to everyone but you," he replied, earning a quick smile. "You had it right the first time I asked you about magic. 'They would know the difference between an aqueduct and astral projection,' you said. Science doesn't have a place in magic, and neither is it an evolutionary step from the dark age of magic and faith into an age of scientific reason or enlightenment. Science and magic were different disciplines on Atlantis, but both were woven seamlessly throughout our history and society. Faith in the Gods that created and protected us was the foundation of our culture."

"So when Thevetat's worship began, it…"—
Penelope seemed to be searching for the right
word—"destabilized?"

"Yes." He was surprised her mind connected it all
so quickly. "It destabilized, splitting communities, families, countries, but most of all, they twisted magic into
something destructive."

Penelope looked ready to ask another question
when Phaidros appeared.

"Here you two are!" he exclaimed, his amber eyes
taking in their linked arms. "Oh, very nice. Off on a date
holding hands while I have to deal with all the drama."

"What's wrong? Has there been another body?"
Penelope asked.

"No." Alexis smiled knowingly. "Aelia is here."

"You might regret agreeing to come and stay with
us," Phaidros said, taking her other arm. "Let's go get
some rooms at the Danieli. I would be more than
happy to be your tour guide, and I'm much more ami-
able company than the Defender."

"Defender?" Penelope looked up at Alexis who was
restraining himself from pushing Phaidros into the
canal beside them.

"Oh yes, didn't he tell you?" Phaidros leaned in,
speaking in a confidential whisper. "Alexis means
Defender, you know. He's the fierce warrior magician,
his magic much more civilized than the death magic
our Lyca can wield, but impressive nonetheless. There's
more to defense than violence. It's about protection.
You feel safe with him, don't you?"

The *moíra desmós* vibrated in Alexis's chest as her fingers curled on his sleeve. The familiarity in the touch made his body hum. *That can't be good.*

"Yes, Alexis makes me feel safe," Penelope replied softly, "and no, I won't leave him to go to some hotel with you because you don't like Aelia." Alexis couldn't hold back a smile as he looked over the top of her head at the other magician.

"You say this because you haven't met Aelia." Phaidros untangled his arm from hers. "Remember I made the offer before you got in too deep. I need to walk if I am going to deal with…*her*." He sulked off, hands in pockets.

"Is he going to be like that the whole time she's here?" Penelope asked, watching him leave.

"Probably. Phaidros might also flirt with you more than usual in front of her," warned Alexis. "If he gets too forward or makes you uncomfortable, please let me know. He's harmless, but if I need to toss him in the Adriatic to cool down, I will."

Penelope laughed delightfully. "You say that like you've done it before."

"More than once."

"Does it work?"

"Not really, but it makes me feel better."

The blue door appeared on the wall, and Alexis reached for the handle.

"What's so difficult about Aelia?" asked Penelope.

The door flew open, and Alexis's eyes were assaulted by a mosaic of purple and gold. Aelia looked them over, gazing openly at their linked arms, fuchsia lips smirking.

"Absolutely nothing," she announced. "You must be the human that has our Alexis so unsettled."

THIRTEEN

THE WOMAN BEFORE Penelope was a goddess. With her dark brown limbs heavy with bracelets and wrapped in a purple silk kaftan, she could have been the love child of Beyoncé and Amun-Ra.

"Hi," Penelope said with a nervousness that only genuinely stunning people could inspire. Self-conscious, she slipped her hand from Alexis's arm, but instead of moving his own hand away, he dropped it to the small of her back. Even through her layers of shirt and coat, her skin lit up with new sensitivity under the imprint of his long fingers. *Don't even think about it, Penelope. It will only end badly and jeopardize your chance at the Archives.*

"Welcome, Princess. I see you have wasted no time in upsetting Phaidros," Alexis scolded her playfully.

"All I did was ask him to help me take my things to my room," she said, before kissing his cheek. "Lucky Zo arrived at the same time. He gave me a hand."

"I needed another two arms to carry all of your bags, so it was no wonder he knocked you back," a cheerful male voice echoed around them as a set of stairs unrolled from the wall, and he appeared.

Where Alexis was tall and leanly muscular, Zotikos was broad and brawny like a Greek nightclub bouncer in a tight black T-shirt. He had curly black hair, a closely groomed beard, and unlike the other magicians, there was something ineffably friendly about him.

"Zeus's dick! You finally caught her, Alexis," he said, looking Penelope over before kissing both of her cheeks. "You're everything I imagined."

"Nice to meet you too, Zotikos," Penelope said.

"Zo. Please. Doctor Bryne in the flesh. I've just arrived from stealing your find."

"You have my Tablet here?" she asked. "How?" The Greek government had refused to let it leave their soil, so stolen was the right word. How he had gotten it out of the country was the real mystery.

"You mean *my* Tablet," Alexis corrected bluntly.

Penelope shot him a look. "If it was yours, you shouldn't have left it at the bottom of the ocean for me to find."

"I like her already. Did you see that, Aelia? The great Defender just got put in his place," Zo said, leaning his arm on Aelia's shoulder.

"Apparently she's very argumentative," Aelia replied, her smirk growing wider by the second.

"Can I see it?" Alexis asked Zo impatiently. "It's been ten thousand years after all."

"I put it on your bed for you." Zo smiled. "Off you two go, but don't play for too long. Aelia and I are organizing dinner and drinks in the floating courtyards."

"I'll come by your room for a girl talk later, Penelope," Aelia said before she and Zo walked away together chatting. *Well, that's ominous.* Penelope hoped she was friendlier than Lyca.

"That's the poet?" Penelope stared after Zo. "I was expecting someone pale and bookish."

"Zo's a lot of things," Alexis replied. "Are you coming?"

"I thought…it's been ten thousand years after all. Don't you want some time to…" Penelope struggled. Despite her comments moments ago, she remembered that young man from the vision when she had laid a hand on the Tablet in the Archives. It had been something infinitely special to him.

"As you said, it's your Tablet too," he replied gesturing toward the stairs. As they walked, the palazzo moved, and she put a hand on the wall to steady herself.

"Why do I feel like I'm going to be trapped in a wall one day?" Penelope remarked nervously. There was something about a sentient house that was harder to reconcile with than living with magicians.

"The palazzo would never do that. I'm surprised you can even feel it. The best way to move about is to picture where you wish to go, and it will find it for you."

"But how do you know how big it is?" she asked.

Alexis shrugged. "I don't. You can't expect a palazzo sitting on top of a repository of magic to act normal."

"I suppose not," said Penelope as they walked past her bedroom and continued up another flight of stairs.

"This is the tower that you so casually projected inside," Alexis told her, and she felt like she was about to be shown something few people had ever had the privilege of seeing. *What does an Atlantean magician's bedroom look like?*

Alexis opened a large wooden door, and Penelope stepped into a space so essentially *him* that her mouth fell open. There were marble pillars, carved bookcases and cabinets, plush Persian carpets, hanging mosaics of cut glass, paintings of strange and beautiful landscapes, tall stands of burning candles, and statues of gods from Greece and Mesopotamia.

"Whoa," was all she could manage. "This place looks like you."

"Forgive the mess," he said a little bashfully. "I've been meaning to get the palazzo to make another room."

It wasn't a mess as Penelope would define it. The room seemed clean of all dust and grime. It was a repository of Alexis.

Books and scrolls sat on any spare surface, with more stacks on the floor. There were scarred wooden work tables with alchemical symbols written in Arabic, low comfortable chairs upholstered in leather, velvet, and silk with Byzantine patterns. A cello and a silver hookah stood in a corner next to an onyx statue of Poseidon; blue glass bowls held stones of different shapes and colors. She loved cello but didn't dare ask him to play anything for her. *What would music composed by a magician sound like?*

The ceiling above her was the blue-black of the night sky, a mural of constellations and symbols of the zodiac moving in golden lines to chart their positions. The entire room smelled of sharp gunpowder and warm cinnamon spice, just like Alexis and his magic.

"This way," he said, and she followed him into a circular room where a huge bed sat covered in saffron pillows and royal blue sheets. Piles of books were arranged on carved wooden bedside tables, and a wall of marble arches overlooking the ocean let in a warm breeze. A shiny black briefcase perched on the end of the bed, looking modern and out of place.

Penelope waited by the doorway, feeling that to go any further would be an invasion of privacy. There was something about Alexis and beds that was dangerous to think about. *You are already thinking about it, otherwise you wouldn't care.*

"You don't need to linger back there," Alexis said as he sat on the bed, lifting the case onto his lap. "Do you want to see it or not?"

There goes that idea, she thought as she went over to him. The wind blew his dark curls back from his cheekbones, and his blue eyes were lost in concentration as he fiddled with the combination locks on the sides.

Alexis wasn't stunning in an intimidating way like Phaidros or Aelia, but the combination of his angular beauty, fierce intelligence, and aura of power made him irresistible. It wasn't a struggle for her to imagine him dressed like a Byzantine prince, armed with a bloody scimitar, and storming confused crusaders like a forgotten eastern god. The thought vanished as he opened the briefcase and lifted out a broken corner of blue-gray stone.

"They've cleaned it better since I last saw it," Penelope said, studying it as he turned it over in his hands. "It was barely recognizable then, covered in pieces of shell and coral."

"But you still saw it," Alexis said, his voice curiously soft. "Ten thousand years under the ocean and yet it was your hands it fell into."

"I don't know how to explain it, but it was like it called to me," she said and sat down beside him. "I hated leaving it behind in Crete, but there was no way they would let me leave with it. I'm glad Zo has managed it."

"He's useful that way. He would've left a replica to confound them." Alexis's ringed fingers traced over the curved lines of script lovingly, eyes far away in remembrance. He passed her the stone block, and she cradled it, feeling the same humming under her fingers as she always had.

"Do you see this scar?" Alexis indicated a long white line over his index finger. "I did that with the edge of a chisel carving that corner." She ran her fingers through the groove.

"What are you going to do with it now?" she asked.

"Reunite it." Alexis stood up and offered her his hand. "Come with me. We'll go the quick way."

Penelope rested her palm in his, clutching the stone close to her chest. Alexis pulled her close, and the same feeling of safety she'd had the night of her kidnapping filled her. *The Defender*, Phaidros had called him. The Tablet between them hummed, and they both looked at each other curiously. *He felt it, too*, Penelope realized.

"Hold still," he said, his arms looping around her back. Penelope rested against him as the air shimmered with glittery black sand. A moment of nothingness passed, and then the Archives and the rest of the Tablet materialized around them.

"That doesn't seem to bother you," he said, his arms loosening from where they'd held her tightly.

"There are far more unnerving things about you than your portaling skills, Alexis Donato," Penelope replied, trying to sound more confident than she felt. She passed him the corner of the stone.

"You wouldn't think there was anything about me that concerned you. You are far too collected considering what you have gone through in the past fortnight." Alexis studied her carefully. "I can't figure out if you're bluffing or not and it's maddening."

"I have a talent for adaptation." Penelope smiled even as he frowned. *And I'm more concerned with my growing desire to kiss you.*

Penelope didn't consider her seduction skills well-developed, but she had no problem showing when she was interested in someone. If he'd been a normal man that made her feel this way, she might have considered it. But Alexis was so very far from normal.

"Watch and see what the Living Language is meant to be like," Alexis said, his voice changing, his eyes brightening with power. The hair on Penelope's body stood on end as the air around her electrified. Alexis reached up and placed the broken corner back into place.

The script flooded with energy, lighting up like a circuit board. The pockmarks and roughened edges rejuvenated, the polish and shine of the blue-gray stone returning. As the writing pulsed with shimmering light, Penelope's eyes welled with tears.

She couldn't read it, but she could *feel* it; the emotion, the care, the promise, the supplication to Poseidon for favor. It had been created with sweat and blood and raw, untrained magic. It whispered to her, words just beyond her hearing, calling out and coaxing her closer.

Penelope moved in a trance as she reached out and placed her hand over the glowing words. White hot lightning shot through her arm and body, filling her mind with images of the temple where it had sat, Nereus looking at it with interest and pride at the young man's talent, Alexis's bare back sweating and covered in stone dust as he chipped away at it...

With a flash of power, the magic from the stone flowed into her hand, strange words lighting up under her skin. Strong arms came around her, pulling Penelope back from the Tablet. Alexis was talking to her, speaking urgently, his blue eyes terrified.

But she didn't hear what he said. She gasped as pain lanced her palm. It was burnt, red and glistening around lines of script. "Christ!" She clutched her hand to her, agony making her grind her teeth. "What just happened?"

"I didn't realize you would try and touch it. I don't know how this could happen—" Alexis broke off.

"Give me a look." He took her wounded hand gently, turning it to inspect her palm.

"I'm s-sorry," Penelope fumbled. "I could hear it, and when I touched it I saw…" She shook her head, trying to dislodge the images now as burned into her mind as her own memories.

"I should have known to keep you back from it." Alexis cursed himself. "Must you always be so curious? Some things shouldn't be touched."

"I can't help it. Beautiful things demand to be caressed," Penelope answered.

The look he gave her was mischievous and disarming, and for a second she forgot all about her aching hand.

"It isn't burnt too badly and can easily be fixed," he assured her. Alexis lifted her palm to his mouth and kissed the burning skin. A hot firecracker smell rose from his skin, and sweet relief flowed through her hand, pulsing up her arm to her shoulder. The damaged skin healed before her astonished eyes, leaving only a pattern of pale scars. He laid another lingering kiss, his stubble sending pinpricks down her arm.

"There, it shouldn't bother you." He ran his thumb over the scars. "Though these will be with you forever now. We should get Nereus to look you over, just in case. Please refrain from touching magical objects, Penelope, no matter how beautiful they are."

"I promise," she managed, her tongue heavy in her mouth. One kiss on the palm of her hand had been more seductive than anything she had experienced in

THE IMMORTAL CITY   199

a long time. The desire to kiss Alexis grew so painful
that she removed her hand from his and took a cautious
step back.

"I'm happy that the Tablet is finally back together,"
she said, looking at it so she wouldn't look at him. "I
understand now what Nereus meant about the language being alive."

"It's a powerful gift, but a neutral one. That's why
Thevetat's followers have twisted it, using its strength
to enhance their spell," Alexis explained. "We need to
stop them, Penelope. There's no way they could've intu-
itively found this knowledge. Something or someone
has been teaching it to them." His eyes softened with
concern as he looked her over. "Part of me wishes you
would return to Australia to be away from this. From
what is about to happen."

"But I've only just found you," Penelope said without thinking. "I mean the mystery, Atlantis, this history,
all of it! I want to stop the Acolyte from hurting anyone else. Don't you even think about trying to send me
back, Alexis. Or trying to Atlantis mind-wipe me again.
We can stop them together. You know the police won't
be able to." She felt the connection inside of her chest
squeeze and pull. What would happen if she left Venice?
Would it be torn from her or lie dormant? Would she
ever be able to feel or find him again?

"I wouldn't dream of trying to send you away. I
know you'd just try and find them on your own," Alexis
replied, placing a hand on her shoulder. "I agree that
we can only stop them together. I only said it because I

don't want you getting hurt, and if I were a better man, I would never have let you find your way here. But I did. I don't have the strength to fight fate anymore. We do this together, Penelope Bryne, or not at all."

"Together then. It's a deal." Penelope stuck out her hand.

Alexis gave it a gentle shake. "Let's get Nereus to look at you before you decide to grab any more magical artifacts."

They found Nereus in her lab, writing furiously in a journal. Her gray head snapped up as soon as they entered. "What's happened, Penelope?"

"I touched a magical object when I wasn't supposed to," she said and held up her palm.

"Come here, let me look at it." Nereus gestured, and Penelope sat down on an old wooden swivel chair. Nereus took her hand and instantly glared at Alexis. "This feels like your magic. What did you do?"

Alexis folded his arms defensively. "*I* didn't do anything. We put the Tablet back together, and when the magic in the engravings was reworking itself, Penelope decided it would be a good idea to run her hands all over it."

"Hades take you, Alexis," Nereus cursed. "What did you think she was going to do when confronted with something like that?"

"It told me to," Penelope mumbled under her breath, and the two magicians stared at her.

"What do you mean?" Nereus asked, her voice gentle again.

"It was the same when I found the corner. It's like it...*wanted* me to touch it," Penelope struggled to explain. "I didn't know it was going to burn me."

Nereus looked back at the scars on Penelope's hand and whispered something under her breath. The smell of lemongrass and ice filled the room, and Penelope felt the buzz of Nereus's magic. "Look there," Nereus whispered. Bright words surfaced on Penelope's skin before disappearing again, leaving it normal-looking once more. "The Living Language from your Tablet has gone inside of her. Fascinating."

Penelope stared at them wide-eyed. "What's it going to do?"

"I have no idea!" Nereus said cheerfully. "It might go away in time, or you might get some ability. Magic is strange that way."

"But she's human," Alexis pointed out.

"So were you once. Magic chooses who it chooses, and it's not very much that's inside of her. A few lines of text at the most." Nereus released Penelope's hand. "It won't hurt you, Penelope. As I said, it will most likely just go away. It could help explain your knot."

"My knot?"

"Oh, Alexis will tell you all about it." Nereus waved a hand impatiently. "Off you two go, I've got something to finish before dinner tonight." Penelope held her hand to her chest as she got up. Nereus's tone was lighthearted, but there was a look in her eyes that made Penelope uneasy.

ALEXIS PORTALED Penelope back to her rooms and with a muttered excuse made a quick exit. He looked unnerved, which did nothing to help convince her that the magic under her skin was nothing to worry about. She paced her rooms, obsessing over his words, Nereus's explanations, the Tablet, and the way she swore she could still feel his lips against her scarred palm.

Penelope had never believed in fate or destiny, but from the moment she saw Alexis in the tower, she knew they were connected somehow. She could feel the line of light growing more prominent, tying her and the magician tighter together. Now the Tablet, *his* Tablet, had marked her. *The magic might just go away, as Nereus said.*

Penelope bit her lip, hugging herself to soothe the anxiety filling her stomach. What would happen after they found the murderer? Would the invitation to the palazzo in Dorsoduro be rescinded? Would she ever be satisfied going back to her old life? What if the pieces of the Living Language inside of her made it impossible to leave? She hadn't liked the way Nereus had said *abilities*. What abilities?

The last few weeks had been dangerous, but they also made everything Penelope had worried about before seem pointless. What happened to the few humans that were given the privilege of knowing about these magicians? Could they ever live a normal life afterward? Or would Alexis simply take her memories away again, leaving a space inside of her that she'd never understand, and never be able to fill?

Penelope leaned against the window sill, breathing in the salty air to try and calm the sudden and painful panic building inside of her. *Get it together, Penelope. You are letting your emotions get the better of you. Find a way to control it. You know you can.*

She kicked off her Doc Martens and folded herself over to touch her toes. The soft Persian rug under her hands wasn't exactly a yoga mat but was thick enough to cushion her as she moved from a downward dog to a plank pose. The tightness in her shoulders screamed as she stretched.

"You need to tuck your hips in a little tighter," Aelia instructed from the other side of the room. Penelope wobbled unsteadily. "May I show you?"

"Ah...sure," Penelope replied.

Aelia's hand pushed gently on her lower back and realigned her hips. "It feels tighter, but it will help your energy flow easier between the crown of your head and your feet." Aelia stretched out next to her. In leather leggings, a bright kaftan top, and heavy jewelry, she was the most glamorous yoga instructor Penelope had ever seen. "Did you forget about our talk?"

"No," Penelope lied. "I was just trying to clear my head. We put the Tablet back together, and I started feeling a bit overwhelmed." *Alexis kissed my hand and a Tablet put words in me and I don't know what to do*, she added mentally.

"I can see from your energy that your mind is split in three different ways. It's almost like you're bottled up. You need to get this blocked energy moving or you'll give yourself a migraine. Come up into a warrior with me." Aelia moved gracefully, placing a bare foot between her hands and spiraling upward.

"You don't seem nearly as terrifying as I was led to believe," Penelope commented. She wondered if Phaidros planned on returning to the palazzo at all.

"Terrifying? No. But I've been known to be intimidating."

"You don't say," Penelope mumbled as she moved into her warrior. Once again, Aelia made microadjustments to her pose. "So what is the nomenclature for a female magician? Surely not a witch."

Aelia made a small choking sound. "A witch? Hardly. Magicians are simply magicians. It never mattered about sex. I like these rooms; sometimes the palazzo and Alexis do get things right."

"Alexis?"

"His tower, his rooms." Aelia smiled, and it was like sunshine. "You're quite pretty, aren't you? What's your blood?"

"Irish, Australian, and a touch Māori," Penelope replied. "Dad is full Irish, and mom is half and half. I was born in Australia." She was certainly more open and friendlier than Penelope expected her to be, even if she jumped topics three times in one sentence.

"An Irish-Australian girl with a Greek heroine's name," Aelia said thoughtfully.

"My father loves the classics. I've always found the name too sweet for my nature."

"Penelope was fierce and clever and steadfast; most cunning and honorable," Aelia argued as they both straightened again. "It's a good person to be named after. You have those attributes from what Alexis tells me. He's very taken with you, but then he's been intrigued since you found his piece of rock. I think it's rather nice you two have come together even if you argue with each other."

"I wouldn't exactly put it that way. It was more me frustrating him to the point he couldn't avoid me," laughed Penelope. "I'm stubbornly persistent when something has my attention."

"Alexis could avoid anyone for a millennium if he wanted to. You're a mystery to him, and nothing frustrates Alexis like a mystery," Aelia said fondly. "I wonder if you would be strong enough to handle the intensity of his affections, Penelope Bryne."

"Affections? What are you talking about?" Penelope dropped awkwardly out of her pose.

"I'm merely asking you, politely, not to encourage him romantically if you only want a holiday fling. He's not that kind of man. He doesn't give his friendships lightly and will let even fewer into his confidence or his bed."

Penelope couldn't hold in her bafflement. "I appreciate your concern for him, but we've only crossed over to being friends. I don't think he's interested in the way you are implying."

"For a clever girl, you're good at ignoring the obvious. You're in his tower, not any old guest room of the palazzo. He's put you under his protection, in his domain. This isn't neutral territory; he's claimed you as his, and he wants Phaidros and everyone else to know it."

"You are reading too much into it," Penelope said as her heart gave a strange little flutter in her chest. Aelia rolled her eyes and started going through the wardrobe.

"Whatever. I know Alexis. Let's hope there is something decent in here for you to wear to dinner tonight," she said, pulling clothes aside. "We haven't been all together in eighty years, and it deserves a nice dress. Let's see what the house has…perfect!" She pulled out a dark green dress, loose and long like a kaftan, and heavy with golden embroidery.

"I don't know. I'm not really—" Penelope began, but Aelia was already finding a matching slip and shoes.

"I haven't had a woman to get ready with in years, Penelope. Let me pamper you for one night in the spirit of sisterhood between us," said Aelia, her violet eyes glowing with good-natured humor.

Penelope relented to her enthusiasm. She missed Carolyn's female company. She needed to get her mind off Alexis and the murders, and Aelia was nothing if not distracting.

TWO HOURS later they walked down the stairs together. Penelope felt like an eastern princess in her dress, despite her initial reluctance. The outer layer was sheer green chiffon, bright gold embroidery framing the neckline, with dripping patterns down her front. Underneath was a flowing shift that moved around her in soft waves.

Aelia had tamed Penelope's dark hair into curls and made up her eyes in greens, golds, and heavy black liner. Penelope loved eye makeup but so rarely had the opportunity to wear it. Aelia had given her heavy bronze bracelets with twisting eastern designs and painted her hands with golden henna.

Aelia wore gold and cream and was as stunning as Helen of Troy. Penelope could imagine her launching a thousand ships and then laughing as she watched them burn. Like the other magicians, there was an unknowable streak in her that made her company exciting and unpredictable. Penelope couldn't help wondering what Phaidros's reaction would be to Aelia's presence. She had tried to raise the nature of their animosity, but Aelia had smoothly changed the subject.

Penelope followed Aelia to one of the most beautiful spaces she had been inside the palazzo. It was designed like a Roman atrium with an elaborate view of the canal and was half garden, half water feature. Penelope stepped carefully over paths built over channels of water to an island with a large, low square table and long flat cushions for people to sit and lounge on. Moroccan lanterns of all shapes and colors illuminated the space in a soft, warm glow.

Zo greeted them both with warm kisses. "You two look divine. I hope you are hungry. Drink some of this wine, Penelope. I pressed the grapes myself." He placed a goblet in her hand, and she sipped, enjoying the heavy notes of citrus and honey. He was dressed in loose pants and a formal *thawb* made of black silk. Enthusiasm radiated off him as she complimented him.

"Be careful of Zo's wine," Phaidros said from behind her. "It's deceptively strong." He was dressed similarly to Zo but in brick red that made his golden hair shine. He bowed to them formally. "You are looking as lovely as always. I'm so pleased you'll be joining us, Penelope. I don't believe I can recall the last time we had a human in attendance at such a gathering. Can you, Aelia?" He was such a vision of politeness that Penelope almost asked him how much of Zo's wine he had already consumed.

"It has been too long," Aelia agreed. "After spending an afternoon with Penelope, I agree with Nereus that Alexis chose his new friend extremely well."

"He did indeed," came Alexis's voice through the greenery. He was in dark blue and had his hair pulled back into a messy knot. Penelope took a large drink of her wine as he stepped barefoot over the channels of water to join them. She didn't know why, but there was something about his naked brown feet that seemed weirdly intimate. His sleeves had been pushed up his long brown forearms, and he wore thin bronze bracelets around his wrists.

His eyes ran up and down her, and everywhere his gaze lingered, her skin tingled. Every platonic thought she had in her head seemed to vanish as he bent down to kiss her cheek, a smile edging the corners of his mouth. Heat flooded from the spot and butterflies started to flap inside her stomach.

"You're looking festive, Doctor Bryne," he said. He took her wine from her, sipped it, and gave it back. "Zo is trying to impress you. This is his favorite vintage."

"Phaidros has already warned me to be careful," Penelope said, sounding awkward even to herself.

"Doesn't sound like something he'd do."

"I'm protecting her virtue from being stolen," Phaidros replied from where he lounged, propped up on colorful cushions.

"I hate to break it to you, but my virtue was fumblingly pick-pocketed years ago," Penelope joked, taking a seat.

Phaidros laughed loudly, lifting his goblet to her. "May the gods bless fumbling pickpockets," he exclaimed, "and to better thieves in the future."

Penelope clinked her cup against his. "Fingers crossed."

"Don't encourage him," Alexis chastised playfully, stretching out behind her on the backless couch, resting on his side in an almost protective position. Penelope caught Aelia's gaze, one that seemed to say, *Didn't I tell you?*

Nereus arrived dressed in dark aqua, Lyca in gray and silver, and Galenos is his customary green and gold. Aelia's determination for everyone to dress up had worked. They looked like vibrant birds of paradise, a sliver of a forgotten time and luxury.

"Alexis tells me your poetry is better than your cooking, Zo. Should I be worried?" Penelope asked as he began to place huge platters and more wine on the table. There was already an elaborate display of fruit and flowers, steaming bread, cheeses, and nuts. He seemed determined to fill every inch of the table.

"It was meant as a compliment," Alexis said beside her. "Zo's food is good, but his poetry is exceptional."

"Stop kissing his ass, Alexis, or he'll start reciting it," said Lyca.

Zo responded with a long stream of smooth Italian verses, as he poured Penelope more wine.

"Quoting Dante with dinner, I'm impressed," she smiled. *Inferno* was one of her favorite poems during her university years, her patchy Italian the result of her loving the flow of the sounds in its native language.

"Sure, *Dante*." Zo rolled his eyes cheekily before disappearing back through the greenery.

"No way," gasped Penelope. She turned on Alexis. "Tell me he isn't."

"The poetry is his, the name isn't," Alexis replied with a shrug. "Even immortals need to get their art out somehow."

"It's all saying one thing and meaning another," Lyca complained. Her pale gray eyes held none of the cold violence Penelope had seen the night she was pulled from the canal.

Galenos stared openly at Lyca's strong figure, shown off in a tight, plain gray dress and adorned with a beaten silver neck cuff and bracelets. It was a stare so hot, it made Penelope think they were lovers, though the quiet, reserved Galenos with the violently beautiful Lyca seemed like an uneasy match.

"You had best pour me a big goblet of that wine, Phaidros," Nereus instructed. "I've got a terrible headache from staring at those spells all day."

"Did you have any luck?" Penelope asked eagerly.

"Some, but I'll tell you tomorrow. Tonight I want a good meal with my adopted children, and Aelia to sing to me."

"Only if Phaidros will play," Aelia insisted, almost shyly.

His golden eyes slid over to and then away from her. "Fine. Whatever you command, Princess."

"Do you think she knows what she does to him?" Penelope whispered to Alexis as she ate some grapes from a platter. Everyone had drifted off into their conversations as the wine flowed.

Alexis chewed a grape, considering the question. "Does any woman know what she does to the man who desires her?"

"He should tell her. You think magicians would be braver."

"He did tell her once. She scorned him harshly, and he never attempted it again," Alexis said softly. Penelope glanced across at the golden Apollo on her left as he lounged in the lamplight. There would be few women alive who would resist Phaidros, let alone scorn him.

"He shouldn't have given up so easily."

"It was a long time ago on Atlantis. Social structures were different then," Alexis explained. "She was royalty, and he was not."

"It was *that* long ago? That is an epic grudge," said Penelope, wide-eyed.

"It's not so long if you love them and it still hurts."

"Hasn't he heard the saying 'Let go or get dragged?' You've all been together for so long, I'd be surprised if you all hadn't been lovers or mortal enemies at some point."

Alexis snorted. "I've slept with none of them. Galenos and Lyca are a couple. Zo and Aelia were lovers at some point in the early days in Egypt, but I think that was boredom more than anything. Magicians rarely couple with other magicians."

"Why not? You would have a lot in common, and you're the only Atlanteans left alive."

"Magicians are naturally solitary and obsessed with their art. They have a strong streak of professional arrogance, and if you combine that with passion and emotion, the results are violent and unpredictable."

"Sounds like me and a million other academics," Penelope said. "There's a reason why we date someone in our field or not at all."

"I can't imagine you don't get offers, Penelope."

"I've had them. I just didn't have time for them." Penelope swallowed a large mouthful of wine. Her love life, or lack of it, wasn't something she was comfortable discussing with someone who could turn a group of female officers into heated cats.

"You two, stop talking! Aelia is going to sing," Lyca interrupted loudly. Phaidros had produced a lyre with seven strings, made of mother-of-pearl and golden wood.

"Aelia uses her voice to weave her magic," Alexis whispered in Penelope's ear, his breath tickling her skin. "She could make you dance and fall in love like a siren does a sailor if she wanted to."

"And you?" she asked as soft, deep stringed music filled the air. The weight of his gaze pinned her, the flir-tatious moment filled with something heavier.

"I'd never use magic to make someone fall in love with me. There can be no external influence, or else the experience can't be trusted, just like magic."

Penelope was saved from replying as Aelia's voice opened into the air. Tingles spread up over her body as the eerie melodies spun silver in her ears. She couldn't understand a word of it, but somehow she knew Aelia was singing of a home they would never see again. Penelope's soul heaved and pulsed, tears filling her eyes.

Behind her, Alexis's hand rested on her back in a reassuring gesture. Lost in the moment, she leaned against him, using the curve of his body like the back of a chair. It was comforting, and the throbbing under the scar on her ribs eased.

Penelope closed her eyes as the song washed over her, and in her mind she could see the string of light pulsing between her and Alexis. She touched it, slow and experimental, and Alexis took a sharp intake of breath behind her. She hadn't imagined it; it was not some new age bullshit she had made up in her head. It was real. He could feel when she touched it, not just when she was afraid or meditating. What was it? How did it come to be there? Why him? She would have to pin down Nereus and ask more questions, since Alexis would probably avoid answering them.

The song finished, and Penelope clapped enthusiastically.

"With a voice like that I'm surprised you haven't wrangled the world," she said to Aelia.

"She gave up on being a pop star after Eurovision," teased Zo.

"You were in Eurovision? Who...where?" Penelope demanded, and then she saw Aelia on stage with blue hair, a sequined bodysuit, cape flapping in the wind machine. "Holy shit—you are Lia Lee!"

"Oh, Zeus," groaned Phaidros. "Don't get her started."

Penelope ignored him. "You should have won that year, hands down."

"That competition is so rigged," Aelia said, flicking her bronze hair over her shoulder. "And I would never use magic to win."

Zo laughed loudly. "She was pretty damn close to doing it that time. I blame the piano playing. Aelia can sing the sky blue, but Phaidros is the true master of instruments. Except cello, which Alexis beats anyone on. You should go and get it. It's been too long since I heard you play."

"Another night perhaps. I haven't practiced."

"Come now, Zo. You know Alexis only plays when he is brooding," Nereus teased.

"It's an instrument of the soul. One must be ready to bear everything if they are to get any real sound out of it," defended Alexis. "I don't brood."

"I've known you for less than a month, and even I know you are the king of brood," Penelope said, tugging at one of his stray curls.

"Start hair pulling at your peril," he threatened playfully.

The night passed in a hazy whorl of drinks and laughter until only Penelope and Alexis remained in the floating gardens. She lay on the platform, head propped up on a large cushion with her hand trailing through the unnaturally warm saltwater that flowed through the channels.

"Do you miss Atlantis?" she asked, staring at the stars through the roof of the atrium. Alexis lay beside her, but they were careful not to touch.

"Sometimes," he admitted. "Other times I feel like I barely remember it."

"Will you tell me about it one day? I swear I'll never write it down."

"If you want to hear of it, I'll tell it," he promised, "but I've drunk far too much to tell such tales tonight. I can do this though." He leaned over her and put his hand in the water. His aura crackled with energy, and an orb of water lifted from the canal and into the air. Penelope reached for it, lightly touching its bobbing surface. He sent a few more up, letting them float around the atrium.

"I didn't think serious magicians did such mindless tricks," she said cheekily.

"We love the tricks," Alexis replied, and the orbs started glowing different colors. "Besides, I like seeing the joy you find in the simplest things."

"Sometimes simple is best," she replied. They watched the orbs silently for a while before Alexis yawned.

"I should escort you back to your room. I'm sure the inspector will want to meet with you tomorrow."

"I think Zo's wine has made my legs disappear," she complained as he helped her to unsteady feet.

"Come on, I'll help you." Alexis held her hand and made sure she didn't fall into any pockets of water. The palazzo moving seemed almost normal as they walked.

"I have a question," Penelope declared loudly.

"Of course you have a question." Alexis pulled her out of the way of a sculpture so she didn't crash into it, and opened her bedroom door.

"The first night you brought me here, Phaidros said my chakras were broken. Is that true?" Penelope asked as she collapsed on a chaise lounge.

"Phaidros can see them, but I doubt they are broken."

"Apparently my red one was out, and it came on when I saw you. What does that mean?" The wine had made her brave, but she wasn't so drunk that she didn't notice the color creeping along his cheeks. He sat on the other end of the couch, lifting her feet, so they rested on his knees.

"Each one of your chakras has a different color associated with it," he explained. "Sometimes certain centers can become more dormant or active than others. They can be balanced with focus and guidance."

"Show me," Penelope insisted. "Prove it, if you can."

"You're very provocative when you've been drinking," he said. "I don't know if you are sober enough to feel it."

"Sure I will." She shut her eyes and said dramatically, "I'm ready, magician."

Alexis laughed, and the sound of it thrilled her. "Don't say you didn't ask for it. Keep your eyes closed, and I'll take you through a quick tour. Breathe calmly and deeply, as you would settling into your meditations."

Penelope did as she was told, the teasing in his voice leaving as the teacher and magician took over.

"We're going to work through each chakra, opening them and allowing the energy to flow," he continued, "I want you to focus on the base of your spine, your root chakra that glows like a small ball of red light. Imagine it turning on like a flame, glowing brighter. Next, I want you to focus on the space just below your navel, your sacral chakra that is orange. Focus on making this orange light glow hotter and brighter until fingers of light reach out and touch the red of your root chakra."

Penelope had never been through energy work before, despite Carolyn's recommendation, and yet she felt something flare low and deep within her as she focused on the light and Alexis's voice.

"We are moving up to your navel chakra near your solar plexus," Alexis instructed. "Feel this sitting in between the top of your ribs, where your instincts and emotions sit. This glows golden yellow, like a tiny sun, burning down to touch the orange light. Next, we will focus on your heart which is the color of vibrant emeralds. This is where love resides, and only you know how to get this one to flare. Focus on what fills you with love and joy, Penelope."

She thought of the sea before her fear of it, the moment she touched the Tablet and *knew* it was going to change her life, that strange thrill of the unknown, and being one step closer to knowing. Her family rose and left her mind. She loved them, but that wasn't what filled her with exhilaration and burning desire. That was knowledge, always. Unbidden, the image of the blue door opening and seeing Alexis on the other side flashed in the forefront of her mind, and she struggled to push it away. The Archives loomed in front of her, the overwhelming joy when she was there.

"It's flared. Just breathe, Penelope. Don't fight it," soothed Alexis. "Next I want you to move your attention to your throat. This chakra glows blue, and while you have no problem communicating, there seems to be an imbalance here. It's like you have been silenced, gagged, whether by yourself or others, out of fear. Focus on taking that gag off, unwind it, and throw it away. Let the intensity of that blue light burn like the center of a flame." Heat ran along Penelope's chest, curling around her neck and the back of her head. Warm fingers lightly touched her forehead, and she shivered.

Alexis lowered his voice. "Open your third eye, Penelope. It's been sitting heavy-lidded for too long. Open it and see the world in its wonder. If you want to know the magic around you, you must look for it. Don't be afraid. I'll be here."

Penelope breathed deeply and tried to imagine an eye opening between her brows. As she did, indigo light flooded her mind, and the other chakras responded as if the new energy made them burn brighter.

"Well done. It's strong, which is a good sign. The last chakra sits on top of the crown of your head; this is where enlightenment and wisdom flow down through you. When you open this chakra, Penelope, all of you will feel it, so be prepared. This chakra is violet and—" Alexis cut off as Penelope shuddered from the intensity of it. She lit up like a street light, energy running up and down, like an invisible hand stroking her insides.

"There you are. You were interested in your root chakra so now that you are fully open I want you to keep your focus on the orange and red bases as they pulse gently."

Alexis's voice had dropped to an even deeper whisper now, sending another tremor through her stomach, making her pelvic floor muscles clench. Desire burned through her skin, making it hypersensitive to every breath of air. She hardly dared to breathe.

"I-I can feel…" she managed as she felt the edges of an orgasm ambushing her. *Oh God please no.* "What are you doing to me right now?"

"I'm not doing it. You are."

Alexis placed a hot hand on the curve of her calf muscle, and she groaned at the contact. His hand slid slowly up her bare skin, the rest of his body moving on top of hers. Her nerves were screaming with a primal need to have his skin against hers, to have him every which way she needed to ease the hunger inside of her. Her lids were heavy as she opened her eyes, finding his blue ones hovering above her. His proximity made it hard to keep her from wrapping her body around his. She was on fire with seven different flames, her breath shuddering.

Very slowly, Alexis kissed her bruised cheek, and she held her breath, hands twisting in the fabric of his shirt. Her skin tingled, as he healed her.

"I can't handle seeing you hurt. I don't care what questions anyone asks about your recovery capabilities," he said, his long fingers stroking her cheeks and tangling in her curls. "May I kiss you, Penelope?"

"Yes," she whispered. His lips were firm and warm against hers, tasting of spiced wine and the tang of smoke as magic jumped from his mouth to hers, healing the cut on her bottom lip as he gave it a slow suck. When he pulled back, she gave a noise of protest; she wanted to kiss him properly, to have her fingers pass through his hair and trace the line of his bare back. *What is wrong with me?* Penelope shoved the voice away. It had barely been a taste, but it set her bones aching and muscles tensing.

Alexis must have been able to read it in her eyes; his smile was gentle but knowing. "I'm sorry to disappoint, Penelope, but I can't allow much more than that tonight."

"Why not?" she asked as he eased off her, leaving her cold. "Is it me?"

"God, no," he said deadly serious. "Don't mistake my actions for disinterest. If I were a lesser man, you would have been naked hours ago. But I am who I am, and we've been drinking. If you come to my bed, I want it to be a very clear and sober decision, and I want you to remember every second of it."

There was an unspoken promise in his words that made Penelope's mouth go dry. "I understand, but whatever you just did to me, you should've put a warning label on it if you didn't want to follow it up with… something else."

"I did try and warn you," he replied innocently. "The good news is all of your chakras are in perfect order."

"Yay," she said unenthusiastically. "You have a great deal more self-control than me if you walk around feeling that all day with your chakras aligned." Penelope pushed her hands through her hair, fighting off embarrassment. "Maybe it's a good thing I didn't go to any chakra meditations earlier if that's what happens. Or maybe it's because it's you, and I'm drunk on Atlantean alcohol."

"Wine and magic are great seducers, and what's between us is complicated enough," Alexis admitted.

Penelope sat up, her whole body aching to have his naked body pressed against hers. She tried to focus. "You mean our weird, glowing string?"

"It's called a fate knot, *moíra desmós*," he admitted. "That's what Nereus meant today about your knot. I originally thought I had caused it when I placed a trace on you years ago—"

"When you were busily crashing my career," she added.

"Yes. But Nereus said it's not due to the tracer spell. Our fates are tied, to whatever end. It would have always been there since birth. After seeing you with the Tablet today, I think it might have connected when you found it, or when it found you. It's only become more noticeable because we are finally together, and in the here and now, our fates are going to be decided."

Penelope sighed with relief. "I'm not crazy."

"You thought you were?"

"What do you think? A man appears in my meditation, turns out to be a real-life magician from Atlantis who wants my help hunting down priests of a demonic cult," Penelope said sarcastically. "Having a logical explanation for why I'm so drawn to you is a good thing. You're gorgeous, but I'm not that much of a sucker for handsome men. You must feel better knowing why you're so curious about a mortal academic, and that I'm not some secret magician who astral projected into your tower."

"Secret magician or *moíra desmós*. Both are intimidating prospects," Alexis replied. He looked sideways at her. "Do you hate me for what I did to your academic career?"

"Yes...and no. Mostly no." Penelope ran a hand through her hair. "I understand your reasons, especially after tonight. They are a moody family of magicians, but they are worth protecting. It's never been about a career or making a name for myself. I just needed to *know*. Do I want to know a lot more? Hell yes. I only published the findings because I wanted funding to find more answers. I have answers, some of them anyway, so I forgive you for being so dastardly and considering killing me to shut me up."

"I hated doing it to you and all the others I've intervened with." He squeezed her foot gently. "You, most of all. I knew I could never physically hurt you even then."

"What I want to know is, why didn't you do something about Madame Blavatsky? That mystical table-knocker founded a whole society, and you ignored her."

"That was Zo's fault! He ran into her in a backwater Russian bar in the 1850s drunk off his head on vodka. She was interested in magic and occultism. He spun her fantastical tales with just enough reality to make it a concern. I kept an eye on the Theosophical Society for a while, but I kept a closer eye on Zo when he was drinking."

Penelope lost it laughing. "What a bastard!"

"He always did like to make my life interesting." Alexis smiled with brotherly fondness. "In regard to my actions toward you, I will make amends, I promise."

"You did save my life and let me hang out in the Archives. That's good amends."

He raised a dark eyebrow. "So, you don't want any more stories?"

Penelope sat up so she could poke him. "Of course I want stories! And I want to hear you play the cello."

Alexis grimaced. "I should hamstring Zo for telling you that. A man has to have some mysteries."

Penelope placed a hand on his chest and said very seriously, "Alexis, you are a magician from Atlantis. That's enough mystery for any person." He looked at her hand, but when she made to move it, he covered it with his own. She could feel his heart beating loud and insistent, and her own responded, matching the rhythm.

"I might be out of line saying this, but of all the people on this planet, I'm glad my fate is tied to yours, Alexis Donato," Penelope said. "I don't know what tomorrow holds, but from the moment I met you I've felt that as long as I'm with you, I'm going to be all right."

Alexis cupped her face with his other hand. "I promise to try and live up to your faith in me, Penelope Bryne. Right now, you are making me wish I was a lesser man so I could take advantage of this moment, but a lesser man would not deserve you." He lifted her hand to his mouth and kissed her fingers before rising to his feet. He bowed to her. "It has been an honor to be your escort this evening. *Buona notte, dolcezza*."

"Good night, magician," Penelope said. He was almost at the door when she exclaimed, "Alexis, wait!"

As he turned, Penelope was there, meeting him on tiptoes and kissing him hard and deep, her fingers threading through the midnight curls at the nape of his neck.

It was a kiss that made promises, expressing the vortex of emotions she had felt since pulling the stone tablet from the sea. She kissed Alexis the way a part of her had wanted to since she saw him in his tower, that wild and graceful thing wrapped in silk and magic. In it, she tried to express the ache of her skin and the need in her chest. The wanting of not just his knowledge but *him*. God, she wanted him, to unlock every part of him like he was a living book filled with deep unknowable secrets, terrifying fairy tales of magic and violence and loss. She wanted to swallow the smoke of his voice and know the feeling of his fingertips on her face.

Penelope pressed Alexis against the door, her softness molded against the hard shape of his long body.

"I wanted a good-night kiss," she said breathlessly after their lips parted. She stepped back from him, shaking.

"If that's how you kiss good night, I can't wait to see how you kiss good morning," Alexis said, brow slightly raised. His smirking mouth was begging to be kissed again, but then he was gone, the door closing gently behind him.

Minutes later, as Penelope lay in bed, the first deep bars of a cello echoed down the tower stairs to her room, serenading her to sleep as something in her soul burned.

FOURTEEN

B Y THE TIME Penelope arrived at their designated meeting spot early the next morning,
Marco Dandolo had coffees and biscotti waiting. He
closed his paper as she entered the café, looking at her
with an amused and measured smile.

"You know what I love about Italy?" she asked as
she sat down opposite him. "There's good coffee wherever I go."

Marco looked her over again, his smile getting
wider. "You slept with him, didn't you?"

"No! Why would you say that?" she said too loudly.
"Of course I didn't. I'm a little hungover, that's all. Some
friends arrived yesterday, so we had dinner and drinks
and…fine! I kissed him, okay? Don't give me a lecture
because I don't exactly know how I feel about it."

Marco laughed at her nervous confession. "Penelope,
you are hardly the first person in the world to kiss someone after they've been drinking. Half the Questura
wanted to make love to Alexis Donato yesterday, so I'm
impressed you stopped at just kissing."

"I still don't know if it was a mistake or not,"
Penelope admitted, dipping her almond biscotti into
the steaming espresso. It wasn't only the kissing that
troubled her; it was the chakra orgasm and the magic,
too. She should have been concerned or afraid. Instead,

she felt more comfortable with a group of magicians than she ever had with normal people.

"I think the paparazzi are more excited about it than you are," Marco commented and handed her a paper. She couldn't understand what the article was saying, but there she was, arm in arm with Alexis, wandering the streets of Venice.

"What the hell? Who took this?" she demanded. She tried to make sense of the sentence underneath the photograph. She and Alexis were both named. "What does this say?"

"Who cares? It's just a gossip rag. Nothing to concern yourself with." Marco tried to take the paper from her, but she tightened her grip on it.

"Tell me now, Marco."

"Fine, fine. In English, it would translate as 'Pseudohistorian spotted in Venezia with illusive bachelor, Alexis Donato.' Really, Penelope, no one reads this garbage. I'm glad that you've stolen their attention, so they aren't focusing on the murders."

"Pseudohistorian! Those pieces of…God, I hope Alexis hasn't seen this. He'll be so embarrassed."

Her nerves tightened as she remembered their intimacy the night before. Did she want to be involved with someone who could land her in the papers every time she left the house? She hated the thought people would think less of him just because he was seen in her company. And she loathed her research being classed as pseudohistory. All of her confidence from the night before fled as she shoved some biscotti into her mouth.

"Don't let it bother you, *Dottore*. No one believes the media," soothed Marco.

"Can we please just talk about the case? You look like you have been up all night. Were you trying to unravel the mystery that is Agent Bianchi?"

"*Buffo*. We can't all succeed in getting our partners drunk like you, though if any woman desperately needs to get drunk and kissed, it's her." Marco handed over a file. "We spent last night profiling, and after much argument, we have a few ideas about who could be behind this."

Penelope looked through the papers. "Where have I seen this guy before?" The picture was of a man in his late twenties with an edgy, expensive fashion sense and a geometric neck tattoo.

"That's Tony Duilio. He's the man I was telling you about who wants to turn Venezia into a floating city. He's been very vocal against the MOSE from day one."

"He's rich and eccentric, but hardly seems a psycho demon worshipper," said Penelope. She remembered the TV coverage she had seen of him a few days beforehand. Nobody would risk such a career just because he didn't land the Venice project.

"We don't think Duilio himself is the killer, but he has been stirring up protestors. People who are passionate and may want to sabotage as much of the MOSE as they can."

"What about the search of local farms for the missing livestock?"

"Agent Bianchi was grudgingly impressed by your insight into that one." Marco flicked through his file and produced a glossy brochure of a boutique farm near Favaro Veneto. "The couple who owns this farm reported the murder of their stud to the local *polizia* two days before the bull's body was found in Santa Croce. They found the butchered remains of it near a local road and the investigators put it down to vandalism."

"And the horse?"

"A racehorse that was reported missing from a property on the Lido. They thought that a competitor had stolen it because it was a week before a race. The horse was worth over a million euro."

"And nobody saw anything?" Penelope shook her head. "Who is this guy?"

"Someone very organized and well-connected. Good at thieving and lying. It was a good lead, Penelope. I have officers who deal with art and antique thefts running checks on the vessels too. Even if we do find it, who knows how many hands they would have changed before our killer stole or purchased them?"

"Keep at it. I hate black market antiques dealing. Any bastard you can charge over it will make me happy."

"I will, don't worry. Do you have any other leads for me to try?"

"Some, but nothing good enough to give to Agent Bianchi. She'll want absolute certainty and might not even care what the killer's religious mind-set is,"

Penelope said. *How am I going to tell them about the Living Language?*

"You are holding something back," Marco said. "Tell me. I'm not Bianchi. It doesn't matter if it's not perfect."

"It's about the script. While I haven't cracked a literal translation, I've found more information about it." Penelope drank some coffee, her mind racing to piece together a nonmagical story. "I found a book of Alexis's that speaks of a written language in Atlantis. It was an account by an Arabic magician who heard it from an Egyptian priest. The Atlanteans believed that this particular script had power and used it to write spells that would help give them the strength to manifest. Thevetat's followers transmuted this language into a shadow script, its opposite. The Living Language's counterpart deals with death and darkness. Pairing it with a human sacrifice makes it doubly strong."

"You're starting to sound like you believe this," Marco said slowly, with surprisingly little judgment.

"I believe the Acolyte believes it," defended Penelope.

"Do you think he is done or that there will be more bodies?"

"At least one more. Three's a magical, powerful number in nearly every race and religion. He won't leave it at two," Penelope said. *I was meant to be the third.* She squashed the thought.

"People connected to the MOSE are under surveillance, if that's how he's picking his victims," assured

Marco. "The ones so far have had a higher profile than many of the other workers."

"What have you got planned? The masquerade is tomorrow night."

"I know, and we'll be ready. Agent Bianchi has already leaked to the media that the members of the MOSE board will be attending, as well as prestigious persons of scientific and historical merit, including yourself," Marco explained calmly. "We'll have eyes on you at all times so if anyone approaches you or even looks at you for too long, we'll intercept them."

"Simple as that."

"*Si.*"

"And I can have Alexis with me?"

"*Si,* you can bring *il innamorato* with you," he teased.

"We aren't lovers," huffed Penelope. "And probably never will be now that it's splashed all over the goddamn papers."

"You never know." Marco shrugged vaguely. "It's Carnevale. Everyone needs or wants a lover at Carnevale."

"What about you? I've yet to see one girlfriend bothering you. I'm sure you have a few."

"Only exes. Doesn't matter. I'm too busy to maintain even a lover at the moment."

"A lot can happen in two days." Penelope drained her coffee. "I'm going to get back to work, so I have something to report to Agent Bianchi. Results are the only things that seem to make her smile."

"That's true. I know it's none of my business, but have you let anyone know you are well since you lost your other phone? I'm sure your family will be worried after not hearing from you," Marco said.

"They probably haven't even looked up from their current projects." Penelope shook her head. "I won't tell them about the kidnapping. My father already has ideas about what I should be doing with my life, but ultimately they care about their academic works, not their daughter."

"In Venezia, we have a saying, *Megio un amigo che sento parenti.* Better a friend than a hundred relatives," Marco said, and Penelope chuckled. "At least more of your friends have come to the city to see you, even if they do get you drunk."

"What kind of friends would they be if they didn't?"

AFTER SAYING goodbye to Marco, Penelope wandered the streets of Dorsoduro. She wasn't ready to go back to the invisible palazzo on the Calle dei Cerchieri. She needed to think and to breathe, and proximity to Alexis hindered both. The picture in the paper flashed in her mind's eye, and her common sense started its warning cry. What craziness made her think getting emotionally involved with Alexis was a good idea? Would she be the object of even more public ridicule?

Her mind went into planning mode, making lists of all the things she should do: get another hotel, call Carolyn and let her know she had lost her phone but was okay, check her emails, give Latrobe University a yes or no about the job offer they had made her. Her real life was starting to feel like it was the unreal one, not the one with magic and Alexis. She would have to go back to Australia eventually. *No one can just run away to Venice and expect to stay there.* That alone was a good enough reason not to let her growing interest in Alexis get too intense.

Penelope brushed her cool fingers against her lips. She had never been kissed like that before. *He's had a hell of a long time to practice, Pen.*

But it was more than that. Maybe it was that their destinies were woven together. At least for the moment. What if it unraveled as soon as they found Thevetat's follower?

Penelope walked down the Calle Avogaria, over a bridge, and found herself standing in front of the gray and white facade of the Saint Sebastian Church. Tourists mingled out the front, but it wasn't crowded, so Penelope went inside. It had been too long since she had studied the rich cycle of paintings by Paolo Veronese that decorated the interior. Scenes from Esther and Saint Sebastian leaped out in gorgeous Renaissance life, but her favorite had always been of Venice's patron saint, Mark, and his brother, Marcellinus, being led to their martyrdom.

The church was almost empty, so she sat down on the edge of a pew, letting her eyes absorb the beauty around her.

Her father had been raised Irish Catholic, but it had never been a strong feature in Penelope's academic upbringing. She'd always loved churches, however, and Italy's places of worship married their love of sensual art and beauty to their beliefs. It was hard to avoid faith in Venice. The story of the famous theft in AD 828 of relics belonging to Saint Mark from Alexandria by two Venetian merchants for protection was strongly embedded in the mythology of the city, even down to the lion symbol they shared with the famous disciple.

Under the sad, watchful eyes of the figures around her, Penelope let her thoughts return to Alexis, their kisses, and the possibility of more.

The few times she had engaged in no-strings romantic flings were almost as unsatisfying as her two long-term relationships. She had decided that some people simply weren't made for that conventionality and her passion was channeled into her work. Pouring time into study bore results every time; pouring time into people rarely did.

Even without his fake celebrity profile, Alexis could not be so neatly slotted into the category of "people."

"You look like you are debating whether to commit a murder," a deep voice said from behind her. Zo leaned over the back of her pew. "Are you going to kill someone? Because I can help if you are stuck on the details."

"What are you doing here?" Penelope whispered, her eyes scanning around him.

"If you're looking for *il stregone*, he isn't here. He's in the tower sulking. I saw you leave and hesitated to follow. But then I thought of all the ways he'd punish me if I failed to make sure nothing happened to you."

"I don't need a damn bodyguard! I was only going for a coffee with Marco."

"And you were only going to bed when you were snatched from your hotel room," replied Zo. "Alexis isn't the only one who doesn't want you falling into the hands of a psychopath. Why are you looking so glum?"

"Just thinking," sighed Penelope. "There's a lot of things I'm avoiding back home."

"Here I thought it was just Alexis you were avoiding."

"I'm not avoiding him. I'm my own woman and will go wherever I like."

"*Dottore*, you snuck out of the house this morning like a guilty lover. I don't want to know what happened between you two last night but if you are fighting, you both need to kiss and…oh, I see, you kissed him." Zo's dark expression melted.

"He kissed me first," she argued.

"He kissed you? I'm impressed and can hardly blame him. You look very kissable."

Penelope glared at him. "It was probably all the wine he drank. I don't want him feeling awkward about it today, so I thought I'd give him some space."

Zo shook his head. "Come with me. The merits of making love is not a conversation I wish to have inside a *chiesa*."

Once outside, Zo held out his arm and Penelope took it. She liked Zo and his easy manner. Last night they had talked for over an hour about all the time he had spent in England, Australia, and America, and subsequently, he understood Penelope's idioms and slang better than the others.

"So the old Defender has finally admitted a soft spot for you." Zo clucked his tongue. "I remember the first time he told me about a university student in Australia writing a theoretical piece on Atlantis for one of her major assignments. You worried him even then."

"But that was ten years ago! How could he have possibly known about that?" Penelope was horrified.

"Alexis has been protecting our secrets for a long time, and he has computers now to help him flag anything on Atlantis theory. That includes university databases. He finds people of interest and keeps tabs on them. He almost busted an artery when you pulled his Tablet from the sea." Zo chuckled at the memory. "I hadn't seen him so agitated in five hundred years. He was impressed with you."

"And then he decided the best way to show it was to bomb my discovery," Penelope said.

"It hurt him to do it, but you were too close. He's a complicated beast. Even on Atlantis, he was difficult to understand."

"Are you going to try and lecture me about not breaking his heart? Because I'm not in the mood."

"We all care about him. You have to understand, he's always been the strongest, the most resilient of all of us. I've seen him walk away from people he cared about, truly loved and admired, because he wanted to protect them from our world. Not every human can take it in, or not want to use the knowledge we hold for their own gain," Zo explained.

"Are you telling me that he's going to wipe my memory and dump me back into a hotel to protect me when all this is over? Because if he tries, he'll have another thing coming."

Zo smiled. "*Bella*, if he wanted to do that there isn't a thing in the world you could do to stop him. But no, what I'm trying to tell you is that he won't do that to you. Maybe he's finally gotten lonely, or you found a chink in his incredible armor. His perfect willpower has abandoned him at last. The fact that he kissed you is groundbreaking. He may have ignored the murders, but the fact that you're involved now ensures that he'll hunt every one of Thevetat's new fanatics down and wipe all memory of them from the face of the Earth."

"Because he's the Defender…"

"Because he cares for you like you are one of us. We are all ungrateful, unworthy assholes. All magicians are. But he's never failed us, even when we deserved to be drawn and quartered. None of us deserve that kind of loyalty. He saw the papers this morning and thinks you have bailed because of them. I have to ask, is your hesitation the media or the magic? If it is the former, there are ways to get them to back off."

The pain in Penelope's ribs tightened, and she stopped walking. "The media thing is embarrassing, but it's not the main problem. You want to know what I am truly frightened of?"

"Tell me. Let me help, if I can."

"I'm worried that once this murder investigation is over our destiny knot will unravel and he'll realize I'm just a plain, boring human that's never been able to maintain a relationship longer than six months. I already feel too much for him and have since he pulled me from that bloody canal. If it's all because of some cosmic bullshit that he likes me and that goes, where does it leave me? *He'll* be over it. He's had a million lives and loves, and I'll still be Penelope, filled with wondrous knowledge that I'll never be able to prove, and obsessed with someone I can never have. *That's* the price of kissing him back."

Penelope didn't realize she was shaking until Zo wrapped his arms around her. He was warm under his jacket and smelled of coffee, leather, and rosemary.

"You're not going to believe me when I tell you this, but he's just as nervous, if not more so than you are about the whole idea. He's been playing the cello non-stop since you left. He only plays like that when he's worried about something deep in his soul. He knows you left the house and I think he's worried he scared you off." Zo gave her back a gentle rub. "Come home, Penelope. End the misery."

"Of course I was going to come back," Penelope said, releasing him. "I just needed some space."

"Good, because Aelia will probably be sitting on the stairs of his tower crying and I can't handle seeing her tears," Zo said, lightheartedly. "Music is her magic, and she's so empathic that when Alexis plays all his melancholy songs, she feels it the same way he does. She loves and hates it, so she'll be crying but won't interrupt him."

"What makes you think I'm going to interrupt it? I love the cello. I'll probably sit beside her."

"No, you won't, because if you do, I'll march you up those stairs myself," threatened Zo.

"Aren't there rules about bothering a magician when he's busy? I know he let me up there before, but that hardly qualifies as a standing invitation," said Penelope as the blue door appeared on the wall of the Calle dei Cerchieri.

"Penelope, that's exactly what it means. A magician lets no one into his sanctum sanctorum unless he wants them to visit again. Trust me on this."

"If he turns me into a toad, I expect you to turn me back, Zo," Penelope said. As the door shut behind them, the whole house seemed to echo with music. It was as if every wall, tile, artwork, and piece of furniture hummed with the deep bass of the cello.

"I told you," Zo said with a shake of his head. "Everyone feels it, even the palazzo, when he gets like this."

"I've never heard anything like it," Penelope whispered.

"You know what's better? Pancakes. I am going to make some, go and retrieve *il stregone* so the paintings will stop crying." Zo pushed her gently toward the stairs that had appeared. Penelope looked up in alarm to see a Renaissance painting of Persephone weeping gently. Clearly, when the house felt something, everything in it did too.

Penelope hurried up the stairs, focusing on the tower. The wall in front of her opened and as Zo predicted, Aelia was sitting on the bottom step looking up toward the notes of music that vibrated in the air. Her impeccable makeup was smeared from the tears rolling down her cheeks.

"About time you got here." She sniffed angrily and got to her feet. "Make him stop before I melt completely."

Penelope brushed past her and climbed the tower steps. The closer she got to his room, the more the music in the air glittered with visible, twisting plumes of silver, gold, and blues. The music rose and fell in deep, graceful arcs. It was the sound of heartache, and it vibrated through the stones and the air and her skin, filling her chest as her heartbeat tried to match the music.

Taking a deep breath, Penelope quietly pushed open the door and stepped inside.

Alexis sat on a small stool with his back to her as he moved the bow in his hand. The tips of his dark curls were damp from perspiration as they brushed his bare shoulders and back. She could see faint blue tattoos moving under his skin, streams of words and symbols that danced in time with the music.

Every word in Penelope's head seemed to vanish as she watched, mesmerized by the sound and energy in the room. She sat down at his workbench, not knowing how to interrupt, or if she even wanted to. A cinnamon, firecracker smell hung thick in the air as his magic weaved into the sounds, turning them into heavy streams of light.

"Alexis?" Her voice was barely a whisper pulled from her tense lungs. The music faltered as the bow jerked off the strings. Alexis turned, his indigo eyes burning with the magic of the music, and as he let the magic go, they faded back to a deep blue.

"Penelope." His voice was like smoke, his accent curling in husky twists. "I'm sorry, I didn't hear you come in." He got to his feet and placed the heavy cello back on the stand.

"Sorry to interrupt. Zo sent me up to see if you wanted breakfast."

He joined her at the table, and the heat and proximity of his naked brown skin nearly knocked all sense from her head.

"I saw the papers this morning and thought you might have…changed your mind about staying here," Alexis said tactfully.

"I went out to meet briefly with Marco. He wanted to share some profiling details with me," she said hurriedly, hating that their mouths were saying one thing while their eyes were saying another. "He showed me the paper. Honestly, it was more derogatory toward you than me. It's your reputation that will be ruined. Mine's already in the toilet."

"I've never particularly cared what others have thought. I especially don't care about the reputation of a mask I wear. I may court whoever I wish, just as you shall." He caught her eye and the hard shell of his gaze cracked. "You are entitled to change your mind, Penelope. I would never judge you for wanting to leave or regretting a drunken kiss."

"I don't regret it," she said defensively. "Do you?"

"No," he replied. He gave the back of his neck a bashful rub. "But I don't want you to feel like you need to reciprocate if you've changed your mind."

"Believe me, I'd have no problem expressing myself if I didn't want you to kiss me," she said with a smile. "Besides, how could I leave when there's the Archives downstairs that I haven't begun to explore?"

"You only want me for my books," he said, sighing dramatically. "I should've known."

"I'm shallow that way."

"Did Marco give you any insight that could help?" Alexis asked, as he stroked the underside of her wrist and made the hair on her arm stand on end. His fingers held indentations from holding down strings for hours.

"He has a suspect, and that's given me an idea about what the spells are trying to do. If you come down-stairs, I'll tell you," Penelope said, the reckless wanting of him from the night before creeping over her the longer he touched her. "As much as I love your playing, I need your brain more."

"So, it was my brain that lured you back," he said teasingly.

"The rest of you isn't so bad either," she replied as her pulse pounded in her throat. "But your brain is what I need most right now." *Lies.* She wanted to kiss the sweat off the back of his neck just to know what it tasted like.

Alexis pressed his lips to the inside of her wrist, and she fought not to tremble.

"Very well, I'll be down shortly. I'm starving," Alexis said, releasing her.

"I'll be in the kitchen…eating," she mumbled, watching him walk to the shower. *Oh God don't think about Alexis in the shower.* Penelope bolted.

Outside the door, she congratulated her iron willpower and hoped like hell that Zo's pancakes were worth turning her back on Alexis wet and naked.

It wasn't until she was back downstairs watching Zo beat a dozen eggs that Penelope reconnected to reality, the music and the need to crush Alexis's body to hers finally leaving her mind.

"That was embarrassingly quick," he said, looking up from his mixing bowl. "You don't look even a little bit tousled."

Penelope shrugged, taking an apricot from the fruit bowl on the bench. She sat down on a stool and watched him move about the kitchen with ease. "I convinced him with words, and he's hungry."

"Thank Zeus for silence," Phaidros said, sitting down beside her. "That music has my energy levels jangling all over the place. The only thing worse than Alexis's playing is Zo reciting poetry."

"Don't listen to him, Penelope. All the best poetry in the world is Zo's." Aelia appeared, her face fresh, and makeup reapplied as if the emotional mess on the stairs had never existed.

"Thank you, my princess," Zo said, kissing her cheek. "Your pancakes won't have spit in them, unlike the ones I'll give to Phaidros."

"Anything to make them taste better," Phaidros retorted.

"I know you supposedly wrote the *Inferno,* but what else?" asked Penelope, trying to get her mind off Alexis.

Zo dramatically slammed down his frying pan, announcing, "Forget youth! But know, the Power above, with ease can save each object of his love; Wide as his will, extends his boundless grace…"

"Homer!" Penelope interrupted, folding her arms. "You're just messing with me now. Next you'll tell me that you were Ovid as well."

"Fuck Ovid, the dirty *coglione*!" Zo shouted, making Penelope jump. "That son of a whore was no better than a thief who stole my lines and ideas…" he continued to rant in a spill of Greek and Latin curses that were so fast and complex, Penelope couldn't keep up with them. He was spouting the stories that had been stolen and the structural vision that had been pillaged until Alexis came in.

"Oh no, you mentioned Ovid, didn't you?" He came and stood behind her. "It was a terrible lover's quarrel. *Never* mention Ovid, or he'll never shut up." He had showered and smelled so fresh and good in his peacock blue shirt, Penelope wanted to hold him close just to breathe him in. *God, girl, you need to get your hormones checked. Men don't do this to you.*

Zo's rant halted when he saw Alexis, his verbal diatribe reverting back to poetry. "The great Odysseus, in his home again, had himself bathed and rubbed with oil and was fitted out in a beautiful cloak and tunic. Athene also played her part by enhancing his comeliness from head to foot…"

"*Stai zitto!*" Alexis rolled his eyes at him. "Hurry up and cook if you are going to cook."

"Where are the others?" Penelope asked as they each took a seat around the large wooden kitchen table, their plates stacked with pancakes.

"They will be in the Archives," Aelia said, handing her a bowl of fresh raspberries. "Galenos is Nereus's assistant for most things, and Lyca is still her guard."

"Nereus doesn't seem to be in danger amongst books," Penelope pointed out.

"Old habits die hard. Lyca has served Nereus her whole life," explained Alexis. "She never leaves her side unless Nereus has commanded her to. Despite her spryness, Nereus is far older than any of us and having someone care for her is no bad thing."

"Are you going to eat all the honey?" Phaidros complained as Aelia poured until her pancakes were almost swimming in it.

"What if I am?" she asked sweetly. "Don't pout. I saved you some." She handed the jug to him, licking her sticky fingers slowly. It was an innocent action, but he blushed around his ears all the same.

"I'm surprised you have any teeth left at all," he said, but without malice. Aelia smiled widely at him, the whiteness of her teeth an affront to her eating habits, and he laughed despite his complaining.

Penelope grinned to herself. Her family meals were such a quiet affair, both parents firmly engaged in whatever they were reading at the time, that to be around playful, squabbling magicians was unusually nice. The normality ended when Zo floated over a fresh pot of coffee, which started to refill everyone's cups.

"If you need to see Nereus, I'll take you to the Archives after you eat," Alexis said to Penelope over the chatter of the others. "She and Galenos have been working nonstop. They are going to know what the walls say."

"Good because I think we are going to have another murder in the next few days."

"I've been thinking about that as well," Alexis said, and something in his tone made the rowdy magicians stop talking. "I summoned you three here for your safety, but also to help."

"What do you need, Defender?" Aelia asked, her expression serious.

"I want you to go out into the city and try and find any traces of magic that are not our own. The *polizia* will be working on the murder sites still, but get as close as you can and see if you can feel out any magical trace leading away. Our killer must be hiding in the city, and if the Demon isn't the one tutoring him, then he'll have a master."

"I can take Santa Croce, and Zo and Aelia can head across to San Michele—" Phaidros began, but Alexis interrupted him.

"No. You all go together. You have different skills and different magic, and what one might not see, the others will."

"I don't need bodyguards. The boys can head to one, and I'll go to the other. We'll cover more ground that way," Aelia said.

"It's not about that. We don't know how many allies the Acolyte has or if he's the only one with magic. Go together. Don't fight me on this." There was a command in his voice that made all of them, including Penelope, sit up straighter. The magician had changed to the general in the blink of an eye.

Penelope and Alexis left Phaidros and Aelia arguing over doing dishes, slipping away to the elevator that appeared in the wall. Penelope's pulse jumped as the doors slid shut behind them locking her in with Alexis.

As the elevator began to pass through the open sea, Alexis pushed the stop button, pressed Penelope up against the glass, and kissed her. All of the churned-up feelings she had that morning vanished, along with her doubts about pursuing a more personal relationship with him. When Alexis kissed her, she felt it with every part of her, and in that moment, she knew she was done for. Just when she felt like she could take no more, he broke off the embrace.

"I've been waiting for that good-morning kiss since dawn," he admitted, his breath warm against her lips. "You sure know how to make a man wait."

Penelope could taste the lemon and sugar he had on his pancakes, and combined with his cinnamon scent, she could've eaten him alive. Penelope gripped the front of his shirt, pulling him back to her lips, and kissing him long and hard as her hands snaked into his thick curls. She could hear the music of his cello again, humming through her and the connection that bound them.

"Good morning, Alexis," she said, as she reluctantly let him go.

"*Buon giorno, cara*," he replied, eyes filled with wickedness. "Time to work." He reached back and pressed the button to get the elevator moving again.

Nereus eyed them suspiciously as they exited the elevator slightly more ruffled than what they went in.

"Took your time. Something wrong with the elevator?" Nereus asked, eyeing them suspiciously.

"Not that I noticed," Penelope replied innocently. "I had a meeting with Marco this morning, and I have a theory." They headed back to Nereus's lab where the projections of the murders still stood in all of their gory detail.

"Penelope! Nereus and I have translated—" Galenos started, but Nereus held up a hand to stop him.

"She already has a theory; I want to see how accurate she is. Go ahead, Penelope."

"Marco has narrowed down the killer to a potential follower of this guy Tony Duilio." Penelope passed

Nereus her phone, the screen showing the smiling millionaire. "He wanted the commission to turn Venice into one of his floating cities. Instead, they went with MOSE. He and his followers have caused several protests and a lot of social media noise, especially in the last month."

"I remember the controversy he made at the time," Alexis said thoughtfully.

"Duilio believes that the MOSE is a haphazard approach that will ultimately fail as the seas continue to rise," Penelope went on. "His floating resorts are anchored with a complicated cabling system that could be lengthened over time to counteract the rising sea level. I believe one of his followers is trying to use dark magic to cause some kind of event, like a tidal wave, to overload the MOSE barriers and sink Venice, proving Duilio's theory right all along."

"My, my, what an excellent theory," Nereus said, handing back the phone. "I don't know about Duilio's exact motives, but the magic aligns with a sea-based disaster." She snapped her fingers and lines of pale blue text appeared over the top of the graffitied walls of the murder scene. Penelope rushed over to them, her fingers scanning the lines.

"Wow, this guy is *pazzo*." She twirled her finger at her temple. "I *knew* it was a petition to Poseidon."

"And a threat," Nereus agreed. "There is a part about Thevetat using his demon fire to heat the waters and kill all of Poseidon's sea life if he doesn't comply with this one request. Having the sacrifice on San

Michele drew on the power of the dead, strengthening the spell."

"'I offer you this stallion, one who will like it as you ride him hard and deep,'" Penelope quoted. "What a pervert. He sounds like a ranting troll."

"Thevetat always did attract the broken and sick-minded." Alexis shook his head. "I hate that they are back again. How could we have become so complacent after last time?"

"You can't blame yourself," Nereus said. "You are not in charge of his influences."

"How did you defeat them before?" Penelope asked.

"We didn't. Atlantis burned and sank into the bloody ocean," Nereus snapped. "Haven't you told her any of this, Alexis?"

Alexis gave his trademark, Italian shrug. "Some."

"Tell her or I will. Just because you have eternity doesn't mean she does. Doctor Bryne, stop giggling. It's unprofessional."

"I'm not giggling," she said, swallowing her smile. "I just love how you tell him off."

"If I didn't, nothing would get done." Nereus pulled down her waistcoat primly. "I will get this printed out for you, Alexis, so you can send it on to Marco Dandolo. I'm going to keep her here with me today." Alexis hesitated, but when Nereus raised a silver brow at him, he bowed and followed Galenos out of the lab.

"You need to teach me how to do that," Penelope said after they had left.

"I'm quite sure you could get Alexis to do whatever you asked if you put your mind to it," Nereus replied as she opened the casings of a long, bronze and silver tube.

"What's that?" Penelope asked, leaning in for a closer look.

"This used to be one of the sacred temple texts on Atlantis." Nereus removed the thick scroll using its bronze ends, whispering a complex series of words under her breath. As she began to unroll it, Penelope could barely contain her excitement. The edges had been illuminated with gold and indigo in intricate geometric patterns. The script in the neat center columns moved, twisting in various illustrations and back again, revealing maps of cities, star charts, gods rising from the oceans, and galloping stallions.

"Alexis will tell you how we ended, so I'll tell you a little of our world before it was dragged into the sea." Nereus touched her finger to a rotating map, bringing it forward. "This is where our beautiful continent once resided. The humans call it the Cyclades Plateau. Yes, you were right about that, Penelope. This is why it was hardly a coincidence that the great tides pushed Alexis's Tablet onto the shores of Crete.

"Most of the Greek mythology had their roots in Atlantis's rich black soils. Their Olympus, land of the gods, was inspired by their ancient memories of us, and was spurred on by Phaidros and Zotikos who spent so much time amongst them."

Penelope gazed at the separation of the ten king-doms that covered the island and the different terrains each one had.

"Poseidon was our founder, and we paid homage to him, as we did Oceanus of the Titans before him. Pose-idon was a great magician, and to people today, as then, he did have god-like powers over water and the seas. His sons were the first rulers of the ten countries of Atlan-tis, with Atlas as their high king. Whether Poseidon still has any authority over the seas, as Thevetat seems to begrudgingly assume, is a metaphysical debate for another time. You'll have time to search our history fur-ther, Penelope, but this, in particular, is what I wanted to show you."

Nereus summoned one of the kingdoms to her. It had mountainous ranges that led out into the sea.

"Are they volcanos?" Penelope asked. She desper-ately wanted to touch the images, but after burning her hand, she knew better.

"Yes, though they were dormant. At the time of Atlantis's destruction, a king named Kreios ruled here. It was because of him and a high priest named Abad-don that the worship of Thevetat emerged."

Nereus sat down on one of the stools at the work-station. She looked surprisingly tired as she played with the glass vial pendant on her necklace. "Alexis told me you saw him at the Temple as a young man?"

"Yes, though only briefly," Penelope replied, remem-bering the way the gold paint shimmered on his skin.

"Every seven years, the best and brightest of our youths came to the capital, to the temple of Poseidon to be assessed. I was Matriarch of the Magicians Guild at the time, Abaddon was the High Priest of Poseidon. We were rivals in the political sense. Faith and magic have always been separate studies, despite their many crossings. Our biggest and most public argument happened over Alexis."

Penelope smiled. "That doesn't surprise me in the slightest."

"We both wanted him. Abaddon saw a raw power that could be molded in accordance with his design, and he was moved by the petition written so eloquently on the Tablet. Even then Alexis had such a gift for words; the Living Language responded to him without training. I wanted to foster his talents, let them grow and expand without being confined to the rigidity of religion," Nereus said, her tone growing hot at the memory. "In the end, Alexis chose us, and Abaddon was forever bitter about it. The Council of Kings and Abaddon never got along either, and after one too many interferences and abuses of power, they sent him to the far side of Atlantis with Kreios to oversee the construction of his new temple."

"If he loved Poseidon so much, how did he turn to the worship of a demon?"

"I'm not sure. All I know is that Kreios always meddled with darker magic, the kind restricted by the guilds. Abaddon wanted power. It has always been his true god. Together they unleashed something that had been hidden since the creation of the worlds."

"Thevetat. They were the ones who set him free."

"Yes. Whether they excavated too close to the volcanoes where he was trapped, or they used blood magic to summon him from whatever hell-plane he was living on, we'll never know. All I know is that Abaddon renounced Poseidon and became Thevetat's high priest. I thought the Demon and his influence had been destroyed when Atlantis sank, but I was wrong."

"Do you think humans, after reading Blavatsky's tales of Thevetat, could have tried to summon him again?" said Penelope. "They may have done it differently to Abaddon and Kreios, but could it have worked?"

"Anything is possible, Penelope. Just look at your destiny knot with Alexis. Ten thousand years apart and yet there it is." Nereus waved a hand over Penelope's chest, and a braid of light appeared.

Penelope stumbled backward. "God, I've never seen it outside of a meditation like this."

"But you can feel it, can't you?"

"Yes, always. The more time I spend near him, the stronger I feel it, like a phantom limb." She wanted to touch its silvery strands, but she didn't want to risk Alexis feeling her exploration.

"That's exactly the way he describes it too; a phantom limb he can't scratch because you will feel it."

Penelope paused for a long moment before she asked, "Do you think this knot can cause strong feelings for the person you are tied to?"

"Not necessarily. Most destiny knots are barely noticeable. Yours is unique, but if you are asking if it's why you and Alexis are circling each other like prowling lions, then no. It's not how they work. You are feeling that way because of how you and Alexis are. He pulled you back from the very jaws of death, you turned up in his heavily warded tower...it's not just destiny at work, it's you as well. You've been intriguing him for years, and he's always been a bit sweet on you, whether he'd admit it or not."

"So everyone keeps telling me. I don't know what Alexis finds so interesting."

"When he came back from Australia, and you were still alive, that's how we all knew he was soft on you," Nereus said, with strange fondness in her expression.

"Do you think he would've killed me?"

"Why do you think no major search for Atlantis has ever happened? Don't think of spiritualists or the mythologists. I mean, an actual archaeological search."

"Because there have never been historically reliable texts that prove it was more than a story."

"Oh, there was. They are upstairs in his Atlantis room. Any scholar who became seriously interested met with an untimely end."

"He killed them all?"

"He defends us and our secrets," Nereus said sternly. "He never enjoyed doing it, but he still did it. You were the closest to Atlantis, but he couldn't kill you, so he sabotaged you. We knew you had to be something rare to stay his hand. Can you live with that knowledge and still feel the same way about him?"

Penelope knew he could kill, she had seen him do it, and he had never tried to hide it from her. She understood his reasons for it. The music of his soul was still in her ears, humming in her very cells.

"It doesn't change how I feel about him," she answered as a fierce protectiveness welled up within her. "This house, this knowledge, it cannot be left to humans. As for the magicians, they would be dissected, experimented on, studied ruthlessly. There are a lot of good people in this world, Nereus, but even I wouldn't trust them with Alexis. I barely trust myself."

"Thank you, I needed to hear it. He's still the most unique magician I've ever seen, and those who are unique in this world are often the most alone. You would know something about that I imagine." Nereus took Penelope's hands and gripped them. "Don't be afraid of it, girl. Don't measure this connection by normal human conventions. He makes your soul sing, I can hear it in your aura, your music and his." Nereus closed her eyes, swaying gently to a silent orchestra. "Protect him, Penelope. Whatever happens, protect him."

FIFTEEN

AFTER AN EVENING meal with the rowdy magicians, Penelope followed Alexis through the courtyard and into the gardens. They walked along the terra-cotta tile path until they came to a stretch of grass that looked out over the lagoon. Tall lanterns stood in the lapping waters beneath the retaining wall, warning boats of the shallow waters and guiding them into the canals. On the grass, rugs woven in reds, oranges, and earthy browns were stretched out around a large cast-iron brazier.

"Have you stolen the weather again?" Penelope asked as she sat down on one of the flat Turkish floor cushions.

"A night from Istanbul, eight years ago. I felt like being outside. Despite the size of the palazzo, magicians are loud and intrusive even when they aren't saying anything," Alexis said, sitting down beside her. He wore another of his elaborately embroidered *entari* robes made of finely woven burgundy wool. With the firelight warming his ruffled black curls and dark face, he looked like he had stepped out of an Arabian Nights fable. Dressed in black leggings, motorcycle boots, and a khaki knit jumper, Penelope felt starkly modern and aesthetically lacking in the setting.

"I saw Phaidros tentatively asking Aelia if she would play the piano for him—that's a good sign, right?" Penelope asked as she stretched out.

"That's a miracle of the old gods and the new," Alexis replied, shaking his head. "Maybe they are finally giving up on their bickering."

"And by bickering, you mean their intense sexual frustration manifesting as arguments."

"That's exactly what I mean, although if they copulate on my favorite pianoforte, I won't be impressed."

Penelope laughed. "Maybe we need to put up 'respect the antiques' signs."

"I'd sacrifice a piano if it stops them fighting with each other."

"Did you send Nereus's translations to Marco?" Penelope asked, changing the subject so her mind didn't start wandering to places it shouldn't go.

"I did. Marco was disappointed that you didn't deliver it in person. He also gave me veiled threats about using you for my playboy satisfaction and casting you aside once I've had my fill of you."

"He didn't." Penelope was going to throttle Marco with her bare hands.

"He did," Alexis said, moving closer to her. "His exact words in English, without the profanity, were 'watch what forbidden fruit you taste, Alexis Donato, even though the taste is sweet. Once you have glutted yourself, be careful not to leave such a tree bare.'"

Penelope's face warmed. "How poetic of him. And what was your reply?"

Alexis's long, calloused fingers brushed her jaw-line as he brought his face closer. "I said that the fruit, when not forbidden, but offered freely,"—he kissed her chastely—"is the *sweetest* fruit of all. And,"—he kissed her again—"that I have no intention of stripping the tree bare when I leave it, as I have no intention of leaving it at all." He sat back, taking his warm hands and lips with him.

"I bet that response pleased him."

"Marco told me he would gut me and toss me into one of the canals," Alexis said, and Penelope broke into laughter.

She propped her head on the pillows, curling her body so she could watch him. He stared in the flames of the brazier, eyes lost. Her laughter died.

"What's wrong?"

"I have to tell you a story, but it's the one I hate the most."

She reached out and took his hand, brushing her fingers over the bronze and antique silver rings with their strange markings, the bloodstones reflecting red and green in the light. "If it's going to cause you pain, don't tell it."

"You deserve to know, and Nereus will make my life miserable if I don't. Ten thousand years and I'm still her student, unable to deny her requests. You are much like her; I find I can't deny your curiosity either."

"You denied my curiosity for the last decade. You knew I was hunting Atlantis and purposely hid from me," she replied, twining her fingers with his. He looked down at her, surprised. "Zo told me you read my uni assignment when I was an undergraduate."

"*Bastardo*! Can you see why I've been so busy all of these years? He never shuts up."

"I'm sure he thought I would find it charming, as opposed to humiliating."

"It wasn't a bad essay. Even then I knew you were going to make trouble for me."

"I haven't even begun to make trouble for you, Alexis Donato."

"Be careful, I don't want you unknowingly manifesting it. I've already had to save you from death once, *cara*. I don't relish the thought of having to do it again." He stretched out and propped his head up on a cushion. "Now, let me tell you how we came to be the seven orphan magicians."

"NEREUS TOLD you how Abaddon went to Kreios to oversee the building of the new temple. I was still only an apprentice when we received news from a magician living in Kreios's capital city that Abaddon had a revelation and was now following a new god.

"The magician, Helios, was disturbed by this. Kreios was now dedicating his new temple to a god called Thevetat and not Poseidon. He also wrote to Nereus about a growing darkness within the country's borders, describing it as the beginning of an eclipse. The High Temple in Atlas discredited Abaddon and voted in a new High Priest, dismissing the new god and his cult as ridiculous and heretical.

"Despite the opposition, Thevetat's followers grew until less than a year later, Kreios declared that all of his citizens renounce Poseidon for Thevetat. Abaddon had always hated magicians, but Kreios finally gave him the power to do what he wished with them."

The hand that still rested in Penelope's trembled slightly, and she tightened her fingers around his.

"I won't go into the details with you, but I will say that they used any means they felt they needed to carry out their experiments. They wanted our magic; to understand where it came from, how it worked. They wouldn't believe that magic could be a Divine gift or something that hard work could achieve. Once they felt a magician had nothing left to give them, they sacrificed them to their demon god. They learned how to steal magic within the sacrifice."

Alexis's expression darkened as he stared out across the water. "When I saw the Bull on the wall of your hotel, it was like being back in those times; nightmares made real. Once news of the killing of magicians spread, retribution was sought. Instead of submitting themselves to the High King's justice, Kreios and Abaddon started a civil war, breaking away from the laws of Atlantis that Poseidon and his sons had established.

"Their war had only one true purpose: convert or kill. Thevetat's warrior-priests were sent after magicians. The magicians began to use battle magic so they could fight back. It became compulsory to be proficient in weapons and warfare and to use your power to enhance your ability to defend yourself and others."

Penelope couldn't imagine what magic could do to a human body if it was used maliciously. She had seen Nereus heal her own fatal knife wound and she had no doubt that she had the power to harm just as easily.

"I hated it. Magicians had always been scholars, innovators, healers, and advisors; now we had to use our gifts for this horrible purpose. Nereus tried to warn the High King that the magical balance of Atlantis was becoming unstable and that it would have consequences. Apart from magicians, no one could see the magical threat, but they saw the destruction the war was causing.

"For seven years, Atlantis tore itself apart, piece by piece. Zotikos, Phaidros, and I worked together as spies for Nereus. We took no country's side, only that of magicians. Our goal was to rescue as many as possible. The day our world decided to erupt, we were on a mission. Galenos, Nereus, and Lyca had heard that the princess and high priestess of Poseidon was being held in a camp on the borders of Atlas and Kreios's kingdoms."

"The princess—Aelia?" Penelope asked.

"Yes, Aelia. In the time before the war, Phaidros had been terribly in love with her, but due to her position and possibly her father's plans for her, Aelia had rejected him. She was still our princess. We knew what Thevetat's priests liked to do to women, especially those with magic."

Alexis looked at his hands and ran them through his hair. Penelope could feel his anxiety and pain through their knot.

She rested her hand on his. "Alexis, don't continue if it's going to upset you."

"I want to *show* you that night, so you know what we are up against if Thevetat's worshippers rise again," he said, lifting her hand to his bearded cheek, "but I'm worried it will frighten you away. It's a horrific memory and…"

"Alexis, look at me." Penelope moved close to him. There was a frustrated helplessness in his eyes that seemed completely alien in someone usually so confident. "Can you feel the *moira desmós* between us?"

"Yes."

"You said our fate is tied. That means not just future; it is past and present as well. I'm strong enough to see it because you were. And I know you'll help me to understand. So show me. I want to see."

Alexis rested his forehead against hers. "Thank you for trusting me. Whatever you see, know that it can't hurt you." His hands tightened on hers and magic crackled around them. Penelope held onto him as they dropped into Hell.

PENELOPE WAS standing on the rocky shore by a sea. Zo, Phaidros, and Alexis moved in front of her, dressed in leather and steel breastplates with pauldrons over their shoulders.

"I can smell the camps from here," Zo said as they hit the tree line.

"Stay focused, the princess is a priority," Phaidros hissed, a bow ready in his hands. Beneath them, the earth trembled, and they stilled.

Alexis's eyes went dark and feral as he drew a curved blade. "We need to move quickly and kill the priests. The magic in this place is about to shatter."

The memory moved, and they were climbing through a fence into a prisoner-of-war camp. Phaidros's hand glowed as fire rose from his fingertips.

Alexis was shadows and death. Penelope moved with him as he cut through guards and priests with detached ferocity. Zo followed closely behind him, breaking locks on cages that held other magic-users and prisoners.

"The southern fence is down," he instructed. "Get moving! Get to the ocean!"

Alexis stilled his attack as the world took a giant breath and the mountain above them exploded, spewing clouds of ash.

"We need to go!" he shouted to Zo and Phaidros. "Break the last of the locks and get these people out of here."

"I'm not leaving without Aelia!" Phaidros glowed with magic, shining despite the ash and blood covering him.

"She isn't here," Alexis said. "We've searched the buildings. They must have moved her."

"No! She is here. I can *feel* her, Alexis. I can sense her magic."

Alexis, blood-splattered and furious, glared the other magician down.

"If it were you, I'd do the same," Phaidros said.

"Poseidon drown you," Alexis cursed. "Zo! Take these people and get out of here. Get to Nereus. Wait for us."

"Alexis, this volcano is going to blow! If Kreios and Abaddon are still here, they will be in the temple at the base of that thing. What use is finding Aelia if you all die trying to escape?" Zo tried to argue.

"Just do as I say!" Alexis commanded, and Zo ran to obey. Alexis held his hand out to Phaidros. "Hold on. We can't waste any more time."

"Thank you, Alexis. I owe you for this."

"Let's survive first, then we can discuss debts." Alexis drew his magic around him and they portaled, reappearing at a marble entranceway.

"Be on your guard. We don't know how many priests are lurking."

"You're right. You should definitely go first," Phaidros said. He knocked an arrow into his bow and gestured at Alexis.

"Unbelievable," Alexis muttered as he went through the door into the mountain.

It was hot inside, the steam heavy with the smell of blood. They found the tunnel leading to the sacrificial areas and Penelope fought not to cover her eyes.

Every few feet was an alcove, and inside of it, a body displayed in a horrific tableau.

"Madness." Alexis's face hardened until it became something Penelope didn't recognize.

"Alexis, some of these people are…they are…"

"Still alive," he answered. He turned on Phaidros, gripping his face. "We are here for Aelia. We can't rescue these people, but you can help them."

"Don't ask it of me, Alexis…"

"You said you owed me. I'm claiming it now. Put them out of their pain." Alexis released him and brought his blade down on a priest who was rushing toward them. "Do it! I'll hold them off."

Phaidros began to glow gold as he pulled the remaining life from the sacrifices around him, and Alexis fought his way through the attacking priests.

Penelope covered her mouth with her hands in awe and horror. She never thought anybody could move as he did. He was death personified as he used his magic and blade to tear them apart. He was indestructible rage. He was justice.

"Let's move, Phaidros!" Alexis shouted as the last priest fell.

"I can feel Aelia's magic spiking. They are trying to rip it from her." Phaidros pushed passed Alexis, taking another tunnel to their right. With each step, it grew hotter and darker.

"There," Phaidros hissed and released his arrows. Two men were standing by an altar in a cavern of rock and fire. The naked body of a woman was strapped down and bleeding. Phaidros's arrows fell from the air as they collided with an invisible barrier.

"You are too late, Defender." A priest with gray hair and a long beard turned to them. His eyes glowed red with magic. "Our master is coming."

"You've doomed us all, Abaddon," Alexis said, raising his sword. "The magic of Atlantis is breaking."

"Yes, and a new power will rise in its place." The second man lifted two blades from the altar stone and smiled maliciously. He was a big man, almost as tall as Alexis, with a long braid of black hair and black eyes.

"You're a fool to follow him, Kreios," said Alexis, his body starting to hum with power. "If you kill Atlantis's magic, there will be nothing left to build upon."

"Thevetat will make sure that there is," Kreios replied as he advanced on them. "I've been waiting for a chance to kill you, Alexis."

Alexis moved, disappearing and reappearing to clash his sword against Kreios's long knives. The ground beneath him shook, and the earth split between them. Abaddon reached out for Kreios, and they disappeared in a hiss of ash and smoke.

Phaidros ducked around falling rock and reached the altar. "She's still alive!"

Alexis hurried to join him, cutting the leather ties that bound Aelia to the slab. "Phaidros, she's dead…" Aelia's beautiful body had been carved to pieces.

"No, she isn't! I can feel the life in her." Phaidros threw his cloak over her, wrapping her tightly and lifting her up, clutching her to his chest. Golden light shimmered under his skin as he fed his energy back into her body.

"Don't let her go," Alexis said as he hooked his arm around Phaidros's waist and the half-dead girl in his arms.

Alexis portaled them out as the cave roof collapsed above them. Out on the beach, Zo paced as small watercrafts filled with passengers launched into the bay.

"We need to get her to Nereus," Phaidros said urgently, and Zo helped them into the small rowboat that would take them out to Nereus's ship.

Alexis helped him launch the boat as the volcano behind them exploded, shooting red fire into the night sky.

PENELOPE CAME out of the memory with a gasp. Alexis held her shaking body as she struggled to reorient herself.

"It's okay, Penelope. I have you, I'm here," he said. She curled into him, fighting the images in her mind.

"Alexis…" What could she possibly say to ease a memory so old and full of pain?

"I know," he sighed, as if reading her mind. "I'll stop if it's too much."

"Just tell me. I don't want to see any more." A part of her hated that she was clinging to him like a frightened child, but she couldn't bring herself to let him go.

Alexis kissed the top of her head and continued. "We had no idea of the full-scale destruction. We only thought of getting away from the explosions. We watched for days as Atlantis sank into the waves and then...there was just nothing. The sea had taken it all."

Ten thousand years later and the shock and surprise of it, the magnitude of the event, was still fresh for him. She could tell by the traumatized look on Alexis's face, the ache in his voice. Penelope didn't say a word, too aware of the horror she would never understand or be able to comfort him over. There was no way to measure that level of loss or grief.

"We had supplies on the ship for the journey we had planned back to Atlas. We only thought about land. It didn't matter where. Phaidros and Nereus worked on Aelia for days to keep her alive and break the black magic of the spell Abaddon and Kreios had carved into her body. Six weeks later, we landed in Egypt."

"And Aelia lived and is so beautiful now," said Penelope, in awe of Nereus's healing skills.

"It took a long time for her to heal, and the wounds she had on her body were nothing compared to what was in her mind. She had magic as a priestess, but she wasn't one of us, not in the beginning. She had dedicated her life to a god that had left us to die. She hated that she lived, and resented Phaidros deeply for loving her so much when she was such a scarred and twisted thing. She wanted to die, and he refused to let her kill herself. The rest of us have done our best to love them both and not interfere. Even as the centuries passed and she moved through her pain, the things she has said to Phaidros, and him to her over the years…well, they both have much to forgive each other for."

Penelope shook her head. "No wonder you were happy they were going to play the piano. Do you think she loves him?"

"I think she has for a very long time, but both are so stubborn and bitter. Phaidros is worried what the appearance of Thevetat's followers after so long will do to her. They are both tiptoeing around each other, but that's better than the fighting."

"He's bribing her with music, it would seem." Penelope smiled.

"He's learned nearly every instrument on the planet, just in case she feels like hearing something."

"That's ridiculously romantic," replied Penelope, her heart aching from the sweetness of it. "You landed in Egypt, I should have guessed. Did anyone else make it who wasn't an immortal magician?"

"There were other ships in the harbor that night, but we lost them in the ash storms. For the next two hundred years we sought other survivors, but we never found any. If they were humans, they must've died long before we reached them. It's just…us. The magic makes us live such long lives compared to humans, but we are not immortal."

"Does that mean if you gave up the magic you would die?"

"I assume so. We would live out the years, age, and die like any mortal."

"And none of you considered doing it? Even after all this time?"

"We have all thought about it at some point," Alexis admitted. "But it wouldn't just be losing magic; it would be having to live without it. It's a vital part of who we are. It would be living a half-life…for what would a magician be without magic?"

"A boring academic like me," laughed Penelope.

"You are far from boring, Doctor Bryne." Alexis looked down at her, his eyes flecked with gold from the firelight. "If you were boring, you would never have found your way back to the palazzo. Your mind works differently from other humans. It fought the spell off out of sheer stubbornness."

"Let's just say, when I saw you in the tower in your epic robe, you made an impression. Tonight is another spectacular edition." Penelope touched the golden stitching of his sleeve. "Ottoman?"

"Egyptian. I had it made when I was living there in 1266 during the reign of the Mamluk sultan Baybars I al-Bunduqdārī," he said. "I had to put a preservation spell on it. They are similar to what we used to wear on Atlantis. Old habits, old comforts."

Penelope loosened her hold on him, relaxing enough to let her arms go, but still remaining close, their sides touching. "And how long were you a part of the Ottoman court?"

Alexis's eyebrows shot up in surprise. "What makes you ask?"

"Your thumb ring." Penelope reached over and twisted the wide band of antique gold, admiring its tiny ruby and emerald stones. "It is a zihgîr, an archer's thumb ring. Only a rich person in the court, one extremely skilled with a bow, would wear such a fine piece."

"You are incredibly observant. I thought you were a doctor of the Aegean." Alexis pulled the heavy band off and passed it to her. It was heavier than it looked, the soft metal still warm from his skin. She slipped it over her small thumb, twisting it so the colors of the stones would catch the firelight.

"Mediterranean and Aegean would probably be more accurate. You can't study Greek legends without inevitably getting caught up in the Egyptians, Byzantines, and Romans at the same time. I've tried to have a wide world view when it came to studying Atlantis." Penelope passed it back to him, too nervous that she might lose it. "So you spent most of your time in the East. Do you hold to a religion at all? Poseidon? Allah? The Christian God?"

"None. I've lived too long and seen gods rise and fall with zealots and holy men of every stripe." Alexis fixed his gaze out on the lights of the city. "If you are asking if I believe in something greater and indefinable that moves through the universe? Then yes, I do, but I wouldn't limit it by simply referring to it with a word as dull and simple as 'God.'"

"What would you call it then?"

He shrugged. "There is no word for it in any modern languages that would properly articulate it. I've walked the world, met with humans who held magic, talked and argued with the holy men of many faiths, and you know what they all had in common? The closer they came to understanding, the less they were inclined to put labels on it. It just *is*."

"Weirdly, I know what you mean. My dad was Irish Catholic but never passed the religion on to me; he felt it was too limiting. I've felt something though. Once." Penelope took a deep breath. She had only ever told Carolyn the story, but after revealing so much of his own personal history, Penelope felt compelled to do the same.

"I was diving in a shipwreck in the Bahamas, and I got trapped. My tank got caught on a fallen beam, and when I struggled, it collapsed onto my leg, trapping it against the reef." Penelope crossed her arms, trying not to let the memory of it overwhelm her.

"I was running out of air and was starting to think I was going to die. It could have been a lack of oxygen, but I began to feel like everything was going to be okay. I got this feeling that whatever I was born for hadn't happened yet, that I couldn't die until it did, and if I calmly waited, something would happen. And then this beam, I'm talking as thick as I am, this barnacle-encrusted thing that would've taken a crane to lift, floated just long enough for me to move my leg. I made it back to the dive boat, and it was nearly a year before I was game enough to go back in the water."

"When I got home, I told my friend Carolyn about it. She's into miracles, divine interventions, crystal healing, guides…everything is possible in her mind. She got me into meditation to try and ease my anxiety over the incident, and it's helped me a lot. I started taking lifeguard classes and slowly began diving again without having a panic attack halfway down. I don't know if it would be classed as a miracle, but I'll never forget it as long as I live."

Alexis smiled widely at her. "The miraculous happens all around us, all the time. Humans of this age hate anything they can't explain, so their mind glosses over it. I once knew a Sufi who could bend time, and it was no more miraculous to him than the sun rising every morning, and even the humans of that time dismissed it. There will always be those who will keep their eyes closed and remain willfully ignorant because the wonder demands too much of them. You're brave to have forced yourself back into the sea. Not many people would have done that."

"Well, I had a stone tablet to find." Penelope grinned. "So, the fairy tale that is Alexis Donato grows from Turkish corsair to Egyptian alchemist, to friend of holy men, to magical philosophizer."

"I have been many things, lived many places, and had many names, but I'm no fairy tale," he replied, leaning over to kiss her slow and soft.

He wound his fingers through her hair, gently touching her ears and neck. It sent shivers across her skin, but this was a time for comfort, not seduction.

"Thank you for telling me about Atlantis," Penelope said, touching his warm cheek. "I know none of this can be easy on you. I never meant to bring any of this to your door."

"You're not to blame. We are the only ones who'll be able to stop them if Thevetat's recruiting new priests to his cause. There is a magic here only magicians can defeat. The *polizia* would not stand a chance against someone with true power. Aelia, Phaidros, and Zo will accompany us to the Arsenale tomorrow night just to be sure that if priests turn up, we can stop them. My only concern is keeping you from their hands, and in mine."

"I'm pretty keen on you doing that too." Penelope bit her bottom lip. "And seeing you in a tux will be pretty great."

Alexis's expression turned devious. "Do you think a magician would wear something as mundane as a tuxedo to Carnevale?"

SIXTEEN

THE NEXT MORNING, Penelope woke early, grabbed an apple from the kitchen, and headed to the Archives. Penelope had fallen asleep by the fire, her head in Alexis's lap as he told her more tales. She had woken in her bed and had passed the night with surprisingly no nightmares.

Worry twisted inside of Penelope as she walked amongst the stacks. She stopped briefly in front of one of the pillars she had seen from the elevator. It was carved with smooth symbols, a golden glyph at the top identifying what section she was in. She reached out and traced her fingers over the smooth carvings, admiring their beauty. Somehow she knew Alexis had made them for Nereus.

Penelope wanted to touch the books, to pull one down and explore the contents but she was so overwhelmed by the choices that she couldn't decide what to pick first. Alexis's warning against touching magical objects also dampened her enthusiasm.

You are in the greatest archive in the world. Stop being such a chicken, Penelope.

She pulled down a thick manuscript with a tan leather cover. When nothing happened, she found one of the many study alcoves and placed it on a reading stand. Golden orbs of light gathered together to hover over her, covering her in light.

"Um, thank you," Penelope said, unsure if the orbs were as sentient as the rest of the palazzo.

The Archives know you love them, Nereus had told her, and maybe providing her with extra light was the Archives's way of proving that. She opened the book, and her hands came up, covering her mouth in surprise.

The pictures moved across the pages in brilliant color. Like the manuscript Nereus had shown her, each page was illuminated, the borders consisting of complex designs depicting life on the Nile River. *It must have been made after they arrived in Egypt.*

Sketches of people on boats tending crops along the Nile filled the pages. The picture moved again, and there were magicians and pyramids.

"No way," Penelope whispered. She turned the page, and the borders turned into the squat complex pictographs of the Mayans. Like the previous page, it seemed to record daily life; growing corn, hunting in the rainforest, and raising children. The magicians revealed themselves again, building pyramids, teaching the knowledge of the skies, aqueducts, and healing.

Every page she turned, the magicians were in a different land, recording their experiences with new cultures. Sudan, India, China, Australia, Turkey. Penelope didn't know how long she sat, mesmerized, until she was interrupted by a deep chuckle.

"How did I know I would find you hiding in a book?" Alexis asked, his hand moving through her hair to rest on her neck.

She smiled up at him. "You can't share a place filled with books with me and expect me not to touch anything. I've been learning about how the first pyramids were made."

"Ah, yes. Typical humans fixating on a good idea and copying it any way they can." Alexis turned the book to look at the shimmering pyramids. "After Atlantis was destroyed, we needed a way to balance out the great hole of magic and energy that was no longer there. The pyramids acted almost like a safety switch system. They helped the power flow the way it should until the world could adjust to the new rhythms. Humans liked them, and over time they forgot their original purpose and made up other uses for them."

"They just forgot?"

"Humans tend to reset themselves," Alexis struggled to explain. "Originally, Nereus thought it had something to do with the loss of Atlantis, but it seems to just be human instinct. Do you ever wonder why humans choose to keep themselves in a permanent state of ignorance? They will learn a great secret of the cosmos; Divinity, the universal consciousness, that the Earth and every living thing falls into a beautiful order, whatever it might be. They learn it, and then it is like the thought is too big, too terrifying, so what do they do? They build convoluted religions, adding barriers and restrictions and rules and concepts around the Truth. They bury the true idea until it's forgotten. But even more perplexing, every couple of generations they will remember the Truth they've fought so hard to forget. Take Atlantis, for example. Only the seven magicians survived. There was a time when Atlanteans traded with all the peoples and continents of the world. All of those people lived their lives and died. I've sought to hide certain information about Atlantis and the others have been extremely selective over the years on who they have told…"

"And?" Penelope interrupted.

"And every couple of generations, something strange happens. Something in the blood, and I have my theories about that, makes a buried Truth or memory be remembered. I believe this's happened with you and Atlantis. You've always known it existed, knew it like you knew the sky was blue. It was real. You had to find it. The memory resurfaced, and you couldn't let go of it and didn't know why."

"So what you're saying is that humans purposely forget anything that's too frightening or important? Why would they do that?"

"Do you ever wonder about the saying, 'It's like history repeating itself'? Why would that be? Why don't humans learn the first time? Or the millionth? Why don't people ever learn? If you can figure that out, you are doing far better than the rest of us." He looked at the pile of books she had been reading and frowned. "I didn't know you read hieratic."

"I don't read hieratic. I've always wanted to learn. Why did you think that?"

Alexis held out a manuscript to her. "This is hieratic."

Penelope scanned the pages, the dense black script messy but familiar. "No, that's English."

Alexis flicked through his journal and held up a page. "Can you read this?"

"It's a list of notes about Tony Duilio's floating city projects. Why?"

"Because it's written in Arabic."

Penelope looked at the page and back to him. "I swear, Alexis, I don't speak Arabic. What's happening? Is it the Archives?"

Alexis took her hand and light streaked down her forearm. He turned her palm over and studied the marks burnt into her skin from when she touched the Tablet.

"Strange," he murmured, turning her hand over again. "The magic from the Living Language still seems to be inside of you."

"I thought Nereus said it would go away. Should I be freaking out?" Penelope demanded, already freaking out.

"Are you in any pain?"

"No."

"Then I don't think it's cause for too much concern. It might be a blessing."

"How exactly?"

Alexis tapped the pile of books. "The magic of the trapped Living Language is automatically translating languages for you. It means there isn't a single thing in this Archive that you can't read."

"Is it permanent?"

"It could be. If you are worried, we could ask Nereus. It won't hurt you."

Penelope clutched at her head. "Magic translating language in my brain without me knowing. Okay, magician, my head is now melting."

"You are worried. Let's find Nereus so she can put your mind at ease." Alexis helped her to her feet.

"NOW THAT *is* interesting," Nereus said a little while later, after studying the burns on Penelope's palm. "I didn't think the magic of the Tablet was going to disappear in you." Words rose to Penelope's skin again, and Nereus smiled. "This is an excellent gift for the Living Language to give to you."

"How long do you think it will last?" Alexis asked.

"Tomorrow, forever, who knows?" said Nereus. She smiled at Penelope. "The Archives have given you the key to their heart, lucky girl."

"I don't know what to say," Penelope managed as she watched the glowing words on her arm fade once more. Her eyes drifted to her Phaistos Disc ring, and the small pictographs started to rearrange themselves. "Whoa. It's changing."

"Doctor Bryne, you are going to have an interesting time studying in the future," cackled Nereus. "You needn't look so worried. Everyone has the potential for magic, Penelope. It's whether or not they have the imagination, inclination, and tenacity to develop it. All of us use it in different ways. Yours is translating language, as is only fitting. Magic will always magnify what is already there, as you've seen with the others."

"What about you?" Penelope asked Alexis who had gone remarkably quiet.

"He's a multi like I am. It's why I fought to have him be a magician and not a priest," Nereus answered for him. "And he was far too good-looking to be shackled by celibacy."

"Multi? As in multidisciplinary?" Penelope guessed, struggling to keep a straight face as Alexis blushed vividly.

"Pure magic of infinite potential." Nereus looked at him proudly. "It means we don't get stuck in one way of using our magic. We can use it by thought and desire. We don't need words or music or any other prop; we think it, and we can make it so."

"That's a gross oversimplification," Alexis managed to say before Nereus cut him off.

"He was the only other one I found like me in all my years of searching." Nereus winked at her. "I simply *had* to have him."

I know the feeling, Nereus, Penelope thought. Alexis's cheekbones were still glowing red, his composure affected by his mentor's praise.

"You had better take her upstairs and get her something to eat, Alexis. She's looking pale, and she's got a big night ahead of her." Nereus hustled them out of her

lab, but Penelope felt her pale blue eyes studying her all
the way to the elevator.

AELIA WAS a Roman goddess, dripping with
gold. On her head, she wore a crown that stretched
out like the halo beams of the sun. Her dress was a styl-
ized breastplate with a kilt of bronzed leather. A cloak
made of a lion skin was wrapped around her shoulders. Penelope hoped it wasn't real fur, but Aelia looked
impressive, regardless. The *gladius* she wore on her hip
was definitely real.

"Alexis warned me about magicians and Carnevale," Penelope said, mouth hanging open. Aelia had
arrived at her room as soon as Penelope had showered.

"I wanted to make sure you didn't arrive in jeans,"
Aelia said primly.

"I was hoping you would have something to fit
me," Penelope said uncertainly.

"Have you checked your wardrobe? Alexis would've
made sure something was presentable in there if the
palazzo hasn't."

"Magic wardrobe. Right. I keep forgetting."

"Well, stop forgetting. You live in tights and jeans,
and that's not presentable for a party like this," Aelia
scolded and opened up the carved wardrobe door. "Athena be praised, Alexis has outdone himself."

"He hasn't even been here to see me, let alone hide
a dress."

"He doesn't need to come into your room to do it."
Aelia pulled out the dress and Penelope's heart stopped.
She had never considered herself someone who lost her
head over fashion, but the dress Aelia laid out on the
bed made Penelope want to squeal with delight.

"I don't think I know how to put that on," she
admitted, eyes wide. There were so many laces and ties
that her mind boggled just looking at it.

"It's okay, I'll help," Aelia said and held out a long
shift of aquamarine blue that tied at the front with
black ribbons. Fine black stitching decorated the neckline and hem in a plethora of magical protection symbols. As soon as Penelope slipped it over her head, she
felt a light hum along her body.

"Alexis is taking every precaution," mused Aelia.
"It's rather adorable to see him so worried about you."

The dress itself was a mixture of greens, blues, and
purples, as iridescent as a peacock's feather. Sea creatures, wild and fantastical, had been stitched in gold
over the silk taffeta. Tiny seed pearls lined the deep
V-shaped neckline to where the bodice laced at the
front, crisscrossing in a way that Penelope would have
never figured out without Aelia's assistance.

Each sleeve had to be laced firmly to ensure nothing came loose in the night. Aelia, who had lived in the
Renaissance, pulled, tied, and arranged each layer to
make everything sit perfectly.

"This is called a *saccoccia*," Aelia said, tying the
pocket around Penelope's waist, hiding the ties under
her bodice. "We are going to put this in it, just in

case." She produced from the wardrobe the distinctly curved shape of a small *koummya* dagger, sheathed in an engraved silver and bronze scabbard. "It will make both Alexis and I happier to know you have some kind of weapon on you."

Penelope rested a hand on her new pocket and felt the hilt of the dagger. After being tortured, experiencing that level of helplessness, she knew she never wanted to feel that again.

"I don't know if I have the personality to be able to pull all of this off," Penelope said softly, as Aelia began working on her hair.

"It's Carnevale. The whole point is that you can be someone or something that you are not. Nuns become whores, men become women, and aristocrats become beggars. It's a living fantasy that you can carry out however you wish."

"Faking it," Penelope said, breathing out slowly to steady her heartbeat.

"Or unleashing what's already there but hidden. Alexis knows the strength of your personality. He knows you will make the dress look *magnifico*. Like all magicians, he loves beautiful things. No matter how overdressed you feel, I can guarantee the men will be even more elaborate. Especially Phaidros, he'll be gaudier and more eye-catching than any decoration in the room."

"I can believe that. He's full of flirtatious bravado, but I think it's covering a sweeter side," observed Penelope. She couldn't shake the memory of Aelia carved and bleeding on a slab.

"He can be sweet when he wants to be, and a right asshole when he doesn't," Aelia replied as she slid gold and pearl pins into Penelope's dark hair. "He does play the piano lovely though, whatever his mood."

"There doesn't seem to be anything you aren't good at. I've always been criticized for being an overachiever, but you all make me look like a dunce."

"We've had thousands of years to get good at the things we love. We have to occupy our time somehow, and magicians are naturally voracious in their need to know more. If you would've been born on Atlantis, I've no doubt you would have been a magician. You have that same hungry curiosity. It's one of the things that draws Alexis to you. You both would get lost in the Archives for days, finally find each other and tell the other everything you had learned, have sex on a study table, and then disappear amongst the stacks again."

Penelope couldn't hold in a wave of embarrassed laughter; the image Aelia had painted was a vivid one. "Probably. I don't know about the sex, but definitely all the rest."

"There would definitely be sex," Aelia said decisively. "It's oozing off the two of you whenever you are in the same room together. I swear if Alexis doesn't make love to you soon, Phaidros will try hugging your leg like a dog to ease some of the frustrated energy you are generating."

"Sadly, for Phaidros, he's not my type."

"When he wants someone, Phaidros is everyone's type."

"Even yours?"

Aelia's hands paused. "Especially mine."

"And you two never have…"

"He doesn't want me that way. Not anymore. We have a complicated past; the best we can hope for these days is a careful friendship."

It was a sore spot, so Penelope changed the subject. "Are they going to meet us at the Arsenale?"

"Yes, they wanted to check out all of the grounds before we arrive. Lyca will escort us to them before returning to Nereus. I know I'm not like Alexis or Lyca, but I want you to know I'm skilled with a sword and can protect us. If there is trouble, you need to stay close to me while Lyca handles it, and if she doesn't, I will. Do you understand?"

"I'll stay with you, I promise."

"Good! Now, let's get started on your makeup and jewelry."

It took more time to dress that evening than any other formal occasion Penelope could remember. Finally, when she had the chance to look at herself in a full-length gilt-framed mirror, she was shocked at the transformation.

A strangely dressed, beautiful creature stood before her, looking like a Renaissance sea witch. Aelia had done her eye makeup with elaborate green, purple, and gold eye shadow, blending the colors in a way that reminded Penelope of psychedelic beetle shells.

The shoes were something Marie Antoinette would've loved; they were elegant, heeled, and made of aqua and purple leather, stamped with shell patterns.

"The final touch," Aelia said, handing her a gold and silver mask. It was a half mask that left her lips free. It was a delicate thing, like golden lace that fit perfectly over her nose and cheeks. The edges dripped and curled in all directions like the spikes of a murex shell.

"You look incredible," Lyca said approvingly when Penelope went downstairs.

"Thank you, I'm really nervous." Penelope smoothed the skirt of her dress with her damp palm.

"Don't be," was all the encouragement Lyca gave. "Come on, we need to meet your *Inspecttori*."

SEVENTEEN

MARCO HAD INSISTED on meeting them at the palazzo as an escort, but with the blue and gold front door disappearing at the slightest provocation, Penelope had to convince him to meet them with a police boat at their dock on the Grand Canal.

Marco looked very suave in his all-black tuxedo but somehow still like a police officer at the same time.

To Aelia's delight, Marco crossed himself when he spotted them moving toward him.

He smiled brilliantly. "*Dottore*, I barely recognized you. You're embracing Carnevale like a Venetian."

"Marco, these are my friends, Aelia and Lyca."

"*Buona sera*," Aelia purred from behind her golden mask as she moved to kiss both of his blushing cheeks. "Penelope has told me so much about you, Inspector Dandolo. Such a noble Venetian name."

"Lady Time still hasn't been able to rid the city of us just yet, *signora*," he said, offering her a hand into the boat.

"*Grazie mille*." She wrapped her fingers around his and smiled coyly. "And it is *signorina, per favore*." His blush grew deeper before he turned to offer a hand to Lyca, but she was already in the back of the boat, checking every inch of it.

Penelope's elaborate dress had made it impossible to step down herself but Marco, as a true Venetian, wasn't bothered by the inconvenience in the slightest.

"Lyca is part of Alexis's private security, isn't she?" he whispered to Penelope as he physically lifted her up, skirts and all, and placed her on the deck.

"Yes, and she's the best. Lyca could kill a god if she were asked to," Aelia said, smiling with her blood-red lips, the only color on her that wasn't metallic. Marco gave a nod of approval before maneuvering the boat into the packed waterway.

It was a cold night, but Penelope didn't feel it under the layers of fabric and shielded by the cape and hood that Aelia insisted she wear to protect her hairstyle from the wind. In contrast, the more tousled Aelia's hair became, the more wildly gorgeous she looked. Marco was visibly struggling to look anywhere else.

"Stop flirting, Aelia. He's only mortal, and if he crashes this boat before I see Alexis tonight, I'll blame you," Penelope whispered tersely.

Aelia pouted. "It's Carnevale, and you are forbidding me to flirt? It's not going to happen. Besides, I have a weakness for Dandolos and this one is a particularly delicious throwback to a more heroic time."

"He has enough to worry about tonight and so do you," Lyca said, her voice cutting sharply through the roar of the engines.

"I'd definitely give him something to worry about." Aelia laughed.

The police boat was allowed to dock at a small jetty at the Torre dell Arsenale, and a uniformed officer jumped in to relieve Marco. He stared openly at the women who got out, but Marco gave him sharp instructions, and his young face became serious once more. Marco produced a traditional black leather *bauta* mask and Aelia tied it firmly into place for him.

"We have nearly fifty officers patrolling the grounds," he told Penelope as they walked along the wide concrete paths. "Bianchi called in some favors, so we have DIGOS here tonight too. They will ensure nothing happens, Penelope, especially to you."

"Thank you, Marco. I'm sure if it does there will be enough people here to stop them. Did you confirm that Tony Duilio is on the guest list?" asked Penelope.

"He is, and he's been attending as many functions as he can while stirring up discontent," Marco confirmed.

People crowded the walkways, some dressed even more intricately than Penelope, and she felt a buzz of excitement despite the business of the night. The closer they came to the main building, the more performers and sellers were spread out on the grounds. It was like an outdoor market of the fantastical, beautiful, grotesque, and bizarre. There were carts selling warm spiced nuts, gelato, thick hot chocolate, wine, and paper cups of deep-fried shrimp and tiny octopuses.

They had only just been ushered through the doors of the party when Penelope felt a little pull inside of her chest. Lyca had vanished the moment they entered the building, but Aelia stayed close beside her, keeping the crush of people away from her.

"I need to find Alexis," Penelope said to Aelia over the thrum of the music.

"Give it a moment, and he'll find you," she said, her violet eyes sparkling. She slipped her arm around Marco's, saying something in Italian that made the inspector laugh loudly.

Penelope looked around her, trying to spot Alexis's tall build over the colorful crowd. She tried to focus on their knot, giving it a slow, mental stroke. She felt a shiver of desire roll back to her and couldn't hold in her smile.

Isn't that interesting?

Penelope stood still as the crowd streamed around her, and very purposely touched the connection again, her mind conjuring the thrumming tingles he had caused when realigning her chakras.

"If you do that again, Penelope Bryne, I'll throw you over my shoulder and carry you out of here," a warm voice threatened from over her right shoulder. "Although now that I see you, I'm tempted to do that anyway."

As she turned to face Alexis, the laughter died on her lips. He wore a Sherwani style jacket of turquoise and purple silk, heavily embroidered with the same creatures and symbols as her dress. The high collar was decorated with tiny pearls in intricate designs. Slimly tailored sea-green trousers disappeared into leather boots. His mask was a masculine version of hers, vividly gold against his black curls. His eyes had been lined with black kohl and glowed with a dark blue fire. He bowed before taking her hand and kissing her knuckles.

"Fuck," was all she could manage.

"I'll take that as a compliment. *La mia bella donna*," he said. He looked her up and down in a way that made heat flare up her spine. "You look outstanding."

"You did warn me that magicians didn't know how to dress mundanely to Carnevale," she said, tilting her head back as he drew her closer. Their lips were almost touching when someone exclaimed, "There you two are! I've been looking all over."

"I'm going to kill him," Alexis rumbled in the back of his throat as Phaidros joined them.

"Later," Penelope whispered. "Jesus, Phaidros. Between you and Aelia, there must be no gold left in all of Venice."

"Why? Is she copying my style again?" the magician asked. "Sol Invictus is a man!" He was dressed in gold from the sunburst crown on the top of his head to the laced-up boots at his feet. He looked like he had wandered out of a Roman orgy with a toga and cape. Like Aelia, he wore elaborate gold and black makeup.

Penelope laughed. "You have dressed to match each other without even realizing it."

"The palazzo produced this costume, and I just went with it!" Phaidros defended. "Where did she go?"

"Find Marco Dandolo, and she won't be far away," she suggested. "They walked away giggling together."

Phaidros narrowed his amber eyes. "Is that so?" He disappeared into the crowd again.

"Poor Marco," Alexis said, shaking his head. "You probably shouldn't have told Phaidros that."

"They can sort it out," Penelope said. "Besides, it got rid of him." She stood on her tiptoes and stole the kiss that had been interrupted.

"You're making excellent bait tonight," Alexis said against her lips. "Good enough to eat." He pulled her closer to him, and they swayed to the gentle music the orchestra had started to play.

"Is that so?" Penelope smiled up at him. "This plan might not be as great as the *polizia* thought. No one is going to know who anyone else is in this crowd."

"This's a private party. The more public Carnevale experience is happening in the next building down," Alexis explained. "Everyone in this room is considered to be someone."

"*Signore* Donato," interrupted a plump man in a tight red brocade coat. "I haven't seen you in a year! Where have you been hiding?" He looked Penelope over approvingly, as if she explained Alexis's absence.

"I've been traveling, Maximillian, hunting new acquisitions," Alexis said vaguely. "Doctor Penelope Bryne, this is Maximillian Ceni, purveyor of the rare and antique."

"Nice to meet you," Penelope said, smiling politely.

"The Doctor Bryne that finds mysterious and beautiful objects in the ocean?" Maximillian asked, his eyes shining with interest.

"The one and the same."

Penelope expected the usual glib comment about her work, but instead, he produced a thick white card with gold edging and presented it to her.

"*Va bene*. I see the picture in the paper the other day didn't do you any justice at all. Those terrible vultures, pay them no mind, *bella*."

"I'm not. Besides, they are more interested in Alexis than me."

"You underrate yourself. If there's anything else of interest that you pull from the sea, please give me a call."

"*Grazie*," Penelope said, knowing she would never sell anything ancient to a dealer.

"Alexis, call me soon, yes? I've items which might interest you. Make sure you give this beautiful lady the night of her life."

"I promise," Alexis said as the man moved away. "Give Maximillian ten minutes, and the entire room will know who you are and that you are my consort. If our killer is here, he will seek you out."

"You don't think the killer could have bought his vessels from him?"

"No. If he had received anything like that, he would have called me first. There are certain cultures and time periods I have the first choice on." Alexis bent down and kissed the tip of her ear. "It was him who told me that you had found my Tablet."

Everyone Penelope met in the following hour wanted to know how she had managed to capture

Alexis, the elusive bachelor, while also passing over business cards to try and get her to secure his acquaintance.

Penelope had been to many seminars and networking events as an academic, so she tried to fall into what Carolyn liked to call her "Meet and Greet" face. She was starting to wish she hadn't drunk her third glass of champagne and sent Alexis away for a fourth when a slender man in a neat black suit appeared before her. He wore a *Medico della peste* mask, the kind that had always given Penelope the creeps.

"*Dottore*, it's a pleasure," the man said. "Tony Duilio, at your service." He lifted the long-nosed mask off so he could kiss her hand, leaving a wet spot she wanted to wipe away. He couldn't have been older than thirty, but his black eyes seemed intense and ageless in his young face. The black, geometric tattoo stood out on his light brown skin.

"Tony Duilio, the brilliant engineer and entrepreneur?" Penelope asked with her most dazzling smile. "What a pleasure. I've heard so much about you."

"From this decrepit old crowd, you probably heard all lies," he said with a cynical laugh. "I'm an admirer of your work; it takes boldness to follow a path no one else can see but you. In that way, we are much alike."

"I've read about your floating hotels. What a fascinating feat of engineering."

"Thank you. What brings you to Venezia, Doctor Bryne? Have you come to watch the great folly that is MOSE come online?"

"No, that's a happy coincidence. I'm here to visit friends," she replied, trying to keep it light and pleasant. There was definitely something unnerving about the young man. He was standing close enough that she could smell the strange aroma of smoky incense coming from him.

"And your friends have left you alone at such a party? Shame on them. This crowd hates anyone and anything remotely new. If they had their way, Venice would be dragged back to the days when the *Libro d'Oro* actually meant something."

Penelope laughed. "Surely it's not that bad. La Serenissima is still beautiful."

"For now, but when the planet gets a little bit warmer, MOSE or no MOSE, Venice will be taken by the sea. I'll watch it happen, and they'll cry they didn't have the vision to support me when they had the chance."

There was something threatening in his tone that made Penelope uneasy. She was saved from having to answer as Alexis appeared, slipping his arm casually around her waist.

"Here you are," he said warmly. "I apologize for leaving you alone, *amore*, but I see you've made a friend."

"Alexis, this is Tony Duilio," she said. "We were just talking about Venice and engineering."

"I've heard a lot about you, Alexis Donato. What an interesting party this's turning out to be," Tony said, without offering to shake Alexis's hand. "Is it true that you are a smuggler?"

"A smuggler?" Alexis laughed loudly. "You've been listening to too much gossip. I admit, I'm a collector and an academic dilettante, but I do it the legal and boring way."

"What a shame. I have a few things on my procurement list I'd have loved a connection to get my hands on, legal or otherwise. It was nice to meet you both, but I have a few clients I really must speak with tonight. If they don't eat up all my time, I might come back and steal your lovely partner for a dance, Donato." Tony pulled his plague mask back over his face and disappeared into the crowd.

"There's something wrong with that young man," Alexis said, the falseness gone from his tone.

Penelope wiped the back of her hand against her skirts. "I know what you mean. Charismatic, but creepy. I doubt he would get his own hands dirty, but I could see him encouraging others to do so."

Marco found them half an hour later, looking harassed. "I don't know what is wrong with these friends of yours, Penelope, but I'm worried it's going to lead to bloodshed."

"What are you talking about?" she asked.

"Aelia's arguing with some golden man," Marco said.

Alexis groaned. "Ignore them. They are always like that. They will be okay."

"Really? Because she told me that sword was fake, but she's pulled it on him and—" Marco didn't finish before Alexis was hurrying through the crowd.

"It's okay, Marco. They are old friends. They won't hurt each other," Penelope said unconvincingly. "Alexis will calm them down."

"They act like ex-lovers," Marco said. "She didn't like that he had dressed to match her...I don't understand women. Speaking of women, I need to check in with Bianchi. Will you be okay by yourself?"

"Of course I will, here's Alexis now." Penelope watched the tall magician move through the press of people.

"I'll meet you back here soon," Marco said. "You two look adorable together."

Penelope groaned. "Oh, shut up."

"Alone at last," Alexis said after passing Marco who gave him a nod.

"That was quick. I thought you would be breaking up that fight for hours."

"Minor misunderstanding." Alexis leaned in closer to whisper in her ear, "Let's find somewhere quieter." His hand was cool and soft as he pulled her around the crowd and through a door behind the stage.

"I don't think we are allowed to be back here," Penelope said.

"I just wanted a moment alone so we could talk. So many people begin to irritate me after a while," he replied, bringing her close. He rested a hand on her back, and Penelope's skin itched underneath it. Something wasn't right.

Usually, when Alexis touched her she felt like she was melting on the inside, but in the anteroom of the museum, his body felt as cold as his hands. Alexis never had cold hands. Reaching inside of her, Penelope pulled on their knot, sharp and insistent. Alexis didn't bat an eye.

"This party is a bore. Let's sneak out and go home," he suggested.

"You know we can't do that," she said, stepping back from him. The knot inside of her tugged back and not by the man in front of her.

"Then we'll have to make our pleasures here."

He smiled and kissed her. His lips were moist, and instead of cinnamon, they tasted of smoke and iron. Penelope stepped back from him, pulling the knife from her concealed pocket.

"Who are you?" she demanded, holding the blade in front of her.

"*Amore*, are you feeling well? What's the matter?" He held his hands up, but something else glinted in his eyes.

"You are *not* Alexis. Who are you?"

"Who are *you* is the real question," fake Alexis replied, prowling around her. "You are a simple human. There's nothing unique about you, and yet you have magicians running to your aid and your bed. You're out of your depth, Penelope Bryne. Join me or be sacrificed."

He reached out to her, and she swiped at him, the knife slicing his fingers.

"Stay away!" she commanded. "Touch me again, and you'll regret it."

Fake Alexis watched the blood drip from his fingers in fascination before looking back at her. "I'm going to enjoy devouring your flesh," he said, his voice distorting into a deep hiss.

"Who are you? Are you the Acolyte?" Penelope asked, carefully staying out of his reach. *Why did I wear this crazy dress!* She needed to keep him talking. Marco and Alexis would find her, and they would have him.

"I am whatever my master needs me to be," he replied.

"And your master? You mean Thevetat?"

A low chuckle rolled up through him. "My God is with me wherever I go. I'm his vessel. I am his hands and his blood and his breath." His eyes flashed a deep red, and Penelope's grip on the knife tightened. She'd seen Abaddon's eyes glow that way in Alexis's memory. He prowled around the displays, circling her like a giant cat.

"What do you want?" Penelope asked.

"I want to be free."

He lunged for her, and she fell backward into a display case. He was on her in a flash, disarming her with a move too fast for her to follow. His bloody fingers gripped her wrists above her head. "Got you, little doctor."

Penelope kicked out at him. Her legs caught in the folds of her dress, so it wasn't as hard as she intended. Fake Alexis laughed and pressed against her.

"Get off me!" she screamed, fighting to loosen her grip. He had been strong enough to create the sacrifices, and the bones in her forearms screamed as he squeezed them tighter.

"You got away from me once. I won't let it happen again, my delicious sacrifice." He leaned in and licked her cheek. Penelope saw red and head-butted him as hard as she could. He stumbled backward, clutching his bleeding nose. "You bitch!"

Penelope dived for the knife as the door into the room splintered open. The real Alexis was there, his mask gone and blue light racing under his skin.

"Defender," the fake Alexis hissed. "You've become slow in your old age."

Alexis rushed toward him, but there was a deafening crack, and only the choking smell of sulfur and smoke remained. Alexis still looked ready for a fight as the smoke alarms in the building sounded. Shouts rose from the rooms behind them as people panicked and rushed for the doors.

Alexis helped Penelope up off the polished floor. "Are you okay? Did he hurt you?"

"No, I'm fine, I'm fine. It's his blood, not mine."

"Hold tight to my hand," he instructed. "Don't let go. Don't get separated from me."

They followed the crowd out of the building and found a space to stand, Penelope with her back to the wall and Alexis standing protectively in front of her. He was on his phone in moments, coordinating with Phaidros, Aelia, and Zo in Atlantean before ringing Marco.

"What happened?" The disheveled inspector found them minutes later.

"Penelope was attacked," Alexis said before she could reply. "I got there in time before he could hurt her."

Marco turned to her. "What did he look like?"

"He was wearing a black mask, I'm sorry," she lied. "He set off a smoke bomb and got away from us."

Marco swore viciously before ringing Agent Bianchi.

"We need to get out of here," Alexis whispered to Penelope. "I've got Zo getting us a boat. Phaidros and Aelia will track Thevetat's follower."

"We can't just leave."

"Yes, we can." His blue eyes glinted dangerously. "There's more going on than I can safely explain here."

Agent Bianchi looked ready to explode as she pushed her way through the crowds. "Dandolo! Where are your men?"

"Clearing the building and searching for explosives," Marco replied. "Yours?"

"On the roofs. They spotted someone fleeing the building before the alarms went off, but they lost him in the crowds. Doctor Bryne, tell me everything."

Penelope relayed the story to the agent, including her attacking him with a knife.

"You're armed?" Marco demanded. "Why didn't you say something about this earlier?"

"Give me the knife, Penelope," Agent Bianchi said, and Penelope reluctantly pulled the beautiful dagger from out of the folds of her dress. "If you managed to cut him, we could have the blood analyzed."

"Is that an antique?" Marco asked, eyes wide.

"Does it matter?" Agent Bianchi replied. She put on a pair of blue surgical gloves and took the weapon from Penelope. She pulled out the blade and smiled at the smears of red. "Got you."

"Once you have what you need, I'd like that knife back," Penelope said firmly. "It *is* an antique, and it's dear to me."

"You'll have it back when the *polizia* say that you can. We didn't catch our man, but it's only a matter of time," Bianchi said. "At least the night wasn't a total bust."

"That's one way to look at the situation. Another way is that Penelope was attacked again, but as long as you got what you wanted…" Alexis remarked, his voice half a growl.

"Thank you for your assistance tonight, Doctor Bryne," Bianchi interrupted. "We no longer require you. I suggest you take *Signore* Donato home." She turned and marched away giving orders into a walkie-talkie.

"She has the manners of a wolf," muttered Marco. "But she's right. I'll get a police boat to escort you home."

"Unnecessary," Alexis said brusquely as a sleek canal boat pulled up beside the busy walkway. Zo was dressed in black SWAT gear, his face like a thunderstorm. "My security will take it from here." Without ceremony, he lifted Penelope up and passed her down to Zo's waiting arms.

"I'll call you if we find anything," Marco called down to her.

"Make it tomorrow," Penelope said. "I've had my fair share of crazy demon worshippers tonight."

Alexis jumped lightly into the waiting boat before Marco could argue. The inspector looked torn between concern and frustration at being so outmaneuvered.

Zo pulled the boat away and drove it expertly between the entertainment flotillas. Alexis helped Penelope inside the warm cabin, shutting the thick, red velvet curtains around them.

"That guy wore your face—" Penelope began but Alexis was already dragging her to him, his strong arms squeezing her tightly.

"Are you sure you're all right?" he asked, the anger in his voice dissolving into worry. His warm, calloused hands flitted over Penelope's face and neck, checking her all over.

"I'm fine, Alexis. I figured out it wasn't you pretty quickly."

"How? He looked exactly like me. I haven't seen that kind of magic since Atlantis."

"Powers of observation. His hands were cold and smooth, and yours aren't," Penelope said. "And he smelled wrong. You always smell like cinnamon and firecrackers. I touched our knot, and he didn't respond at all."

"I did. I felt like the floor had fallen out beneath me and I knew something was wrong. Tell me what else happened."

"He kissed me." Penelope grimaced. "And then I pulled a knife on him because I *definitely* knew it wasn't you."

Alexis's lips twitched, the tenseness finally leaving the curves of his mouth.

"You knew it wasn't me because of kissing?"

"I only felt it with my lips and not the rest," Penelope admitted vaguely.

"What is the rest?" he asked innocently. A loud tap on the glass roof above them made Penelope startle. Zo saluted to Alexis and vanished.

"He's going to help Phaidros and Aelia," Alexis explained.

"Then who is driving the boat?"

"Magic," he replied. "Humans will see someone driving who isn't real. I want Dorsoduro to be searched before I take you back to the palazzo."

Penelope sat down in the wide-seated lounge. "Plenty of time for you to tell me what got you so panicked back in the museum."

"You mean apart from someone I care about being threatened by a worshipper of Thevetat?" He sat down next to her. "Or the fact that you were plucked right from under our noses? That is embarrassing and frustrating."

"You said that you hadn't seen magic like that since Atlantis. You can't blame yourself for that," Penelope argued as she untied the mask from her face. "What else?"

"That voice!" Alexis pushed his hands through his wild dark hair. "The man, he was possessed by Thevetat. On Atlantis, there were certain priests the Demon could enter whose bodies he could use. They were called Vessels. It looks like he has found one again."

Alexis pulled a small lever on the side of the boat, and a tray slid out with a selection of drinks.

"Yuck. That's what he was mumbling about. He called himself a Vessel and said his hands were the Demon's hands. Give me some of that water. If what you say is true, I need to get the taste of demon out of my mouth." Penelope gestured at a bottle of Pellegrino. She didn't normally drink champagne either and wanted both tastes off her tongue. "So the Acolyte's a Vessel as well. I suppose it explains the threats in the petitions at the murder sites. Do you think the human he's possessing has any idea that his body is being used?"

"Vessels have to offer their body in service. Like all demons, Thevetat needs permission to possess a body. Whoever he is, he's been groomed for it."

"Which means there are more of Thevetat's priesthood alive than you imagined." The weight of the realization pushed down on her. "This isn't only about Venice, is it?"

"No, some other design is at work here. Venice might just be the beginning." Alexis slumped against the back of the chair. "Nereus is going to go ballistic."

"I can't say that I can blame her. I knew I was bait, but we couldn't have known he'd have magic. What can we do?"

"Right now? Nothing. We need to wait for the others to do their work. Thevetat wants you, tonight revealed as much. But I won't let him have you."

Penelope kicked off her shoes and moved so she could sit on the carpeted floor under the glass roof, her skirts flowing out around her. "There are worse places we could be waiting." She looked up at the clear sky, the light of the city dimming the stars, but they were still visible enough for her to enjoy.

"It will be better a few minutes from now," he said, his voice softening.

"Where's the boat taking us?"

"To get a better view, of course."

Penelope jumped as the sky exploded in bright gold and green fireworks above them. "Oh my God, it's beautiful!" she said, staring up in delight.

"Yes, it really is," Alexis replied, and something in his voice made her turn. He looked like a feral sea god given a human body for one night; his eyes dark with hungry desire. No one had looked at her that way before. His hands gripped the sides of his chair like he was unsure whether or not to touch her.

The air in the cabin grew hotter the longer she held his gaze, the spicy smell of his skin filling the air. Very slowly, she ran her hands up his legs, positioning herself between them.

"May I kiss you, Alexis Donato?" she asked, as politely as his request had been two nights before. His hands found her waist, bringing her closer still.

"Yes," he whispered as his lips lowered to hers.

When Alexis moved his hands to the soft skin of her shoulders, Penelope fought the urge to pull him to the floor with her. Sensing it, Alexis lifted her into his lap.

"Thank you for coming to my rescue yet again," she said, her fingers tracing his sharp cheekbones.

"You were doing a good job without me, as usual," he replied. "At least now I know how much of an impression my kissing has made on you." She wanted to say something tart and clever, but he chose that moment to fasten his lips on the soft skin below her ear. Her whole body shuddered in response.

His lips smiled against her skin. "That was surprising."

"Be very careful not to start something you don't plan on finishing, *Signore* Donato," Penelope warned. "My body can only handle so much teasing before it spontaneously combusts."

"I plan on teasing your body in ways it can't possibly imagine," he said, lips moving along her exposed collarbone. The soft stubble of his beard raised goosebumps over her chest and along her breasts.

"If that's your plan, I hope you know how to get me out of this ridiculous dress," she said breathlessly.

Alexis's warm hand found her bare leg under the mountain of taffeta. "I'm sure I will find a way when the time comes."

The fireworks were still going off around them, unobserved. What was going on above Penelope seemed irrelevant to what was going on beneath her. She felt a delicious helplessness as his hand moved higher in frustrating slowness.

Penelope unbuttoned the top of his jacket, exposing more of the dark brown skin of his throat. She had seen what lay underneath the layers of clothes, and she wanted to explore every inch of his body, trace every groove, and learn what every tattoo meant.

His skin tasted as she imagined it would, like spicy cinnamon and sin. She couldn't believe she had permission to touch him in such a way, that this ancient magician who had seen empires rise and fall would be interested in someone like her.

"Where are you?" Alexis asked softly.

"I'm here. I just can't believe that you are, too," Penelope admitted.

"*Amore*, what's not to believe?" Alexis took her hand and placed it over his heart. "Am I not flesh and blood and spirit, the same as you? The only things that separate us are time and my ability to do magic, which is the culmination of lifetimes of learning. Don't put me on some pedestal, Penelope, or lower yourself. What's there not to love about you? You are courageous, intelligent, kind, and extraordinary. There's nothing undesirable about you, and I'm honored that it is my arms you have chosen to be in, even if you only choose it for tonight."

Penelope rested her face against his neck, too overwhelmed to look at him in case he saw how much his words had affected her. She listened to his heart beating, and as she did, the memory of his music mingled with it. She wanted him, not just for the night, but for as long as she could keep him. She wanted to spend long nights arguing over every subject imaginable, to explore the Archives with him, to hear all of his stories as if he was a palimpsest to read and learn at her leisure.

"Thank you, Alexis," she whispered before kissing the top of his shoulder.

"*Prego*," he replied before his lips found hers, the kiss gentle at first and then building in intensity. Her hands fought with the buttons of his coat, desperate to feel the heat of his body.

"Are you always this impatient?" he asked lightly.

"Some of us don't have an eternity to wait. You're a tease, I can't help it," Penelope replied. "Messing with a lady's chakras and then leaving her to suffer for days is disgraceful."

He grinned. "I promise to make it up to you."

Penelope forgot what she was going to say as the hand under her skirts moved to lightly brush against the lace of her underwear. Heat seeped through her, and her breath hitched. He kissed her neck slowly, as if gauging every reaction to be sure it was welcomed. She moved softly and encouragingly against him, her hands sliding under his shirt.

"Let go, Penelope, let go," he whispered as his hot fingers moved under the lace and stroked her. Hot, moist heat flooded her, and she could feel her wetness on his hand as she thrust against him. When his fingers moved inside of her, she bit down on the cry that rose inside her throat.

Alexis rolled her onto her back, his long weight resting on top of her, his hand not stopping. Her hands pulled his face to hers, their kisses muffling the helpless sounds coming from her. She came in full, body-shuddering gasps, the tenseness that had been in her muscles for days leaving in a rush of pleasure. She shuddered again as he slowly slipped his fingers free.

Alexis's breath was warm as he kissed the tops of her breasts. "I think it is time I get you home, *Dottore.* Hold onto me." She wrapped her arms and legs around him, earning one of his wicked smiles.

The boat and the lagoon vanished, and suddenly they were in his tower, Alexis holding her up in his arms. Candles and lanterns filled the space with a warm golden light.

"What about the boat?" she asked.

"Damn the boat," he replied as he kissed her roughly. He carried her easily across his gallery of the fantastic, moving toward the bed with its saffron and royal blue sheets.

"For the love of God, get me out of this dress," Penelope begged as he lowered her to her feet. She pulled off the sleeves in frustration.

"Easy, there's an art to it," he said, sitting down on the bed. "Stop fidgeting and let me show you." His eyes glittered roguishly, and she humored him, letting her arms fall to her side. "Stay still."

The flash of a knife appeared in his hand, and with one swift slice, he slit the laces of her corset and it slipped off her and onto the floor.

"You see?" His arms came around her again, his cheek resting on the soft shift covering her chest. "There's another bundle of laces hidden here if I remember correctly." His hands searched the small of her back. There was a soft *snick* and mounds of fabric hissed to the floor as her skirts fell. "That's much better."

Without the armor of the heavy dress, Penelope felt strangely bare, her senses heightened. Alexis released her only so he could toss his jacket and shirt to the floor. In the boat, Penelope had been ready to pounce on him, but now encountering him in the privacy of his room, she wanted to take her time. Her fingers explored the hard ridge of his collarbone and down the grooves of his chest.

"You really are beautiful, Alexis," she murmured, moving to straddle him. His torso was hot against the bare skin of her thighs. Her shift came up and overhead, goosebumps breaking out at the change of air temperature.

Alexis ran his hands down her spine, gripped her hips and rolled her onto her back. His eyes ran appreciatively down the length of her body, as he lazily stroked the curve of her stomach.

"You're the one who's beautiful, Penelope. You should see your aura right now. It's…incredible."

"Show me," she insisted. He traced a symbol on her stomach, and her vision swam. They were both glowing in a sea of colors, like waves of heat over the desert sand. Where they touched, the light merged and changed, their energies mingling.

"Do you see the world like this all the time?" she asked, propping herself up on elbows.

"Not all the time. I can turn it on and off as I need to," he replied. His hand slipped up her raised back and unclipped the back of her turquoise bra. She moved so he could slide it from her arms, and he bent his head to lay a kiss on the scar over her heart, making her aura flare.

Penelope's eyes fluttered shut as his mouth left a hot line of kisses under the curve of her breast before he moved to suck gently on her nipple. The blind desperation from the boat was back, and her hands searched for the waistband of his trousers. He kicked them off before helping her slip off her underwear. His mouth was still busy on her chest, his soft curls tickling the sides of her ribs. She buried her hands in his hair, fingers tightening every time he made her body twitch.

"Come here," she said, and he shifted so his face met hers in slow, demanding kisses. His long body melted against hers and she smiled, tracing her fingers down his spine. When he moved inside of her, both of their auras flared brightly, and she could barely keep her eyes open. They moved together, bodies adjusting to each other as their energy did, creating something new together.

"Look at us," Penelope managed. "Alexis…"

"I see it," he replied, moving deeper inside of her, and causing her to shudder around him. "Stop trying to analyze and just feel."

He rolled them over so she was now on top of him, and she steadied herself by placing her hands on his chest. Their auras, his body, the color of the bed sheets—her senses overloaded. She shut her eyes and let instinct take over, her body screaming to take what he offered as her hips moved in a demanding rhythm. She had wanted this, wanted him underneath her and deep inside of her from the moment she saw him. Wanted to claim every inch of him as hers, to be so close that she didn't know where he ended and she began.

Alexis sat up, hands gripping her hips tightly, his lips kissing hers. "Look at me, Penelope," he whispered, and she obeyed, opening her eyes to lock on his raw gaze. In them, she read the control he was losing, and her body convulsed. They climaxed together, their souls as raw and open to each other as their bodies.

After, they clung to each other, Penelope trembling in his lap, unable to let him go in case she shattered. His breath ragged, Alexis kissed her forehead gently before she buried her face in his shoulder, losing herself in him once more.

PART THREE

THE
CANTICLE
OF
HEARTS

*"Of Love the standard-bearer I; My hopes
are ice, and glowing my desires. At once I
tremble, sparkle, freeze, and burn..."*

~ Giordano Bruno ~

EIGHTEEN

PENELOPE WOKE IN a mound of sheets, the strong aroma of coffee teasing her eyes open. A colorful cup and saucer sat on the carved bedside table, steaming prettily in the Venetian sunshine. The roof above her was a stunning dome of marble featuring an intricate gold and blue mosaic of such dizzying design that it made her head swim. Her hand reached out along the mattress but found it empty.

I wonder what time it is. Penelope pushed her disheveled curls from out of her face and sipped her coffee. A robe of green silk had been placed strategically on the bed, and she wrapped it around herself, tying it at the waist. The remnants of her Carnevale dress had been cleaned up from where the layers had been tossed across the thick Persian rug. Sipping her coffee, she hunted her magician through the sprawl of rooms.

Alexis sat at one of his scratched-up wooden workbenches, scribbling in a large leather journal. His laptop rested on a pile of ancient-looking manuscripts.

"It's a little early to be working so hard," Penelope commented. He looked up, and the frown between his dark brows vanished.

"I was starting to worry you were never going to wake up," he said, lowering his fountain pen.

Penelope went over to see what he was working on and he looped his arm around her waist.

"I had an exhausting night," she replied. "Do you know how hard it is to move about in a dress like that?" He grinned as he bent to give her cheek a whiskery kiss. "What are you working on?"

His notebook was a mass of intricate writing that looked like a hybrid between written Atlantean and Arabic. A half-finished sketch of long lines was in the middle of the page.

"Tony Duilio's floating cities." Alexis scrolled through the underwater photographs and artistic renderings on his laptop. "Something isn't quite right about them. Something to do with the cables. Perhaps I need to step away from it for a few hours. I did promise Lyca a training session…"

Penelope couldn't hold back the smile that appeared on her face. The distracted rambling of an academic with a problem to solve was familiar territory.

"Go and train with Lyca," she said, kissing his broad shoulder. "I need a shower and to make a few phone calls. I'll meet you in the kitchen when you get hungry." As she tried to untangle herself, the arm around her tightened, pulling her close so he could kiss her in a way that had her toes curling in the rug at her feet.

"I'm already hungry," he complained, eyes full of mischief and sex.

"Stop that!" She pinched him playfully.

"No," he replied. "Go on, I'll see you at breakfast."

Smiling to herself, Penelope walked down the tower steps to her bathroom. Her exotic makeup from the night before was smudged into metallic panda eyes, but the knowledge of how she got into such a state made something inside her glow with happiness.

Showered and dressed in clean clothes, Penelope found her phone and rang Carolyn.

"Mother of God, I thought you were dead," her friend answered the phone almost instantly.

"Not quite. Sorry for not checking in, it's been a strange few weeks. I dropped my phone in a canal, and all sorts of things have happened."

"All sorts of things, like work or a guy? You have a weird *he he* in your voice," she said shrewdly. Carolyn was not one for subtlety, a fact that had gotten her into more than one heated argument with the university's academic board.

"I don't have a *he he* in my voice," Penelope retorted. "There is a guy, yes. I told you about him."

"The hottie copper? I knew it, the man is—"

"God, not Marco. His name is Alexis."

"I know of no Alexis, liar."

"He's the guy I saw in the meditation," Penelope spilled. She couldn't tell Carolyn everything but this one detail she could share.

"*What the hell*?" Carolyn's voice was giddy. "The Turkish Corsair? How—when—fuck—tell me everything!"

"You were the one that told me to ask him questions if I saw him again."

"So you asked him out on a date? You metaphysical hussy."

"It wasn't like that. I saw him in the meditation and our paths crossed, and I recognized him. It turns out he's another academic nut. Oh God, Caro, you should see some of the artifacts he has in this house."

"You are in his house!" Carolyn was incredulous. "Pen, this guy could be a total serial killer."

"Stop being so dramatic. Alexis isn't a serial killer. The house has other people living in it too, so it would be hard to get away with murdering me. Stop worrying."

"You meet this guy in a meditation and you are shacked up with him already. Of course, I'm going to worry. You said he was an academic? In what field?"

"Esoteric mysticism in ancient civilizations." *In a manner of speaking.* "Funny story, he was at the Atlantis Tablet lecture."

"You're kidding me! That's spooky, even for me. Did you talk to him at the lecture?"

"Sort of." Penelope hesitated before admitting, "He was the guy that asked about magic."

"The crackpot," Carolyn said deadpan. "You went to Venice and hooked up with the magic crackpot that you cursed so viciously and articulately afterward."

"Yep. Funny coincidence isn't it? He's also not a crackpot. Magical history is a part of his research portfolio, so he had a legitimate reason to ask."

"What's magical crackpot's full name?"

"Alexis Donato."

"So Italian." Carolyn was silent for a long moment. "Jesus girl, you sure can pick them."

"Are you stalking him?"

"You know it's my superpower. Google is a powerful tool. You should use it sometime. He looks like a Euro playboy, Pen. Not something you would be dumb enough to go for. Holy crap, there are pictures of you with him! Wow, you look taken with him."

"Yeah, the media's everywhere here at the moment. It's embarrassing, actually. Also, don't believe everything you read on the clickbait Internet," Penelope said.

"Off clickbait and onto Google Scholar. He's published a hell of a lot," murmured Carolyn. "No wonder you are crushing on him, this guy has been circling your field for years. I'm sort of surprised you haven't clashed with him before."

"I'm raiding his library to try and help out with these murders. The books he has…I can't even begin to describe them. I'm scared to touch anything without white gloves on."

"Well when you have more money than God, you need to spend it on something. Your judgment's always been so good, don't get too distracted by all the pretty things around you not to see through any of his bullshit," Carolyn advised sagely. "I'm really happy you rang. Stuart has been hounding me about where you are and, I quote, 'You need to talk some sense into her Ms. Williams, she is too caught up in wonderland!'" The similarity to Stuart's frustrated brogue was disturbing. "He's really worried about you."

"He's really worried about the research grant he applied for with Latrobe University. Having a daughter on the faculty would help cement it and make him look good," Penelope replied. There was no sting in her voice, merely a fact, which was even sadder.

"He wants to see you settled, not running around the world after murderers. I have to admit, I'm not 100 percent down with that either, but I know better than to try and stop you."

"Wise, very wise," said Penelope.

"I know you feel useful over there and are having an exciting romance in the most beautiful city in the world, but have you given any thought to what happens once it's over? If you find the psycho killer, what then?"

Penelope pulled at a loose thread on the hem of her shirt. "I don't know, Caro. I can't see that far ahead. I don't even want to look."

"Penelope Bryne without a plan? Wow. What's going on over there?"

"Let's just say I've had some things happen in the last few weeks that's made me take advantage of the present."

I was tortured, stabbed, and thrown into a canal. I made a stranger bleed, I watched people die, magic is real, and it's more terrifying and beautiful than you can imagine. She wanted to say the words, but they died on her tongue. *Alexis saved me. He's the missing piece of who I am. He makes me feel like I'm not alone, that I belong somewhere. I have magic words living inside of me.*

Carolyn sighed. "Who am I to naysay a fabulous, exciting trip to Venice? As I said, you look like you are having a good time with him and that makes me happy. I hope you're taking advantage of his library and not just his body."

"I'm heading down to visit the collection as we speak," Penelope said, pulling on her boots.

"That's something at least. Text me if you find anything excellent, okay?"

"I promise."

Where would I start? I die every time I go down there.

"And Pen? Call your parents. If you can't handle Stuart, call your mom. You're their only child, and you're playing cop. They have valid reasons, not just grant reasons, to be concerned."

"Fine, I will. Thanks for the chat, Caro."

"You sound like you are having fun. I haven't heard a smile in your voice since you found the Tablet. Be careful, okay?"

"I promise."

Penelope headed down the stairs and touched a wall painted the color of oxblood. "Good morning, House," she whispered, and it opened a doorway to the kitchen for her.

After making another coffee, she steadied her emotions and opened emails on her phone. Ignoring her groaning inbox, she sent a message to her father:

Stuart,

I am fine. Please stop harassing my friends. I have another two weeks to think about the Latrobe teaching position. Relax. I'll let you know when I decide.

Love to Mom.
Penelope.

P.S. Met an expert on Homer. You would like him.

Penelope pressed send before she could chicken out. She couldn't believe he had tried to get Carolyn to do an intervention! *He knows you've stopped listening to him.* She would have to deal with him one day, but it wasn't today. She intended to have breakfast and go for a leisurely walk around Venice with Alexis.

Aelia was in the kitchen looking unusually casual in loose black trousers and a tank top, her bronze hair piled carelessly on top of her head. Even without makeup, she was stunning, perhaps even more so.

"Would you like a glass of juice?" she asked as Penelope sat down at the counter.

"I'm okay, thanks," she declined as Aelia put kale into the juicer.

"You can't live off coffee alone," Aelia chastised.

"I can and will. At least I know what's in it. How was the rest of your night?"

"Not nearly as enjoyable as yours," Aelia said, smiling wickedly. "It was mostly telling Phaidros to get over himself and trying to find the bastard who attacked you."

"Did the palazzo give you matching costumes? It's kind of nice when you think about it."

"Phaidros doesn't see it that way."

"Only because I make a better Sun Deity than you," a stubborn voice said from behind Penelope. Phaidros wandered in, picked up a glass of green juice, and sniffed it. "What's this disgusting mess? It smells like mulched grass and sadness."

"If it smells so bad, don't drink it," Aelia replied primly.

Phaidros took an experimental sip, and his face lightened in surprise. "That's surprisingly good. Raspberries and green apple?"

"And carrot and ginger and a whole bunch of other things," Aelia said, her violet eyes watching him as he stole a couple raspberries, eating them before she could stop him. Despite their bickering, there wasn't anything malicious about it, and a blind person could see most of the time, they were trying to get the other one talking.

Penelope pulled on the knot inside of her to hurry Alexis along. She tried not to think about him in the shower and failed. She imagined his bare skin gleaming with sweat from training, his dark hair tied back from his face as he moved all that graceful muscle...

"Whoa! Look at that glow, Aelia!" Phaidros commented, bringing Penelope out of her daydreams. "Her aura is positively vibrating."

Aelia sipped her juice and leaned on the bench beside him. "Oh yes, I see what you mean. At least the tension has broken in the house."

"Not only in the house," Phaidros chuckled.

Penelope rolled her eyes. "Don't you have anything else to do but speculate about my sex life?"

"No speculation needed. It's written all over you. It's good to know Alexis didn't let you down. I'd say, it's been a few hundred years," he teased. "You can't blame it on Carnevale like everyone else is this morning."

"I've no intention of blaming it on Carnevale. Speaking of which, I'm surprised you didn't end up moving out of the house and into a hotel like you said you were going to. What changed your mind?" Penelope said innocently.

"All my things are here. I couldn't be bothered," Phaidros answered nonchalantly.

"Uh-huh, whatever you say." Penelope looked pointedly at Aelia, and both she and Phaidros blushed.

"What an awful-looking drink," Alexis said, arriving in time to spare Penelope further uncomfortable conversation. He was dressed in dark jeans, a navy-blue sweater, and a thick, gray scarf to ward against the gray Venetian day that awaited them outside of the palazzo.

Penelope made a small sound in the back of her throat, part growl, part choke, and quickly covered it with a cough. Phaidros nudged Aelia playfully, and they both grinned.

"I'll have you know that this juice is extremely healthy for you," Aelia told Alexis.

"Does it kill or cure?" he quipped. "Penelope doesn't know about your culinary experiments, Aelia. Her body is human; it won't be able to digest your creations."

"Mother of Zeus!" Zo squealed in horror. "What have you done to my kitchen?"

"Time to leave," Alexis whispered in Penelope's ear, and they departed amidst a torrent of curses and tantrum magic. "Walk or Archives first?"

"Walk," she said decisively and took his hand.

Outside, the wind was cold and fresh, a film of damp settling on the paving stones and the buildings. Even in its gloomiest weather, Venice was still beautiful.

"What story would you like today, Doctor Bryne?" Alexis asked as he hooked arms with her.

"Whichever you'd like to share," she replied, knowing no matter which he chose, it would be fascinating. They passed a seedy looking group of tourists, still wearing their disheveled outfits and drooping Carnevale bells from the night before as they searched for their hotel.

Alexis smiled with an unexpected brightness. "I'll tell you a story about a spectacle on a scale that was absurd even for Venezia. It was 1530 and Venice, which has never celebrated half-heartedly, outdid itself in a grand display of wealth and naval prowess."

Alexis's voice came alive as he described a naval battle that took place in the middle of the Grand Canal. A wooden castle was built on rafts out on the water opposite the entrance of the Palace of the Great Council.

"It was painted to look like marble and had four big towers on each corner, and a larger tower in the middle," Alexis explained. "Zo was involved, and under his direction, they loaded the towers with artillery. He had a captain of the city, Gattino, and some of his men watch over it before entering it early the next day. At midday, thirty armed *brigantini* sailed in from the Arsenale and with fireworks and other tricks of gunpowder, they attempted to take the castle. Zo, who has always loved a fight and the sea, was in the thick of the play-fighting, rallying men from the boats to bring the castle down. The Doge and the Dukes of Milan and Ferrara watched the grand display from the portico of the palace. With the fortresses captured, the festival finally began."

Penelope's mind filled with gilded battleships, exploding firework cannons, Zo hanging from a crow's nest in full regalia as his pyrotechnics thrilled Venice, from the Doge and the golden families of the *Libro D'oro* to the lowest vagrant, drunk on cheap wine. She stopped and pulled Alexis in for a kiss when her phone started vibrating angrily in her coat pocket.

"You should just turn it off," Alexis suggested.

"*Buongiorno,* Marco," she answered. "How's my favorite *inspecttori* this morning?"

"Hungover and pissed off," he said sternly. "I need you to meet Agent Bianchi and me. Bring Donato if you want to."

"What's happened? Have you identified the owner of the blood?"

"Three bodies were found this morning. I can't let you in at the site, but I'll bring you photos."

That knocked Penelope's good mood right out of her. "Damn it. Tell me when and where to meet, and we'll be there."

BY THE time they arrived at the bar on the Calle de Carro in San Marco, Penelope's dream of spending a lazy day with Alexis was gone. She spotted Marco and Agent Bianchi, heads pressed together over a pile of papers and half-empty coffee cups.

"They are looking a lot friendlier," Alexis observed.

"A common goal. They're finally working together," Penelope replied, noting with a feminine eye that Agent Bianchi's ponytail was messy, and the perpetual frown was gone. When she looked up and gave them a small smile of welcome, Penelope almost fell over in surprise.

"*Buongiorno*," Penelope said, taking a seat next to Marco. "What's all of this, Agent Bianchi?"

"Please, call me Gisela," she replied, her brown eyes flicked unexpectedly to Marco. "This is everything we know about the bodies we found this morning. Marco can run you through it? I'll get us all some more coffee."

Penelope waited until she had gone before she raised an inquiring eyebrow at Marco. "Inspector Dandolo, I don't wish to alarm you, but I think Gisela Bianchi is drunk."

"Close. We are both hideously hungover," Marco corrected. "We had too much of my cousin's grappa last night and were in the process of sleeping it off when we got the call about the murders."

"Sleeping it off…together?" Penelope's eyes widened.

"Not together. She was on the couch you rejected," Marco replied. "I don't sleep with people I work with. We were both in need of a drink last night after getting yelled at by our superiors."

"This is rage," Alexis said, breaking up their conversation. He was holding one of the photographs, his eyes filled with frustration. "Do we know who the other victims are?"

"Three random revelers pulled off the street," Marco replied. "They were the first murders not connected to MOSE. You said rage, but someone would have to be very quick and thorough to kill and display them in such an obvious place and not get caught."

Penelope took the photo and forced herself to look. Three bodies hung from the bridge of the Ponte de L'Arsenal o del Paradiso, their stomachs slashed and intestines displayed.

"Alexis is right. This's a tantrum. There's no careful sacrifice or ritual prayers. This is quick and messy and meant for us, not Poseidon," Penelope said. "It's because I cut him." Alexis found her hand under the table and gave it a gentle squeeze.

"She's probably right," Gisela said as she sat back down. "He saw you as an easy target and didn't plan on you having the dagger."

"None of us did," Marco added. "Although if you didn't, then we wouldn't have had the blood."

"We found more DNA on the ropes that he hung those people with. We have evidence to match him to the attack and these deaths."

"How long before it is finished getting analyzed?" Alexis said.

"They promised me by lunchtime," Gisela replied looking at her watch. "Shouldn't be much longer."

"Good. I'm looking forward to having a conversation with this killer," Alexis said.

Gisela glared. "This is a police investigation, not some vendetta because he touched your girlfriend."

"I'm merely interested in how he came to know so much of the forgotten language," Alexis said, his face guileless. "You think I have it in me to be violent?"

"Of course not," Gisela apologized quickly. "I'm sorry. Even I want to beat this bastard up, but we need to keep cool heads if we are going to catch him."

Alexis lied smoothly, but Penelope could see Marco wasn't buying his innocent act. Marco had seen Alexis's face the night Penelope was tortured, and he still suspected Alexis was involved somehow in the murders of the *Sangue di Serpente*. If the Acolyte had magic, if Thevetat was once again recruiting and providing his followers with power, nothing would stop Alexis and the other magicians from taking him.

"Oh, God," Gisela muttered as she checked her phone. Marco's rang at the same time.

"What is it?" Penelope asked.

"The blood. It belongs to Tony Duilio and not one of his protestors," said Gisela. "Marco, call Adalfieri. I need to organize a warrant."

"Tony Duilio. So he was in front of us all along." Alexis looked calm, but his blue eyes were filled with fire.

"He's so well-connected, Gisela's going to have a hell of a time getting permission to arrest him." Marco shook his head, his frustration palpable. "You two should go home. We can take it from here. I'm not putting you in front of the firing line again."

Penelope gave him a brief hug as she was leaving. "Please be careful, Marco. Duilio isn't what he seems. You don't know what he is capable of when cornered." *He's possessed by a demon god that will show no mercy.*

"Don't worry, *Dottore*. This isn't the first time I've had to arrest a killer. Besides, Gisela will protect me." His grin was wide, but his eyes betrayed his anger.

"We need to get back to the palazzo," Alexis said to Penelope as they hurried away. "The wire construct, I know there is something there I'm not seeing. Duilio may be brilliant, a follower of Thevetat, but he isn't capable of orchestrating all of this. Someone's pulling his strings, and I intend to find out who it is before the *polizia* interfere."

NINETEEN

TONY DUILIO IS *the killer.*

Penelope had a hard time aligning the brilliant but strange man she had met with the sheer violence of the murders. To be able to hide that part of himself from a world who admired him…Penelope couldn't imagine the effort that must have taken. Alexis was right. Something didn't seem to fit. Duilio was an instrument. The conductor was another matter entirely.

Penelope curled up in a chair in the Archives with her notebook and began writing about Duilio, speculating about how someone who had such public social and business reputations could've been exposed to Thevetat's influence. If Alexis was right and someone was controlling him, how many new priests and followers were out there? Penelope remembered the long corridor of sacrifices in Thevetat's temple and brought her knees up to her chest. How many more people had been sacrificed and gone undiscovered?

When Marco had Duilio in custody, Alexis would find a way to talk to him and, with any luck, find the others he was working with.

"I thought I might find you down here," Alexis said, more than an hour later. "I've hit a wall and wanted to see if you could see something I can't." He held out a battered leather notebook to her, a sketch of Duilio's hotels drawn in black ink. The script on the page shifted and rewrote themselves in English for her. *Am I ever going to get used to that?*

"Engineering-wise, it's structurally sound. The way the cables and pylons move is quite brilliant, but there's something about it, like an itch in my brain whenever I look at them," explained Alexis.

Penelope took the notebook from him and studied the curving black lines of the cables. She turned the book from one side to the other with a frown. "You think there is something magical happening?"

"Depends on how long Duilio has been groomed by Thevetat. But yes, it wouldn't bother me so much if it was just a normal structure."

Penelope picked up her pen and notebook. "Maybe you are looking at it the wrong way."

"What do you mean?"

"You've been looking at it from the side when you should've been looking at it from above," Penelope said as she sketched. "How many of these cable-cluster structures are there per hotel?"

"Hundreds."

Penelope held the drawing up of an interlocking circular loop. "Birds-eye view of one."

Alexis studied it for a moment before tracing it with his finger. It glowed a light blue, and he lifted it into the air. He flipped through his notebook and found the specifications of the floating resort. The glowing circle multiplied in a great connecting pattern.

"Holy shit," Penelope said as she stared at it. "It looks like a giant web."

"Exactly like a web. Why would a follower of Thevetat build a city with a web under the water? What would they be trying to catch?"

Penelope looked at the drawing, and she remembered the way the magicians had built the first pyramids after the fall of Atlantis to help balance magic, the way the magicians had laid out the pyramids in such a way...

"Magic." Penelope touched the shimmering lines. "They're using the webs to somehow catch magic."

Alexis smiled broadly as he reached down to kiss her. "Brilliant girl! They are going to try and harness the power of the magical high tide. Come, we need to show Nereus. There are two of these resorts already under construction, and we need to ensure they don't get finished."

"This doesn't make sense," Penelope said as she followed Alexis through the stacks. "Tony Duilio, who I'm assuming has a different name, has a huge reputation and empire, as well as the brilliance to make these magical webs. You said yourself that he's probably got a mentor, someone guiding him, teaching him magic. He sacrificed those people, made a real show of it, stirred up the protestors."

Alexis halted. "And?"

"He did all of this. Created all of this fear and chaos. He couldn't have been so clever and still believe he wouldn't eventually get caught. He must have known it was only a matter of time." Penelope froze and then patted herself down frantically. "Phone! I need a phone!" Alexis took his mobile from his pocket and passed it to her.

"What is it?"

Penelope searched through the numbers. "Marco! They are going to arrest Duilio. He won't be there. They are walking into a trap."

"*Pronto*," Marco answered. "What is it now, Donato?"

"Marco! Thank God! Where are you?"

"Duilio's palazzo in San Marco. The team has just gone upstairs to arrest him."

"Get them out of there, Marco! Call them back, don't let them—" Penelope didn't finish as an explosion burst over the line before the call went dead.

TWENTY

THE BOMB SCENE in San Marco was bedlam. Logistically difficult at the best of times, the canals were now crammed with police, Carabinieri, and fire and ambulance crafts as they struggled to keep the public and the reporters away while assisting the injured. The bomb hadn't been big enough to take down the entire building, but it had been enough to make it structurally unsound, the threat of it falling into the Grand Canal making rescue efforts difficult.

Alexis, Penelope, and Phaidros pushed through the dust-covered crowd of *polizia* who were helping the wounded to ambulance boats. Panic was riding Penelope as she searched for any signs of Gisela or Marco.

"That Duilio is a right bastard," Phaidros muttered as another officer was carried by on a stretcher. "Why would he do something like this? How could anyone do this to Venice? Even Napoleon, the pompous little ape, could not hurt her in such a manner."

"He wants the shock to distract people," Alexis replied. "Hurting La Serenissima, disturbing her serenity in such a violent manner, will send a shock wave that extends to all who love her. To make war on Venice is to make war on the psyche of the world. It's the exact kind of chaos Thevetat's followers thrive on."

"We need to check what's remaining inside the apartment," Phaidros insisted, "before the *polizia* or anyone else can get in there. If another bomb or magical trap has been laid, maybe we can find it before the humans do."

"I'll find Marco," Penelope suggested, squeezing Alexis's hand.

He kissed her gently. "Be careful, *cara*. I'll be back in a few moments."

"Don't get blown up," she added hurriedly. Alexis's smile was beautiful, even in the sooty chaos around them, and then he was gone.

Penelope heard Marco before she saw him. He was giving instructions to men moving rubble, each sentence punctuated by violent cursing.

"Marco!" Penelope waved at him from behind the police tape. Holding a bloody cloth to his head, he waved her in. Abandoning any formalities, Penelope hugged his dusty body.

"Thank God you're okay," she said, looking him over. "I heard the explosion from Dorsoduro."

"My phone broke, so I couldn't call you back. Are you here alone?" Marco looked over her shoulder.

"Alexis and Phaidros went the other way looking for you," she lied. "I was so worried about you. Did everyone get out?"

"No, the blast was rigged to the inner doors so four men died and at least ten others were injured," he said, voice low.

"Gisela, is she—?"

"She wasn't in the building. Her boat got hit by some debris, but she's okay. She is around, giving orders to other DIGOS agents, no doubt. That bastard Duilio."

Penelope squeezed his arm. "You'll get him, Marco, I know it. Do you think he's placed any more bombs?"

"I pray that he'll be satisfied, but I doubt it. Gisela's on it. Major tourist areas are already being swept by agents, and they are talking about shutting down the city."

"What a nightmare," Penelope said. "He knows what he's doing, and that's what makes it more frightening. He's going to whip everyone into a terrified frenzy."

"Inspector Dandolo? We've almost made it through," an officer interrupted.

"I'm coming," Marco said and rested a hand on Penelope's shoulder. "Go down to the water and wait with Gisela. I'll join you when I can."

"Be careful," Penelope replied. As she watched him hurry into the building, she hoped that Phaidros and Alexis had found what they needed.

Penelope headed along the side of the building to where the jetties jutted into the Grand Canal. Gisela appeared in black SWAT gear, saw that it was Penelope and hurried to hug her. Penelope stilled in surprise. Gisela wasn't a warm person, and she certainly wasn't a hugger.

"Penelope, I've been looking for you," she said with a friendly smile.

"Marco sent me to find you. They are about to get through the wall into the apartment."

"Come with me, this way," she insisted. "It's not safe here."

"*Grazie*. I feel like I'm in everyone's way."

"That's because you are." Gisela's voice changed slightly. "I mean that in a nice way. We need to keep these paths clear."

Something snapped like static under Penelope's skin as she followed Gisela through the press of officers. She pulled back at her sleeve to see the glowing lines of the Living Language rising to the surface of her skin, the Greek word κίνδυνος shone before rearranging itself to *kindunos*, and then finally to *danger*.

Penelope pulled her sleeve down quickly and checked behind her. It hadn't warned her when she was attacked at Carnevale, so why now? Her hand went to the small oyster knife in her coat pocket. She had never taken it out, and it reassured her as she continued to look around.

"Are you coming?" Gisela called ahead of her. Something moved across her face—annoyance mixed with want. Penelope's hand tightened on the knife.

"I'm waiting on Alexis and Marco. They said they'd meet us here." Penelope offered the excuse casually.

"They could be hours yet. At least come down to my boat where you can sit down." Gisela pointed to a sleek, black vessel at a small, wooden dock.

"Marco said you were on the boat when the bomb went off."

"That's right, it was terrifying," she said.

Penelope looked over the boat's pristine paint job. "He also said that it had been hit with rock and dust. Doesn't look like it to me."

Gisela's perfect face slipped, her eyes changing from brown to black. *Mirroring magic.*

Penelope didn't hesitate. She turned and ran back the way she had come, but something heavy slammed into her, tackling her to the cobblestones.

"Clever little wench, aren't you?" a man said as he hauled her to her feet and spun her around. It wasn't Duilio. He was taller and broader, and his deep bronze skin shone under a mane of long, black hair.

"Let me go! Who are you?" Penelope demanded. The stranger's smile was cold and vicious. Penelope stilled. She had seen that smile before as the earth shook, and rock rained down inside a stifling hot cavern.

"Kreios," she whispered.

He chuckled, his voice full and rich. "He must love you if he's told you about me."

"Who?"

"The Defender, who else?" Kreios replied. His grip loosened ever so slightly on her wrists as he laughed, and Penelope twisted her right hand free, trying to pull herself away as she fumbled for her knife.

"No, you don't." Kreios pulled her back to him, and Penelope drove the small knife into his shoulder. He only laughed harder as the bloody blade pushed itself free and fell to the ground. "We'll have plenty of time for knife games later, Penelope Bryne."

He made a complicated gesture with his free hand, and she slumped into his arms, paralyzed. Eyes wide, Penelope could do nothing as Kreios swung her over his shoulder, unable to cry out or even touch the knot that bound her to Alexis.

"HAVE YOU given any thought to what's going to happen when we catch Duilio?" Phaidros asked as they climbed over a broken marble pillar. "The *polizia* aren't exactly going to hand him over."

"We need to find him first, then the *polizia* can have him," Alexis replied as he crouched down to study a burn pattern on the floor. "He isn't an amateur bomb maker. He knew exactly how much power to put in it."

"If he's the Acolyte, then he has plenty of under-world connections. We already know the *Sangue di Serpente* were being used by him, so maybe he's Sicilian," Phaidros said, returning from what remained of a bathroom. "I'm not picking up anything magical, Alexis."

"Me neither. I don't think this is where Duilio performed any of his worship. If he's like any of the other priests, he'll have a place underground. This is his persona, not who he is."

"There'll be no sign of his master either. You're thinking it, Alexis, so we might as well talk about it while Aelia can't hear us." Phaidros folded his arms.

"You think some of the priests survived? You know that isn't possible, right?"

"Isn't it? We survived."

"And we searched the world for others. How many magic-users and wise men have you chased after over the years trying to find ancestors or students of ones who could've survived?"

"I know, Phaidros, but it was mirroring magic. You *know* who used to use that as a weapon," Alexis said. "I don't want to believe Abaddon could've survived any more than you do, but everything was chaos. He could have had another escape tunnel we didn't know about."

Phaidros ran his hands through his golden curls. "Say you're right and he's been training people ever since. Hiding them. We need to be *sure*, beyond any shadow of a doubt, that it's him before we mention it to the others. Aelia…"

"I promise not to say anything, but if I find proof, you need to be prepared for that. She will need you, Phaidros."

"She doesn't need or want me, Alexis. All I do is aggravate her."

"Well you *are* aggravating, but you are also wrong. One day you'll get your head out of the past to see that for yourself. We are going to all need to stay together if Thevetat's power is growing again."

"What are you going to do about Penelope?" Phaidros sat down on a block of concrete. Alexis stood up from where he was inspecting a wall. "She doesn't have the proper magical training to defend herself, Alexis. You can't protect her every second of the day while you race about the world hunting priests."

"I don't know," Alexis replied, his voice low. "She doesn't understand what a war with Thevetat means. We can give her some magical training if we have to."

"We can't teach someone and hunt! She's not a book, Alexis. You can't leave her locked up in the Archives for years while you search. She's human, she only has so long to—"

"Don't you think I know all of this? This isn't the time to argue about it. Once Duilio is dead or arrested, Penelope will be safe from him, and then I'll decide. Until that happens, I can't make a choice."

"Don't forget that it's her choice too. She's not the type of woman who will fall in line because you command it, Defender."

There was a shout from behind a wall of rock and Alexis held up a hand to silence him.

"They are almost through. There's no magic here."

"Then get us out."

Phaidros took his arm. They vanished in a cloud of black sand and reappeared in a doorway, a street back from the site next to the water of the Grand Canal.

"Let's hope Penelope has found Marco in all this mess. I would hate for her to have to suffer the loss of a friend," Alexis said. They stopped dead as a dark figure in SWAT gear appeared in front of the canal, a woman slung over his shoulder. Long hair tumbled around the face of a ghost. *Kreios.*

"As always, you are too slow, Defender," Kreios said. "I promise to enjoy your woman."

Alexis and Phaidros moved together, but not before Kreios and Penelope disappeared, faster than a blink of an eye. Phaidros turned white as he gripped Alexis. "We need to go. *Now*. We don't know how many of them there are."

Alexis couldn't breathe, the image of Penelope slumped over the shoulder of his old enemy burnt into his eyes.

"I told you, Phaidros. I told you," he managed to say between choked breaths. "I knew they weren't gone." Phaidros grabbed him by the shoulders and shook him.

"Get it together, Alexis. Falling apart won't help her." He glowed with fury and magic. "You just had both of our worst suspicions confirmed, so what do we do next?"

"We go back to the palazzo, track her with magic, kill anyone who tries to stop us." Alexis balled his hands into tight fists. "We don't tell Aelia it was Kreios until Penelope's back."

"Agreed," Phaidros said as they hurried down the streets.

Alexis found Marco and pulled him aside roughly.

"What the hell, Alexis? Let me go," he demanded. "What's happened? Where is Penelope?"

"Duilio took her from right under your nose," Phaidros half lied so Alexis wouldn't have to.

"He was dressed in black tactical gear. We saw him just as he disappeared with her in a boat."

"He was here? What kind of man is he?"

"A very clever one. Send out an alert for everyone to look for Penelope," Alexis demanded.

"And what about you?" Marco's eyes narrowed. "What are you going to do, Donato?"

"Make calls to people you don't want to know about," growled Alexis. "I would advise you not to get in my way."

"Are you going to kill him?" Marco asked bluntly.

"Only if I have to. If not, I'll give him to you," Alexis promised.

Marco nodded grimly. "Find her. Do your best. But if the decision comes down to you killing Duilio, then lie to me afterward."

"You're a good man, Marco."

"No, I'm not, and neither are you. Go, Alexis, before I feel obligated to stop you."

NEREUS WAS waiting for them in the doorway of the palazzo, a set of long daggers in her belt. "What am I feeling, Alexis?" she demanded.

"Phaidros, find the others," Alexis said, and Phaidros hurried away. "He's back, Nereus."

"Name him," she hissed, her eyes shining with fury and power.

"Kreios is in Venice. We can't tell Aelia until we have Penelope."

"He took her?"

"Right from under our noses. We couldn't reach him in time." Cold rage settled in Alexis's veins. He could blame himself for his failures later. He had no time to indulge them now.

"So that's who has been mentoring Duilio," Nereus said wearily, sounding impossibly old. "And what of Abaddon?"

"No sign, but they were together when the mountain exploded. If Kreios managed to get out, it's possible his master did too. I don't know how they managed to hide from us for so long."

"How doesn't matter. They have Penelope," Nereus said. "What do they want with her?"

"The third sacrifice? To taunt me? Who knows? She's gone, and we need to find her."

"And the destiny knot? Can you feel her?"

Alexis reached deep inside of himself and searched for the connection. "It's there, but dim. She's unconscious, so perhaps when she wakes, we'll be able to use it."

"If it's there, she's still alive—"

Nereus was cut off by the cracking of thunder overhead that shook the walls of the palazzo. They hurried outside to the inner courtyard and looked up at the sky. Static crackled along Alexis's skin as the air convulsed above them.

"This isn't a natural storm," Nereus said, vocalizing his thoughts. "They are moving on us."

"Alexis!" Zo's voice was urgent as he joined them. "I just picked up another bombing on the police scanners."

"Where?"

"The Arsenale. The main headquarters of the MOSE project," Zo replied.

"They're going to try and flood us," Nereus said. Phaidros, Lyca, Aelia, and Galenos joined them, armed and ready for a fight.

"Duilio and his followers have declared war on Venice," Lyca hissed. "Orders, Defender."

They stood straighter, watching him as they instantly fell back into the chain of command from ten thousand years ago. There had only been a handful of times it had happened since.

"Duilio wants to destroy Venice by sinking it into the sea. He destroyed the command center, so we go to the gates themselves," Alexis said. "Phaidros and Aelia, head to the inlet mouth of Malamocco. Zo and Lyca, take Chioggia, and I will check the Lido."

"You can't go alone, Alexis," Aelia replied.

"Galenos and Nereus must protect the Archives. We don't know if they know about the palazzo, but we must assume that they do. Hitting Venice was a strategic move. We can't leave it unprotected."

"Take the cop," Zo suggested. "He's mortal but seems cleverer than the others."

"I'll consider it. We don't know who Duilio's allies are, so be on your guard. Expect Thevetat has taught them some forms of magic and will put up a fight.

Penelope is a priority. Once we have her, we need to regroup to hunt the others. If the MOSE gates are damaged, try to fix them, but don't take any unnecessary risks."

Thunder cracked again and again overhead, and rain started to fall in heavy drops that tasted of iron. The magicians looked at the skies uneasily, collectively remembering the last time they smelled blood in the rain. It had been during the largest magical high tide they had ever experienced, and only days before Atlantis disappeared into the sea.

"Go now," commanded Alexis. "Before there's nothing left to save."

TWENTY-ONE

PENELOPE WOKE TO the sound of dripping water and the smell of mold. Her eyes blurred as she tried to open them. She sat up slowly, her head pounding. Her hands and ankles were fastened with thick, black zip ties.

"Oh my God," she whispered.

She was in a catacomb, with dusty bones shelved in stone around her. The floor of the chamber was still damp from the tides and covered in a sticky layer of mud. She struggled away from the wall she was leaning against, afraid of the rats and spiders who no doubt called the bones home.

"So you are awake at last." The lithe figure of Tony Duilio stood in the entrance to the tunnel. His stylish hair had been shaved off, and his geometric neck tattoo was gone. He even held himself differently, straight and calm as a soldier.

"What do you want from me, Tony?" Penelope asked, her voice trembling.

"My name is Antonio," he replied coldly. "I don't want anything from you, Doctor Bryne, although I do owe you for this." He held up his hands to show the red line her knife had made.

"I should've put it in your throat," she snarled. "All of those officers were innocent. The people you sacrificed—"

"I didn't sacrifice them, Thevetat did. My body was just another tool for his will. Just as yours shall be."

Penelope tried to calm her racing heart. "I don't get it, Antonio. You had a billion-dollar business and an amazing career. What can you possibly get out of all of this that you haven't just thrown away?"

"Anything I have or don't have is at my master's pleasure. He created Tony Duilio. I played the part."

"I still don't understand."

Antonio's smile was sarcastic as he crouched beside her. "Of course you wouldn't understand. A privileged girl like you, brought up by academic parents in a nice house, in a safe neighborhood. It made you weak, and you don't even realize it. You know what I was doing when I first met my master? I was trying to pick his pockets in a Sicilian back street. I was eight, and I had already seen my mother murdered. I was living on the streets for over a year when he saved me. When you have nothing, you learn how useless things like degrees and companies are."

"So your master cared for you? Is that what you think? He turned you into a murderer!"

"I was already a murderer. He just gave me what I needed to focus on and to believe in."

"A demon? You set the bar way too low." Penelope shook her head. "You know the police will find us. You

AMY KUIVALAINEN

let me go and come with me, and no one else needs to get hurt."

"It's not going to happen, Doctor Bryne. I told you, Thevetat has a plan for you and those magicians you can't seem to stay away from."

"I'm never going to help you."

"You won't have to," a second voice said, and Kreios entered the chamber behind Antonio. She struggled against her bonds again. "You should've seen Alexis's face when he realized I had you. The Defender I knew would never have let himself become so vulnerable over a woman." His smile was sharp and vicious. "I've waited a long time to get my revenge on that bastard, and the fact that I have you is an unforeseen enjoyment. He'll make stupid mistakes in his efforts to get you back."

"No, he won't. I don't mean anything to Alexis. He was helping me find who was responsible for the murders. He won't lift a finger to get me back even if he knows you have me. He isn't that stupid."

Kreios lifted her to her feet. "You aren't fooling anyone. I know my enemy as well as I know myself. I've taken what he treasures, and he'll let all of Venice sink into the sea just to get you back."

"You're wrong. Alexis is coming for you, Kreios, and he'll bring all of his friends. You had better slither back into whatever hole you've been hiding in before—"

Penelope's head rocked back as he hit her hard across the face. Blood filled her mouth, and she spat it out at him. He raised his hand again when an old man in dark red robes stopped him.

Penelope's eyes went round. His long beard and hair had been cut, but she would recognize those carmine eyes in any nightmare. *Abaddon.* Thevetat had saved his High Priest from the collapsing caverns.

"That's enough, Kreios. Beating a woman is beneath you," he said. "Look at her face. She knows who we are, so the magicians have told her something at least. The sacrifice is now complete. Bring her with you, and we will see how brave she is."

The ties around Penelope's feet were cut so she could walk between Antonio and Kreios. She wished she knew of some way to get a message to Alexis. If he had seen Kreios, he would know who the real enemy was and what he was up against. She tried to touch the knot inside of her, but she couldn't feel or find it.

Bright, flaming oil lamps filled the space in front of her as Penelope was lead forward into a chamber. She pushed backward in horror, but only hit Kreios's chest. He grabbed the back of her head and made her see. She wanted to vomit, but her stomach was clenched too tightly in fear.

A bull stood on a stone altar, its throat cut, and its blood was dripping into a beaten copper bowl between its front hooves. The hooves themselves had been wrapped around and around with bright golden wire to ensure it remained upright. Its horns and eyes were painted gold, and a garland of flowers hung around its broad neck.

Surrounding the altar, six youths had been arranged in a frozen dance. They had been killed by a swift blow to the back of the head, the gory mess partially disguised by headpieces of bull's horns and flowers. Their feet had been removed and replaced with dancing feet of clay. Golden wires held their hands joined and raised, so they looked like joyful worshippers, dancing for their bull god. The walls and stone pillars were covered with dark script, the alchemical glyphs for boil, salt, and sulfur painted amongst them. *The third sacrifice. The spell is completed.*

Penelope choked, even as she was unable to look away. "You sick bastards…"

"Don't be so naïve, Doctor Bryne," Abaddon chastised lightly. "This is how worship was born; in the darkness, with promises and blood. It's the only language the gods truly understand. This was the final sacrifice, and even now, far above us, my god is answering this prayer."

He was breathy with awe and love. Beside her, Antonio watched Abaddon with adoring eyes as the old man dipped his hand into the copper basin. "Bring her to me."

Penelope kicked and struggled as Antonio and Kreios wrestled her forward, knocking her to her knees in front of the bull before ripping the sleeves of her shirt.

"She's had magic touch her," Abaddon commented as his fingers stroked the soft skin of her forearms. Thankfully, the Living Language stayed hidden. Penelope knew what they did to people with magic.

Abaddon whispered something, and her arms shot outright and rigid from her body. She tried to move them, but they held firm as he dipped his hands into the basin.

Penelope screamed as Abaddon drew glyphs on her skin, the blood searing her like hot wire where it touched. The men stood by impassively as she squirmed, the blood scorching her flesh black.

Delirious with pain, Penelope watched Abaddon produce a triptych of finely beaten lead sheets, covered with markings. She recognized them from her studies of ancient Greece. It was black magic used to curse people, often petitions to the gods to maim or kill their enemies. It was one of the reasons why competitors in the Olympics used to swear an oath before Zeus that they hadn't used black magic to give them an edge.

When Penelope had first heard of the lead petitions, she had laughed at the superstition. She had seen too much in the past month to laugh now.

Antonio took a small shovel and loosened the muddy paving stone next to the altar before digging a hole in the silty clay underneath it.

Abaddon and Kreios started to chant in long stanzas, and the writing on the triptych glowed the yellow-orange of a forge fire. Nausea and disgust crept over Penelope's skin like a layer of invisible filth. Once they had finished chanting, they placed the triptych into the hole. The smell of sulfur and rotting flesh filled her nose, and she knew their spell had been activated.

Kreios took a bronze knife and goblet from the altar and knelt beside Penelope.

"You've been inside the sanctuary of magicians," he said, voice dangerously soft. "Let's see what protection you have in your blood." He cut a long gash in her wrist and made the blood drip into the goblet. Satisfied there was enough, he cut his own arm, letting his blood mix before passing the knife and goblet to Antonio. Penelope's body locked, but if she could have moved she would have gouged Kreios's black eyes from his head.

Once Abaddon's blood was added to the mix, he used his finger to mix them and sketched a symbol onto his chest. Penelope's eyes widened as the glyph glowed before being absorbed into his skin, leaving a silvery mark, unlike the bloody wounds laced around her forearms. He tipped the rest of the blood on top of the triptych, and Antonio filled in the hole and replaced the paving stones.

In the stories Penelope had read, the lead plates were buried in graveyards so the dead could carry the curses to Hades. Had Antonio buried plates at the other sacrifice sites that were completely missed by the police? If she could get a message to Alexis, he could go to the sites and destroy them, and it might stop the spell from working. Penelope tried to find the knot, but it was as if a barrier was in her way, preventing her from reaching him.

"She's trying to summon him," Kreios warned.

"She won't succeed," Antonio said, his voice changed, now sounding deep and ancient. His black eyes turned to silver and red as something inside of him came forward.

Abaddon bowed to him. "My lord, you honor us."

Antonio ignored him, instead kneeling down to sniff at Penelope like a dog snuffling meat. "She smells of magic and sex. The magician has tasted of her. He'll fight to get her back."

"Then we use her to trap them as I retrieve what's rightfully ours," said Abaddon. "Lift her up, Kreios. We must leave here before it floods."

Her body was still chained by invisible bonds as Kreios tossed her over a shoulder and carried her out of the crypts.

It wasn't until they were above ground that Penelope realized they had been in the depths of San Zaccaria, located in one of the busiest tourist districts of Venice. People paid them no attention as they hurried to get out of the rain. It was as if Penelope and the priests of Thevetat had been rendered entirely invisible.

Antonio followed them, so she had nowhere else to look but into the hungry eyes of the Demon.

ALEXIS HADN'T gone into his war chest for nearly one hundred years. He tried to push away all thoughts of Penelope as he said the binding spells over the locks. She would be afraid, but she also would show courage in her recklessly brave way. She had to know that he would come for her, that he always would.

Kreios would use her to draw out and distract the magicians from whatever his true plan was. Tony Duilio had wanted her all along. Maybe they wouldn't use her as bait, but as a sacrifice.

Alexis pushed the thought out of his head. It wasn't only Penelope's life at stake. Venice was packed to capacity at this time of year, and there would be no time to evacuate everyone. All those lives sacrificed to Thevetat would only make the Demon's worshippers stronger. He couldn't let that happen, not even to save Penelope.

From his chest, he took out a leather baldric, crossing it over himself. It held two swords on his back and four knives securely. It held two swords on his back and four knives on his chest. The blades had been made by one of the royal smiths in the city of Atlas. The steel hummed against his skin. Normal blades didn't guarantee death to a priest or vessel of Thevetat, but these were designed with only that purpose in mind, imbued with a form of magic that would slice through any supernatural protection.

Nereus was waiting for him at the front door. The other magicians had already gone to their designated inlets.

"You have murder in your eyes, my son," she said. "I'm glad to see it. Listen to me very carefully: you must get her back."

"Of course I'll get her back," Alexis replied. "She doesn't deserve to die because of our failures."

Nereus took his hands and squeezed them. "It's not only that, Alexis. She's important. The Living Language is moving inside of her. It chose her. It doesn't do that with just anyone." The hair on Alexis's neck rose. Nereus had performed an augury concerning Penelope's fate, and she had kept it quiet.

He didn't like it when she kept secrets from him, but he still leaned down and kissed her papery cheek. "I promise I'll find her and kill Kreios."

Nereus touched her fingers to his forehead, tracing out a protection rune like she used to before every mission. "I'm very proud of you. Never forget that."

Alexis saw her safely into Galenos's care before he took out his phone, calling the Questura first and then the phones of police officers on the scene in San Marco until they located Inspector Marco Dandolo.

"Alexis Donato, have you killed anyone this afternoon?"

"Not yet, but the night is young, Inspector. This is a call to warn you. Two followers of Thevetat, including Tony Duilio, intend to override the MOSE gates and flood Venice. The bomb at the Arsenale was either him or one of his associates from the *Sangue di Serpente*."

"The Serpents are still in Venezia! How do you know this? No, don't tell me. What can I do?" he asked urgently. "We need to evacuate—"

"There won't be enough time to evacuate the city, so a few friends and I are going to the gates themselves. I believe they'll have Penelope at one of them or close by, should they wish to use her as a bargaining chip."

Marco's voice dropped to a whisper. "Take me with you. Not as *polizia* but as someone concerned for Penelope. Let me help."

"I'm going to the Lido inlet. If you can drive a boat in this weather, you can join me there. I have people checking Malamocco and Chioggia."

"How are you getting there?"

"I have my ways. It's your choice whether or not you follow me." Alexis hung up and stepped out into the rain.

Very carefully, he let go of all the checks and locks that he had bound and hidden his magic behind. Like a starving man suddenly placed at a banqueting table, Alexis sighed with relief as magic filled and energized him. He noted the power of the magical high tide was already making him stronger, but it was a mixed blessing. Kreios would be able to feel it and use it against them.

Alexis unsheathed his swords, gripping the hilts tightly. Lighting struck the buildings around the city, and he disappeared on a clap of the thunder.

TWENTY-TWO

PENELOPE SHIVERED WITH fever and pain as Kreios dropped her unceremoniously to the ground. The piers at the Lido inlet stretched out like two long, accusatory fingers in the water, the powerful yellow MOSE gates hidden under the choppy, black water.

Abaddon stretched his arms out to the ocean, and the concrete shuddered beneath her, responding to the magic flowing around him.

"Can you feel the power humming in the air?" Antonio sighed as he closed his gray and red eyes. "The humans have forgotten the power of the old gods. They have forgotten why they feared the sea. Tonight, they will remember; tonight, we will show them all. This icon of debauchery and self-importance, this sanctuary for the magicians, will suffer."

"And what do you gain from all of this?" Penelope asked between shivering lips. "You're meant to be a *god*. Shouldn't you already be all-powerful?"

"I'm taking back my world once and for all," Thevetat whispered from Antonio's mouth. "Before the humans, it belonged to me and my kind. It was given to them, to be protected by the likes of Atlantis. It was their corruption that led to the destruction of their land. Humans have slowly been killing it ever since.

It's time for me and mine to have control over it before there is nothing left to save."

"If that's what you wanted all along, why did you wait so long? Ten thousand years is a long time to be a sulking coward because you lost," spat Penelope.

"Little child, you have much to learn about magic." Antonio squeezed her face tightly. "It has taken ten thousand years for the tide of magic to rise again. For the first time, it's back where it needs to be. I will not wait for this moment again. This world will be mine to walk upon." He let her go with a rough shove.

Kreios and Abaddon chanted over another lead tablet before throwing it into the sea. The waves lurched around it, sucking it down to the seabed.

"The ritual's completed," Abaddon declared. "Stay and watch our victory, my sons. I have business with the old witch tonight, and thanks to Penelope's blood, I'm going to walk through the front door." There was a pull of magic through the air, and Abaddon disappeared, red coals falling from the space where he had been.

Antonio knelt down beside Penelope, his cold face twisted into a smile. "You'll die screaming, knowing that the Defender and his traitorous brothers are buried under the ocean where they belong. I want to feel your suffering as it feeds my power and ecstasy."

Penelope pulled back, but he gripped her shoulders and put his iron and blood lips to her mouth. She tried to bite him as something slithered from his mouth and into her. She gagged and spat while Kreios watched with a fascination that made her skin crawl.

There was a crackle of white light, and something silver flew over Penelope's head and sliced open Antonio's throat. He collapsed, wide-eyed with shock, gasping bloody breaths as he gripped the gushing wound.

Feel the power in his death, Penelope. You will never feel helpless again if you just say yes and let me in. Penelope clutched her head, trying to dislodge the voice.

There was another flash of white and silver, and Alexis soared into view, daggers flying at Kreios. He dodged one, but the second caught his thigh, opening a large gash. Unlike Penelope's knife, it made him stumble in pain.

"You're too late!" Kreios exclaimed. "Can you not feel it? The tide's rising and our time has come again."

Alexis drew his sword and charged, the pale blue light of his magic licking the blade. Smoke poured around Kreios's hand, and a sword materialized in time to block Alexis's attack. They fought so quickly in between the flashes of lightning that Penelope couldn't follow their movements. Power made the air crackle with static and smell of ozone. Penelope crawled over to Antonio's dead body and pulled his knife from his belt. She cut the black ties at her wrist before Thevetat made her drop the knife.

Let me in, and I will give you the power to stop this. You will be able to save his life.

"Get out of my head," Penelope demanded. Her hand shot up, and she smacked herself across the face, the glyphs on her arms burning hot.

You bear my marks, which means you are mine to use as I see fit. Let me in, or I'll make you kill the Defender yourself.

Through the driving pain in her head, Penelope found the knife that had made Kreios bleed and stumbled through the storm to help Alexis.

Alexis had driven Kreios to the end of the pier, his escape blocked by the ocean.

"This isn't Atlantis," Kreios said over the crash of waves. "We shouldn't be enemies anymore, Defender. The humans had their chance to make this world better, and all they have done is kill it. They need to be ruled before the planet dies completely." They clashed again, Kreios's blade slicing Alexis's forearm, making him retreat two steps.

"You're still too stubborn to see that it doesn't matter if you kill me, we've already won. Penelope is dead, and so is the rest of Venice."

"I'm not dead," Penelope growled, the long knife in her hand.

"You really are perfect for each other." Kreios lifted his sword. "And that's why you will fail to stop us." An invisible hand of power tried to push Penelope backward as Alexis charged Kreios again. The Demon inside of her fought back, operating her like a marionette, positioning her in front of Alexis to stop his attack on Kreios.

"Penelope, move!" Alexis shouted.

"I can't!" she managed to say, and the burnt glyphs on her forearms glowed. Kreios's laughter echoed over the crash of the waves.

"You see? I told you that you would fail." He came and stood behind her. "The Demon has her, and he'll always protect what's his."

Kreios hooked an arm around her waist, using her body as a shield. The knife in Penelope's hand began to heat, but she held it tighter. The scars on her palm burned, and the power Thevetat had over her arm faltered. Penelope drove the knife backward and into Kreios's side. He roared with pain and anger as she tried to drag her feet forward.

Kreios tried to grab her but lurched backward as a bullet hit him in the right shoulder, his sword falling from his hand. Another bullet hit his left shoulder, and he collapsed to the ground, clutching his bleeding side. A figure appeared in the rain, running toward them, gun still raised and trained on Kreios.

"Marco!" Penelope exclaimed. "What are you doing here?"

"Alexis said he might need help." Marco stepped through the mud and crouched down next to Antonio. "Tony Duilio. Damn him."

The fury left Alexis's face, and he sheathed his sword before stepping toward Penelope.

"Don't!" she cried, holding out a warning hand to Alexis. "Don't touch—it's in—"

She screamed and lashed out. Alexis pulled back from her, his blue eyes taking in the charred glyphs on her forearms. Her hands jerked up and gripped his throat.

"Fight it, *cara*," he urged her. "It doesn't have a right to be there. You are no Vessel."

I haven't permitted you to be in my body, Thevetat, so get out, she thought, but the Demon only laughed.

Penelope reached inside of herself and touched the tie that bound her to Alexis. She could feel him again, the connection calling out to her. Her hands released his neck. Alexis made no move toward her, but inside of her she felt the slow pull of him tugging back.

Stop that! Let him go, Penelope, I command it. I will give you whatever you want, whatever you wish...

The voice in her head was drowned by a rush of music. Low bass notes of a cello swept through her in an elegant, heart-wrenching melody of love and loss. It was the sound of Alexis reaching out to her. Penelope gripped tighter to their connection, holding onto it like a lifeline. The music became louder and louder.

"I can hear your heart," she said, dazed. "Can you hear it? It's singing to me."

"It's because it belongs to you," Alexis replied simply.

Get out, Penelope commanded as the Demon squirmed at the sound of the music and the rush of love she felt through the knot. The darkness left her in a powerful gust, and she fell forward, heaving up blood and ash.

"Is she going to be okay?" Marco asked, his voice trembling.

"She'll be fine," Alexis murmured, as he held her to him. He kissed her face, murmuring endearments in relieved Atlantean.

Laughter cut through the night and Kreios sat up, his black eyes changing to gray and red. Marco fired his gun again but Kreios held up a hand, and the bullet fell to the ground. The gun crumbled in Marco's hand. Alexis drew his sword and stood between Kreios and Penelope.

"Your special steel won't protect you against the deluge, magician," Kreios promised. "Never believe that I'm gone for good, old enemy." Alexis threw the sword, but it sailed through air and coals as Kreios and Thevetat vanished.

"What the hell was that? Where did he go?" Marco demanded, hurrying to the sizzling coals on the ground.

"I don't know, but they will return when Kreios is healed," Alexis said.

"Abaddon said he had business with the old witch tonight—do you think he meant Nereus?" Penelope asked in a rush. "He buried lead tablets at San Zaccaria. You have to warn the others."

"Nereus can look after herself. Abaddon won't get through the front door," Alexis assured her as he pulled out his phone and called Phaidros. "I need you and Aelia to get to San Zaccaria, Penelope says that tablets have been buried there." There was loud cursing on the other end of the line before they hung up. "Phaidros is on it. They found Kreios's men burying them at the Chioggia and Malamocco inlets. Do you know where the other one is buried here?"

"It's not buried," Penelope replied. "He threw it into the ocean."

Alexis looked out at the churning dark sea, his eyes burning with blue fire.

"The surge will come through here. I need to get the gates up."

"But that's impossible—"

"No, it's not." Alexis's face softened as he looked at her. "Whatever happens, I am glad I had the chance to know you, Penelope." He kissed her softly before stepping back.

"Wait, what are you going to do?"

"Stop Venice from falling into the sea. Go with Marco, in case I fail." Marco tried to take her hand and lead her back, but Penelope shoved him off.

"I'm not going anywhere. Alexis!"

Penelope's cries were cut off as the wind picked up around them and Alexis stepped down the large, uneven stones to the ocean, pulling energy from the air. Light began to dance under his skin.

"*Dio mi salvi!* What's going on Penelope? What *is* he?" Marco asked.

"He's a magician," Penelope whispered. She watched in numb fear as Alexis became something unrecognizable. He was a god, thrumming with power, magic swirling around him in a haze of gold and blue light.

Penelope could hear his voice, but the wind pulled his words away, making them indiscernible.

Alexis lifted his hands up toward the ocean, and the ground shuddered underneath them. The water churned and heaved as something yellow rose from the depths.

"The gates," Marco said in awe.

Visibly shaking from the effort, Alexis's magic streaked through the water before wrapping around the heavy walls and pulling them up against the waves. As they came up one at a time, the water behind them calmed.

"How many are there?" Penelope asked Marco.

"About twenty," he replied, not taking his eyes off Alexis. "Do you think he can last that long?"

"I don't know what he's capable of." Penelope was shaking, the trauma of the last few hours catching up to her. The thunder and lightning above them lessened, whatever had been powering the spell suddenly broken.

"Phaidros must have broken the tablets at San Zaccaria," Penelope said, watching the dissipating storm.

Alexis's cry snapped her attention back to him and the line of yellow barriers. The magic that had been riding him left with a flash, and he pitched forward into the waves. Penelope shoved Marco off her and scrambled down the rocks.

"Alexis!" she shouted, scanning the surface of the water.

"Penelope—don't!" Marco called after her.

Penelope reached the swirling black water and her fear of drowning, of being pulled under with no escape, momentarily overtook her, stopping her short.

"Alexis!" she called again, still searching the waves for any sign of him. She felt the knot between them flicker and begin to fade. Penelope pushed aside her fear and dove into the freezing sea.

Her lungs squeezed painfully as she fought the waves, but Penelope dove, again and again, reaching around her as she searched desperately for Alexis.

The knot inside of her thrummed sharply, pulling her down as if they were physically tied together. Just when she thought she couldn't hold her breath any longer, she snagged the leather baldric around Alexis's shoulders and kicked forcefully toward the surface. She broke free with a loud gasp, sweet air flooding into her tight chest.

Her months of lifeguard practice took over, and she pulled Alexis's head above the water and kicked backward toward the rocks.

Marco scrambled out into the water, grabbing her arm and heaving them both in. He was cursing and exclaiming in Italian as they struggled to lift Alexis's huge body over the stones and onto a flat surface.

"Alexis?" Penelope pushed the wet hair from his face and listened to his chest. "He's not breathing." She placed her lips over his and blew into him before starting CPR.

"Come on, Alexis! You can't just save the day and die on me," Penelope snapped through her tears, pushing harder on his chest.

"Penelope, move over, I'll do it," Marco said, moving her out of the way. He took over, pressing down on Alexis's chest. "Alexis, if you don't wake up, I'm going to make love to Penelope, and she will forget all about you."

Penelope breathed into Alexis's mouth again, and Marco resumed pumping.

"It's not working!" she cried. "God, I don't know what to do."

"Then we do it the Venetian way," Marco said and slapped Alexis as hard as he could across the face. Alexis jerked violently, and they rolled him to his side as he spewed salt water. Penelope cradled his head, smoothing his black hair back from his face.

"I hate…fucking Dandolos," Alexis wheezed, and Marco and Penelope laughed weakly.

"Hate me all you like, you still owe me your life." Marco held out a hand to help Alexis to his feet. "I'm sorry, Penelope. It looks like our lovemaking will have to wait another day."

TWENTY-THREE

PENELOPE HUDDLED CLOSELY to Alexis on the deck of the police boat as Marco navigated through the rough waves and back to the city. On the other side of the deck, Antonio's dead black eyes stared accusingly at her, his throat a bloody ruin. She didn't know what story they could tell when they arrived at the Questura. The only thing she was concerned with was getting Alexis back to Dorsoduro where the other magicians would be able to help him. He rested against her, his eyes shut and breathing shallow. *What happens to a magician who has used all of his power?*

The docks at the Questura in Santa Croce were swarming with *polizia*, Carabinieri, and DIGOS. Officers were busy changing boats, refueling, and heading back out again. A familiar blonde was shouting orders as they pulled in. When she saw them, her instructions faltered, and she jumped from the jetty and into Marco's arms.

"You bastard! You just left me here without saying a word," Gisela exclaimed, letting him go with a shove. "I saw you leave in the storm and thought you would capsize for sure. *Vaffanculo*! Is that Tony Duilio? Penelope, your arms are bleeding."

"I'll be okay. Help me get Alexis out of the boat," Penelope said, and the three of them helped support

Alexis onto the jetty. Gisela hurried away to find officers to get the body out of the patrol boat.

Alexis gripped Marco by the shoulder. "You know you can't tell anyone about tonight."

"What do you mean? Everyone should know how we took down Duilio and foiled his plans to sabotage the Lido gates. How lucky for us that you are an electrical genius and knew how to override the systems manually from the island," Marco said, his face a picture of innocence. "Penelope, go home and get someone to look at those burns. I know the ambulance isn't qualified to deal with them." He gave them both a stern look before heading into the Questura.

"He's a strange man." Alexis shook his head. "I don't know if we can trust him yet."

"Give him some time to prove himself," Penelope said. "How are we going to get back to Dorsoduro? You look spent."

Alexis pulled her close and with the last ounce of his magic portaled them into the house at Calle dei Cerchieri. They landed roughly in the courtyard—and into a pool of blood.

Penelope stumbled backward. "Oh my God."

"Phaidros!" Alexis called as they followed bloody footprints. "God, Nereus!"

He slid to the marble floor next to Nereus's still body. Even from where she was standing, Penelope knew Nereus was dead. Her skin was waxy gray, her torso a torn mess of wounds.

"Zo!" Alexis shouted helplessly as he wept, cradling Nereus's body close to him. "Where is everyone?"

"Alexis? Are you here?" Zo crashed through the blue front door, and his eyes found them. "Fuck, fuck, fuck."

"Go and find Galenos! Where is Lyca?"

"She's right behind me. She's with Phaidros and Aelia. They are docking now."

Zo hurried away, calling out to Galenos and searching the rooms.

Penelope stood frozen with shock as the three other magicians entered the house to find Alexis covered in blood and sobbing.

Lyca's silver eyes and face turned feral. "Priests. I can smell them." She took off at a run.

Phaidros hurried to Alexis, wrapping his arms around Alexis's shaking shoulders.

"What happened?" Phaidros asked urgently.

"We just found her like that," Penelope murmured through numb lips. Aelia took one look at the wounds on Penelope's arms, and her violet eyes grew round with fear.

"Stay still. We'll ghost the last hour," Phaidros said, his voice trembling. He whispered under his breath, and a shimmering projection flared around them.

There was no sound as they watched Nereus come through the Archives's elevator doors. Her hands and mouth moved rapidly, and the doors sealed over with stone and iron. The blue door exploded, and Abaddon appeared. His expression looked like he was gloating, but Nereus simply smiled and spat at him. Abaddon's face changed to a mask of fury. He lifted his arms, and with a flash of red light, Nereus fell dead. Abaddon walked from the room, his projection fading.

Aelia stared at Abaddon's retreating back, and a scream of such nightmarish fear and horror came out of her that the palazzo shuddered around them. Penelope collapsed to her knees, clamping her hands tightly over her ears as the sound shredded her eardrums.

Alexis covered his head with his arms, shouting something at Aelia. Phaidros crawled along the floor toward her, blood spurting from his nose. He reached up and pulled her down into his arms, holding her face to his chest until the scream broke apart into sobs. Phaidros kissed her forehead and hair, his arms locked tight around her.

"I have you, my love, I have you, it's okay," he crooned to her. "They won't ever touch you again. I'll die before I let them anywhere near you."

Penelope curled up on the marble floor, blood dripping from her nose and ears, the wounds on her arms burning as she clutched her knees to her chest.

"Alexis," she whispered, as her eyes shut on the heartbreak and terror around her.

ALEXIS SCRAMBLED to check on Penelope. He reached for her, but his hands were covered with Nereus's blood. *So much blood.*

Zo crouched down beside her and lifted her into his arms. "Don't give me that look, Alexis. You don't have the strength to lift yourself, let alone her," he snapped. "Lyca's looking for Galenos. Let's get you upstairs. Phaidros and Aelia will see to Nereus's body."

Zo took charge, and Alexis was so grateful that he started to cry again. He didn't know how long it had been since he had been so depleted of magic and energy.

Zo placed Penelope down on her bed and Alexis slumped into a chair, head in his hands, his whole body aching and cold.

"What happened out there?" Zo asked softly. "You look like death."

"I was dead. Penelope saved me," he murmured. Zo waited expectantly, and the rest of the story tumbled out.

Zo glanced down at Penelope with a frown. "If she was possessed, even temporarily, we'll have to watch her, and those glyphs will have to be cleansed."

"Aelia should do it," Alexis said. "I don't know what else Penelope went through. She might not want a man near her, even me."

"You don't think—?" Zo bit his lip. "I have to tell you, the crypt at San Zaccaria was harrowing. I don't think they ever stopped sacrificing. They just managed to hide it from us."

"I should've known. I should've paid closer attention."

"Alexis you're a great man, but there's only one of you. You can't carry the weight of this."

"We'll have to hunt them. Nereus's death needs to be avenged. We need to map out how they have been hiding, how deep their operation is."

"You need to sleep," Zo pressed. "I can watch Penelope."

"No." Alexis shook his head. "I'll stay. I'm not ready to let her out of my sight."

"Okay, but rest." Zo took a blanket off the end of Penelope's bed and wrapped it around Alexis's shoulders. "The world can wait, Defender."

WHEN PENELOPE woke, it was dark again. Aelia sat in a chair next to her bed dressed in loose yoga pants and an oversized shirt. She was watching Penelope carefully, noting the slightest change.

"What happened?" Penelope murmured.

"You passed out, and we thought it best to let you sleep."

"Where's Alexis?"

"I sent him away to rest. He's been here most of the day, but I didn't want him here for what happens next."

Penelope sat up, alert. "What the hell does that mean?"

"You were held captive by Abaddon," Aelia said coolly. "You need to be cleansed, and we need to talk as women. Men have no place here, not even Alexis."

"Did you find Galenos?"

"Lyca did. I'll run you a bath, and we can talk about it."

Aelia disappeared into the bathroom, and Penelope climbed out of bed. She was still in her musty, dirty clothes from the day before, and she felt cold and clammy. The scabs on her forearms hurt every time the skin stretched. Tentatively, she reached inside of her and touched the knot. She was reassured to find that it was still there.

Penelope rubbed her chest, exhausted and heartsore from everything she had seen in the past forty-eight hours. She went into the bathroom where Aelia was tipping ingredients into the steaming water. The bottles didn't look like normal bath oils.

"What's all that?" she asked.

Aelia lifted a brilliant blue bottle and tipped out the contents. "This and that. It'll help. Get in."

"With you here? I'm sure I can take a bath alone."

"Until those glyphs are healed and you are cleansed, you'll be escorted everywhere. If you want it over quickly, get in."

"Fine." Penelope pulled off her dirty clothes. "Why do you need to do this again?"

"You have been touched by an evil older than you can comprehend. From what Alexis told me, you managed to fight off a possession. That's all well and good, but there is still a taint on you." Aelia paused, taking an audible breath. "Penelope, I need to know if they hurt you sexually."

"No, they didn't. They slapped me around, terrorized me some, and then glyphed me, but that was it. I got the feeling they were running out of time. Abaddon had a sense of urgency about him."

Penelope slowly lowered herself into the tub. The hot water smelled of myrrh, rosemary, cloves, and very faintly of salt.

"He was worried we would sense the magic and stop him. And we would have. He had to move quickly. Zo and Phaidros have already been out in the city, but they are long gone. The bastards." Aelia frowned. "Put your arms in the water."

Penelope looked down to see her hands gripping the sides of the cast-iron tub so tightly her knuckles had gone white.

"I-I can't—" she said, struggling to move them. Aelia hissed before ripping them from their sides and plunging them into the water.

Penelope screamed and thrashed as the glyphs steamed, turning her bones to lava. Aelia was stronger than Penelope expected and held her down until the pain dissipated. Penelope vomited over the side of the bath into a strategically placed bucket. Aelia handed her a glass of water once she had finished.

"What's in it?" Penelope asked.

"A little salt only. It'll help."

Penelope guzzled the water, desperate to cleanse the taste of ash from her throat and tongue. Aelia pulled off her soaked shirt, and Penelope's throat closed at the sight of her skin. On her stomach, under a violet-pink bra, was a mass of scars with fine lines of Atlantean script written over the top of them.

"Aelia—" She didn't have the words. The air shuddered around Aelia's arms, and on her forearms more glyphs appeared, matching Penelope's fresh wounds.

"This is why Alexis wanted me to be the one to help you tonight. He didn't know how far Abaddon had progressed with you. The arms were just the beginning." Aelia turned so Penelope could see the scars on her back.

"I'm so sorry, Aelia," Penelope managed to say. Her bruised heart ached for what Aelia had gone through even as she felt dizzy with relief for having been saved from the same fate.

"I don't want you to think you are alone in this, Penelope. It took Nereus, Alexis, and Phaidros a long time to find a cleansing process that worked for these kinds of injuries. You'll have scars, there's no magic that can stop that, but you'll be alive, and your mind will be free."

"Tell me what I need to do."

"For now, enjoy your bath. Once you are done, I'll perform the healing, and you will probably sleep for a few days." She smiled before turning back toward the bedroom.

"Aelia, is Galenos—"

"He's not dead, but Abaddon mangled him. Lyca is with him, and Zo and Phaidros are helping with his injuries. When Alexis wakes, he'll join them. He was always the best healer after Nereus."

"Will it take long for Alexis's magic to return?" Penelope swallowed the tears in her mouth as she relived the terrible moment he was pulled from the sea. "I thought he was dead."

"It will take a lot more than a high tide to kill Alexis. He's exhausted, but he will be fine."

Once alone, Penelope wept quietly at the state of her mind and body. The last few days were a blur of terror and blood. Her adrenaline and nerves were shot, and for the first time since stepping through the blue door of the palazzo, she wondered if it had been a good idea. She had brought chaos and death back into the magicians' lives, and Nereus and Galenos had paid the price for it.

Come home, Penelope. Step off this dangerous path before it gets you killed. Stuart Bryne's ghost rose around her with uncanny timing. The weird thing was, after almost dying, she felt like hugging the old bastard.

Penelope scrubbed herself as best she could, climbed out of the bath, and wrapped herself in a thick bathrobe. She wanted to crawl under the covers and stop the accusing, cajoling voices in her head. Aelia was waiting for her outside of the bathroom, dressed in dry clothes once more.

"You won't want food yet, but I brought you some mint tea," she offered, holding out a steaming cup. Penelope sat down on the chaise lounge opposite. She had brushed her teeth twice to rid her mouth of the ashy taste, but she accepted the tea, hoping it would stop her stomach from feeling so hollow.

"Why do I feel like none of my limbs belong to me?"

"Combination of high trauma, exposure to huge amounts of dark and light magic, no food for days, dehydration...shall I go on?" Aelia gave her an amused look. "You aren't invincible, you know. It's okay not to feel 100 percent after the last few weeks."

Penelope drank her tea, wondering if Alexis was awake. She ached to see him, but she was also worried he blamed her for Nereus's death. She would never forget the image of him weeping over his master's bloody body, as if his world was now irreparably broken.

Her hands shook, and she set down her cup before she spilled tea all over herself.

"Let's do this," she said, holding her arms out to Aelia. "I don't know how much longer I can stay awake."

Aelia put down her own tea and took Penelope's shaking hands. Penelope expected the bone-melting pain of the bath again as Aelia began to sing. Her song was in Atlantean, a complex melody of soothing and healing. Penelope inhaled the temple smell of frankincense and rose petals as golden words filled the air in glittering bands. They twisted down to wrap around Penelope's forearms like bandages. Joy filled her, and she smiled at the wonder of it. Aelia finished the song before blowing on the words, turning them from gold to dark blue. Penelope touched them gently. "I don't think I'm ever going to stop being surprised by magic."

"I can't help you with nightmares, but whatever influence Abaddon's magic had over you is gone."

Penelope leaned forward and hugged Aelia. "Thank you so much."

"You're welcome." Aelia patted her back gently before they broke apart. "Go back to sleep. We can talk again in the morning."

GALENOS'S ROOMS smelled of blood and the salty sweat of pain. Alexis had woken with a jolt, Penelope's pain registering through him. He had promised Aelia he wouldn't interfere, but it tore him apart to not go to her. *It is your fault she is going through this. You should have never let her through your door.* Aelia was with her, he reminded himself, and Galenos needed him more.

Lyca sat beside Galenos's bed, twisting small curved knives about in her hands as she watched the rise and fall of his chest. Alexis knew the expression in her pale silver eyes; she was premeditating all the ways she was going to kill Abaddon in explicit detail. She wasn't the most nurturing of lovers, but she was a protective one, and she would avenge every mark Abaddon had left on Galenos's body.

"How is he?" Alexis asked from the doorway.

"How do you think you would feel if you lost a hand and a leg in one night?" Lyca's knives stilled. "I'm sorry, Defender."

Alexis waved the apology away. "May I examine him?"

Lyca was more animal than human when she was grieving and angry, and he wasn't about to take a step toward her mate without her permission. Lyca nodded, but the muscles in her shoulders bunched, alert and protective.

Galenos was swathed in bandages, from the stub of his right arm to the deep wound in his torso, and down to his missing left leg. They had watched the projection of Abaddon stroll through the palazzo in horror and fury. After killing Nereus, he had stalked the gentle Galenos. He had been thrown out of the Archives as Nereus had sealed it, and in Galenos's disorientated state, Abaddon had attacked him. He would have died had Alexis and Penelope not arrived at the house when they did.

Alexis's magic wasn't completely restored, but he couldn't leave Galenos in so much pain. Nereus had been their greatest healer, but Alexis had studied under her and would do what he could. He placed one hand on Galenos's smooth forehead and let his magic pour into him. Galenos's aura glowed as Alexis joined his energy and, with their combined magic, began to heal his wounds. It would take more than one session, but he could begin tonight.

Galenos's black eyes opened, and when he saw Alexis, they filled with tears. "Defender, I'm so sorry I couldn't protect her."

"It's okay, Galenos. It's not your fault," Alexis soothed. "Nereus knew the cost of protecting the Archives from Abaddon."

Galenos groaned. "They are sealed so only Nereus's heir can open them."

"How about you get well first and then we can get you to reopen them, hmm? It can wait," Alexis assured him.

Galenos shook his head. "You don't understand. I'm not the heir."

"What are you talking about? You have been at Nereus's side since we first created the Archives. Of course you are the heir."

"I tried Alexis! I *tried*. They are sealed tight. Why do you think Abaddon did this to me? It was because she sealed them, and I couldn't reopen them," Galenos insisted, wincing at his own urgency. Lyca hissed softly, and Alexis took the message.

"Calm yourself, brother. We will sort it out. Rest now and heal."

"Don't treat me like a child, Defender. I know what I'm saying. I know the Archives as I know myself and I'm telling you, it didn't want me entering them. Without its cooperation, we'll never get back into it again."

"I believe you, but you should only be worrying about getting better now. That is your only job."

Galenos looked as if he would argue further but Lyca's growl silenced him. Galenos settled back in his pillows and Lyca gestured at Alexis to follow her outside. She closed the door behind them.

"You are going to have to make some decisions, Defender," Lyca said bluntly. "Nereus is dead, and you are unmistakably our leader now. We need a plan."

"Lyca, I know you are upset, but we need to decide as a group what to do next. We have to put Nereus to rest and—"

"She would want us out there hunting them!" Lyca shouted. "Nereus wouldn't care what we do with the empty shell of her body; it's just meat. Her magic left with her spirit. She is gone. Abaddon and Kreios won't be idle while we sit here pulling our hair and wailing."

"What would you have me do? Call us all to war against an enemy we've only just rediscovered? I agree that we need a plan, but I won't rush out blind. They have had thousands of years to rebuild their numbers, and they obviously have the resources, too. We need to figure out how they are operating and dismantle their organization one step at a time," argued Alexis. "We can't do that if we can't get into the Archives. That's the first thing we need to resolve."

"I don't understand why the Archives rejected Galenos. It doesn't make sense. That has hurt him deeper than any wound Abaddon inflicted."

"Nereus didn't do anything without good reason," Alexis said, but suddenly he wasn't so sure. "I'm going to need you to check the warding on the palazzo too. No one does protection wards like you."

"They weren't enough to stop Abaddon," Lyca grumbled. "He wanted something from the Archives, and he wanted to kill Nereus. If he still wants Penelope, I don't know if my wards will be enough."

"It was Duilio who wanted Penelope, and I killed him."

"You hope." Lyca's silver eyes were vicious. "You need to stop being a coward and do what's right for her. The longer she stays here, the more at risk she is. She's a human in the middle of a magical war. Do you love her? Then send her away, so she doesn't end up more wounded than she already is."

Without waiting for a reply, she went back into Galenos's room, shutting the door firmly behind her.

TWENTY-FOUR

THE FOLLOWING MORNING, Zo insisted on everyone coming together for breakfast to eat waffles as big as the fine china dinner plates he served them on.

Penelope had slept better the previous night, the combination of Aelia's magic and Alexis coming to lie quietly beside her finally calming her anxiety. She was the first one to arrive in the kitchen, and Zo had given her a hug almost tight enough to break bones.

"It's good to see you are standing upright," he said, looking at the new tattoos on her forearms. "They suit you."

"Thanks. I bet my dad is going to love them." Penelope had tried and failed to imagine Stuart Bryne's inevitable reaction to the dark bands of Atlantean script.

"Fathers disapprove of everything." Zo hesitated before adding, "Alexis is going to blame himself for them, just to give you a warning."

"Why? He didn't burn me."

"He failed to protect you, and he'll take it extremely hard. I know broody and moody is a part of his charm, but I don't want you to get hurt by it."

"I'll do my best not to take it personally," she assured him even as her stomach clenched. *How could he fight Thevetat's priests if he was always worried about protecting her?*

Alexis came into the kitchen and started making coffee, ignoring Zo's protests.

"I already made some," he said stubbornly.

"Penelope likes it better with cinnamon," Alexis replied, winking at her over Zo's forehead. The tightness in her stomach eased ever so slightly.

"Don't worry, Zo, I'll drink both. I haven't had coffee in three days, if I don't replenish my caffeine stores soon, I think I'll go into shock."

"Did someone say coffee?" Aelia appeared like a drop of sunshine in a yellow kaftan. Phaidros follow her in, his face soft and besotted. He kissed Penelope on both cheeks.

"I swear you have nine lives," he said. "I was beginning to think Alexis was never going to let you out of that tower."

"Aelia told me I had to sleep."

Phaidros clicked his tongue. "I suppose the princess must be obeyed in all things."

Lyca's snort echoed through the kitchen. "Unlikely." She was watching Penelope with cold, silver eyes.

"How is Galenos?" Penelope asked.

"He isn't dead, which is more than I can say for Nereus," she snarled.

The magicians went deathly quiet.

"And you blame that on me?" Penelope held the back of a chair to stop herself from swaying.

"We didn't have any of these troubles before you walked through our door and started screwing Alexis, distracting him from his duty."

Alexis opened his mouth to argue, but Penelope beat him to it. "The murder happened before I stepped foot in Venice. Abaddon already planned to come for Nereus and the Archives, and you still wouldn't have known he existed. I get that you're angry and you're grieving and looking for someone to blame, but back the hell off me." She held Lyca's gaze until the magician stood quietly, her whole body poised to attack.

"Have your breakfast. Laugh. Pretend that none of this has happened. The Archives are sealed, and you had all better check to see if your magic will unseal it. Pray to the gods that it does, or we might as well open our throats. As for you, *Doctor* Bryne, go home. You aren't a magician. This's not your business. Leave before you get yourself and Alexis killed."

With a swish of her silver braid, she was gone.

Penelope let out a breath and released her hands from where they clung to the back of the chair.

Zo whistled softly. "Wow, I've never seen anyone but Nereus stand up to Lyca like that and live. Ovaries of steel, Doc."

"What did she mean about the Archives being sealed?" demanded Penelope. "How?"

"Nereus sealed them behind her when Abaddon came for her," Phaidros explained. "It was to protect the knowledge down there. It threw Galenos out and right into Abaddon's path."

Penelope sank into her chair. "How do you reopen them?"

"Only the heir can. The Archives will only accept who it wants."

"But what about Galenos? I thought he was Nereus's apprentice."

"He was, but he said that they wouldn't reopen for him," said Alexis. "It doesn't matter who Nereus's apprentice was. Only the Archives can choose its protector."

"No wonder Lyca is so pissed."

"Lyca is *always* pissed," Aelia responded, sitting down beside her.

"She was Nereus's bodyguard, and she wasn't here to protect her." Penelope pushed the hair from her face. *God, what a mess.*

"For being the bravest of us, you get the first waffles," Zo announced, placing a stacked plate before her, piled high with fresh strawberries.

"Thanks, Zo," she managed and made an effort to eat even though her stomach protested.

"Take it slowly," Alexis advised, sitting down beside her.

"What's going to happen to Nereus's body? Are you going to bury her?" Penelope asked when everyone was entering their second round of waffles.

"We will build her a pyre and burn her," Aelia replied. "Magicians are always burnt. It stops them from coming back or their magic being..." She stopped and looked sadly down at her plate.

"What is it?" Penelope asked.

"I think Abaddon stole some of her magic," Phaidros said. Alexis gave him a warning look that shut him up.

Penelope didn't have to be a magician to figure out that the power dynamic in the palazzo had shifted from Nereus to Alexis. He always seemed to be Nereus's second, and now she noticed how they seemed to be wary of him. The knot inside of her stomach tightened again.

"If you are going to figure out where Abaddon has been hiding all these years, you all better figure out how to break the spell on the Archives," Penelope said, changing the subject. "No one is untraceable, not anymore."

"We'll need Galenos on his feet to help with the tech side of things," said Zo. "One thing at a time."

"We'll try after breakfast," Alexis interrupted, quieting the table. "I still believe Galenos is the heir. He just hasn't had an opportunity to properly bond with the Archives yet. He seems to believe it isn't him, but it can't be anyone else. We'll do it to try to put his mind at ease."

"Good idea," Aelia said, a little too brightly. "As Penelope said, Abaddon can't stay hidden forever. We can start with the *Sangue di Serpente* and flush the snakes out."

Phaidros grinned at her. "I'll book our tickets to Sicily."

"No one is leaving until I say they can," Alexis said, the authority in his tone undeniable. "There will be no half-baked plans. If we are going after them, we do it strategically."

THE WALL where the elevator used to be was a seamless line of marble and lead. The magicians studied it, but none of them seemed game enough to touch it.

"Is there no other way into the Archives?" Penelope asked.

"One way in or out. It's easier to defend that way," Zo replied. "Having it under the seabed was Nereus's idea, so if there was no other option, it could be flooded."

Penelope shuddered at the thought of all those beautiful manuscripts and artwork floating in the gray lagoon. Alexis nodded to Zo who stepped forward and placed a hand on the smooth surface. His scent of rosemary and leather grew stronger as he sent his magic into the wall. When it didn't respond, he shrugged and moved back.

Aelia stepped forward next, placed her hand on the wall and sung a few soft bars. The smell of frankincense and rose petals filled the air with a gold mist, settling on the wall with no response.

"I don't think that's a surprise to anyone," Aelia remarked before shoving Phaidros forward. He made a frustrated sound before touching the wall and whispering softly to it. Penelope's nose tingled as she smelled Phaidros's magic for the first time; olive groves, spiced wine, and something sweet that reminded her of the taste of apricots. The Archives ignored him as it had the others.

"Go on then, Alexis. You are destined to be our leader. Maybe she expected the Archives to submit to you too," said Phaidros.

"She wouldn't have been that stupid," Alexis replied, stretching his hands out to the wall. Pale blue light danced under his skin and streaked through the wall. Everyone held their breath, but the wall pushed the magic out of it.

"What the hell were you thinking, Nereus?" Alexis growled in frustration. The light under his skin flared brightly, and he punched the wall with such force that the plaster molding fell from the roof. Without looking at any of them, he threw up his hands and stalked angrily from the room, leaving only the smell of scorched spice behind him.

"That went about as well as could be expected, I suppose," Zo said softly, breaking the bubble of tension in the room. "I've got a kitchen to clean up."

Phaidros put a hand on Penelope's shoulder. "You had best go after him, Penelope. He's his own worst enemy when he gets like this."

"And you think I'll be able to talk him out of it?" Penelope frowned. "He probably just needs some time alone to process. Getting stuck with all this responsibility is a lot for anyone to take in."

"Alexis has been in charge of us since Atlantis, whatever he may think. He's always deferred to Nereus because she was his master on Atlantis, but he's always been more powerful than her."

Penelope remembered the Lido and the way the storm and sea had bent to him, how he had pulled the gates from the ocean floor. She had seen what he could do, and it terrified and thrilled her, making her love and fear him even more. Now he had to take on his old mantle to hunt the Demon's followers.

"He's suffering from magic depletion as well, which is never fun, but he needs someone to anchor him, and he will only listen to you."

"I'll give it my best shot," she promised.

"And don't listen to Lyca. None of us blame you for what happened here," Phaidros added.

"Thanks."

He gave her an encouraging smile before leaving her alone to stare at the gray wall. The thing was, Lyca hadn't been entirely wrong. Penelope *was* a liability because she couldn't protect herself. She wouldn't be able to live with herself if she got Alexis hurt. She had seen him almost drown, and that was enough to give her nightmares for the rest of her life.

She walked slowly through the palazzo, her scarred hand rubbing over her forearm. Kreios and Abaddon knew they could always use her to get to Alexis because she was a weakness. He would always be of two minds when he went after them. *The priests won't stop just because Venice failed. How many other cities are they planning to attack the same way?* Only Alexis and the other magicians could stop them. Not her.

PENELOPE FOUND Alexis sitting at a work-bench in his tower, head in his hands. His whole body tensed when she approached.

"Are you okay?" Penelope asked, tucking her hands into her pockets, so she didn't reach out to him. "Stupid question. I know you aren't, but I'm worried, and so is everyone else."

"And yet it's you they send like a sacrifice," he said, lowering his hands. "This is a nightmare."

"I know, but you will work it out. You have managed to keep them alive since Atlantis. It's not going to change as much as you think."

"We are going back to war."

"I know. That's why I'm leaving." Her voice didn't crack as she said it, but her heart did when she saw the look in his dark blue eyes.

"What? You can't…"

"I can, and I'm going to," she said, crossing her arms tightly over her chest. "You can't fight this war properly if you are distracted by trying to keep me safe. It's not how war works. Kreios was right, Alexis. We are weak when we are together because we will always try and save each other before anyone else."

"Kreios is a psychopath. You can't believe anything he says." Alexis held his hand out to her, but she stepped back from him. If he touched her right now, she would never have the strength to go. "I can understand why you are afraid, Penelope, but if you leave, they may come after you again."

"They were only after me to get to you, don't you see that? If I'm away from you, they won't give me a second thought. I'm just another human. If I'm with you, I'm in more danger."

"Please, think this through. Don't leave," Alexis added in a tortured whisper. "I've only just found you."

"The tide of magic is rising, what use is an academic? I'm not a soldier or a magician." Penelope stepped forward and kissed his cheek, breathing his cinnamon smell in, searing it in her mind. "We are bound together, Alexis Donato. After this war is done, you will know how to find me."

PENELOPE HURRIED down the stairs to her room, stuffing her clothes into her bag and arranging her laptop safely on top. She picked up her phone and shot out a message before slinging her bag over her shoulder.

The palazzo led her straight to the front door as Phaidros came through it. He looked at the bag over her shoulder, and the smile on his lips vanished.

"What's happened?" he demanded.

"Nothing. I'm going home." Penelope hoped she sounded resolved and not ready to cry at the drop of a pin.

"Why? What did he say?"

"It doesn't matter. Please be careful and stay alive."

"Don't leave. He's better when you are around. He needs you. Whatever it is, you both can work it out."

Penelope kissed his cheek softly. "Take care of him Phaidros."

She stepped past the blue door onto the Calle dei Cerchieri and didn't look back.

TWENTY-FIVE

MARCO WAS WAITING for her as Penelope jumped off the crowded *vaporetto* and onto the pier in Castello. His smile fell as he took stock of her tattoos and the exhaustion written on every line of her. When he took her in his arms, the tears she had held back came out in a flood.

"*Dottore*, what's wrong?" he asked gently. When she didn't answer, he patted her back gently. "It's okay. You don't have to tell me just yet. Come on, let's get you a drink."

Marco took her bag, and she followed him through the streets to the Dandolo palazzo. In a daze, she glanced around the magnificent marble foyer.

"This place is incredible. Maybe I should've chosen your couch in the beginning," Penelope said as they climbed the wide sweeping staircase.

"It's beautiful, but it costs murderous amounts to keep it maintained. It's been in the family since 1512, so I can't let it go on my watch. My sister, Isabella, and her wife have good heads for business, and rent out the rooms to rich tourists. Otherwise it would have sunk by now," Marco explained as he opened the doors to his rooms. "Take a seat. I'll get us some wine." Penelope sat in an armchair and watched him pull out glasses and a bottle of red wine.

"It must be my month for having beautiful women as drinking partners," he said, handing her a glass. "Although I have to admit, I'm surprised to see you here. I thought you would be hiding under a pile of overpriced sheets with Donato."

"Yeah, me too," Penelope said, drinking her wine in one gulp.

"You want to tell me what happened? You two seemed so close."

"If I tell you, you have to promise not to tell anyone."

"Penelope, I watched Donato pull the MOSE gates from the sea. Even if I could tell someone, who would believe me? Besides, I know how to keep secrets."

"Okay, let me fill you in on what's really been going on since I first landed in Venice."

Penelope laid it all bare, from that first meditation to their meeting in Australia, the Archives, and everything in between. She told him about how Alexis had rescued her from being sold to Duilio and the way Nereus had died and Lyca blaming her. With a lump in her throat, she told him how she had walked away from Alexis.

"I came here because I wanted to see you before I fly out tonight." Penelope poured herself another glass of wine.

"Do you think it's such a good idea to go so soon? You are still healing, and it sounds like you are making a rash decision that will be bad for both of you."

Penelope shook her head. "I bought my ticket on the way over here. Alexis won't stop me. He knows, strategically, it's the best move."

"Strategy is not always best, especially when it comes to the heart." Marco shook his head. "I know better than to try and dissuade you, but health-wise, I still think you are flying too soon."

"I have no job to return to. There will be plenty of time to rest back in Melbourne." She didn't sound bitter about it either. Stuart was going to lose it when he found out she had never responded to Latrobe's job offer. She had filed it under future problems, but now the future was staring down at her, angry and disapproving.

Marco disappeared into the downstairs kitchens, returning with steaming bowls of fresh pasta, another bottle of wine tucked under his arm.

"I'm not going to put you on a plane without being properly fortified," he stated, handing her the pasta despite her protests. "Plane food is the worst, and Isabella makes the best pasta in all of Venezia."

"You are an incredibly good man," she said. "I'm so grateful that I met you."

"So am I. You have been good to work with. I'll miss you."

"And what about Gisela? Will she be heading back to Rome soon?"

"I don't know. She still has a lot to finalize concerning Duilio's case. It has finally been given to the media, and all of Italy is going crazy about it. I have kept you out of the articles as much as I can."

"Thanks. I don't think I could handle reporters right now."

"They are scavengers, but Gisela is good in front of the cameras."

"Have you asked her out yet?" Penelope smiled across the table at him.

"Of course not. You don't ask women like Gisela Bianchi out on dates. Besides, she is too clever to date someone like me, and I'm too old to deal with such a high-maintenance woman."

"Don't wait if you want to do it, Marco. Despite how it ended today, I'll never regret what I had with Alexis." *Will I ever have it again?*

"Hmm, we'll see if we can be friends first," he replied lightly.

Marco insisted on escorting her to the airport and seeing her safely through customs. His ID meant that she got processed in a separate line without all the usual jostling and hoop jumping.

"Can I say something without you getting too upset?" he asked as they stood at her boarding gate.

"Depends on what it is," Penelope teased.

"Alexis is not a normal man. He has different burdens and insecurities. I know how he looks at you, how he'd do anything for you. You cannot expect a normal relationship with one such as him. Despite the idiotic way you two are going about it, I think your future is with him."

Penelope hugged him. "Thank you for everything, Marco. I hope you come and visit me in Australia soon. You'll always have a place to stay."

"I'm owed a lot of time off after the last few months, so I might take you up on that." He kissed both of her cheeks. "I know you aren't much of a believer, but I bought you this. Everything happened so quickly I had no time to give it to you. I figured if you were going to fight demon worshippers then you need some protection." He draped a long silver chain around her neck. Hanging from it was a pendant of St. Mark, on one side a saint with a scroll pictured and on the other a roaring lion. "He has always protected Venezia. He might help protect you too."

"*Grazie*, Marco, it's perfect." Penelope kissed his cheek, her hand clutching the pendant tightly.

PENELOPE'S STOMACH lurched as she stepped onto the plane and took her aisle seat. She would fly to Rome and connect to a flight that would take her all the way to Melbourne. The flight attendant handed her a small bottle of water and Penelope downed it. The knot inside of her chest that connected to Alexis pounded like an extra heartbeat.

"It's all in your head," she whispered to herself. "Alexis is perfectly safe."

She reached into her satchel for her laptop just as an envelope fluttered down and landed on her plastic tray table. Sitting up, Penelope ran her finger along the cursive twists of her name. She looked down the aisle, but there was no one around who could have placed it there.

With nervous hands, she opened it and pulled out the letter written on thick paper. A necklace with a small glass vial tumbled out after it. She recognized it instantly. It was Nereus's necklace that she had worn every day since Penelope had met her.

Dear Penelope

I hope this letter and my pendant arrive on time. I'm sure by now I am dead, and the palazzo is in an absolute uproar. I do apologize for my family; magicians are as moody and impolite as cats.

I foresaw my death five years ago as I sat feeding pigeons in Saint Marco's square. Codussi's folly, the great Torre dell'Orologio, chimed its bells and death opened out in front of me. After so long, you can't imagine how relieved I was to see it. I didn't only see my death, but a human woman who would enter our lives and bring the greatest of us to his knees. I longed to see my sweet Alexis happy and in love once more, but I knew that every ounce of that happiness would cost you both. He is stubborn and often misguided in his need to protect, but someone must defend the Defender, and I'm so happy that it is you.

The magicians will not understand my actions or my death. They will be uncomfortable that the Archives want a human to be its guardian. The Living Lan-

guage chose you, the scars on your hand and your new abilities to translate language prove that the Archives want you to know its secrets. I saw the way you looked at the Archives and how it loved you back. I know you will not abuse it, and I'm at peace knowing that the sacred knowledge will pass on to you.

The vial in your hands contains a small part of my magic to unlock the seal the Archives and myself placed over it. Should you decide to take on the charge of Archivist, you will need to listen more to your heart than your head. The purest of magic is in your veins, and my only regret is that I won't be able to train you myself in what you will need to learn.

This decision, as always, is yours entirely. No one can force you into this, and your feelings for Alexis cannot influence you. If you decide to go and live a quiet life without magic, send the vial to Galenos. He will know what to do, but first remember this; a home is where you belong, and you do not belong in some dusty corner of academia.

Now, get off the plane, Penelope Bryne.

Nereus

Penelope reread the letter, the vial warming in her hands. She shut the letter, took two deep breaths, and read it again.

"*Signorina,* you must put your tray up, *per favore,*" the stewardess said, making her jump.

"Sorry," Penelope stammered and pushed it up. Her heart was pounding as she twisted the vial in the light. *What are you going to do, Bryne?*

She looked down at the tattoos on her arms and remembered the pain and fear of the last few weeks. Her little finger, snapped by Giacomo, would always be crooked, and she would always have nightmares of pulling Alexis's lifeless body from the sea.

In between these memories, however, were flashes of having coffee with Marco, quoting poetry with Zo, talking action movies with Phaidros, and doing yoga with Aelia. She thought of Alexis's face while he slept, the thrum of the cello as he moved the bow across the strings, and the line between his eyebrows that deepened whenever he concentrated.

The love for them all pulled at her. The Archives wanted her because the magic of the Living Language had chosen to leave Alexis's Tablet and live inside of her. As if the thought had summoned it, pale light raced under her skin.

Just then, Stuart Bryne's brogue cut through her recollections like a rusty razor blade. *You need to put aside all of this fairy tale nonsense and come home.*

Home is where you belong, Nereus's letter had said, and Penelope had never felt like she belonged to her own family or within the structured confines of a university.

The only place she had ever felt a sense of belonging was at the palazzo in Dorsoduro. Her life would never be boring or safe again. She couldn't fight with magic alongside Alexis and the other magicians, but she could use the Archives to arm them with knowledge.

She would find a way to live with that. Penelope opened the vial and tipped the shimmering contents down her throat.

The plane that had been lifting off was suddenly filled with a flash of white light, and it hit the tarmac, the engines and the electronics instantly fried, and the passengers knocked out.

In the ensuing chaos, the emergency door to the plane fell open, and Penelope climbed out before anyone could stop her.

TWENTY-SIX

$\mathcal{A}$LEXIS DIDN'T BOTHER to get up as the door to his tower shattered, and a furious Phaidros stormed in.

"What the hell did you do?" he demanded, ignoring the piles of rubble around him where Alexis had torn the contents of his tower apart.

"She left me, Phaidros, not the other way around. It's okay. It's safer this way."

"You think she will be safer out there alone? Undefended? You think that if you let her go that Abaddon won't kill her out of spite? She is mortal, Alexis!"

"That's right. She *is* mortal. She deserves to live her short life away from all of this. Lyca is right."

"Lyca is as crazy as a bag of demented cats! She's guilty and grieving and seeks to blame Penelope for all of our failings. Penelope's an archaeologist, a scholar, she can help us! You keep talking about how we are at war and acting like some kind of a general, but a true leader doesn't throw aside his best assets because he's afraid."

"I'm not afraid of Abaddon," Alexis snarled. "I defeated him once without the aid of a human and I'll do it again."

"I wasn't talking about Abaddon. I was talking about Penelope." Phaidros sat on a broken hunk of table. "Alexis, you *love* her."

"I have loved other humans before."

"Not like this and not for centuries. You feel the intensity of it, and it scares you as nothing else has before."

"Do you think she deserves this life? We are going back to war, Phaidros. How can I subject her to that?"

"She isn't some silly girl. She knows her own heart and mind. You should've stopped her from leaving, not given up."

Alexis gripped his head in his hands. "You didn't see her. She was on her knees before Kreios, powerless and burnt and broken."

"You saved her, Alexis." Phaidros put his arm around Alexis's wide shoulders. "And then she saved you. It doesn't matter how far you send her. She's a part of you."

"I would be too worried for her safety if she were here."

"You'll be worried about her safety on the other side of the world. That's Lyca talking, not you. Use your brain. You're meant to be the smart one."

"Nereus always knew how to manage every situation. I've lost my path and my compass. What am I going to do?"

"You know what you need to do. You are just too frightened to do it." Phaidros squeezed him. "Don't make my mistake and give up so easily. Penelope doesn't have a thousand years for you to suck up your pride."

"She won't come back, and I can't make her," argued Alexis.

"You don't have to make her, but you at least have to fight for her." Phaidros got to his feet and offered him a hand up off the floor. "Maybe clean this mess up before you bring her back. You always were such a trasher when you were angry. I'm going to find Aelia." He paused by the door and gave Alexis a meaningful look. "You aren't the only one that cares about the doctor. If you don't go after her, Zo will."

Alexis knew he was teasing but the thought of Penelope in Zo's arms, or in the arms of any other man, made jealousy spread its spikes in his chest. He had taken two steps when an envelope fluttered from the mural of the stars above him. He caught it in surprise.

His name was written on the front of it in a hand he would have recognized anywhere. *Nereus*. He slid a shaking finger underneath the flap and tore it open. Inside was a single slip of paper:

My stubborn Defender,

I told you that her destiny was tied to yours, and still, you let her go. Foolish boy, you can't hide your heart like a relic in the Archives forever.
Don't follow her, as I always said; it must be her choice. It was never yours.
Try not to take it too personally, and watch out for them all. I doubt they will understand.

Ever your proud mentor,
Nereus

"God damn it, Nereus," he muttered before shouting, "Phaidros!"

Alexis was halfway down the stairs of the tower when the palazzo shuddered around him. He could feel the wards straining. Abaddon and Kreios had wasted no time in returning.

Alexis drew his power around him and portaled into the front foyer as the blue door shimmered to life. Phaidros and Zo joined him, swords ready.

"Let the bastards come, I'm ready to spill their blood," Zo growled.

The great blue and gold door swung open, and instead of two priests of Thevetat, there stood a woman crackling with new power. Alexis's breath rushed from his body.

"Penelope?"

Her smile was slow and shy when it came. "I do believe I found a part of Nereus's lost magic."

Alexis's shock fell off him, and he dropped to his knees in front of her, wrapping his arms tightly around her hips. "I am so, so sorry. I should never have let you leave."

"No, you shouldn't have," she said, lifting his face so she could kiss him long and hard. He could feel the thrum of magic inside of her, feel the strength and love running through the knot that bound them. She smiled radiantly down at him. "Release me, magician, so that I can go to my Archives."

"Your Archives?" Zo's voice was small and confused.

Alexis released her, and Penelope went to the wall of stone where the elevator used to be.

"Yes. *My* Archives," she said, placing her hand on the wall. It shuddered and crumpled beneath her hand, and the art deco doors to the elevator reappeared.

Penelope fixed Alexis with a look that made him feel weak and invincible at the same time.

"Come along, Defender," she said primly. "We have work to do."

ABOUT THE AUTHOR

Amy Kuivalainen is a Finnish-Australian writer who is obsessed with magical wardrobes, doors, auroras, and burial mounds that might offer her a way into another realm. Until that happens, she plans to write about monsters, magic, mythology and fairy tales because that's the next best thing. She enjoys practicing yoga and spending her time hanging out with her German Shepherd, Duke in the beautiful city of Melbourne.

CPSIA information can be obtained
at www.ICGtesting.com
Printed in the USA
LVHW031539061021
699703LV00006B/37